SHAPING OF STONE

ALSO BY HALEY RYLANDER

LIFESTONE TRILOGY

Essence of Stone

Ashes of Stone

Shaping of Stone

LIFESTONE TRILOGY BOOK III

SHAPING OF STONE

HALEY RYLANDER

Aspen Leaf
Press

Published in the United States by Aspen Leaf Press

Paperback ISBN 979-8-9856103-6-9
Hardback ISBN 979-8-9856103-7-6
eBook ISBN 979-8-9856103-8-3

Edited by Alfred Bagdonas
Cover art and illustration by Grace Crandall

Printed in the United States of America

First edition December 2022

Aspen Leaf
Press

CONTENTS

For Emma

Faeran
Semestrial Sea
Terulian Mountains
Riverseep Forest
The Wildwood
Ard Gael
Lay Hills
The Grasslands
Ciel
Morcanan
Yavran
Maramor
Lake Orhirion
Rone
Remsgraen
Telem Fier
Calafor
Tura
Orhiri River
Braided River

CHARACTER LIST

ELVES

Fieri

- Auralia (uh-rah-lee-uh): Kindom Council Member, Lady of Rone
- Caerlyn (kair-lihn): Sira performer, friend of Renyra and Firas
- Cuvan (koo-vahn): Kindom Council Member, Lord of Telem Fier
- Renyra (reh-neer-uh): Sira performer, hunter, Firas's wife, guest to Turi Council

Morcani

- Aryn (ahr-ihn): builder, vierstone master of Daro, deceased
- Dulon (doo-lon): Lord of Daro, host of the last Kindom Council, deceased
- Firas (feer-ahss): Renyra's husband, shipwright, Sira performer
- Miyela (mee-yel-uh): Kindom Council Member, Lady of Morcanan

Remsgri

- Rhosti (rah-stee): Kindom Council Member, Lord of Remsgraen

- Trali (trah-lee): Sira performer, friend of Renyra and Firas

Turi

- Alos (al-ohss): Turi Council Member, Master of Trade in Tura
- Alsena (al-sayn-uh): Turi Council Member, Master of Guilds in Tura
- Alura (uh-lurr-uh): Sira performer, Raren's sister, friend of Renyra and Firas
- Coren (korr-ihn): Master of Sport in Tura
- Dorian (dorr-ee-an): Turi Council Member from the southern Wildwood region
- Eldian (ehl-dee-an): Lord of Maramor, father of Gellion, deceased
- Farra (fair-uh): Veldon's wife
- Gellion (gehl-ee-un): Kindom Council Member for Daro, metalworker
- Kaelo (kay-lo): metalworker exiled by the Turi before the Great War
- Kyna (kihn-uh): visiting elf to Daro, guest to Turi Council
- Liera (lirr-uh): Kindom Council Member, Lady of Tura
- Raren (rahr-ihn): Sira performer, Alsena's brother, friend of Renyra and Firas
- Reanan (ray-uh-nahn): Turi Council Member, Master Builder of Tura
- Saethir (sayth-ihr): Turi Council member from eastern Ard Gael
- Tenille (tehn-ihl): Kindom Council Member, Lady of Maramor, Gellion's mother
- Tornac (tor-nak): Gellion's older brother
- Valder (vahl-durr): Gellion's younger brother
- Veldon (vehl-duhn): Gellion's youngest brother

HUMANS

- Vensure, Justus: Albaren, military commander of Tradira
- Eurig: Dierna, Lawgiver of the Elder Clan
- Heleena: Kayda, old woman from Suri Ranta

PART I

1

CLOSED GATES

The gates of Tura were guarded. Gellion's steps faltered when he saw the teeth of spears outlined against the sky. It had been centuries since the Turi guarded their gates. Just seeing the city still standing was a relief of which Gellion had not dared to hope, but the spears sent shivers of cold over his skin. Was this merely a precaution against what had happened in Daro, or had Kaelo already begun to enact his plans here? Gellion glanced at his brothers. Valder and Veldon had seen the guards, too, and were watching them warily.

"How long do you think it's been?" Valder said.

"Nearly two months, I think." Veldon's eyes were fixed on the gates, as though trying to see what lay beyond them.

Gellion couldn't find his voice. Every day of those two months away from the elves, he had imaged what could be happening in Tura, wondering what his family must be feeling at his presumed death, wondering which of his friends had survived the battle at Arvain. The answers awaited him at last.

The cold over his skin spread to his lungs, constricting his breath. There was only one death he was certain of—the one he had witnessed with his own eyes. The sharp pain that had once accompanied any thought of Dulon was beginning to dull, but Gellion knew from his experience in the Great War that it would never leave him entirely. He was not prepared to begin the process anew if he found Firas had died, or Renyra, or—

His chest gave a sickening lurch. Could Kyna be behind these walls? So close after all this time? After all he now knew? It was possible she had died at Arvain. It would be better for the elves as a whole if she had. Yet the thought of the possibility still broke something inside Gellion.

She betrayed you. She betrayed all the elves. She never loved you.

A thousand times, Gellion had agonized over what he would do if he found Kyna alive in Tura, still in the confidence of the elves. Could the Turi have discovered for themselves that Kyna was Kaelo's accomplice?

Not accomplice. Daughter.

Gellion could still not comprehend the fact. Would anyone believe him? A part of him still doubted the revelation, but the evidence he and his brothers had found in Suri Ranta was too perfect. The spy had to be her. She had to be Kaelo's daughter. Gellion had decided to go directly to Liera as soon as he arrived. He would tell her everything. If all went well, he wouldn't even have to see Kyna, though what may happen to her when the rest of the elves knew of her treachery sent a chill through his bones.

It was useless to speculate, especially when the reality of all his imaginings was mere minutes away, but the habit had become so ingrained in Gellion, he could hardly seem to stop himself. He closed his eyes, trying to escape the turmoil and focus on the present. He turned inward. In his mind, he ran through the first steps of the A'vaeri, picturing his own body moving with precision and balance. His jumbled thoughts narrowed, aligned. The memories and worries were still present, but they bent to the immediacy of the now. Gellion sighed.

"Let's go." He spoke more to himself than to his brothers. Opening his eyes, he strode toward the gates.

The guards peered down at them as they drew closer, then one of them exclaimed and disappeared behind the gates. A few moments later, the thick sheets of metal that shaped the gates of Tura opened before them.

"Gellion!"

The voice sounded familiar, but it wasn't until the elf was nearly upon him that Gellion recognized Reanan, the Master Builder of Tura. Gellion had not seen Reanan since leaving the Turi Council two hundred years before, when he had sailed for Daro.

"Riu above," Reanan breathed. He stopped in front of Gellion with wide eyes. His skin was a deep tan—Gellion had always assumed he held some Remsgri or Fieri blood—but now his face was nearly as pale as Gellion's own.

"They said—" Reanan faltered, shaking his head as his eyes took in Valder and Veldon standing behind Gellion. "They said you were dead. All of you. Tenille—" The look of pain on Reanan's face made Gellion's throat constrict.

His mother.

So she has mourned us.

Gellion had known his mother would assume he and his brothers were dead when the rest of the elves of Daro returned without them, but somehow hearing it confirmed made the situation seem immeasurably worse. Had his mother blamed him for the deaths of Valder and Veldon? She had every right to. Tenille had been perplexed by Gellion's decision to accept the infamous Albaren alliance that had led to a near massacre of the elven army, but she had honored his choice at the time. Now he had brought her incomprehensible pain.

"Is our mother here?" Veldon asked.

Gellion's eyes locked on Reanan, his pulse racing.

"Yes," Reanan said. "All the Turi Council is." He was still staring at Gellion and his brothers as though expecting them to blow away in the breeze at any moment. "Tenille has been in Tura for weeks. So has Tornac."

Gellion stiffened. In all his visions of his homecoming, his older brother had always been safely back in Maramor, seeing to the running of their family's city. His mother had been there too for that matter, though Gellion had considered the possibility of her presence in Tura if Kaelo's return had become public knowledge. The heat in Gellion's blood began to drain until he could feel his face paling. The full Turi Council was in Tura. The gates were closed and guarded. Clearly something had happened to cause alarm. Was it more than simple precaution?

"But ... but how?" Reanan still seemed to be having trouble forming his thoughts into words. "How are you here? How did you get across the sea?"

Gellion disregarded Reanan's questions with the wave of a hand.

"It's a long story, and one I intend to tell in full before the Turi Council, but not now. Reanan, what has been happening? Why is the Turi Council here? And the gates—"

Reanan's mouth had been hanging open, but now he slowly closed it, the shock in his face turning to what Gellion could only interpret as dread.

"I fear you will not believe me if I tell you," Reanan's voice was weighted with weariness.

Valder snorted. "We'll believe your story if you believe ours." A corner of his mouth twitched up. "I think you will find us a less skeptical audience than you imagine."

Reanan did not smile. "It is not a story you will want to believe in any case." He glanced behind them, then back to the gates. "Come inside. It will be easier to show you."

Every step Gellion took behind Reanan increased the tension in his muscles until his heart was hammering with the stress, yet when he walked through the gates of Tura, the Great City looked exactly as he remembered it. A swell of affection rose in his chest at the familiarity of the flower lined streets and beautiful buildings. Above the homes and shops, Gellion could see the Central Tower gleaming alabaster in the sunlight. Elves passed through the streets around him. No beards, no beggars, no children, no backs bent to age. Gellion nearly laughed with the joy of being among his own kind once more.

It had not been an easy journey from Suri Ranta to Faeran. Gellion and his brothers had spent nearly two weeks in the mountain village across the Semestrial Sea. The Kayda people had been undeservedly accommodating to the small company of elves, but even among the Kayda, there had been suspicion, and Suri Ranta was far from a peaceful oasis.

Some of Gellion's joy at being back in Tura melted away as he thought back to the mountain cave west of the human town, where he and his brothers had spent sleepless nights uncovering the past and plans of the foe that now threatened Tura—if Reanan's responses were any indication. His joy dimmed further when he looked more closely at the elves walking with quick strides through the streets. The elves were nervous, many of them glancing toward the sky at regular intervals, or else keeping their heads lowered as they moved to their destinations.

Gellion looked at his brothers. Valder was beaming. He clearly hadn't noticed the air of solemnity in the city. Gellion didn't think Valder had given much thought at all to the dark knowledge they had learned since their departure from Suri Ranta.

Valder alone had immensely enjoyed the long days of sailing across the Semestrial Sea with nothing but sailcloth and a rudder. Gellion had sorely missed a motor at the back of the boat and had never crossed the sea with so few hands on deck. It had been a wet and slow journey, each moment more agonizing than the last as they made their painstaking way back to Faeran. More painstaking still had been their trek along the coastline for days until they arrived in Tura. Gellion was exhausted and salt crusted, and his nerves were wound tight as harp strings, but Valder seemed to feel none of these discomforts. Not for the first time, Gellion longed for his brother's easy resilience.

Pleasure was evident in Veldon's face as well, his eyes taking in all around him with an analyzing gleam, but a line creased his brow as his gaze locked on several spears and halberds latched to the back of elves who walked in a clear cadence of patrol. His eyes dropped to the ground. He stopped in his tracks with a sharp intake of breath.

A part of Gellion knew what Veldon's reaction meant before he followed his brother's gaze. Why else would a stone street procure such dismay? The suspicion did not soften the blow when Gellion lowered his eyes to the ground. The street was smooth—unbroken and grey—but through the grain of the stone, a latticework of ebony spread in every direction. Gellion lowered to his knees and brushed the stone with the tips of his fingers.

Dead. Lifeless.

He harbored no doubts that the rest of the city was the same. Every street, every building. His hand balled into a fist against the stone.

Gellion had been expecting this. Of course Kaelo had come to Tura, Gellion had always known he would, yet like his mother's grief, this confirmation of his worst fears brought more dread than he had anticipated.

He took slow breaths against his mounting anxiety. It was gone. All the vierstone in Tura. He knew it in his bones. They had arrived too late. Their warnings would fall on deaf ears. Their explanations would be useless. Gritting his teeth, Gellion rose to his feet and faced Reanan. The Master Builder was watching him.

"You know what it means, then," Reanan said softly.

"He destroyed it all?" Gellion said.

Reanan nodded. "The elves from Daro warned us, but it did no good. We couldn't stop him." He closed his eyes as though in pain. "We were such fools."

"What happened?" Gellion tried to control his voice, to keep frustration and panic from coloring his words. "What did he do? Please, Reanan, tell us plainly."

"I will, though I hardly think I am the best elf to do it." He glanced back at the closing gates. "But first let us go to the forges. We can speak there and you can see for yourself how the tale ends."

Gellion exchanged a look with his brothers. They were clearly as perplexed by Reanan's words as he was, but they followed Reanan to a pile of levit boards without further questions.

The boards were stacked next to a smooth metal path. Reanan stepped onto one of the boards and activated it with the press of his heel. The board rose off the ground with a barely audible hum. Gellion mounted his own board and felt his weight lift off of the path. He smiled despite himself. The levit boards seemed such a normal thing—a comforting thing. He had gravely missed Remsgri technology in his months crossing Tala.

A breeze swept Gellion's hair from his face as his levit board glided forward. He followed Reanan into the Scholar Quarter of Tura, his brothers close behind. Gellion forced himself to focus. Everywhere he looked, he saw black lacing the streets and buildings, but nowhere did he see other signs of damage. He frowned. In Daro, blackened vierstone had always accompanied earthquakes that had cracked the foundations of the city. Buildings had crumbled and split, roofs had caved in, Rale paths had broken. But Tura looked exactly as it always had.

They passed the glittering glass of the Archives and crossed a bridge into the Guild Quarter. Where was Reanan taking them? How could he show them what Kaelo had done when there seemed to be no damage to the city? Gellion longed to shower Reanan with questions and refuse to move another foot until the Master Builder answered them, but he bit his tongue and followed in silence. The forges were not far by Rale path.

Reanan banked his board right to follow a street running north along the Orhiri River. After a few blocks, he began to slow.

With Reanan in front of him, Gellion did not immediately see the forges. Hearing Veldon's gasp, he leaped off his levit board and stood to face the source of his brother's dismay. His stomach dropped. The forges of Tura were one of the Great City's wonders—huge and open to the air, with a sturdy roof to keep out rain and sun.

The roof was gone. A massive slack tub lay on its side next to the river. Some of the furnaces still stood, but their sides were scorched and pieces of stone crumbled from their edges. Several furnaces were nothing but heaps of rubble, surrounded by splintered planks of wood, twisted metal, and ash. It looked as though there had been an explosion.

Gellion swallowed past his tightening throat. He had spent years working metal in those forges. Had Kaelo done this?

"What happened?" Gellion's voice was a hoarse whisper. He felt Valder and Veldon step up on either side of him, but he could not seem to pull his eyes from the wreckage to see their expressions.

"What remained of the elves of Daro sailed into our harbor nearly two months ago," Reanan said. "Two days later, Kaelo made his presence known in Tura."

Every nerve in Gellion's body seized at the name. By now, he had no doubts whatsoever that his old mentor was behind these attacks, but he had been unsure whether the elves of Tura would have discovered the culprit's identity in his absence. A glimmer of hope lit in his chest. Had Renyra survived the battle, then? Had she carried Gellion's message to the elves?

"It began with an earthquake," Reanan continued. "But there was no more shaking after that. He just silently drained the city of vierstone until there was nothing left. We tried to catch him, threaten him, track him. Liera confronted him once, and it ended in a whole street's destruction when Coren launched an ambush against him. But nothing we did ever had a chance of succeeding. We were playing into his hands the entire time. Following the prophecy." Reanan nearly spat the last word. His face darkened, but there was something else in his eyes. Shame?

"Prophecy?" Veldon said sharply. "What are you talking about?"

Reanan hesitated. "There was an elf—from Daro. A Turi woman."

Gellion could feel his skin starting to chill.

"Kyna," Reanan said.

It was like a punch in the gut. Gellion struggled to keep his face under control. He could feel the eyes of his brothers boring into him, but ignored them.

"What did she do?" he said softly.

Reanan narrowed his eyes. "Did you know her?" he asked.

"What did she do?" Gellion repeated, enunciating each word. He was not about to explain his relationship with Kyna now.

"Liera brought her on the Council," Reanan said slowly. "Along with a Fieri elf from Daro—Renyra. They told us all that occurred in Daro. The earthquakes, the vierstone, and the alliance. Renyra warned us about Kaelo, though it was not until Liera saw him with her own eyes that anyone believed it. Anyway, Kyna brought a prophecy to the attention of the Council. She said she found it in the Archives." He shook his head. "It was perfect. Too perfect. We should have seen there was something wrong with it from the beginning, but we were desperate, and Kyna played her part well."

The pain in Gellion's stomach was starting to twist and transform. So the elves already knew Kyna was a spy. That gave Gellion a strange relief. Kyna must surely have left Tura by now if her secret had been revealed. He wouldn't have to speak with Liera after all. Not about this. But what had Kyna done? By Reanan's tone, the elves had learned of her treachery too late.

"The prophecy spoke of all that had been happening in Daro and in Tura," Reanan said. "It led us to melt what vierstone remained to us in a furnace. Kaelo couldn't destroy vierstone he couldn't touch. It made sense. But the prophecy went further. It spoke of a weapon—something forged 'from his despise.' We eventually interpreted it to mean a sword of vierstone. Kaelo wore armor that no arrow could penetrate, so we assumed a vierstone sword may succeed where no other weapon could. Kyna urged us along all the while, and we ate it up like sweet bread. It was all part of Kaelo's plan."

Gellion looked back at the destroyed forges. The Council must have made the vierstone sword here. His eyes moved to the overturned slack tub, then to the crumbling furnaces. An idea was forming in his mind. Memories of a lamp-lit study swam before his eyes. Two words, traced over and over and circled. Pages of notes on phoenixes and volcanoes.

"Vierstone ash." Gellion whispered the words. His mind whirled. Melted vierstone in the furnaces—meant to protect from Kaelo. Cold water from the river—a slack tub to cool the metal of a forged blade. He thought back to Kaelo's notes on volcanoes. There had been stacks of books on geology in those shelves, and Kaelo had pulled from them, written pages of his research on magma and ash.

Reanan stared at him. "How do you—"

Gellion cut him off. "What did he do with it, Reanan? What did he do with the vierstone ash?"

Reanan had gone pale again. He looked between Gellion and his brothers.

"He raised a phoenix."

Ice poured through Gellion's body and solidified in his veins. He stared at Reanan, willing the man to to take back his words, to say it was a joke, but the despair in his eyes was unmistakable.

A phoenix.

Gellion clenched his fists and closed his eyes. They were too late, and it was worse than they could have ever imagined.

"We need to go to Liera," Valder said again.

Gellion had refused Reanan's offer to bring them to the Lady of Tura. He wanted to think first, to process all that Reanan had told them, but how could he process the reality that a monster from his deepest nightmares had come to ravage his world once more, this time controlled by an elf he had once admired more than anyone in the world? It was ridiculous. It was impossible.

"We need to put this in perspective first." Gellion ran a hand through his hair. He was standing on a side street in the Guild Quarter, where Gellion had dragged his brothers after speaking with Reanan. Tura was a big city, but Gellion had once known many of the elves who lived here. He did not want the story of his or his brothers' return circulating the streets just yet. Not if their mother was here.

He shook his head.

One thing at a time.

But where to begin?

Veldon's voice cut through Gellion's thoughts.

"What did we learn in the Falspires that the rest of elves do not yet know?"

Gellion could feel his anxiety easing at the calm in his brother's eyes. He took a breath.

"We know how Kaelo played the Albaren and the Dierna, though that will offer little help to the elves now." He sighed and reached into an inner pocket of his shirt. "And we have this." He held out a roughly cut piece of stone, crimson and smooth with ripples like glass where it had cleaved. The stone cooled the tips of his fingers. He could feel his heartbeat slow and his anxiety dampen. The vierstone in his ear flared with heat, as though in protest.

Gellion had experimented with the redstone during their long hours of sailing. The stone both repelled him and drew him. He had begun to understand some of its workings, though he had not yet allowed himself to use its true power again. Well did he remember the rushing current that had flowed through his body when he used the stone as Kaelo had. He had ordered a rock to break in his hand and the rock had obeyed without a moment's hesitation. It had been a heady feeling, a powerful feeling, but so too had there been something *wrong* about it. Was it only because Gellion had seen Kaelo use that power to destroy his home?

Veldon eyed the redstone warily. He didn't like it when Gellion brought it out so casually. Of the three of them, Veldon seemed to be most sensitive to the mysterious substance. Gellion assumed it had something to do with Veldon's affinity to vierstone. All his life, Gellion had thought himself well attuned to the workings of vierstone. He could use its channel to make incredible works of craftsmanship and could influence the very properties of metallic elements under its influence, but Veldon understood lifestone itself in a way that Gellion could never hope to emulate—the same way their father had.

"I wish you would keep that hidden." Veldon pulled his eyes away from the stone to glance around the street.

Gellion shrugged. "No one here knows what it is."

"I still think we should be careful with it—both the stone itself and our knowledge of it. We still do not know where it comes from, or fully understand what it does. It could be dangerous, and not just in the hands of an elf using it for destruction."

"I am being careful," said Gellion. "I've brought it safely this far haven't I? Do you think I plan to start exploding rocks throughout the city? Challenging Kaelo to a duel at the top of my lungs?"

Veldon said nothing. He looked away.

Gellion sighed and slipped the stone back in his shirt.

"Veldon, I am taking it seriously, alright? I just don't see the harm in looking at the thing, or trying to figure out how it works. The better we know this stone, the better we can understand Kaelo's power."

"I'm not sure Kaelo's breaking stones is the power we need to worry about now." Valder raised an eyebrow. "He has a *phoenix*, and from what Reanan says, Kaelo can destroy all the vierstone in a city without causing any further damage or drawing attention to himself. It sounds to me like his use of redstone just paved the way for whatever he's doing now. It's nice to know how he did it, but I can't see how that," he motioned to Gellion's chest, "is going to help us against the same flying fire beast that kept the elves at war for two hundred years."

Gellion fell silent. Valder was right. Having access to Kaelo's weapon had offered a perfect solution to fighting him one on one, but Kaelo was not their only enemy now. What good was controlling the stones of a city when combatting an armored bird the size of a ship that could reign fire and fly? Gellion might be able to use his command of stone to trap the beast if it landed near him, but it was an unlikely hope.

"So we have nothing," Gellion said. "We can tell the elves why the army of Daro came to be massacred between two human armies, but not until months after the threat has passed. We can tell them that Kyna is Kaelo's daughter, but not until she has succeeded in leading the elves on a false chase and ensured the success of her father. We can tell them how Kaelo sent Daro into the sea and destroyed all the vierstone in Tura, but not until after he has raised a weapon far more powerful." A laugh escaped Gellion's lips, though he had never seen a situation less humorous. "The elves would have been just as well if we'd never escaped Tala."

"That's not true," said Veldon. "Any information about Kaelo could be valuable in stopping him. We don't know what he will do next. If he still intends to use redstone to enable his plans, our knowledge could still prove instrumental in his undoing. We may not have returned to the elves as saviors with all the answers, but we have returned with information that warrants hope, and we have returned to help."

"What makes you think anyone here wants my help?" Gellion said. "I just led a thousand elves into the worst disaster since the Battle at Mathtier and let my city fall into the sea without recognizing its destroyer was my old mentor who is—oh, yes—is only alive today because I spoke in favor of his life centuries ago!" Gellion's voice came faster and rose in pitch with each word. He could feel his emotions starting to pull him under again, his hands starting to shake. He had the sudden urge to take the redstone out of his shirt again.

"Gellion." From the gentleness of the voice, Gellion assumed it was Veldon who had spoken, but he was surprised to see Valder looking him in the eye. "You have to stop doing this to yourself. You constantly live in the past, torturing yourself with your failures and every decision you wish you had made differently. It does no good. You have the power to do something about what is happening *now*, and if you let the consequences of your past experience stop you from doing that, it will only add to your regrets and lessen the chances of the elves getting out of this."

Heat prickled up Gellion's neck. Was he so easy to read?

"He's right," said Veldon. "I have told you this before, Gellion, though you have done little since then to heed the advice." A sad smile curved his lips. "We can still tell Liera all we know and get a more complete story of what is happening among the Kindoms. I very much doubt this is an issue only afflicting the Turi now. We will learn what we can and go from there, making the best decisions we can with what we are dealt. It is all we can do."

Veldon's smile became more genuine. "Besides, you're forgetting the best benefit of our return that has nothing to do with what information we've gathered or what problems we have solved." His eyes lit with the innate joy Gellion had always envied in his brother. "We get to show mother we're still alive."

The thought only brought a fraction of the same joy to Gellion. Of course he was looking forward to seeing his mother again, but how quickly would her relief and happiness wear off after the initial reunion? How soon would that joy turn to anger, that relief to blame? He couldn't bear to see either emotion in his mother's eyes, not when he deserved them both so thoroughly.

As for his reunion with Tornac, Gellion felt only dread—deep and gnawing. There was so much more between Gellion and his eldest brother than this latest fault. Gellion could never do anything right in Tornac's eyes, and the last few months would have only proved Tornac's assertions of Gellion's irresponsibility and selfishness correct. Gellion wouldn't be surprised if Tornac was disappointed by the revelation of Gellion's continued existence. At least he would be happy to see Valder and Veldon, though Valder had likely earned some of his own enmity by following in Gellion's footsteps.

The excited spark remained in Veldon's eyes, though it was tempered by sympathy when he saw Gellion's face. Gellion did his best to appear pleased.

Valder hadn't noticed his elder brother's discomfiture. A wicked smile stretched across his face.

"We can 'show' mother however you want, but I say we scare Tornac witless with our resurrection."

2

RESURRECTION

Any plans of going straight to their mother and Tornac dissolved as soon as Gellion and his brothers walked back into the bustle of Tura's main streets. Gellion had almost forgotten how massive the Great City was.

"Not exactly Daro, is it?" Valder eyed the distant buildings against the horizon and the maze of streets before them.

Gellion smirked. Valder had never lived in a city this big. It took some getting used to, though travel within the city had become markedly easier since Rale paths were installed along the streets. Gellion remembered his distant youth—how incomprehensible Tura had seemed to him then. That had been long before the Remsgri invented the Rale, and travel had been restricted to walking the streets or floating up and down the river. All the same, he had loved Tura with all his heart. He still loved it.

"Any idea where they're staying?" Gellion asked Veldon. While Gellion and Valder had been living in Daro these last centuries, Veldon had remained with Tenille and Tornac. He had briefly stayed in Tura with them before sailing for the Kindom Council.

"In the Public Quarter, I'm sure," Veldon said. "There are guest rooms across from the Central Tower, but finding the right one would be a guess in the dark. We stayed in a different one each time we visited."

Gellion sighed. Given the tumultuous state of the city, it was unlikely they would find Tenille or Tornac in their rooms at all. Gellion should have asked Reanan where his mother was staying. Surely an active Council Member would have known.

"I'd say we have two choices then," said Gellion. "We go back to the gates and find Reanan, or we go to Liera." Gellion hated the thought of Liera knowing of his and his brothers' survival before their own mother, but he could see little way around it.

"We may as well go to Liera now," said Valder. "We need to talk to her anyway, and if there's not much chance of finding mother and Tornac on our own, we should do something useful. Do you know where to find her?"

Gellion nodded. "Most likely in the Central Tower, or else in her home a few blocks away. She's no Dulon, walking twenty miles a day through the streets of her city." Gellion grimaced, images of Dulon's long stride and flashing smile squeezing his chest. He wished it was the Lord of Daro to which he was about to confide all of this information. Dulon had always been infinitely more approachable than Liera and had always had an answer to any problem.

Until the Albaren came to us.

"Let's go," Gellion mumbled, walking to the nearest levit boards.

The Central Tower of Tura was an elegant pillar of white against a clear sky. Glass windows curved around its surface, reflecting the sunlight in a gleaming starburst. It was easily twice as tall as any building in Daro.

Gellion scrutinized the ground as they crossed the fan shaped expanse of stone before the tower. Like the rest of the city, this stone was laced with black, only here, Gellion thought he could make out seams where Builders had filled in cracks. A shiver shook his frame as he thought of the Court of Daro, split and crumbling before the partially collapsed Domes of Rhelyon. He was horrified by what Kaelo had done here, but grateful Tura still stood in reasonable repair.

A rush of cold air washed over Gellion as he walked through the glass doors of the tower. Summer in Tura was even hotter than in Daro, and the city's cooling systems were more a necessity than a luxury. Valder and Veldon let out sighs behind him. It had been months since any of them had felt the comfort of a controlled indoor environment.

"There are meeting rooms on the third floor," said Gellion. "It's the best place to start. If Liera's not there, I would wager there's an elf who knows where she is."

"Lead the way, oh Lord of Tura," Valder said with a bow.

Gellion rolled his eyes and began to walk toward the nearest lift. It was glass on all sides, offering an incredible view of the city from the upper floors.

The base of the lift descended as the brothers approached, revealing two pairs of feet, then legs and torsos. A man and a woman it seemed. It was not until the doors of the lift opened that Gellion registered who the woman was.

His feet froze in stride as a rush of adrenaline spread to his limbs. His arms seemed to reach out of their own accord to stop his brothers in their tracks. He heard the intake of breath from each of them as they looked up to see their mother just a few strides away.

It felt as though Gellion's heart was trying to climb out of his chest and up his throat. This was not how he had pictured his reunion with his mother—in the middle of a hallway where neither party had expected the other. She was not even alone. Gellion recognized Alos, the Master of Trade in Tura, walking next to her. Gellion grimaced. He had never much liked Alos and had no desire for him to be a part of this.

"—ridiculous," Tenille was saying to Alos. "I don't care where the phoenix is or what Kaelo is doing, we need to convene a Council beyond Tura. Physically protecting the cities doesn't require every Lord and Lady of the Kindom Council." She looked up then, and her eyes slid over her sons, then past them down the hallway.

Her eyes widened. Her voice choked off in a strangled gasp.

Tenille stopped walking so suddenly that Alos smashed into her back, sending them both stumbling forward.

"What the—Tenille!" Alos cursed and grabbed at Tenille's shoulder to keep himself upright.

Tenille ignored him. She untangled herself from Alos with a shove and straightened, her eyes locking on Gellion, then darting back and forth between her three sons.

Slowly, Gellion lowered his arms, which were still outstretched like barricades against his brothers' chests. A heavier silence than Gellion had ever known pressed against his ears, somehow amplifying the beating of his heart.

Tenille closed her eyes and took a shaking breath, then opened them again with deliberate slowness. She seemed shocked to see her sons still standing before her.

"Riu above," Alos whispered behind her. He had recovered from his anger enough to look at the object of Tenille's attention.

Veldon was the first to find his voice. "Mother." There was a smile in the word, almost a laugh.

Tenille's eyes widened still further at the spoken word. She was nearly grey she was so pale, and she opened her mouth in a silent 'o.'

Gellion lurched forward as her knees gave out, catching her under her arms. Valder and Veldon were beside him in another moment, helping Gellion lift their mother back to her feet.

No sooner had she regained her balance, Tenille collapsed into Gellion's embrace, sobs shaking her body.

So great was Gellion's shock, it took him several moments to muster the sense to clasp his arms around his mother. Never in all his life had he seen such a show of emotion from the stoic woman, not even when his father had died in the Great War. Heat spread over his skin, and he could feel the prick of tears behind his eyes. He blinked them away.

Tenille was beyond words. She pushed back from Gellion and her eyes roved over his face. She held up a hand and touched his cheek. Gellion smiled as comfortingly as he could, and Tenille's eyes flooded with fresh tears. She turned to Veldon then and threw herself against him with fervent desperation.

"It's alright, mother." Veldon fought for breath within her crushing embrace. "We're fine." He managed to extricate one of his arms and patted her on the back. He looked at Gellion over the top of Tenille's head. He was smiling, but his expression showed sadness beneath the joy. Relief this violent bespoke how much pain they had put their mother through.

By the time Tenille turned her attentions to Valder, she managed to choke out a few words.

"Riu's mercy. But ... but how? Dear heaven above. It can't ... you can't. I—"

"Careful now," Valder said. "You wouldn't want any of those words to make a coherent sentence."

Tenille shoved backward from Valder, glaring at him through water-rimmed eyes, but her anger melted when she saw his grin, and she collapsed into his arms again.

Alos was still standing to the side of the hallway, gaping at the scene before him. Gellion met the man's eyes and raised an eyebrow.

"Right," Alos mumbled. "I'll just ... I'll just go on to—" He trailed off and hurried toward the main entrance to the Central Tower, though he glanced back several times.

Tenille was standing on her own now, scrubbing her face with both hands.

"I don't understand," she said.

"We'll explain it all," Valder said. "But perhaps somewhere a bit more comfortable." He glanced around at the stark hallway, then looked at Gellion. "Take us to one of those meeting rooms upstairs?"

Gellion nodded. His skin was still hot, his breaths coming in shallow spurts. The guilt he had felt imagining his mother's grief from afar was nothing compared to seeing that grief now, so painfully plain before his eyes. For weeks, Tenille had been nearly alone in Tura, grieving for three of her four sons and fighting against the elf she had once mentored to one of them. Reanan had said Renyra had been on the Council. Had she told Gellion's mother of the battle? How he and his brothers must have fallen?

You're doing it again.

Gellion let out a sharp breath. His brothers were right. This constant obsession with the past would do the elves no good moving forward. He needed to focus, to shove his guilt and pain away from the present and do all he could to fix the consequences of his decisions. He owed it to the elves, and he owed it to his mother.

Forcing a smile on his face, Gellion held the doors of the lift open.

———

"Have you used it?" Tenille eyed the stone Gellion had sat on the table between them. Bright sunlight from the windows reflected off its crimson surface.

Gellion didn't answer her at once. It seemed a somehow shameful thing to admit, that he could do the same thing as Kaelo.

"Gellion did," Veldon said when several silent moments had passed. "He made a stone break in his hand, and he's been studying it since we left Tala."

Tenille only nodded, her expression blank. Red rimmed the edges of her eyes, purple circles beneath them. The colors seemed obscenely bright against the pallor of her face. Gellion shifted in his seat, looking away.

He and his brothers had told their mother everything that had happened in Tala, not just since the battle at Arvain, but since the Kindom Council had left Daro. Tenille had listened in stunned silence, her mind clearly working at top speed to keep up with the events they described and the implications of what they had experienced and discovered. Gellion was as honest as he could bear, leaving out only the nature of his relationship with Kyna and the details of his disastrous trip to Tradira.

He was impressed by how coolly his mother took their news, until he saw the tremor of her hands and the unmoving focus of her eyes. The poor woman was half in shock, and here they were telling a tale fit for legends.

"We probably should have waited a while to tell her all of this," Gellion said to his brothers in a low voice. He saw a measure of his guilt reflected back in their eyes.

"I'm fine." Tenille's voice was a hoarse whisper and cracked on the second word. A corner of her mouth turned up. "I will be fine," she amended, but her eyes welled with tears once more as she looked between her sons.

Gellion's stomach twisted into a tighter knot. He was suddenly possessed of the nearly unbearable desire to beg for her forgiveness, to grovel like the disgraced son he knew himself to be, but the presence of his brothers tempered his tongue. At least, that was the excuse he told himself. He couldn't be sure his courage would have held even in their absence. Instead, he said the only words he could bare to utter, inadequate though they were.

"I'm sorry. We came as quickly as we could."

Tenille's smile held no hint of betrayal or pain. "I know. And I am so grateful."

"If we had been here sooner—"

"Then we would not now know the secret to Kaelo's power, and in all likelihood, a phoenix would still fly over these lands," Tenille said. "You have nothing to be sorry for."

Gellion could hardly stand to look at the understanding and forgiveness in her eyes. Would she say nothing of his role in causing the situation in the first place?

She is waiting to be alone with me. She doesn't want to shame me in front of my brothers.

"Does Tornac know?" Tenille said.

Gellion stiffened.

"No," Valder said. "We didn't know where to find either of you. We were going to Liera when we ran into you in the hall."

A strange look came over Tenille's face.

"What is it?" Veldon said.

Tenille knit her brows. "I would not set your hopes too high where Liera is concerned."

"What do you mean?" Gellion said.

"She has been—" she paused, as though unsure of the right word. "Distant, since the ordeal with Kaelo. She tried to kill him with that sword before she knew it was all part of his plan."

"It's not the first time she's tried to kill him," Gellion said.

"No, but this time was different I think. An attempted public murder rather than an execution. Even if Kaelo had been condemned to death as she planned centuries ago, I doubt if Liera would have carried out the sentence herself. But I do not think the confrontation with her son is the only thing unhinging Liera. Some of the other Kindoms have been rather frank in their opinion of Kaelo and the threat he has brought to the elves. They blame Liera, thinking Kaelo is doing all of this for vengeance upon her, and by extension, the Turi. Only now he is threatening the elves as a whole."

"Did he say nothing of his purpose, then?" Gellion said. The heat of anger was beginning to seep through his guilt. "In all the time he was in Tura, or when he raised the phoenix, did he still say nothing? Are we as blind as we have been since Daro?"

A shadow fell over Tenille's face. "Reanan didn't tell you?"

"Tell us what?" Gellion said.

Tenille glanced between Gellion and his brothers. "Kaelo did reveal his purpose, at least in part."

Gellion felt the blood drain from his face. It was a question he had desperately sought the answer to for months, yet now that he was about to learn it, a strange dread rose within him.

"What is it?" Valder's face was alight with excitement.

Veldon looked almost as wary as Gellion.

"I do not think this is simple vengeance upon the elves who exiled him," Tenille said. "Kaelo said he sought justice for all elves, but that justice could not coexist amid passion and partiality. He said vierstone was a weakness and a curse among the elves. He said ... he said he will rid the elves of it. Completely and permanently."

3

PLANS

The trees of Riverseep Forest felt somehow more alive than trees should. Renyra couldn't decide if it was because of their sheer size, the myriad of living animals that seemed to be in constant movement through their branches, or something more. Maybe the terra spirits of this forest were more active or numerous than in most places Renyra had been, giving a feeling of heightened life to the canopies and all that was shadowed beneath them. Maybe it was just Renyra's imagination. Legends from a war fought before she was born had returned to Faeran, why not sentient trees?

"Where do we start?"

Renyra blinked and forced her gaze from the forest. Caerlyn raised an eyebrow at Renyra. In the dim lighting of their platform, Caerlyn nearly blended with her surroundings. Only the bright green of her eyes shone from the shadows. The rest of the troupe was watching Renyra, some with expressions of polite interest, others grim determination. Firas just looked worried.

"I don't know," Renyra admitted. She had thought of little else the last day, but she was no closer to coming up with any clever plans that would lead her and her troupe to Kaelo and the phoenix. How did you track something that could fly?

"As far as I know, the phoenix hasn't been seen since Kaelo flew it out of Tura, but then we are so far flung from the rest of the Kindoms, I doubt we would hear anything for some time if something happened."

She sighed and slumped back against a branch. Its bark was smooth and damp. The moisture seeped into her shirt, but it felt good in the muggy heat of the jungle. As beautiful as the trees were, Renyra wished there was a breeze to cut the stagnant air. The effect seemed to add to the sense of isolation she felt in Remsgraen—the Great City at the center of Riverseep Forest.

"I don't know what we should do," Renyra said. "But there's no reason to stay in Remsgraen."

"I'm more than happy to move on." Caerlyn eyed the thick branches over their heads. Renyra's mouth twitched. Caerlyn, like Renyra, had lived much of her life under the open skies of the Fieri grasslands. The forest did start to feel claustrophobic after a while.

"We have Trali now." Raren grinned and jerked his head toward a thick-limbed elf with a waterfall of dark braids. "I say we go back to Telem Fier, at least for a start."

Trali nodded slowly. "I will go to Telem Fier with you, though I do not like leaving my people in this time." His voice was deep and rich.

A smile broke through Renyra's worry. She hadn't seen Trali in centuries. Reuniting with Alura and Raren in Tura had been wonderful, but having all six members of their past troupe together again was more than she could have dreamed. It almost made the current situation of the world worth it. Almost.

"I know this will be hard," Renyra said. "I'm asking you to leave behind ties to your Kindoms, but this is a threat that transcends Kindoms. The elves will attack Kaelo with armies, and I hope to Riu that works, but I just can't see a head-on attack stopping him and this phoenix any more than it did in Tura or Daro."

"I agree," Alura said. "But what are we supposed to do that the rest of the elves can't? What happens if we succeed in tracking the phoenix and find ourself face to face with it?"

"It is a good question." Worry was still deep in Firas's eyes. His gaze was not on Alura, but on Renyra. "We do not know how to kill a phoenix. Or is our goal not the phoenix?"

"Kaelo would certainly be an easier target," Renyra said. "But I had something else in mind as a first attempt." Though Renyra was as lost as the rest of the troupe as to how they would track the phoenix, she had a better idea of her plan once they had found it. "There is another possible element to all of this." Renyra looked around at all of them. "Kyna."

An undercurrent of hostility emanated from the troupe at the name. Renyra ignored it.

"What if she's still with him?" she said. "We don't know what her tie to Kaelo is, but Tornac said she rode the phoenix *with* Kaelo out of Tura. What if we were able to find her alone—talk to her?"

"Talk to her?" Caerlyn scowled. "Are you serious?"

"Yes," Renyra said.

"And what would we say?" Raren looked about as convinced as Caerlyn, though with a less aggressive expression.

"I want to ask her about the phoenix. And Kaelo. I want to know why she is helping him and see if we can bring her to our side. For all we know, Kaelo forced her to help him under threat. I'll bet she knows how to stop them."

"I know you want to think the best of her," Firas said gently, "but we have no reason to believe Kyna did not act of her own free will. If we find her, she could very well attack us, or turn us over to Kaelo. It is a great risk to take on the little hope of her cooperation."

"We won't rely on her cooperation," Renyra said. "In fact, I say we go in to this expecting her to attack us. But of the three of them—the phoenix, Kaelo, and Kyna—Kyna is our best bet."

"It is something to consider," Firas said. "And if the opportunity arises, we can try. Very carefully. But if we are going to undertake this— tracking Kaelo and following a phoenix on its path of destruction—I think we need something more. We need a plan for confronting the phoenix, or Kaelo, as Alura said. We need a plan to stop them."

"Kill them," Caerlyn said.

Renyra bit her lip and looked down. A ripple of unease moved through the troupe. Killing was not something taken lightly by the elves and was the very reason Kaelo had been exiled centuries before. Renyra still wished there was another way to end this.

"We all know that's our goal," Caerlyn said. "We may as well say it out loud. I know it's distasteful, but it is necessary. We need to not only kill the phoenix, but Kaelo as well."

The silence that followed twisted Renyra's gut. Finally, she nodded. "I know."

"We'll need better weapons," Raren said.

Renyra took a deep breath. Had she not already tried to kill Kaelo twice? Why did it still bother her?

"I'm not worried about weapons," she said. "It's getting past Kaelo's defenses that's the problem. I've attacked him twice now. Both times, he was completely prepared, *expecting* me. In Daro, he caught my javelin and bent it in half. In Tura, he dodged an aerial attack and incapacitated me with a touch to the wrist before I could even touch him. It's his senses we should focus on."

"But we've all heard how that armor he wears repels normal arrow-heads and blades," said Raren. "How are we supposed to get past that, even if we do manage to get close to him without him knowing?"

"Armor does not stop us hitting his head," Trali said. "We knock him out. Then take him and do what we must."

Renyra nodded. "And he may not be wearing armor at all if we find him in the right situation."

"Alright," Caerlyn said. "But what about the flaming bird that will undoubtedly be with him? I doubt we can just smash it on the head, or stab it unawares."

Renyra knit her brows. She had always found it odd that the elves had taken so long to kill the phoenix during the Great War. She had always assumed the bird was just well protected by armies, or strategic in its attacks, but it seemed as though *someone* would have managed to stab the beast before the end of two centuries.

"Why is it so difficult to kill a phoenix?" she said.

No one answered at first.

Renyra was the youngest member of the troupe. Almost all of the rest had been alive during the Great War. Firas had been born long before its beginning.

"It is not a normal creature," Firas said. "I cannot say I was ever close enough to see it well, but those elves that did claimed it's feathers could repel weapons like no armor they had ever seen. Metal would bounce off, bend, or melt when set against the monster, and non-metal weapons, like ropes or wooden stakes, would burn."

"Oh." Renyra looked down. She felt a fool for expecting their destruction of the phoenix to be so simple as a stealthy stab with a spear. If the solution had been so easy, the elves would have done it long ago.

"Well," she tried to muster a semblance of confidence. "We set Kaelo as our primary target, then. And we try to get information from Kyna about how to kill the phoenix."

"It is a good plan," Trali said. "But first we must find them, yes?"

Renyra's confidence sagged. Yes, that was the real difficulty.

"I say we go to Telem Fier," said Raren. "Cuvan will be as informed as anyone about the phoenix's whereabouts, and Telem Fier's within easier reach of the other Kindoms. If nothing else, I'll bet the city itself will be a target before long. We can meet Kaelo and his phoenix there if we wait long enough."

The plan was met with general consensus from the troupe. Renyra nodded her agreement, but still found herself dissatisfied by how little any of them knew about the phoenix or its whereabouts. It could be weeks before information about Kaelo reached Telem Fier, and how would they ever be able to find him alone if they waited for him in a Great City? But it was the best they could do. At least they would be doing something.

<hr>

A thin mattress dominated the central floor space of Renyra's room. It sat on no supports, but lay directly on the metal floor. Somehow, it was every bit as comfortable as a bed stuffed to the height of Renyra's knees. Everything about the Remsgri was efficient and simple. A few of Renyra's belongings lay strewn on the floor beside the mattress. Two metal javelins and a bag of accoutrements and extra clothes, recently obtained in Telem Fier. None of these objects had belonged to Renyra for more than a few weeks. She missed her house, her things, her life.

"May we talk?" Firas walked into the room.

Renyra nodded and sat down on the low bed. Firas lowered himself next to her. His long legs bent upward so his knees were nearly level with his chin. Somehow he made the position appear graceful.

"Why is this so important to you?" he said.

"Important?" Renyra stared at him. "What could be more important than stopping a mad elf and the phoenix he recently brought to life from destroying all the vierstone in Faeran?" There was a note of hysteria to her voice, and she took a steadying breath.

"I am not saying that stopping Kaelo is unimportant," Firas said calmly. "I am wondering why it is so important that you stop him yourself."

Renyra looked away from Firas's penetrating eyes.

"It doesn't have to be me," she said. "I just think the elves will go about this all wrong, like they did in Tura. Someone has to think differently, and I don't trust anyone else to do it."

Firas nodded. His eyes narrowed in thought.

"They will go at him with force," Renyra said. "Throw weapons as fast and hard as they can and get as many numbers as possible to attack him. They will lose. I know it. I *feel* it Firas. What happened in Tura will happen on a larger scale—the biggest scale. If we couldn't stop a single elf in a single city, how much more impossible will it be to stop an elf with a phoenix set against an entire continent? I'm scared, Firas. I fear that I'm leading all of my friends to their deaths, and if anything happened to you—" Renyra's voice cracked. The horror of losing Firas was something she could never consider.

A warm hand cupped her shoulder. Firas pulled Renyra against him and pressed his face into her hair. Renyra breathed in his scent and concentrated on his presence. The vierstone in her ear warmed, and she felt an echo of his love for her, his concern and his own fear.

"But what other choice do we have?" Renyra said against Firas's neck. "I can't bear to lose any of you, but if we do nothing, I will lose you anyway."

Firas cocked his head in question.

"I went without vierstone for a week," Renyra said, "and while you assured me it would have no effects on me in so short a time, it did. I couldn't feel you. There was something between us, some barrier. It was like a piece of me was missing, and I couldn't entirely reach you. Over time I fear I would no longer even remember what it was to feel you there. I wouldn't even mourn the loss anymore."

Renyra hugged her knees to her chest, leaning harder into Firas.

"You are right," Firas said. Both of his arms were wrapped around her now, the steady beat of his heart comforting against her head. "It is not a future we can allow to happen without giving all we have to stop it. I just wonder if it would not be better for us to join with Cuvan, or even return to the Turi Council. I see your point of looking at the problem from different angles, but that is a conversation that could still happen among the leaders of the Kindoms. You don't need to put all of this on yourself."

Renyra shook her head. "They won't listen. We've tried to work with both Liera and Cuvan, and it didn't work. I understand their reluctance to take risks and think beyond the scope of what they know, but it would only hinder us and take too much time as the Councils gave input and opinions and argued."

Pushing herself up, Renyra turned to face Firas. "Caerlyn said the last phoenix was killed by just one elf. It wasn't force that killed it, it was something else. Do you know anything more about it?"

Firas looked down, his big eyes laden with sadness. "No. Only that it was Gellion's father who killed the beast. But Gellion won't ... wouldn't talk about it."

Renyra's eyes widened. "It was Gellion's father?"

Firas nodded. "But I know no more than anyone else what happened."

Silence stretched between them for a moment while Renyra let this revelation sink in. Then she shook herself and returned to their previous point.

"Well whatever happened, it shows that killing this phoenix is possible, and that it is possible with a small group of elves. I think we are meant to do this, Firas. We've been caught up in every part of Kaelo's journey so far, and we probably know more than any elf alive what he's capable of because we've seen it. And we know Kyna."

"I still do not think that should be viewed as an advantage."

Renyra narrowed her eyes, and Firas held up his palms in surrender, a small smile tugging at his lips.

"I hope I am wrong," he said. "If anyone can force Kyna into friend-ship, I daresay it is you. In fact, I would not be surprised if you bested Kaelo through simple force of willpower. You will have him groveling for forgiveness before Liera in two weeks' time."

Renyra glared at Firas, unsure how much he was mocking her.

Firas's smile held more sorrow than amusement. "You do make good points, and you know I will follow you to whatever end you set your heart to. I am only asking that you be careful. If you would believe it, I am as afraid of losing you as you are of losing me."

Renyra's face softened. "We will be careful. I just know this is some-thing we're meant to do."

"Then we will do it." Firas's face grew serious. "And if three centuries together has taught me anything about you, we will succeed."

4

PHOENIX FLAME

The afternoon was wearing to evening by the time Gellion and his brothers followed their mother out of the Central Tower. Tenille led the way through the streets of the Public Quarter—not toward her apartment, but to the Markets across the river. She said she had made dinner plans with Tornac earlier in the day and was determined that he should know of his brothers' survival with no further delay, despite Gellion's half hearted suggestions that they find Liera first.

As she walked, Tenille's glance continued to drift back toward her sons. Gellion suspected that she feared she was imagining all of this and had to constantly reassure herself that Gellion, Valder, and Veldon were really behind her.

Gellion avoided her eyes. He couldn't decide which conflict was greater within him, the fear that Kaelo was bent on destroying all the vierstone in Faeran, or that his own elder brother was just a few streets away. Veldon kept glancing sideways at him, probably guessing his internal struggle.

"Are you alright?" Veldon pitched his voice so Tenille would not be able make out the words.

Gellion grimaced. "I think I'd rather confront Kaelo."

Veldon raised an eyebrow. "What are you going to say to him?"

"I'm sorry?" Gellion suggested, shrugging. Veldon's other eyebrows rose to meet the first, a sort of incredulous hope on his face. "For not being dead," Gellion continued.

Beside him, Valder snorted, but tried to cover it as a sneeze when Tenille turned around.

Veldon sighed, but showed no shock at Gellion's response. Veldon had seldom known a time when his two oldest brothers were not at odds. Even before the end of the Great War, Tornac and Gellion had held a tenuous relationship. From Gellion's earliest recollections, Tornac had taken the role of father and protector upon himself, determined to groom Gellion into a responsible and accomplished elf in the best way he saw fit. Never mind that their own father had been alive and well at the time. Gellion had long since accepted that he and his brother were as alike as wind and stone and had given up trying to understand Tornac even before their infamous last parting. He could not imagine that their centuries apart, or the near deaths of their younger brothers on his watch, would have done much to repair the relationship.

When the Markets of Tura came into view, the corners of Gellion's mouth pulled up despite himself, his bearing softening in the warm embrace of reminiscence. Tables and chairs sprawled along the riverbank, stringed lights linking the branches of trees overhead. The sizzle of hot oil and the hum of conversation met his ears before a waft of breeze brought mouthwatering aromas to his nose. He had not had a freshly cooked meal since Suri Ranta. The thought of food that was not dried or stale made his stomach clench with anticipation.

"There he is," Veldon said. Excitement laced his voice and his eyes shone bright with joy.

Gellion followed his brother's gaze.

Like most of the Turi elves around him, Tornac had dark hair—brown, rather than the rich ebony of Valder and Veldon. It fell loose beside his face and his brow was furrowed as he looked across the river. Gellion read his own features in the backlit profile of Tornac's face, though he could hardly guess what thoughts lay within the dark expression.

"Wait," Valder said, though the whole group had stopped upon seeing Tornac. "Come this way." He jerked his head back toward the

Markets with a mischievous gleam in his eyes. Veldon gave Valder an exasperated look, but smiled and followed him.

"What is he doing?" Tenille said, looking at Gellion.

"Being Valder," Gellion muttered.

"Mmm." Tenille pressed her lips together, but there was a hint of amusement in her eyes as she watched her two youngest sons bend their heads together in conspiracy. "Aren't you going to join them?"

Gellion realized with a thrill of panic that he was alone with his mother, with Tornac so close that the turn of his head would give him away.

"I don't know if Tornac wants to be surprised by me. And there's a knife by his plate."

Tenille did not smile, or roll her eyes as Valder and Veldon would have. The look in her eyes was something closer to sadness.

"He was crushed when he heard about you. It has been as difficult for him as for me."

"He mourned for them." Gellion indicated his younger brothers, now waving at him frantically to join them.

Tenille's lips made a thin line. "Whatever there is between you and Tornac, he would never wish you dead, Gellion."

Gellion was unconvinced, but could no longer ignore the gestures of Valder and Veldon, who were now flailing their arms and attracting stares from passersby. He hurried to join them, giving his mother a last look of doubt.

Valder whispered his plan to Gellion.

"Are you sure we should be doing this here?" Gellion said. "In public?"

"If it's Tornac's wrath you fear, it will be more tempered in the company strangers," Valder pointed out. "Besides, everyone loves to witness a good, heartfelt reunion. It's like public betrothals—makes everyone around feel warm and happy and involved."

"I don't think 'warm' and 'happy' have ever been used to describe Tornac," Gellion said.

"Gellion." Veldon's voice was uncharacteristically hard. "Sometimes I wonder if you've ever taken any time to know him in all the centuries you lived together. He is a good man."

Gellion gritted his teeth and said nothing.

"Well, now's as good a time as any," Valder said, unfazed by the less than friendly sentiments of his brothers.

Tenille was still hanging back outside Tornac's field of view. She was never one to outright condone their brotherly antics, but she rarely interfered.

Valder walked in front with Veldon and Gellion trailing behind. When he reached the back of Tornac's chair, Valder turned so that his back was to Tornac. With a wink to Gellion and Veldon, he stumbled backward into Tornac's chair. Tornac cursed and grabbed the sides of the chair, bracing his feet to keep from falling over. While he was distracted, Veldon and Gellion slipped into two of the chairs at the table. Valder had spun away from the side Tornac leaned to and took his own seat before Tornac had recovered himself.

Tornac's head whipped behind him, trying to locate the elf who had so rudely smashed into him. When he could find no culprit, he turned back to the table.

Tornac jerked backward so violently he nearly toppled over the back of his chair. He gasped in so much air he looked like he nearly choked on it, and his eyes darted between his three brothers as though preparing for an attack.

It was difficult to discern what emotions lay behind those eyes. Chief among them was shock, but Gellion thought he could see fear beneath the surface—fear and pain. Did Tornac think he was going mad? Gellion would have. He also would have punched Valder square between the eyes for pulling something like this.

Standing on unsteady legs, Tornac took a step backward, shaking his head.

"Hello, brother," Valder said with a broad grin. "Did you miss us?"

Tornac's eyes widened, fixed unblinkingly on Valder.

"Valder." The word was barely a breath. "I—"He looked to Gellion, then to Veldon.

Bracing himself, Gellion waited for the explosion, or for Tornac to simply walk away, but there was no hint of anger in his face as shock gave way to realization.

Tornac stepped toward Valder, the nearest brother. Valder sank back against his chair, his smile faltering slightly under the intensity of Tornac's gaze. Tornac grasped him by the shoulders.

"It was only a joke!" Valder flinched as though expecting a blow and put his hands up in surrender.

Tornac lifted Valder onto his feet like a limp doll, looked him straight in the eye, then pulled him against his chest and clasped his arms around him with a force that knocked the breath out of Valder with an audible *whoosh*. Valder gasped, then visibly relaxed and wrapped his own arms around Tornac.

"You bastards." There were tears in Tornac's eyes.

Valder laughed.

Relief washed through Gellion, but it was quickly replaced by a fresh wave of anxiety as he realized Tornac would soon make his way to him. Veldon was on his feet now and met Tornac's furious embrace with several claps on the back.

Gellion's heart was hammering. Over the pounding in his ears, Gellion thought he heard what sounded like raised voices. He knit his brow, diverting his attention to the elves at the surrounding tables. Several of the elves were watching Tornac and his brothers with curiosity, some with gratifying smiles, but more elves were turned away, looking across the river with alert expressions.

Gellion stood. The hair on his arms stood on end, and his anxiety intensified. He strained his ears, but as he turned to follow the direction of the elves' attention, he caught Tornac's eye over Veldon's shoulder. Gellion froze, all worry of distant shouts forgotten.

A measure of reserve spread over Tornac's features. His smile lessened; his grip on Veldon loosened. Tornac disengaged himself from Veldon, giving his youngest brother a firm shoulder squeeze and a look of fondness that only increased the turmoil within Gellion's chest. Gellion shifted his feet. There was no one between himself and Tornac now. He raised his eyes to meet his brother's gaze.

"Gellion." Tornac's voice was hesitant, his expression unreadable.

Gellion's mind had gone blank. Under his brother's stare, he could think of nothing to say, nothing to do. He just stood dumbly, hoping his face was as impassive as Tornac's.

Distant shouts came again, but closer this time, and much louder.

Gellion tore his gaze from Tornac, whipping his head to the side and looking in the direction of the eastern city gates. He could hear frightened whispering around him now. Elves were standing and pointing.

The air had gone still. Even the sound of birdsong had ceased, leaving only the far off rush of waves against the sea cliffs.

A sudden pressure on his shoulder nearly made Gellion leap sideways, but he managed to retain control of himself when he saw his mother standing next to him. The look on her face turned Gellion's blood to ice. He could see dread in her eyes, a fear full of memories. The same memories came to Gellion's mind as the hair on the back of his neck joined that on his arms, sticking straight out with a charge pulled from the air. The silence. The instinctual fear. He felt like a rabbit in an open field, trying to find the shadow of the hawk he knew hovered beyond his vision.

The shadow came.

It was a shadow far bigger than a hawk's—far bigger than the largest eagle to ever take flight in Riure. An unearthly screech echoed off every building around him. The sound was terrifying, but somehow beautiful at the same time. Gellion felt an innate terror rise in his breast, yet he longed to hear the sound again.

Shaking his head, Gellion automatically searched around him for anything that could be used as a weapon, though he knew almost anything would be useless against the beast that flew above them.

"Has it come here before?" Gellion shouted over the tumult rising from the elves around him. "Has it come since Kaelo raised it?" Seeing nothing else, he grabbed one of the dinner knives sitting on the table.

"No," Tenille said. "This is the first time anyone's seen it that I know of. It's been a week of silence. We had no idea what Kaelo was doing." Her words came fast. She, too, was looking around frantically, but not for a weapon. Grabbing Gellion's arm, she dragged him closer to her other three sons, pulling them together with a look that dared any of them to try and go off alone.

"What do we do?" Veldon's eyes roved the sky.

"Find shelter," Tornac said.

Gellion was surprised to see Tornac now held a sword in his hand. He had not even noticed the blade at his brother's hip before now.

There was an uncomfortable twinge in Gellion's stomach as he recognized the blade as Vyra's. Tornac had taken the weapon upon himself when his wife had died in the last months of the Great War.

All five of them ran toward the metal roof that covered the markets. The space was already choked with panicked elves.

"What does he want here?" Gellion yelled. "I thought he already destroyed all the vierstone in Tura!"

"He did." Tenille shook her head. "I don't know. I don't know what this is."

Veldon and Valder were both looking at Gellion. Valder's eyes flicked to Gellion's chest, where the redstone lay hidden beneath his shirt. Gellion reached for the lump, but his hand paused before he took the stone out. What was he supposed to do with it, raise pillars of stone toward the beast and hope one hit?

A shadow fell across the river, and Gellion gasped involuntarily as a bird the size of a ship soared into view. All of Gellion's muscles went rigid. The assault of memories hit him like a block of stone, and he thought his teeth must surely shatter under the strain of his jaw.

The phoenix looked just like the one that had plagued the elves for two centuries during the Great War. Its metallic feathers were crimson, mottled with pinks and blacks in mesmerizing patterns reminiscent of magma. Fire trailed from the tips of each feather and from the lashing tails behind the beast.

Next to Gellion, Tornac took a step forward. His knuckles were white around the hilt of his sword, and rage burned in his eyes as he watched the phoenix. Gellion reached for Tornac's arm as he took another step.

"Are you mad?" Gellion said. "You can't kill it with that and you know it!"

Tornac turned his glare on Gellion, and his eyes seemed to simmer with emerald fire.

"Let go, Gellion." If Tornac's eyes were fire, his voice was ice.

Gellion pulled harder against him. Before Tornac could respond, the phoenix let out another cry, and Gellion released Tornac reflexively to clap his hands over his ears. Tornac remained where he was, cringing away from the cry.

The great bird was flying over the Public Quarter. It stilled its wings and dropped in altitude so it was nearly even with the Central Tower. Then it opened its beak wide enough that Gellion could see the glowing inside of its throat from across the river.

"No!" The shout escaped Gellion's mouth before he was conscious of thinking it, but he knew his cry would do no good.

Flames flowed from the phoenix's mouth like a torrent of water. The fire was not the orange and yellow of normal fire, but a deep, shocking crimson. The flames bathed the Central Tower, then the buildings surrounding it. Screams carried across the water, and Gellion felt gorge rise in his throat. Panic was building within him. He tried to push it down. He had to do something. He couldn't just watch Tura fall by fire. But what could he do?

The phoenix banked gracefully in the air, letting out another flow of flame below it. The screams continued, but they were not the shrieks of agony Gellion would expect from burn victims, nor did he see any lingering flames coming from the Public Quarter. Gellion narrowed his eyes, squinting across the river. Most of the Turi buildings were made of stone, metal, and glass, but trees lined every street in the city. Surely they would be charred to bits in the inferno emitted by the phoenix? Yet the wake of the phoenix remained seemingly untouched. No smoke rose from the buildings or the trees.

The falling flame came closer. The phoenix was heading for the river, directly toward the markets.

Gellion reached for the redstone in his shirt. He had no idea what he would do with it, but holding it gave him some comfort against the horrific beast flying toward him, a sense of power.

"We have to move!" Valder shouted.

There was nowhere to move. Elves were scattering, falling over each other, blocking each other.

"Get to the river!" Valder yelled, but Gellion remained in place. There was something strange about this fire.

"I don't think it will make any difference," Gellion said. "Those flames—I don't think they burn."

Valder looked at him like he had just suggested water did not make one wet.

"Listen!" Gellion pointed across the river. "Those are screams of fear, not pain. Even the trees are not burning." He looked again to the eerily scarlet fire. It was nearly to the river now. "There is something wrong about those flames, but I don't think water or shelter will do anything to save us from them."

As Gellion spoke, he saw the fire douse a building. It behaved more like smoke than flame. The inside of the building seemed to glow red from within the fire's outline, but then returned to normal when the phoenix had passed over.

"He's right," Tornac said. He was still holding his sword, but his look was more calculating than bloodthirsty now. "Whatever devilry is in those flames, I do not think there is anything we can do to stop it."

The phoenix banked again. Gellion could see the wicked point of its beak now. Its eyes glowed as brightly as its feathers. But there was a shadow between the arches of its wings. Gellion's eyes widened. Was Kaelo riding the phoenix over the city?

Before Gellion could get a better look at the figure on the bird's back, a wall of red flame touched down on his side of the river, enveloping the table where he had sat with his brothers just minutes before.

"Get down!" Tornac shouted.

Gellion felt himself pulled forcefully to his knees. He opened his mouth to protest Tornac's manhandling, but the words died on his lips as the fire consumed him.

It was warm. Gellion felt no pain, no burning flesh or lack of oxygen. Instead, he felt a mind numbing shimmering of the air. The same current ran through him that he had felt countless times in Daro, only stronger. It was more akin to the splitting of reality he had felt in the vierstone quarry when a quake hit while he was touching an entire cliffside of vierstone. His head reeled, and his skin seemed to vibrate. He fell to his hands, shouting and holding his head, trying to still the waves of vertigo wracking his mind and the humming current traveling across his skin, through his blood.

Then it was over. The flames had passed. Elven screams still surrounded him, and he heard another ethereal shriek from the phoenix, but it was further away. Gellion pushed himself to his knees.

"Is everyone alright?" Tenille said in a quavering voice.

"Fine," Valder said faintly.

Veldon nodded.

"What was that?" Tornac looked as shaken as Gellion felt.

"It was like Daro," Veldon said. "Like the earthquakes." He was looking at Gellion, eyes full of meaning.

Gellion knew what that sensation had meant. It had been a current, similar to the current that flowed from vierstone, but markedly different in one vital way, he was sure—it had an exactly opposite frequency. That had been the same current Kaelo had extended from redstone in Daro to stop vierstone's current—to kill it. But there was no vierstone left in Tura.

Not in the foundations.

Gellion swallowed the dread rising in his throat. With sickening certainty, he lifted his hands to his right ear and unfastened the vierstone earring pierced through the cartilage. He placed the stone in his palm and looked down at it.

It was black.

He looked to his brothers, eyes locking on each of their earrings.

All black. All dead.

He held his earring up to his brothers and watched understanding dawn on each of their faces.

"I think we have our answer," Gellion said in a hoarse whisper. "We know the next piece of Kaelo's plan."

5

STORIES OF PRESENT AND PAST

Ever since Gellion had determined he would return to Faeran, it had been his plan to rejoin the Turi Council to confront whatever threat Kaelo posed to the elves. For weeks he had expected it—longed for it—yet now that he sat in the familiar meeting room with curving walls and a window overlooking the city, he itched to leave. It was not that he had disliked his time on the Turi Council in those years preceding the Great War, nor that he dreaded returning to his role of leadership now. It was the room itself.

Two memories clung to its walls—one of a trial and one of a dream. Gellion could not decide which disturbed him more.

"We kill the phoenix. It is the only plausible option."

Gellion blinked and forced his attention back to the meeting. Tornac was speaking, his brows low over his eyes. The meeting had only been going on half an hour, but Gellion was already annoyed by Tornac's authority in the group. Tornac deserved it, he supposed. He was essentially the acting Lord of Maramor, and Liera had taken little initiative thus far to enforce order upon the meeting. Someone had to step up, and Tornac had been on this Council for decades while Gellion was in Daro. It still rankled him.

Gellion, Valder, and Veldon had not yet had the chance to recount their story to the Council. The sudden arrival of three elves presumed dead was somewhat overshadowed by the magnitude of the event that had occurred that evening.

In less than an hour, the phoenix had unmade every scrap of vierstone remaining in Tura, namely that pierced through the skin of the city's inhabitants. It was a horror beyond anything Gellion could have imagined. If Kaelo's goal was to rid Faeran of vierstone, it seemed he had a nearly unstoppable and fool proof way of doing so. Suddenly, the discoveries Gellion and his brothers had made in Tala seemed useless.

The Council had convened late in the night. Amid the panic, there had been little uproar at the arrival of Gellion and his brothers. Four of the seven Council members in attendance had already seen the brothers earlier in the day. Saethir and Dorian had not know them well enough to do more than smile congratulations at the news of their continued existence. Then there was Liera.

Tenille had not exaggerated about the precarious mental state of the Lady of Tura. Liera's skin resembled milky parchment, and her eyes were bloodshot and unfocused. She had drawn back in shock upon seeing Gellion, but had shown little other emotion, only eyed him warily throughout the meeting.

"Of course," Alos said with a soft snort. "Just kill the phoenix. A simple solution."

"It is not simple," Gellion said before Tornac could respond. "But it is possible. It has been done before."

"Yes, but no one knows how!" Alos said. "All evidence of how Eldian defeated that phoenix burned away when it died."

All evidence. Including the man who achieved the impossible.

All these centuries later, the pain of losing his father could still touch Gellion. Gellion had not been in Maramor during that final battle, but keeping the phoenix's armies at bay on the other side of the mountains. He had returned to the charred remains of a tower and the news that his own father had killed the beast of terror—and died in the ensuing inferno.

Gellion could see the same memories haunting Tornac's eyes across the table—but there was something else in his face. His brows were drawn together, and a slight frown pulled at the corners of his mouth. He seemed more frustrated than grieved.

"We know something that might help," said Veldon.

Everyone in the room turned to look at him. A flush had begun to creep up his neck.

"We found something while we were in the Falspire Mountains of Tala," Veldon said. "Information on Kaelo. It ... well, it may not give us the key to killing the phoenix, but it could be helpful." He looked at Gellion.

All attention turned to Gellion. Valder cocked an eyebrow and nodded to him. Gellion took a breath. So far, his mother was the only elf they had told of their adventures and discoveries. He had no idea how the Council would take their revelations. He still felt his news would fall on uncaring ears. What use was knowing how Kaelo came to be where he was in the face of the effortless destruction he now wrought? But the eyes that watched Gellion now were hungry. The Council wanted to know their story. They deserved to know it, even if it would solve few of their problems.

"It was a long and strange journey from Arvain to Tura," Gellion began, staring at the table. "We convinced the lawgiver of the Elder Clan to release us and travelled across half of Tala with Dierna traders to the northern Falspire Mountains. There, the Kayda people helped us. The humans of the mountains knew more of the elves than we could have guessed, though they themselves did not know the full importance of their encounters. We stayed in the Falspires to research the stories we heard. We followed the trails of legends and superstitions and found far more than we imagined.

"We know what happened in Daro. We know what happened with the Albaren and the battle at Arvain. We know what Kaelo has been doing these last centuries, and now we know how he destroys vierstone and breaks cities."

The Council stared at him, some with open mouths. Liera sat unmoving and pale. There was more fear in her eyes than interest.

And so, Gellion told their story in full. He did not go in order, as some discoveries had not made sense until weeks later. First he spoke of the Kayda's wary reactions to Valder and Veldon and the story of the selkie. He explained how he and his brothers had surmised the selkie was an elf, and he described Kaelo's notes and the letters from Commander Vensure. Then came the more difficult parts. He told the Council about the elven spy to the Dierna.

"The spy was a woman. We agonized over who it could have been, until we came to Suri Ranta. The Kayda described a little girl—a changeling child among the humans fathered by a selkie—by an elf. Kaelo catalyzed the alliance with the Albaren and sent his daughter to tip off the Dierna. He was only playing the humans off of each other to get us out of Daro. But I think it spiraled beyond his control. I still cannot believe he planned for the Albaren to betray us. If he wanted us dead, he could have accomplished it in Daro."

Stunned silence.

"A daughter?" Reanan's eyes were round. He was shaking his head. "But why? How? You mean to say he had a child with a *human*?"

A chorus of muttering moved around the table.

"What proof have you of this?" Liera's voice was a sliver of ice. Her eyes burned with more spirit than Gellion had seen since his return.

"The Kayda are proof that the child existed," Gellion said. "And there were two beds in Kaelo's cave. Then there is the proof you all have just told us." He looked straight at Liera. "Kyna convinced you of that prophecy. She helped Kaelo raise the phoenix."

Liera's face turned a subtle green. Her eyes unfocussed. Was she imagining Kyna's face? Making the same mental confirmation Gellion had when he had first come upon the revelation? The resemblance was obvious when one was not blinded by impossibility. Eventually, the Lady of Tura raised her eyes to Gellion, and the truth of his statement was evident in their depths.

"So Kyna has been pulling the strings since the beginning," Tornac said. The bitterness in his eyes surprised Gellion in its fervor. He looked almost as betrayed by Kyna's identity as Gellion. "That explains some of Kaelo's success. But it does not explain how he has raised a phoenix and purged an entire city of vierstone. You said you know how he is doing it. Explain."

Tornac's eyes were hard as he looked at Gellion. Though his face still softened each time his gazed passed over Valder and Veldon, Tornac's shock at seeing Gellion alive had clearly worn off. Heat welled in Gellion's chest. What had he expected, instantaneous forgiveness of all of his faults? Tears of joy and a heartfelt embrace like that of his brothers? Gellion nearly scoffed aloud at the thought. It would never be that way between them. He should be grateful Tornac was even acknowledging his presence, but gratefulness was not one of the emotions currently writhing under his skin.

Gellion kept his face carefully neutral. He inclined his head to Tornac, then glanced at his younger brothers. Veldon sat straighter than necessary. He looked profoundly uncomfortable as Gellion reached into his shirt. Valder nodded his encouragement with the quirk of his lip.

"We found this in Kaelo's cave." Gellion placed the redstone on the table in front of him. His fingers were cool when he withdrew his hand.

The Council members leaned forward. The rock was not particularly impressive, just a roughly cut hunk of glassy stone no larger than a palm. Gellion watched the expressions surrounding him carefully. No one gasped or drew back in surprise. Most looked at the rock with tilted heads and drawn eyebrows, clearly confused. Then Liera's eyes widened.

"Red." It was all she said, but she looked like she had seen a ghost.

"If you look closely," Gellion said. "It has the same cut and texture of vierstone. It is identical in every way, except—" He nodded to Liera. "It is red."

"The sword." Comprehension dawned on Tornac's face.

This gave Gellion pause. "What sword? The vierstone sword?"

Tornac shook his head. "It was vierstone, but he changed it. He touched it and it turned red."

"What?" Veldon said, eyes round with horror. "He *turned* it red?"

"Yes." Tornac raised his eyebrows at Veldon's reaction.

"What is it?" said Dorian. "You are saying this rock here is connected to what Kaelo did to that sword?"

"It must be." Gellion took a breath to steady himself, but this news rattled him as much as it did Veldon. They had not know where the redstone had come from, but Gellion had assumed Kaelo had found it as it was, maybe in the ruins of the Great War, or in the dark recesses of the shadows of the world. Could he have *created* it? Cold prickles spread down Gellion's arms. He thought he had known Kaelo. How could an elf change so much? What had happened to Kaelo in those centuries to make him what he was now?

"Will someone please explain what this stone is?" Alos looked between Gellion and his brothers with a raised eyebrow.

"We believe it is the opposite of vierstone, so to speak," Gellion said. "Kaelo can use it in a similar way to vierstone, only instead of seeing into stone and metal—increasing his awareness and understanding of it—he can blindly control it. It is how he breaks stone. But there is more." Gellion nodded to Veldon. "Vierstone contains a current. It is constant, and oriented in a single direction. This stone," He gestured at the redstone on the table, "has the same current, only it is oriented in the opposite direction. Kaelo uses that current. He extends it into vierstone and the frequencies clash, stopping the current in the vierstone permanently."

"Riu above," Reanan said. "You ... you have tried this? You know it to be true?"

"I have tried to the extent of verifying our theory," Gellion said. "But I have not destroyed vierstone with it."

"And you say he *made* this abomination?" Alos said.

"The possibility never occurred to us," Gellion admitted. "Until Tornac mentioned the sword. You say Kaelo turned it red with a touch. If it is the same as this stone, here, it is the only logical conclusion."

"Perhaps he can make more of it using its own power," Tenille said. "He could have found the original stone."

"It doesn't matter where he got it." The stone reflected in Dorian's eyes as he leaned closer to examine it. "We have it now. We can use it against him. We can stop him."

"That is not why we brought the stone from Tala." Veldon spoke softly, but Dorian drew back into his chair when he saw his expression. "We do not understand this stone. We do not know how it works, or what consequences may come from its use. There is something wrong about it, that much is obvious from any interaction we have had with it. What we do know is that Kaelo has redstone with him and has been using it to achieve his goals. It is possible that the stone even has a role in his control of the phoenix, or at least his ability to create that flame we saw tonight through the phoenix. If we can get the stone off of Kaelo, it may not solve all of our problems, but it would hinder him."

Most of the elves were now staring at the stone as warily as Veldon had. All but one. Liera looked not at the stone, but at Gellion. She turned away when Gellion caught her gaze, but not before he saw a flicker of suspicion in her eyes.

"We will not tell the elves of this stone," Liera said.

"Excuse me?" Tenille said in a mock-polite voice.

"This is not something that should be common knowledge," Liera hissed. "Can you imagine if other elves discovered how to make this? I will not have a weapon this powerful hanging above my Kindom."

"Do you remember what happened the last time we kept information about Kaelo to ourselves?" Tenille said. "Without outside council, we gave Kaelo exactly what he needed to raise a phoenix!"

Liera blanched.

"We must warn the other Kindom leaders," Tornac said. "But I agree with Liera."

Tenille gaped at Tornac. "But—"

"Listen," Tornac said. "We have already established that we know little about this redstone. That makes it dangerous. I am not saying we shouldn't use it, but we need to learn more about it before shouting of its existence to all the elves. It would only cause trouble among the Kindoms if we tried to explain what we have found now. We must warn the other Kindoms, but only about what really matters—the cleansing flame of the phoenix. We must prepare the other Great Cities for similar attacks."

"And how are they to stop the phoenix, even knowing what is coming?" Alos said. "With this stone—"

"This stone will not stop a phoenix," Gellion said. "Think what Kaelo has done with it. He has made impressive damage, but it has all been within cities, on the ground. Breaking streets and buildings will do no harm to a beast that flies, let alone one with feathers hard as stone. If it was a standoff against Kaelo alone we faced, we may have a chance, but our biggest problem now is the phoenix. For all we know, killing Kaelo will not harm the phoenix in the least, and then the beast will be under no control. The phoenix is our first priority, and we cannot rely on redstone as a solution."

It took a moment for his words to settle in. Alos looked disappointed, but bowed his head in assent. Veldon relaxed his shoulders and gave Gellion a small smile. There was a line between Valder's brows; he was looking at Liera.

The Lady of Tura was skewering Gellion with her gaze. A measure of sharpness had returned to her clouded eyes, but they bore a strange light Gellion had not seen there before. She did not look away from Gellion this time, but held his gaze.

"Very well," she said, still not taking her eyes off Gellion. "Let us plan."

By the time Gellion awoke, light was spilling into the room from every crack in the curtains. He marveled that he had slept in such bright conditions. Upon checking the position of the sun, he gasped. It was well past noon, the day cloudless and bright.

Gellion blinked. His eyes felt swollen, and his muscles still struggled through the weakness of prolonged inactivity. He watched the street below. Two elves glided past on the Rale path, another walked with brisk steps and pushed through a metal door. It took a while for Gellion to replay the last twenty–four hours in his head. Coming back to Tura had been like jumping on a speeding Rale line. No time to acclimate, no time to rest, just a wild and rushed onslaught of emotions.

Dawn had begun to break just a few hours after the Council meeting ended last night. After over a week of traveling by boat and then by foot, it was no wonder Gellion had slept half the day. The rest was a good thing, he knew, yet a thrill of panic still gripped his insides. What could have been happening in Tura all the time he was asleep? Why had no one woken him? He shook his head and ran his hands through his hair, trying to force himself to shake the dregs of sluggishness that still dragged at him like weights.

Gellion pulled off his wrinkled shirt and pants, rummaging in the wardrobe by his bed for something suitable to wear. His hands found only one garment, and he remembered with a jolt that all of his clothes were degrading in the sea under the rubble of Daro. It was still a difficult thing for him to accept, having never seen the broken remains of Daro with his own eyes. His fist tightened around the supple fabric. His clothes were the least of what had drowned with his city.

With a deep breath, Gellion forced himself to relax his grip and pull Tornac's set of clothes from the wardrobe. He took the redstone from inside his bedside table and slipped it into his pocket.

The guest quarters Liera had provided for them were far more spacious than anywhere Gellion and his brothers had resided since their imprisonment in Arvain. Gellion walked into a sitting room with a fireplace, a couch, and a neatly upholstered armchair. Valder and Veldon sat on the couch, each with a cup of tea.

"Morning." Valder grinned. "We were about to go make sure you didn't run away in the night—or morning that is."

"You only woke up half an hour ago," Veldon said to Valder.

Valder only widened his grin.

"There's food in the kitchen," Veldon said. "And more tea."

Gellion's stomach growled at the thought, and he hurried past his brothers without a word to pile a plate with whatever he could find in the kitchen. He sat across from them and took a large bite of spiced sea bird wrapped in flatbread.

"Veldon's been up all day." Valder rolled his eyes.

"I have been talking to Tornac."

Gellion nearly choked. He struggled to swallow his dry mouthful. "About what?"

"Everything that's happened. We heard the most important points last night, but there is more. Details." He cocked an eyebrow at Gellion. "You will be happy to know Firas is alive and well."

Gellion slowly lowered his food back to his plate, a stab of guilt in his stomach. He had hardly given a thought to his best friend since the phoenix attack the night before.

"Tornac said Renyra was on the Council," he said. "I suppose I assumed Firas was here as well." He jerked his head up. "Is he here now? Are they both here? Have you seen—"

Veldon was shaking his head before Gellion could finish.

"That is the story Tornac was telling me," he said. "Firas and Renyra went to the Fieri and Remsgri before Kaelo raised the phoenix. They were supposed to go to Telem Fier and then to Remsgraen. They are presumably still there."

"Oh." Gellion relaxed back into his chair, disappointed but relieved to know his friends were alive and in no immediate danger.

"Tornac went with them as far as Maramor," Veldon said. "And," He glanced at Valder, his face suffusing red. "Kyna did too."

"What?" Gellion sat up again.

"Kyna and Tornac brought vierstone back from Maramor to make the sword—well, to make the phoenix. It is likely she had to make sure they had enough vierstone."

Gellion closed his eyes, heat burning in his chest.

"Of course she did." Had she feigned feelings for Tornac as well? Lured him into her plans with the same callous, unfeeling ease? The heat burst and spread through Gellion's limbs. He took a breath, bracing himself for the rage that was sure to overwhelm him, but the heat did not reach its usual intensity. After its initial burst, it turned cold inside him, leaving him not comforted, but controlled.

Veldon was watching him with concern. Valder carefully studied his tea.

"Have the birds been sent?" Gellion said. The lightness of his voice pleased him. This cold anger was easier to push down.

Veldon seemed taken aback by the change of subject.

"I ... I think so. I haven't talked with anyone else on the Council today."

Liera had ordered letters sent to the Great Cities to warn the Kindom leaders of the phoenix's newfound power. Gellion had been shocked to learn that the Rale line out of Tura had been unusable for weeks—Kaelo's work—but the Fieri had since sent a ship with birds so the Turi could contact the other Kindoms.

"I suppose all we can do now is wait." Gellion sighed. The Turi Council had decided on little else at the meeting. It was difficult to plan any attacks when the movements of one's enemy were so unpredictable, and the Council members had grown irritable and muddled with the late hour.

"I thought we were done with that when we left Tala," Valder said. "Getting to Tura was supposed to mean action and excitement, not more waiting."

"Was yesterday not enough action and excitement for you?" Gellion said.

Valder paused with his mouth open. "Well, yes, but I doubt Kaelo will be coming back here if destroying vierstone is what he's after. There's nothing left here to destroy. That means we'll need to leave Tura before long if we want to do anything against him."

"We will leave as soon as we know where to go."

Valder laughed. "That's an enigmatic answer if ever I heard one."

Gellion couldn't help but smile, though it faltered when he looked at Veldon. His youngest brother was twisting the black stump of dead vierstone that was still pierced through his ear, staring ahead with unfocussed eyes. Gellion doubted if Veldon had heard any of their conversation past Valder's mention of destroyed vierstone.

"We'll stop him, Veldon," Gellion said.

Veldon jumped slightly at his name, dropping his hand from his ear. His face flushed.

A knock at the door tore them all from their thoughts. Valder shouted for the newcomer to come in, and Tornac stepped through the door.

Gellion's teeth clacked together with an audible snap.

Tornac closed the door behind him. His hair was pulled back from his face, revealing circles under his eyes and agitation plain in his expression.

"What's up?" Valder said, his brows drawing together at Tornac's appearance.

"I want to talk to you about something," Tornac said.

He looked from Valder to Veldon, then more slowly to Gellion. He walked closer to them, looked at the couch, almost sat, then apparently decided standing was better. He stood stiffly in front of the fireplace.

A prickle of unease moved down Gellion's spine. Rarely had he seen his older brother so discomposed.

"When—" Tornac said, then stopped, closed his mouth, and began again. "I was there when father went into that tower. Before he killed the phoenix."

Gellion exchanged a look with Valder and Veldon. They were clearly as confused as he was.

"We know," Veldon said.

Tornac nodded. "Well, I tried to go with him, but he wouldn't let me. He was acting strange, distracted, and when I refused to remain behind, he told me— " Tornac broke off again.

"Told you what?" Gellion leaned forward. Tornac had never said anything like this after the war. Of course, Gellion had not stuck around long enough to hear many stories. Veldon seemed as surprised as Gellion, however, and he had been with Tornac for centuries after their father's death.

"He told me he knew how to kill the phoenix. He wouldn't explain anything—the phoenix was right above us, trying to kill us at the moment. But it wasn't an accident, whatever happened in that tower. Father knew what he was doing. It didn't seem important, not—afterward. The phoenix was dead. Father was dead. But now—"

"What are you saying?" Gellion said

"I am saying that our father knew something that we did not. It was no fluke that he killed the phoenix that day. He knew something none of the other elves did, and he used it to destroy the phoenix. We have to find out what it was."

6

FATHER AND DAUGHTER

The spires of Maramor were exactly as she remembered. Of course, it had only been two weeks since Kyna last saw them. Somehow they were less majestic when viewed from above, robbed of their backlit silhouettes and dwarfed in size by the surrounding mountains. Even the floating platforms of the city seemed smaller than they had when they loomed above her. Had the city ever been as impressive as it seemed, or had Kyna simply been caught off guard by its architecture, rattled by the nearing inevitability that awaited her in Tura?

It was impossible to tell if any of the elves in Maramor saw the approaching phoenix. From this height, the city appeared deserted, but as the great bird banked lower, Kyna could begin to make out moving specs on the pathways and bridges. She wondered if word had spread of Tura's cleansing. Would the elves here know what was happening when they first spotted the outline of the phoenix in the sky?

Kyna blinked against the air rushing past her face and tightened her grip on her father's waist. It was difficult to grip the woven metal of his armor, though it moved like liquid silk beneath her fingers. No blade in Faeran could pierce the material, yet Kyna could feel the muscles of Kaelo's back through it, shifting and tightening to accommodate the phoenix's movements. Kyna's legs cramped with the effort of gripping the bird's body. Its feathers were hard as stone and smooth as glass, but emitted a pleasant warmth that was not altogether unwelcome. Even in the midst of summer, the air of the mountains was cool at this height, and Kyna's skin puckered beneath her light clothing with each gust of wind. The wind was discomfiting in more ways than one. Each blast made her tighten her thighs around the phoenix and squeeze her fists until her father's armor bit into her fingers. She wished she could strap some sort of saddle to the phoenix, or at least a strap that she could hold on to, but the thought of presenting such a request to her father or the phoenix sent a shiver down her spine.

Kaelo gripped the bird with his bare hands as they flew. Kyna had touched the beast with bare skin once before and never desired to again. The sensation was disconcerting to say the least. She shook her head and pulled her mind back to their current mission. The phoenix was only a tool, a means to an end that would benefit all the elves. She would just have to endure its unnerving presence until their plans—and her life's purpose—were accomplished.

The phoenix dropped in height again. Kyna held her breath; she hated descending. Worse than the roiling of her stomach, however, was the pounding of her heart. The first sounds of elven shouts and screams already rode the streams of wind that slipped past the phoenix as it neared Maramor. As though in answer to the cries of terror, the phoenix let out a hair raising screech, and a ripple of flame coursed from the metallic plumage on its head and down its body. Kyna flinched as the fire passed through her, though it was not painful.

Folding its wings close to its body, the phoenix dove. Kyna gasped and threw her arms around her father's middle before she could stop herself. Every muscle in her body ached with tension, and she thought surely they would float off the bird's back as it raced gravity to the ground, but the beast's wings had folded over her legs and pinned her in place.

"She will not let you fall," Kaelo shouted over the roaring of the wind. "Watch forward, now."

Tears streaming out the corners of her eyes, Kyna forced her gaze to focus beyond the phoenix's head. She could see the docks of Maramor rushing toward her and the first level of buildings just above them. Then the phoenix's body swelled beneath her. Its glassy feathers glowed and emitted a burst of heat, and everything before Kyna was doused in a brilliant torrent of flame. Kyna gasped. The flames were impossibly red and brighter than any fire she had ever seen. It was not the first time she had witnessed the phoenix's cleansing breath, but seeing it this close was like being plunged into a storm-tossed ocean having only seen calm waters from a distance.

Since Kaelo had created the phoenix in Tura, Kyna had only ridden the beast a handful of times. Her father had not allowed her to ride the bird over Tura two days ago, but that first experiment of cleansing had gone without a hitch, and he had determined Maramor to be safe enough for her to experience the phoenix's power firsthand. Kyna tried to tell herself the pounding of her heart was born of excitement, but the tremors in her hands betrayed her as she watched the crimson flame bathe streets and buildings and elves. Elves screamed each time they were consumed by the flames, though Kyna knew it did not harm them. Not that she blamed the elves for their terror.

The phoenix flew back and forth across Maramor, slowly ascending with the terrain until only the top tier of the city remained untouched. It was then that the arrows came.

Kyna let out a yelp the first time an arrow flew past her. She tried to duck down, but Kaelo sat straight backed in front of her and did not move.

"They won't hurt us," Kaelo said.

"They won't hurt *you*!" Kyna tried to suppress the panic threatening to overwhelm her senses. Unlike her father, she wore simple cloth, and would make a much more porous target for arrows than either her father or the phoenix.

More arrows were coming. Out of the corner of her eye, Kyna saw one bounce off the phoenix's right wing.

"She will let no arrows near you," Kaelo said.

Kyna heard a chorus of shouts from below, orders spoken in unison with eerie precision. Then a grey cloud rose before her. She squinted in confusion, then gasped as she realized it was a volley of metal arrows, aimed straight at them.

Before she could so much as scream, the phoenix threw its wings out to its sides, buffeting the air with a powerful beat and arching its neck. Crimson fire poured from the beast's beak. The wake of flames seemed to shimmer as it hit the volley of arrows, and through the haze of the fire, the arrows' shapes blurred, then disintegrated. When the air cleared, Kyna saw a cloud of ash floating on the breeze—all that remained of the arrows. Her eyes widened in shock, and cold rippled along her spine.

With a final beat of its wings, the phoenix breathed flames over the regiment of archers, then tilted sideways, catching an updraft of wind that carried it up and over the last row of spires in the city. Kyna glanced behind her as the phoenix crested the mountains above Maramor. The city appeared just as it had upon their descent, yet it was forever changed.

It will be forever better, Kyna thought with forced resolution.

The phoenix shrieked once more, and its cry echoed through the forest of rocky peaks stretching to the horizon.

Kyna leaned back against the wall of the cave. The stone was smooth as marble and cut into the shape of a chair beneath her. The ceiling of the cave soared to a height disproportionate to any natural processes that may have made the original cave. These details were small luxuries compared to the accommodations Kyna had grown accustomed to in Daro and Tura, but the cave lent a sort of nostalgia to her exhausted mind that she clung to with desperation. She had spent the first decades of her life in a cave. Those years had been simple—laden with the hope of things yet to come. The reality of those things was not so simple.

A cool breeze blew from the mouth of the cave, sending a spray of water droplets onto the glistening stone. Kyna wrapped her arms around herself.

We had to choose one of the highest mountains in Ard Gael to shelter?

"If you came nearer, you would be warm."

Kyna cringed. The voice was feminine, alluring. It sounded as though the words had been spoken in plain air, yet Kyna knew it was a trick of her mind. The phoenix did not make any physical noise when it spoke. It had not opened its obsidian beak, but its eyes bore into her now, leaving no question as to where the voice came from.

"I am fine, thank you." Kyna dropped her arms and straightened against the cold stone, fighting the shivers that threatened to shake down her back.

The phoenix cocked its head with a twitch. Its eye did not rotate with the movement. Kyna looked pointedly at the fire crackling against the back of the cave. The phoenix rarely spoke to her. Kyna often heard it whispering to her father and suspected it might be able to make its thoughts heard only by him when it chose. Kyna felt no loss at the phoenix's preference for its creator. The looks it gave her were calculating, its molten eyes steeped in an intelligence that was not animal. She often found herself staring at the beast with fascination, but not without a tightening in her chest, a trail of goosebumps down her arms.

"She will not hurt you." Kaelo was watching Kyna from behind the fire. Its smoke curled lazily toward the vent Kaelo had carved through the ceiling.

"I know." Kyna tried in vain to keep defiance from her voice. She felt like a pouting child.

Kaelo raised an eyebrow, then turned to the phoenix. The beast's head swiveled to regard him, and a ripple of light traveled underneath its mottled feathers. Kaelo's eyes shone. There was a hunger in them, almost a fervent joy, though Kyna could not recall ever attributing the word 'joyful' to her father and did not venture to do so now. It was not joy he felt, she was sure, but exhilaration. Pride. Anticipation.

Heat moved up Kyna's face. The phoenix bore no expressions, but that same calculating intensity emanated from its eyes as it watched her father.

Why does it have to stay inside the cave with us? The rain evaporates before it even hits the thing. It would be perfectly comfortable outside.

Kyna looked to the mouth of the cave and watched the falling water glisten in the firelight against the darkening sky. She tried to think of something, anything, that didn't make her want to grind her teeth until they wore away, but there was nothing. To think of the last few months was to bring an onslaught of emotions Kyna had sworn she would never face again. To think ahead should have brought her satisfaction, excitement, but in any imagined future, she now saw only the glowing eyes of the phoenix. She shivered.

"You have hardly spoken since Tura."

Kyna looked up, surprised to see her father had returned his attention to her. A faint line creased his brow as he regarded her.

"Have I ever been a font of words?" Kyna shrugged. "Did you expect the elves to rub off on me?" Memories of a Fieri woman smiling and talking for hours on end made Kyna flinch. She passed the lapse off as a cough.

Kaelo's face darkened. "Of course not. All the same, you're not acting yourself."

Kyna swallowed the words that came to her tongue. The phoenix was staring at her with unblinking eyes. She wanted to talk to her father alone, but in the week since she had returned to him, he had never once been away from the phoenix.

"I'm just tired," Kyna said. "These last months were—difficult."

"Did you expect them to be otherwise?" The words were not spoken callously, but nor was there sympathy in Kaelo's face. Kyna had never noticed the absence before.

"No." Kyna bristled. "I'm not complaining. You asked why I'm quiet and I told you. The elves were exhausting. Silence is something I have not enjoyed for some time."

The hard lines in Kaelo's face smoothed. "It is good you lived among the elves before the cleansing. I hope you understand better now what we do."

Kyna nodded, though her insides squirmed. She wished her father had never sent her among the elves. Before mingling with the elves, Kyna had understood what her father planned and why. At least, she thought she had. All her life, her father had told her of what the elves had done to him and how the elves' lives and emotions worked. It had all seemed simple—straightforward. At first, living among the elves had affirmed all that her father had ever told her and strengthened her resolve. Then *he* had come and confused everything. Gellion. Kyna clenched a fist. She had tried to banish the name from her thoughts, but it still managed to plague her in moments of weakness.

He is dead. He is meaningless.

But Tura had been no easier.

Without conscious thought, Kyna reached for the cuff at her wrist. The smooth stone embedded within pressed against her skin, and she felt her shoulders relax as her tangled emotions cooled and leveled.

Kaelo was watching her with a satisfied expression. The phoenix ruffled its feathers with the sound of shaken chain links and readjusted its legs beneath it. In the darkening shadows, the bird's red and orange mottling glowed like embers, and its eyes seemed to burn hotter than the flames of the cooking fire. Kaelo was staring at the beast again. His eyes rarely seemed to stray from it—his greatest achievement, his greatest pride.

"You did well," he said.

After a long silence, the phoenix swiveled its gaze to Kyna, and she realized her father was talking to her.

"Me?" she said.

Kaelo snorted softly. "Yes, you. Dealing with the elves at all is tasking, but the Turi Council is an animal all its own. You handled them well."

Kyna flushed and looked down, ashamed by the force of her pleasure. Praise from Kaelo was no small achievement, and she had begun to fear it would never come after all she had been through.

"They weren't exactly cunning," Kyna said with a shrug. "I had to shove the prophecy down their throats to get them to understand it, but they never suspected anything. I don't think they even would have believed any of it was you if Liera hadn't affirmed your presence herself."

A shadow fell over Kaelo's eyes, and Kyna immediately regretted bringing up Liera's name. Her father had not so much as mentioned his mother since the woman had tried to kill him, not even when planning the attack on Tura.

"So, how long will all of this take?" Kyna said into the lingering silence.

Kaelo looked back at the phoenix as he spoke.

"I do not know. The Great Cities will be simple, but we will need to be careful with the countryside. Ard Gael went quickly, but the grasslands and Riverseep will be more difficult."

"Difficult?" Kyna thought of the cloud of arrows disintegrating in the phoenix's fire, of the crimson flames that had engulfed two cities and nearly a dozen villages in a matter of days. "How do you mean?"

"Difficult to ensure we reach every town—every elf," Kaelo explained. "Much has changed in the Turi lands since last I dwelt here, but the lands of the other Kindoms were never familiar to me beyond the Great Cities. We will have to be meticulous."

"But surely the large cities are the most important?" Kyna said. "What does it matter if we miss a few villages?"

She knew she had said the wrong thing. Kaelo's eyes were nearly black when he turned them to her, and the hard lines had returned to his face.

"After all we have been through to get here, you would leave our job half done?"

Kyna bit her lip and shrank against the stone behind her.

"Of course not. I was only—"

"There can be no vierstone left," Kaelo said. "None. Or all we have worked for will be pointless. What would happen if a few villages retain their vierstone?"

Kyna turned her eyes down.

"What would happen?" Kaelo repeated.

"I—those villages would become powerful," Kyna said. "They would barter for vierstone like the humans barter gold, or use it as a bargaining chip or symbol of status."

Kaelo shook his head. "It is more than that. Those villages and elves would become pillars of resistance. The elves will not accept the release this new world provides until none of the old remains. You ask how long that will take—it will take as long as it needs to. Until there is not a sliver of vierstone left to tempt the elves. A thorough cleansing is far more important than a swift one."

Kyna didn't respond. It was not the speed of their success that concerned her. A month ago, she wouldn't have cared if the endeavor took them years to complete. But now—

The hair on the back of her neck stood on end, and she risked a glance up to see the phoenix staring at her. The longer this mission took, the longer they would be with the phoenix. A swift cleansing sounded far better than a thorough one to her.

"It will not take long." The phoenix's voice carried softly to Kyna's mind, more a whisper of a thought than a voice.

Kyna tore her eyes away from the phoenix and pressed her cuffed wrist against her thigh, trying to drain away the fear coursing through her blood like poison.

7

FRAYED NERVES

Renyra could not keep her eyes from the silhouette of Telem Fier's wall. The straight line was broken at regular intervals by the outlines of bodies holding spears. They were pillars to the peril that flew unseen countless miles away, reminders that the peace in Telem Fier was nothing but an illusion of time. Renyra should have been used to the sight of elven guards by now, but seeing them here, in the Great City of her own people, weighed her heart with a different sort of dread.

"We need to go to Cuvan," Raren said again. "Any information we hear from the streets is filtered through elves and time. If we want to stay ahead of the phoenix, we have to have more immediate sources of news. Cuvan will hear of Kaelo's movements before anyone else here."

Renyra sighed. "Alright."

Raren's eyebrows rose. For two days, Renyra had been resisting all suggestions of talking to Cuvan, convinced he would brush them off as he had before, or even discourage them from their plans. It was becoming increasingly clear, however, that Telem Fier was too large a city to rely on hearsay.

"You're right." Renyra shrugged. "I still don't relish the thought of allying with Cuvan, but living off of scraps of rumors is obviously not working. Unless any of you have new information?" Renyra cocked her head at Caerlyn and Alura, who had just emerged from the current of the crowd passing through the street.

"Not really." Caerlyn sat at their table with a heavy exhalation. "It's the same talk. I think we can assume the rumors about Ard Gael are true though. Elves from Maramor have started arriving in Rone with their stories. Sounds like there's no vierstone left in any Turi lands."

"So fast." Renyra shook her head. "It's been what, two weeks since Kaelo raised the phoenix? At this rate, we'll only have a month or two to stop him before all of Faeran is lost." She let out a huff of frustration and raked her hands over her face.

The last weeks had worn Renyra's nerves to frayed bits of wire, and she found herself struggling to keep her emotions reined in. There was too much at stake. There were too many courses of action and they all relied on events out of her control. Every decision seemed as though it would alter the course of elven history, and the cost of failing was too much to fathom. How was she supposed to remain calm and rational during all of this?

"We can't act on information that is even a day old at the speed Kaelo's going," Renyra said. "We have to figure out where he's headed next and get there as fast as we can. And for that—" She rolled her eyes. "I guess Cuvan is our only option."

Renyra pushed her chair back and stood.

May as well get this over with.

She turned her feet to the center of Telem Fier and started walking.

Renrya led her troupe to the nearest stack of levit boards. She dislodged the boards and handed them to her friends, then dropped her own board onto the smooth path and mounted it, activating it with the press of a heel.

They were a strange group, gliding through the streets of Fieri elves. Renyra and Caerlyn fit in perfectly with their dark skin and patterned wraps. Trali's cropped garb was unconventional for the grasslands, but his braids and caramel skin disguised his foreignness well enough. Alura and Raren stood out far more with their light skin. Then there was Firas. His willowy form and pale hair were almost laughably out of place in Telem Fier. He looked like a ghost on stilts floating above the milling heads around him. Renyra giggled and winked at Firas, whose eyebrows rose.

"What?" He said.

"Oh, nothing." Renyra's grin widened. "You're just lovely."

One of Firas's eyebrows lowered, leaving the other arched above in a look of amused suspicion.

"Oh?"

Renyra giggled again, unable to suppress the bubbling feeling she had not felt in weeks.

"Do you know what I think?" Firas said. "I think you are making fun of me."

"I would never!" Renyra laughed.

"Mmm." Firas regarded her with mock solemnity. "I think someone should wipe that grin from your face. It does not do to laugh at other elves' expense." He wrapped a hand around her upper arm.

"Firas!" Renyra tried to swerve away from his grasp, but he pulled her back to him with ease. Then he leaned down and pressed his lips to hers. The suddenness of the sensation sent a shiver down Renyra's spine, and she stopped struggling against him. Their levit boards were still moving forward, and with closed eyes, Renyra relished the feel of the breeze against her skin and Firas's mouth on hers.

"Ugh." Caerlyn's voice sounded behind them as they broke apart.

Renyra ignored her.

"It didn't work," she said to Firas, a smile still stretching across her face.

"I didn't expect it to." Firas shrugged. A corner of his mouth drew up, and behind his teasing exterior, Renyra saw the depth of his love— or maybe she felt it. Firas's hand was still on her arm, and all of her skin was so flushed with heat, she couldn't tell if her earring was warm or not.

It was a moment before Renyra realized the rest of the troupe had stopped their boards. She slowed and looked back in confusion, only to see the entrance to the city hall gaping beside the Rale path.

"I believe this was our destination?" Caerlyn smirked. "Unless you two wish to carry on. We can go on alone."

Renyra rolled her eyes and stepped off her levit board, taking Firas's hand and strolling to the carved doors. Caerlyn's smirk softened to an amused smile as Renyra passed.

Cuvan was not in the city hall. Renyra asked any elf she encountered if they knew his whereabouts, but the only help she got was from a messenger also asking after the Lord of Telem Fier. He could tell her where Cuvan was not, but was little help otherwise, and ran off on his own shortly after their encounter. It took nearly an hour of following leads and directions before they tracked Cuvan down in the city forges, overseeing the metalworkers making spears, swords, and arrows.

It took more than one glance for Cuvan to recognize Renyra, and when he did, trepidation showed in his eyes.

"You have returned from Remsgraen, I see." Cuvan's voice was heavy, resigned.

"Lord Cuvan," Renyra said. "We need to speak with you."

Cuvan moved his gaze from Renyra to each of her companions, then sighed.

"Very well." He led them out of the heat of the forges and to a side room lined with weapons and tools. It was not the most diplomatic of venues, but Renyra supposed she couldn't be picky.

"Are you on your way back to Tura?" Cuvan said.

"No," Renyra said. A flicker of annoyance heated her words. "Tura is lost, as I understand it."

No thanks to you.

Cuvan seemed to hear the implication in her tone. His face darkened.

"There was nothing anyone could have done for Tura. Though that has not stopped Liera from summoning the Kindom Council to convene there."

Renyra's eyebrows rose at that.

"I doubt if anyone will go," Cuvan continued. "I certainly have no plans to abandon Telem Fier under threat."

"A threat you gave no credit to just a week ago." Renyra spoke the words before she could stop herself. The whole troupe went still, and Cuvan's eyes narrowed.

"I did not discount the threat you warned me of, and if you will remember, that threat was very different from the one we now face. The *suggestions* I declined to act upon would have done Telem Fier no good in the present situation." He drew himself up, his broad shoulders seeming to inflate. "The Fieri have done more than should be expected of us. We sent messenger birds and supplies to Tura, though it is the fault of the Turi that any of this has happened."

"That isn't true," Raren said through gritted teeth.

"None of this matters, now." Alura placed a hand on Raren's arm. The heat behind his gaze cooled, but he did not relinquish his glare at Cuvan. "We didn't come here to argue or place blame." She shot a meaningful look at Renyra, who looked down. "We came to request information."

Cuvan regarded Alura in stoic silence, waiting. When no one else spoke, Alura continued.

"We want to track the phoenix's progress, to know exactly where it has been sighted and when, as soon after the fact as possible. As the Lord of Telem Fier, you are bound to learn this information before anyone else, and we only ask that you would share the news with us as you learn it."

Alura's gentle voice had smoothed the lines from Cuvan's brow.

"What do you intend to do with this information?"

"Intercept him," Firas said. "Sabotage him in any way we can."

"I have scouts, guards, and troops doing exactly the same thing," Cuvan said. "If you would like to join them—"

"No," Renyra said. "Thank you." She tried to sound gracious. "All we ask is that you relay any information about the phoenix to us as quickly as possible. Please," she added with what she hoped was a humble expression.

Cuvan let out a long breath. "I cannot guarantee the speed with which I will hear about the phoenix's movements beyond Fieri lands, but I have scouts throughout the grasslands and in the major cities. If anything happens within our borders, I will know within the day, and if you stay near the city hall, I will relay the information to you if I can find you."

"Thank you." Renyra smiled with relief, shame building in her chest from her earlier churlishness with the quiet man. He had only ever done what he thought best for his city, even if it had clashed with Renyra's opinions.

It was then that the messenger came running into their room. He cast an annoyed glance on Renyra and her friends, as though reprimanding them for finding Cuvan and not telling him.

"My Lord," he said to Cuvan. "I have urgent news from Auralia." He shoved a folded letter toward Cuvan, who took the paper and opened it with a worried frown. His face went leaden as he read the words.

"What is it?" Renrya blurted. "Do you know where he is?"

Cuvan folded the letter back as it had been before answering.

"The phoenix's flames have fallen over Rone. Kaelo is in the grasslands." He turned to the messenger. "Find the Fieri Council members. We must prepare the city."

For days, Cuvan had the metalsmiths working day and night forging weapons robust enough to combat a phoenix, though from the reports pouring in from those cities now drained of vierstone, no weapon, no matter how well made, could cause any real damage to the beast.

"I hear its fire can turn metal to ash." Alura looked out the window of their rooms with apprehension, as though expecting the phoenix to swoop from behind a cloud any moment. "How can you fight such a beast?"

"It can't shoot fire out both ends." Raren smirked. "I expect attacking from all sides would give you a better shot of hindering the thing. I think Cuvan has a chance, to be honest. So far, no city has really fought back against the phoenix, have they? Kaelo took the Turi cities by surprise. They had no time to make any attempts at defense."

Renyra wanted to agree, but could not let herself hope that Cuvan's defenses would succeed where all others had failed. No one knew when

Kaelo would get to Telem Fier. At first, she had thought he would come straight to the Great City of the Fieri before making his way through the rest of the grasslands, but the day after Rone's attack, messages had begun to trickle in from other towns, coming faster each day. It seemed Kaelo would save Telem Fier for last, biding his time and making thorough work of the rest of the Fieri lands in the mean time.

"Will we stay in Telem Fier for the attack?" asked Trali.

"We'll never get near the phoenix while it's attacking the city," said Caerlyn.

"Should we try to head the phoenix off in the grasslands before it arrives here?" Alura said.

"I don't think so." Renyra ran her hands over her face. "It just moves too fast. The phoenix is unhindered by terrain and it probably flies high between cities."

"What, then?" Caerlyn threw her hands in the air. "We are useless in Telem Fier, but leaving is as foolish as staying?"

"I only said searching the whole grasslands for the phoenix wouldn't work," Renyra said. "I didn't say we should remain in the city until the phoenix comes."

Caerlyn raised an eyebrow. "What are you thinking?"

"I think we should scout," said Renrya. "Keep a rotating watch for the phoenix outside the city until it comes. Then we can at least see what we're up against. Maybe follow it from here."

Firas's eyes shone with the light of an idea.

"Yes," he said. "We wait outside the city for the phoenix to leave after its attack—assuming the Fieri do not bring it down. Then we follow. Tracking the phoenix blindly over large areas of land will get us nowhere, but tracking it when we can see it, follow its direction, and know something of its next destination, might just work. Kaelo and the phoenix will almost assuredly go toward Riverseep Forest after Telem Fier, toward Remsgraen. We can try to intercept it before it reaches either."

Renyra found herself smiling. "Yes." She stood, setting her tea down with a slosh onto the wood of the side table. "Yes! It's perfect. We may even be able to get Kyna on her own if we can catch up with them at night."

"How will we follow it, though?" Caerlyn said.

"We'll make a plan for that," Renyra said. "At least now we have a foundation, and I like where it's going." She winked at Firas, then clapped her hands together and turned to the face the whole troupe. "Now we can get to some real planning."

8

FLAMES IN THE GRASS

Heat bled into Renyra's back as she leaned against the rock. She pressed herself harder into its surface to spread the effect. The day had been far from cool, but in Renyra's opinion, one could never be too warm. The sun was beginning to turn scarlet to her right, painting the strips of cloud near it in pinks and light oranges. Renyra smiled. Sunsets in the grasslands were unrivaled in their bold beauty. Within the hour, the whole sky would be the color of flames. If she had to spend all evening watching for the smudge of a phoenix against the sky, she supposed this was not so bad.

For over a week, Cuvan had kept Renyra and her friends informed of Kaelo's whereabouts. They had held their watches on the horizon but had not expected any sightings with the phoenix so far away.

Yesterday had taken away their sense of security. The phoenix had reigned its fire upon Calafor, a port city to the south of Telem Fier, and was reportedly moving north. By the time word had reached Cuvan, the troupe feared their plan would come to nothing, as the phoenix would surely be upon them any moment. Yet night had fallen, dawn had broken, and still the city sat in silence.

"How long can it take to fly from Calafor to Telem Fier?" Renyra squinted against the southern horizon. The Braided River twisted into the distance, beginning to reflect the sunset like rivulets of spilled paint.

"Maybe he is taking his time to approach Telem Fier with caution," Firas said.

Renyra let out a snort. She was tired of waiting. It had been nearly four hours since Cuvan's bird had come. Its message had been simple: 'Phoenix was in Calafor—Telem Fier is the last.'

There was no vierstone left in the grasslands apart from its Great City. There was nowhere else for Kaelo to go. Telem Fier would be next. Renyra's stomach roiled. She lifted a hand to brush her vierstone earring with her fingers, and a tingle emanated over her skin. Would she lose her contact to vierstone so soon after being reunited? The thought was hardly bearable. Part of her—a cowardly part, she knew— hoped that by remaining outside the city, she would avoid the phoenix's fire and retain the life of her vierstone, at least for a little while longer.

"Look."

Firas's voice made Renyra jump, and she automatically looked to the southern sky. No winged silhouettes marred the horizon.

"What—"

"There." Firas pointed to a gnarled tree down the river a ways. From the shadow of its branches flared a light. A fire. The flames flickered, then extinguished, only to reignite a few moments later.

"They've seen it," Renyra whispered. Ice trickled into her stomach.

Firas bent to a small cage near his feet and lifted the latch on its door. A little orange bird flitted out into the air, paused to orient itself, then darted toward the city. Its leg bore a warning for Cuvan. The phoenix was coming.

"Don't move yet," said Firas.

It was a needless warning. Renyra hardly thought her legs capable of movement just now. The flames had come from the scouting location of Caerlyn and Trali. She looked back toward Telem Fier, where Alura and Raren watched further to the east, but saw no sign of light coming from their hiding place. It appeared the phoenix was coming straight north from Calafor. Kaelo was almost here.

"Do you see it?" Renyra gripped Firas's arm and leaned forward, as though the few inches of distance would allow her better sight miles away.

"Not yet. Get behind the rocks and we will watch from there."

Renyra reached for her bag and climbed over the rock that had formed her chair. She peered over the top of it, her heart starting to flutter.

It was nearly a minute before she saw anything unusual, and it was not what she had been expecting. She did not see a winged shape high in the sky, but a haze of red along the horizon, like an approaching dust storm, but glowing. Renyra's breath caught in her throat.

"The fire," she said, her voice faint. She felt Firas tense beside her. He slipped his arm around her shoulders.

The wall of flame moved slowly and seemed to cover far more area than Renyra would have expected from a single creature, even one as large as a phoenix. Were the flames consuming the grasslands? But she had heard they did not truly burn.

Then the dark shape she had been waiting for materialized against the sky. Each time a new wave of flames lit the horizon, the outline of the phoenix was obscured, but between bursts of fire, the clear shape of a flying monster was revealed. The bird's location changed each time Renyra saw it, and she understood. It was flying back and forth, covering all the land in its path like a cultivator making horizontal sweeps of a wheat field with fertilizer.

There were houses, farmsteads, even small settlements just south of Telem Fier. The phoenix was leaving no stone unturned in its crusade against vierstone.

No wonder it took so long to get here from Calafor.

Yet if the phoenix had done this over all the grasslands in ten days, its pace was still shockingly, devastatingly fast.

The reality of what she was seeing suddenly hit Renyra. A phoenix was flying toward her. A *phoenix.*

Riu have mercy.

She drew the sign of the three pointed star over herself and felt Firas's hand tighten on her shoulder. She drew comfort from his touch, but still her eyes did not flicker from the avian shape moving toward them with steady progress.

Would it touch down before it reached Telem Fier? Had it already done so out of their range of view? Renyra looked around her. There were no buildings or elves near them. To the west, the shifting riverbed barred settlements, to the east were rocky outcroppings, fit only for livestock, and to the south, crop fields stretched to the nearest villages—those now being doused in phoenix flame. If they could remain hidden from the phoenix's sight, it may pause its outpouring of flame before descending on Telem Fier.

Renyra couldn't keep still. Each minute seemed an hour as she watched the phoenix come nearer.

Finally, the flames subsided.

The phoenix rose in the air, then hovered, beating wings that even from a distance Renyra knew were impossibly large. The fire from its mouth had ceased, but still the creature seemed to radiate flames.

"What is it doing?" Renyra didn't know why she whispered, but she was convinced that to speak aloud would draw the attention of the monster, even a mile away.

"It is facing the city." Firas's tone matched Renyra's own.

Renyra looked behind her at the distant walls of Telem Fier. Could the phoenix see the guards posted along the walls, sense the resistance brewing within? She hoped their messenger bird had reached Cuvan by now.

"Watch." Firas's hand gently pulled Renyra back to face the south.

The phoenix had begun to fly again, but not toward the city. It was heading for the rocky outcroppings to the east. Renyra knit her brows and squinted toward the phoenix. What was it doing? A sudden spark of hope lit in her breast.

"Could the phoenix be too exhausted from Calafor and the villages to attack Telem Fier?" Her eyes shone as she looked at Firas. "What if it remains hidden through the night, assuming itself unseen, planning to mount its attack in the morning?"

"It is possible." Firas did not sound hopeful.

The phoenix disappeared among the jagged shards of stone. Renyra itched to run after it.

"They could be resting for only a short time," said Firas. "Whatever Kaelo is, he still needs food and water." His brow furrowed. "I don't expect they would stay this close to the city all night. It would be foolish to assume Cuvan doesn't have scouts."

"Then we should go to them now! If—"

But Renyra's words died in her throat as a flurry of fiery wings rose from the rocks. The phoenix had launched itself into the air once more, and this time, it let out a scream that Renyra was sure carried for miles in all directions. She clapped her hands over her ears at the grating sound. The phoenix gave two more beats of its wings to gain altitude, then flattened itself parallel to the ground and flew forward, directly at Telem Fier.

Renyra stared at the beast and only ducked below the rock when Firas pulled her down.

Why had the phoenix stopped for so short a time? Had it only needed to rest its wings for a moment? But then why go to the shielded rocks out of its way?

"What was it doing?" she whispered, watching the bird bear down upon them. Her pulse began to race against her throat. The phoenix was terrifying in a way that she could not explain. Its presence made her skin crawl.

The phoenix's wings undulated through the air, trailing wisps of flame with every movement. Renyra kept her eyes locked on the beast, trying to see behind its head. She thought she could discern a shape there, a lump that did not belong to the phoenix's lithe form. Kaelo? The phoenix banked to the left, angling toward the southern gates of the city. As it turned its back to face her, Renyra saw the shape upon its back more clearly. It was Kaelo. She could just make out the color and shape of his armor, which she had seen glimpses of in Tura and heard about from those who had seen him more clearly.

Was Kyna not with him, then? Had he left her somewhere after spiriting her away from Tura that day? Was her role in all of this finished? Or was she somewhere else? Somewhere near?

"Firas." She grabbed Firas's arm with both hands. "Why would the phoenix have flown off course to touch down in those rocks for only a few moments? What if it didn't stop for itself, or for Kaelo? What if it was dropping someone off?"

Firas's brows drew together. "Dropping someone off?"

"Yes!" Renyra stood. "I can't think of any good reason for what it just did, but if there was someone *else* on the phoenix's back?" She raised her eyebrows at Firas, and a measure of understanding dawned on his face. Renyra grinned. "Someone who would weigh the phoenix down if it had to maneuver through a Great City and fight an assault. Someone without Kaelo's impenetrable armor or power over vierstone or the phoenix, but who is obviously connected to all of this."

Firas looked to the shards of rock, brows hooding his eyes.

"You think she was with him. You think she is there."

"If she is, it would be the perfect opportunity! We could find her, talk to her."

"And hope she doesn't kill us, or call the phoenix back."

"How would she call it back?"

"We know little of this beast, and nothing of its connection with those it answers to."

"But this is what we've been waiting for! We would have to deal with all three of them if we catch them between Telem Fier and Remsgraen. This is safer. This is better."

Firas was slowly nodding, though anxiety shone in his eyes.

"I suppose it is worth a try." He glanced back at Telem Fier.

"Let's go on to Raren and Alura," Renrya said. Her mind was whirring as plans and possibilities scrambled over each other. "Those rocks are at least a mile from the city, and it will take too long for all of us to run there and back if we still want to catch the phoenix north of the city when it leaves. If it leaves." She amended. They could all hope that Cuvan would somehow manage to finish off the beast, or at least Kaelo upon its back, but it was a hope they could not rely upon, let alone act upon.

"Then what are you thinking?" Firas had fallen into an easy lope next to Renyra. Her own legs were pumping in a sprint.

"I don't know!" Renrya had not settled on any functional plan yet. Her eyes darted from the rocks to the city, from her friends to the cloud of crimson flame that had just risen from the depths of Telem Fier. She didn't want to risk the plan they had agonized over prior to the phoenix's arrival. It was a good plan, and it lay ready for them. But this was an opportunity she could not bear to pass by. If she could talk to

Kyna, understand why she had done what she had done, maybe even convince her to come with them, it could change everything.

Closer to the city, Raren and Alura were waiting for them with wide eyes. Alura seemed to be struggling to tear her gaze from the phoenix. Even from a distance, Renyra saw thin weapons flying through the air against the bird's wings. The beast's shrieks continued to echo through the fields, but it did not appear to be hurt.

"Some bird, eh?" Raren's face was ashen.

"Come on!" Caerlyn and Trali had caught up to them.

Renyra was still scanning the walls of the city, trying to find something that would spark an idea, give her some kind of inspiration. Then she saw it. The city stables jutted out from the walls, not within the city like those of Daro, but open to the fields to allow the horses pasture.

"I will go," Renyra said as she ran. "You all continue north of the city as we planned. Wait with the boat. I'll take a horse and ride to the rocks. Whatever happens, I will meet you outside the walls before you leave, or catch up behind you."

Firas whipped his head to look down at her. "No."

Renyra let out a huff of frustration. "We can't all take horses out there. Do you have a better suggestion?"

"What are you two talking about?" Caerlyn was staring between them as she ran.

Renyra slid to a stop and gestured at the rocks behind them.

"The phoenix touched down in those rocks," she said. "I think Kyna is there, and I want to find out."

The rest of the troupe had paused to listen.

"And you plan to gallop off alone on an animal to do so?" Raren said.

"No one else here knows how to ride."

"What if I rode with you?" Alura said. "On your horse. It could surely bear us both?"

"And if Kyna comes back with me? We can't ride three to an animal."

The silence that met this argument made clear the opinions of the troupe regarding this possibility.

"I will take a horse and go with you." The anxiety in Firas's face now was deeper than when he had watched the phoenix. Like most elves, Firas bore no understanding of or fondness for horses.

"Look," Renyra said. "This is not negotiable. I'm going alone."

Renyra stopped running, and Firas slowed his gate to look at her. The anguish in his eyes nearly broke Renyra's resolve. She knew how she would feel if Firas had suggested leaving the group on his own.

"I will come back to you, whatever happens." She took his hands and squeezed them. "I promise you, Firas. Kyna may not even be there, and if she is, I will be careful. I will find you outside the city before you leave, or I will follow you until I find you."

Firas just stared at her. Renyra did her best to meet his eyes with confidence, but the emotions radiating from his hands to hers were nearly crippling.

"We need to go," Caerlyn said with uncharacteristic gentleness. "Whatever Renyra's decision, we must go on."

"Go," Renyra said, forcing a smile. "I'll see you soon." She rose onto her toes and kissed Firas on the lips, then set off at a sprint toward the stables.

It was somehow comforting to be on the back of a horse again, though the last time Renyra had galloped bareback across long distances was when she had traversed all of Albarad to warn the elves about Kaelo, and of Daro's fall. She never would have imagined stakes could get higher than that, yet now a phoenix doused her people's Great City in flame behind her, and before her was a possible meeting that could as easily end in disaster as salvation.

The rocks drew nearer with every stride of the chestnut animal beneath her. The horse was gasping for breath, clearly not accustomed to be ridden so hard. Renyra felt bad for the animal, but urged it faster all the same. A part of her hoped she would find nothing and no one in those rocks. Certainly it would be easier to return to her friends and continue with their preconceived plan than to involve Kyna in all of this, but Kyna presented one of the only advantages Renyra felt she had in her pursuit to stop Kaelo. If Kaelo had dropped her off in some obscure mountain range to hide while he flew through Faeran, that advantage would mean nothing. If Kyna was here, now, Renyra had to try to find her.

Renyra kept glancing back at Telem Fier, though doing so threatened to throw her off balance on the heaving horse beneath her. Each time she saw a similar sight—clouds of red flame, just like she had seen on the horizon to the south, and the occasional flash of fiery wings. She saw no smoke, nor any visible destruction. Still, it did not seem as though Cuvan's weapons were working. Renyra bent lower over her horse and squeezed her knees tighter.

The rocks were larger up close than she had expected them to be. They rose on a hill that seemed more a mountain from her vantage, jagged hunks of stone that jutted to the sky at angles both shallow and steep. Renyra slid off the horse's back, now slick with foam, and tied its reins to a twisted bush, hoping the animal would not pull itself free. She ran to the nearest boulder and began to climb. The rocks were close enough together that Renyra could move between them easily, always finding a new surface to grab or launch herself off of. She moved with the smooth grace of a Sira artist, relishing the physical challenge.

As she progressed up the hill, she listened and she watched. All she saw were rocks. They made perfect hiding places. Renyra was sure that a dozen elves could have hidden on this side of the hill alone and she would have been hard pressed to find any of them in the time frame she now faced.

She tried to remember where the phoenix had landed. Had it been between those two vertical stones to her right? But there were two similar stones further up the hill. Renrya paused, catching her breath. She scanned the terrain above her, trying to detect any color, shape, or movement that did not belong.

A bird took off in a flurry of feathers from one of the twin pillars up the hill, and Renyra nearly shouted in surprise. She tighten her fingers against the stones and took a slow breath. Her heart was making a valiant attempt to break out of her chest.

It was only a stupid bird.

But then she saw another shift of movement below where the bird had flown. She doubted she would have noticed it if she hadn't been staring at the exact place, but as she watched more carefully, she thought she caught it again. A shift of black amid the grey—a shadow? Renyra tensed, suddenly unsure how to proceed. She was a hunter, skilled at stealth and agility. It should be easy to sneak up on an elf, especially in this obstacle course of stone, yet Renyra could not stop thinking about how easily Kaelo had always thwarted her attempts at sneaking. Would Kyna be the same? Was it even Kyna, there between the rocks?

Renyra started to climb again, but with slow, deliberate motions. Her shoes did not so much as scuff against the rocks, and her hands found purchase without scraping. There was some vegetation between the stones, brittle and crunchy from the drought of summer. Renyra avoided the noisy plants and kept to rocks, creeping toward her goal one stone at a time. She did not see any other signs of movement and heard nothing but the distant call of birds.

One more rock to squeeze beneath. Renyra began to scale the side of the pillar. Half way up the stone, another rock leaned against it, forming a sort of bridge. Renyra raised herself onto the platform, flattened against the pillar, then edged her face around its side.

She nearly fell off the rock.

Kyna stood just out of arm's reach and was pointing a red sword at Renyra's chest.

Any exultation Renyra may have felt at having her theories proved right vanished upon seeing the grim snarl on Kyna's face. Renrya gasped and took a step back, reaching for a dagger at her waist before she could think about what she was doing.

Kyna took a step forward as though to rush Renyra, but then her step faltered. Her body stiffened. She stared at Renyra, recognition wiping the snarl from her face.

"Wait!" Renyra held both hands up, leaving the dagger cinched at her waist. "Please, I just want to talk."

All color had leached from Kyna's face. Her lips parted and moved in soundless words, and her eyes widened in shock. It was more than disbelief in Kyna's expression, however. On the guarded face Renyra had come to know, was fear.

"Please," Renyra said again, fighting every instinct that told her to match Kyna's weapon with her own.

The tip of Kyna's sword wavered. Her eyes darted behind Renyra, and she took a step back.

"Go away," she said.

"I'm alone." Renyra wanted to recall the words as soon as she spoke them.

I'm alone? What better thing could I possibly say to a potential enemy pointing a sword at my face?

Yet Kyna did not look like a formidable enemy at the moment. Had Renyra been right about more than Kyna's location? Had Kaelo coerced or threatened her into this role?

"I only want to talk to you." Renyra pitched her voice low, like she was talking to a frightened horse.

"You are a fool." Kyna was holding the sword with both hands now. Her stance was wide, her eyes bright. "Get away from here now. Go back to your life. Do not try to stop him."

"If Kaelo has done anything to threaten you, we can help, we can get you away."

"No!" Kyna was backing away in earnest now. "I don't want to hurt you, Renyra, but I will. I will if I have to. It's for your own good. Go back." The fear had not left her eyes. Her knuckles were white around the hilt of her sword.

"For my own good?" Renyra couldn't keep the heat from her tone, though she knew it would only hurt her chances of appealing to Kyna. "You *want* to destroy all the vierstone in Faeran? You want to abolish the elves' only tie to each other? To love and joy? To Riu?"

"You don't know what you're talking about," Kyna said in barely more than a whisper.

Renyra swallowed the retort that rose to her lips. This was not going how she had imagined. Could Firas have been right? Was Kyna as much a part of this as Kaelo? But a shadow of fear still lingered about Kyna's expression. There was something more to this. Renyra took a breath and gentled her voice.

"Please, Kyna. Tell me what has happened to you. I want to understand." Renyra took a step forward, moving to climb down from her perch to Kyna's level.

Kyna stared at her a moment longer, and for a fleeting second, Renyra thought she would agree

Then she turned and ran.

"No!" Renyra shouted. "Wait!" She leaped off the leaning boulders and chased after Kyna, not knowing what she would do if she caught her. Could she force Kyna to talk? A dagger and a javelin against a sword? Renyra shoved the thought away. It would not come to a fight. She would not let it.

The rocks were larger here and spaced more widely. Renyra ran on flat ground, leaping over and ducking beneath rocks as she followed the sounds of scuffing and the glimpses of glossy hair flying before her.

"You are afraid!" Renyra said as she ran. "I can see it! I want to help you. Please."

Kyna did not answer. She did not pause. She was running down the hill now. It was getting more difficult to keep sight of her. Renyra slid down the face of a rectangular boulder and dropped to a rock six feet below, crouching to absorb the impact.

Plants crunched under her feet as she ran. Pebbles flew to either side of her. She was almost down the hill now. Would Kyna keep running? Would she turn to fight if Renyra didn't give up the pursuit?

Then Renyra heard a sound that raised the hairs all over her body. She looked across the fields before Telem Fier. The phoenix had left the city and was heading straight for them.

Kyna was still running, making for the fields.

"Kyna!" Renyra cried, putting on a burst of speed.

Kyna had seen the phoenix. She slid to a stop and turned to face Renyra. Before Renyra could slow her pace, Kyna knelt and flattened her hand against the ground. The ground beneath Renyra's feet shuddered, then pitched. Renyra careened off balance, but before she could regain her footing, the stone around her broke upward with a loud crack, and Renyra felt herself thrown into the air. She landed on her back, head swimming and lungs devoid of air.

For several moments, Renyra lay gasping on the ground, trying to muster the strength and mental capacity to push herself up. Kyna was surely long gone by now, running to join the phoenix that had come back for her. Finally, Renyra was able to draw in a full breath. After several lungfuls, she managed to position her hands behind her and push.

Her mind did not have time to register what she saw before it happened. The phoenix was almost on top of her, hovering in the air on wings so large Renyra could not fit them into her field of vision. Then everything was red—brilliant, glowing, all consuming. A flush of cold moved through Renyra's body, and her very cells seemed to vibrate with the air around her.

She was back in Tura. Kaelo's hand was gripping her wrist. She was lying in the street enduring waves of inexplicable terror.

Then it was over. The flames were gone. Renyra was huddled not on a cobbled street but on stone in a field. Telem Fier lay before her, drained of lifestone, and a phoenix was flying away into a darkening sky.

9

LOYALTIES

Kyna tried to steady her hands against Kaelo's waist. One hand still gripped the redstone sword. She had not had time to return it to her father and bore no scabbard for the weapon herself. Her fingers cramped around its hilt, but she did not loosen her grip.

The phoenix rode an updraft of air higher into the sky and flew over Telem Fier. No weapons came at them. They were beyond the range of even crossbows now. The sun had dipped below the horizon, and the city was glowing with a soft light. From this height, it looked peaceful. There was no smoke, no rubble, nothing at all to suggest anything out of the ordinary had occurred minutes before. Kyna could picture the elves below her walking about their evening tasks with smiles and easy movements, a typical night.

It could be a typical night if they would let it be.

The phoenix had caused no lasting harm to the city and had not killed any elves in its crusade, even though the elves had tried their best to kill it. The residents of Telem Fier were free to continue with their lives now—better lives—though the elves would not yet accept it.

The lights of Telem Fier receded behind them with startling speed, and the ground below blurred into twisting waterways glistening in the twilight. Kyna was relieved to leave the grasslands of the Fieri behind them. The land had been too open, too revealing. If there was an oppo-site to claustrophobia, Kyna was convinced that she was afflicted by it, and traveling a quarter mile high in the air did nothing to relieve her insecurity. Riverseep Forest would be much more to her liking, she was sure. Far to the north, she thought she could see the smudge of trees, but it could have been her wishful thinking.

Even at this altitude, the air was markedly warmer in the grasslands than in Ard Gael, for which Kyna was grateful, but her eyes were dry and scratchy from a full day of flying, and she was hungry. Surely they would rest soon. Even the phoenix could not fly all night after a day like this. Kyna didn't dare ask her father to stop. He had said nothing as she clambered up the phoenix's side in the fields before Telem Fier. He had not even looked at her, his gaze locked instead on the small Fieri elf lying on the ground behind her.

Another tremor of nerves shook through Kyna's body. How in all of Riure had Renyra found her? And *why*? Kyna had long since accepted that Renyra was strange in her ways, but to seek out the elf who had coerced, lied to, and betrayed her just weeks before and ask if she needed *help*? It was madness. That had to be it. Renyra's mind was so addled by vierstone, she could not make rational choices based upon self preserva-tion or logic. Well, if that was the case, she would be cured soon enough. The phoenix had seen to that.

Still, visions of Renyra's face haunted Kyna in the growing darkness. She tried to focus on her surroundings, on the of glow of the phoenix's feathers against the black water below, but her mind drifted to the smell of spices in Renyra's apartment, to sitting in a hoop in the Sira training grounds, to that retched pulling sensation in her chest she had tried to burn away after each encounter. Kyna had never expected to see Renyra again; she had relied upon never seeing her again. Would the Fieri woman haunt her the rest of her days? Pursue her until Kyna descended into the same madness as her own?

Kyna's stomach dropped, and she realized the phoenix had begun to descend. Her muscles relaxed at the thought of food and sleep.

Liera had sent Renyra to Telem Fier before creating the vierstone sword that had led to the phoenix's creation. It was only natural the woman should have been there. Kyna could not understand how

Renyra had found her in those rocks, but the woman could not possibly follow her beyond Telem Fier. Kyna would shove the memory into the same recesses of her mind as everything else that had happened the last months. She would not let it disturb her. Her days were filled with more than enough action to divert her mind from such unpleasantries.

The phoenix touched down among a sea of reeds. A chorus of snapping accompanied the bird's landing, and the creature shrieked its protest at the uncomfortable footing. All at once, orange flames engulfed the phoenix's tail with a *whoosh,* and it lashed its body back and forth, reducing any reeds within reach to ash. Kyna gasped and held on to her father, feeling as though she were sitting atop a bucking horse. Then, blowing a huff of smoke out its nostrils, the phoenix settled down and extinguished its tail, though the feathers still glowed at the edges, ready to ignite again at the slightest provocation. Kyna slid to the ground, now a warm pillow of reed ash, and moved to the far side of the cleared circle.

A pressure in Kyna's ears made her stiffen, and she turned to see her father standing behind her. He had made no sound on the bed of ash and now looked at her expectantly. Kyna swallowed. Would he berate her for what had happened outside Telem Fier? But how could the blame lie on her? It had not been her decision to lie hidden in the outcropping of rock. Kyna bit her lip, preparing a defense, but then Kaelo's gaze shifted to her hand, and she remembered she was still holding his redstone sword. Shoulders relaxing, Kyna placed the sword's hilt into her father's waiting hand, flexing her cramped fingers once its weight was gone.

Kaelo held the sword in front of him and ran his fingers along its edge. His eyes were narrowed, his chin raised.

"Who is she?" he finally said.

Kyna sighed. There was no point pretending she did not know Renyra. The phoenix would have told Kaelo of Kyna's mental cry for help. It would have seen the end of Renyra's chase, maybe even heard her shouted accusations, and told him that too.

"She is an elf from Daro," Kyna said. "We were both in the Turi Council meetings."

Kaelo nodded slowly. He was looking beyond Kyna now, as though thinking to himself. Then he sheathed his sword and walked to the center of the circle. His bearing left no question that Kyna was supposed to follow. She did.

The phoenix bowed its head at Kaelo's approach, and he lay a hand on its neck. Light rippled from his touch, and the beast's eyes flared crimson. It took off in a flurry of wings.

"She will bring us fish." Kaelo watched the bird with shining eyes. "Though wood will be impossible to come by here, and the reeds are too green to burn."

Not too green for a phoenix to burn.

Kyna did not voice the thought. She knew incinerating something and making it burn for a cook fire were not comparable, but something in her cringed at the thought of another dinner soaked in phoenix fire. It did not make a difference, she supposed. Any cook fires they made were set aflame by the phoenix anyway, but it somehow seemed different to eat something heated directly by the beast's throat, like remnants of the bird's essence remained within the meat.

Kyna looked at her father out the corner of her eye. He still faced the phoenix, watching its light recede into the growing darkness. A ghost of a smile tugged at his lips, and his eyes were bright in the silvering light from the moon. Two weeks, and his reverence for the cursed bird had not abated. He was obsessed with it. Of course, he had been obsessed with phoenixes most of Kyna's life, but it was a different thing in the presence of the living, breathing incarnation, rather than the distant hope of an idea. Kyna's chest burned, and she shook her head at her own absurd emotions. Who was she to be jealous of an *animal*? She had been instrumental in bringing the stupid thing to life. Kaelo may have raised it from the vierstone ash, but Kyna possessed as much responsibility for its existence as her father.

She set her jaw and pressed the stone at her wrist into her skin. The heat in her chest cooled. Kyna frowned. The heat had never been there at all before she went to Daro. She had hoped distancing herself from vierstone and the elves again would have made her constant reliance on redstone's touch go away.

It will just take time. You were with the elves for months and have only been away a couple of weeks.

"Did she follow us here from Tura?"

Kyna started. Kaelo was still looking out across the winding river.

"No," Kyna said. She had hoped her explanation of Renyra had satisfied her father. "She was already in Telem Fier. Or Remsgraen. I don't know. Lier—" Kyna caught herself. Mentioning Liera would do her no favors when her father was already annoyed. "She was sent to bring messages to the leaders of the Fieri and the Remsgri."

A muscle was working in Kaelo's jaw. He glanced at her with unreadable eyes.

"You did not arrange to meet her?"

"Of course not." Kyna tried to keep the panic from her face and her words. She had nothing to be ashamed of. She spoke nothing but the truth—Renyra's presence had been an unwelcome shock.

Kaelo eyed her, then nodded. "But you spoke to her? How did she find you?"

"I have no idea. I knew no more than you coming into Telem Fier. I was in the rocks and heard something coming toward me, and then she was just there."

"And she spoke to you."

"Yes."

"What did she say?"

Kyna opened her mouth and shook her head. "I—she just wanted to know why I did what I did."

"That is all?" Kaelo's eyes narrowed. "She went to the trouble of finding you and risked speaking with you only to ask why you betrayed her?"

Kaelo's voice was level and low, yet Kyna detected an undercurrent of ice. Was he suspicious of her? She shrugged, avoiding his eyes but trying to impart nonchalance into her voice.

"She thought I was following you under duress and wanted me to come with her. I quickly disabused her of the notion."

"By running from her?"

Heat flushed Kyna's skin. "I was running to the phoenix."

Kaelo had gone still. He was no longer looking at Kyna, but staring at the ground. One hand traced the hilt of the sword at his hip. Kyna shifted her feet, unsure what else to say. She could not determine what direction her father's questions were taking. Was he accusing her of weakness for running rather than incapacitating her pursuer? For humoring the conversation of an enemy rather than cutting it off before it could start?

"Do you follow me under duress?" The question was calm and cool, but Kyna could see the tight lines around her father's eyes.

"No," Kyna said quickly. Too quickly? But no. Nothing was forcing Kyna to remain with her father. She had chosen this. She had always followed him willingly.

"Father," she pleaded. "The Fieri woman is sentimental to the point of madness. The very picture of what you have warned me of all my life. You sent me to the elves to act as one of them, and I did. Convincingly. She was entirely taken in by my ruse. She could not understand how I could be so different from what she thought she knew. That is all. She was fooled. She is a fool. She will not bother us again."

Kaelo's eyes followed a far off glimmer of red, now growing larger. The phoenix was returning.

"Do you still want to do this?" Kaelo said in the same quiet tone.

"Do what?" Kyna could feel adrenaline starting to leak into her blood. She forced herself to look at her father.

"All of it. What we are doing." Finally, Kaelo met Kyna's gaze. His eyes were opaque. His face a mask of stone.

"Of course I do," Kyna said. The adrenaline was coursing stronger now. She pressed her wrist to her thigh and felt the cool release of her shame, but the fear remained. Had he sensed her reluctance? Did he know how she watched the phoenix out the corner of her eye?

"You have not," Kaelo paused. "Changed your mind?"

She hadn't. There was nothing for her to be ashamed of. There had been moments of doubt and weakness, yes, but she had fought them. She had come through stronger than before.

"You think I am so easily swayed?" Kyna forced of measure of heat to her words.

"I had hoped not. I had hoped you were different." The muscle worked in Kaelo's jaw again. Disappointment hung on his brow. "Perhaps I underestimated the influence of vierstone. Perhaps I should not have sent you among the elves."

A new fear laced through Kyna's veins. How closely had her father watched her in Daro and in Tura? Had he seen her moments of weakness first hand? Guessed at the struggles she had undergone?

"Father, please. I was not affected by it. Or them." Kyna's words grew more frantic. "I haven't changed my mind. Of course I will stay with you. Through all of it. I'll help you. I've done all you asked of me. Why do you doubt me now?"

Kaelo's face softened, but before he could answer, a blast of warm air fell over them, and the phoenix descended, settling itself in the ash with a low hum that almost sounded like a purr. The smell of charred meat wafted through the space, and Kyna felt her stomach grumble in anticipation of hot food. Kaelo diverted his attention from Kyna to watch the phoenix. He stepped forward to take several fat fish from the its beak.

The phoenix ruffled its feathers, sending dancing reflections of light across the ground. Kaelo watched the beast hungrily for a moment, then brought the fish over to Kyna and extended one toward her. Kyna took it without comment and sat down in the ash, pulling out a knife to slice open the fish.

The phoenix always gorged itself before bringing them food and now settled in a satisfied perch to watch the two elves across from it. Kyna did her best to ignore the bird, but focusing on the tense silence between herself and her father was not much more comforting. The smoking fish had cooled enough to eat by the time Kaelo spoke again.

"I do not doubt your loyalty."

Kyna lowered the fish from her mouth and looked at her father. He was regarding her with something between weariness and wariness. Kyna had never thought of her father as difficult to read until she had lived among elves so transparent she could have listed every emotion on their faces any moment of the day. Just now, she wished her father were so obvious.

"I only want to ensure that you still understand," he said. The ice had receded from his voice and posture. "That you still believe in what we do."

Kyna's eyes flickered to the phoenix before she could stop them. Kaelo's gaze followed her own. Kyna regretted not confronting him about the phoenix while the beast was out of hearing range. Now, its eye was fixed upon her with unwavering intensity. If a bird's face could hold expression, Kyna would have said it was smug.

"I still believe in it," Kyna said. She forced herself to think of Liera's unfounded accusations against Kaelo, of the bloodlust in the eyes of elves who condemned without forgiveness even as they claimed their own morality to the highest standard.

"They are hypocrites." She thought of the pain she had seen in the elves on the ship from Daro. She thought of the roiling emotions that still lingered beneath the surface of her own skin every time she thought of Gellion.

"And they are dangerous. The stone is dangerous." Kyna raised her chin, staring the phoenix straight in the eye. She straightened her shoulders and set her face in grim determination. "I understand. Now more than ever."

Kaelo's eyes moved over her face, then he relaxed and nodded.

Kyna nearly sighed aloud in relief. It was as good as an apology coming from her father. The adrenaline in her veins began to recede, and her appetite returned in full when a breeze wafted the aroma of smokey fish into her face. Kaelo reached into a bag and tossed her a metal flask. A smile stretched up half of Kyna's face as she unstoppered it and smelled the heady spice of liqueur, probably from Tura. She tipped some into her mouth, and liquid heat flowed down her throat, hitting her chest and spreading almost instantly to her limbs. Kaelo pulled a second flask from the bag.

"We are halfway done." He smiled at her and took a drink. Kyna raised her eyebrows. Her father never drank. Then again, he never smiled either, and the elusive expression had graced his face more in these last weeks than Kyna had seen in most of her life. Kyna let out a breath. Her muscles relaxed, and she took another sip of liqueur, savoring the heady fog that had begun to creep over her thoughts.

Maybe she was thinking too much, worrying too much. Her father was obviously pleased with how things were going. Maybe after all of this, he would find a measure of peace at last, and they could live a normal life in the improved world of their making. Renyra was nothing, just as the rest of them were nothing. Two Kindoms were now cleansed of vierstone, and after the destruction of Daro—and select mayhem in Tura—they had inflicted no further damage upon elves or cities. Everything was going as her father had promised. She should be content, thrilled. Proud.

"Half done in number, maybe, but not in the war." The voice cut through the heat enveloping Kyna like a cold knife. The phoenix had cocked its head and seemed to have an eye locked on both her and her father.

Kaelo's hand froze with the flask against his lips. His gaze fell on the phoenix, and his face darkened. Any remaining heat in Kyna's veins cooled, replaced by a new tension. Kaelo pushed the stopper back into his flask, and his fingers tightened on the metal. From the brooding, blank look in his eyes, Kyna got the impression the phoenix was sharing more with him than it was with her.

"What?" Kyna directed her question to her father.

Slowly, he dragged his eyes away from the phoenix.

"The elves of Telem Fier were—uncooperative." His voice was guarded.

None of the cities had been 'cooperative.' Kyna looked from her father to the phoenix. The bird's throat was glowing yellow beneath its plated feathers. Kyna had learned to associate the effect with agitation or anger.

"What happened in Telem Fier?" Kyna asked. Her view of the Great City had been marginal at best from her rocky refuge and abruptly interrupted by the arrival of Renyra. She had seen what appeared to be arrows and spears above the city walls, but this was nothing new. Elves had shot at the phoenix in most of the larger cities they had cleansed. None of the weapons had posed any real threat to the phoenix.

"Nothing we could not handle," Kaelo said stiffly.

"But more than we have faced thus far," said the phoenix. It had begun to preen its wings, its obsidian beak clicking against its feathers.

"No elves can stop us," Kaelo said. "We knew they would try, and they have not disappointed, but they will not succeed. Their resistance is an inconvenience, nothing more."

"An inconvenience that could become dangerous if left unaddressed." The glowing along the phoenix's throat had intensified, heating from orange to red.

Kaelo said nothing, but Kyna did not like the brooding look that had returned to his eyes.

"They have united against you," the phoenix said in a silky voice. "They try to kill you—to kill us—yet you offer them no consequences for their actions or repercussions for their hatred."

"They act in desperation," Kaelo said. "They do not understand. They are children fighting back against a perceived injustice that is for their own benefit. Killing the child that defies you would not make them achieve the end which you envision."

"Still, young must be corrected, or they will continue their inexcusable behavior. It will get worse as the elves' desperation increases and as they have more time to prepare retaliation against us. So too will their hatred of you grow, a hatred that has followed you for centuries and matured within their minds. A hatred you do not deserve."

The dread in Kyna's core had been mounting with every word the phoenix spoke, but now that dread was laced with fear. How did the phoenix know her father's past? Had he told it everything? From the moment Kyna had first heard the beast talking in her mind, she had been disturbed by its ability to think and speak like an elf, but the thing was more than just sentient. It was intelligent and cunning. Its very presence rang with an age entirely disproportionate to its newly awakened state. Did the phoenix also possess a talent for manipulation? Kyna had heard stories of the persuasions of the phoenix of the Great War, but that bird had been controlled by Olcon, hadn't it?

"What is it that you propose?" Kaelo watched the phoenix with shrewd eyes. "Destruction? Death? Punishment?"

"Discipline." The phoenix's head swiveled to the side so one massive eye was facing Kaelo. "Correction. I am merely warning you. Do not let this resistance grow beyond your ability to suppress."

"That is why I created you," Kaelo said. "To overcome resistance."

"Yet you set limits upon me." A harsh undertone entered the phoenix's mind-voice, and smoke began to curl from its nostrils. "I cannot both achieve your goals and follow your rules if the elves continue along this path."

Kaelo opened his mouth, then slowly closed it. His glare cooled to a semblance of calm once more.

"Then we will continue this discussion if and when there is a threat that our current methods cannot surmount."

A final puff of smoke rose from the base of the phoenix's beak. It tucked its wings flat to its body, then bowed its head toward Kaelo.

"As you wish," it said.

Yet as Kyna looked from her father's stiff shoulders to the seemingly complacent bird, she saw its eyes gleam with a light of satisfaction.

10

TO FIX A FORGE

Damp air blew through the forges, raising wisps of dust and ash into the air. The lights from across the river stretched in thin beams through the misshapen mounds of bricks, stones, and wood. It reflected in mesmerizing undulations across Gellion's body as he moved through the shadows and floating particles. The forges were deserted. The entire area was devoid of movement or sound save the soft scuff of Gellion's boots. There was no longer scattered debris to impair his steps. Any rubble that could be repurposed sat in neat piles organized by material, and the remnants of the roof were gone entirely.

A breath of satisfaction eased Gellion's shoulders away from his neck.

His feet halted in front of a furnace—not one of the collapsed heaps of rock, but a standing furnace with several deep cracks and crumbling stones on one side. It would do.

The breeze blew again, and the sound of scattering pebbles and rustling leaves made Gellion go rigid. He turned in a slow circle, watching the shifting shadows for any sign of movement or stillness where either did not belong. It was late. Most of the elves of Tura were long in their beds, including Gellion's brothers. Any elf sneaking about the forges this time of night would be as suspicious as ... well, as suspicious as he was.

After nearly a minute, Gellion dropped his shoulders again and turned to face the furnace. Lifting a hand, he ran his fingers along the cracks in the stone. He felt nothing but cold, rough rock. There was no warmth permeating his ear, no thrill of awareness through his fingertips. He could not tell what kind of stone this was, how it was structured, or how it had been crafted. It was like he had lost one of his senses. The loss twisted his gut, but as a blind man hears all the more acutely without his sight, Gellion's connection to the redstone's energy was now as easy as drinking water without vierstone to interfere.

Gellion clasped his fingers about the rock. Its wild current rushed into him. Gellion sucked in a breath and closed his eyes in concentration. With no outlet yet defined, the current vibrated and bounced within his body. It was nothing like the subtlety of vierstone. It was forceful. It was eager.

Gellion let his hand trail against the cracked stone of the furnace once more. He still felt nothing from it. Frowning, he lay his palm flat against a deep crack. He pictured it whole, repaired, reconnected. Then he channeled the current through his fingertips.

A soft snap rent the air and the broken stone jerked beneath Gellion's hand. He stepped back with a sharp breath and looked around. Nothing stirred.

Taking a breath, Gellion lay his hand back on the furnace. The crack was gone. There was not even a seam of repair, just solid, unbroken stone.

He smiled and lay his hand against the next crack.

It was nearly dawn by the time Gellion left the forges. His eyes hurt with the strain of darkness, and his hands shook, though he could not tell if this particular ailment was from a night without sleep or the effects of using redstone for hours straight. He felt disoriented in his own body. Detached. He shook his head and blinked in the weak light suffusing the forges from the eastern horizon. Exhausted or not, he was supremely satisfied with what the light revealed.

Every furnace stood in perfect repair. Even stains and damages centuries old were gone, replaced with smooth stone, neat bricks, and flawless metal. The roof was still missing, and damaged tables remained in scorched piles of wood, but the forges were recognizable for the first time since Gellion had arrived in Tura. They were more than recognizable. They were perfect.

Gellion's eyes shone as he admired his work. It had been wonderful to work with his hands again. He had hardly thought of Kaelo all night. He had hardly even thought of Tornac. His smile broadened. Alsena and Reanan would be rendered speechless when they saw this. Liera would be furious.

Rubbing the grit from his eyes, Gellion took one last look at the forges before turning his feet toward home. If he hurried, he may be able to get a few hours' sleep without rousing suspicion of his late night.

He stepped onto a levit board and breathed in the fresh air rushing past him. It began to clear his head.

Veldon would probably have a panic attack when he found out Gellion had used redstone for something so large without telling anyone, but that was precisely why Gellion hadn't told anyone. He had not even known if it would work. Now, the forges stood as close to new as any elf could accomplish, and Gellion was no worse the wear for his efforts. It had been an experiment, and one that had succeeded beyond Gellion's hopes.

The Central Tower stood silent and empty as Gellion passed it, though a few elves wandered through the nearby streets on their way to the markets. As he veered to the east toward the guest quarters, Gellion hesitated on the street that led to Liera's family house. She may not be in her offices yet, but he would bet the Lady of Tura was awake. She did not seem the type to sleep in.

Liera's behavior had become increasingly concerning over the last weeks. As Tenille had warned him, the Lady of Tura was frazzled and distant, with a hunted look lingering about her eyes and an apathy toward action that Gellion had never seen in her before. It was her refusal to repair the forges that had led to Gellion take the matter upon himself, presiding over Alsena, the Master of Guilds, and Reanan, the Master Builder, to bring the forges to their former glory. Naturally, Gellion's overnight repair using redstone had not entered their plans. He had just saved the elves weeks of labor.

It was not Liera's attitude toward the forges that made Gellion pause on her street, however. More alarming than Liera's behavior as Lady of Tura was her behavior toward Gellion himself. Gellion had never considered himself to be *friends* with Liera, but they had always worked together with civility, if not respect. In the last two Council meetings, Liera had not spoken a word directly to Gellion and watched him constantly with narrowed eyes and sideways looks. She acted as though Gellion himself was what hunted her. Gellion was not the only elf to notice Liera's suspicion. Valder and Veldon had both asked him about it more than once, but Gellion could think of no plausible reason for Liera's behavior. Would she explain herself if Gellion caught her alone and asked her outright?

The levit board beneath Gellion's feet lifted and sank in a steady rhythm as he stalled on the path. He stood with his arms slack to his sides, reviewing possible ways to approach the subject and directions the conversation could go, but his sleep deprived and muddled mind stumbled over the imagined words. Finally, he leaned forward and continued toward home. Confronting Liera in his present state would do nothing to make the encounter easier.

A light glowed from within the apartments when Gellion arrived. Gellion let out a breath of frustration.

So much for slipping up to my rooms unnoticed.

He pushed down on the door handle and walked into cool, dry air. The temperature was a shock to his damp clothes and skin. The gentle scrape of wood drew his eyes to the sitting room, where Valder was reclined on a couch, whittling wood.

"Morning," he said, not looking up from his work. "Where have you been?"

"The forges." Gellion tried to match Valder's casual tone.

Valder's hands paused, and he looked up with a raised eyebrow.

"In the middle of the night?"

Gellion hesitated. "Yes."

"Mmm." Valder nodded and lifted his other eyebrow, then looked back at his hands with a shrug.

"I'm going to lie down for a few hours." Gellion hurried past him before he could ask more questions.

"Don't sleep too long," said Valder. "Mother and Veldon should be back from Maramor before noon."

Gellion's steps paused. He had forgotten.

"I know," he said. "Wake me up before you leave to find them. Or," he added, "if Tornac comes by." He would not have Tornac thinking he slept his mornings away.

Valder's mouth twitched. "I will."

Gellion fell into his bed with a whirling mind and leaden limbs. He spent too much of his time these days thinking. If he wasn't contemplating Liera's bizarre suspicion, he was orchestrating his day to avoid being alone with Tornac, talking with Council members about Kaelo's progress and ideas to stop him, or studying redstone in attempt to unravel its secrets. Yet the thing that occupied Gellion's mind as often as any of these was Tornac's suspicions regarding their father. Gellion and his brothers had talked circles around the subject, trying to understand what Eldian could have meant by his last words to Tornac and what could have possibly happened in that tower. No amount of speculation had given them any insight. Tornac had already scrutinized the possibilities for centuries and come up with no plausible theories. His younger brothers were proving to be of no more use.

Gellion could not understand it. Why would his father have kept information from the elves that might have saved them all? That *had* saved them all, if what he had found had indeed been the phoenix's downfall. With so few leads, it was useless to guess at what Eldian had discovered.

Raking his hands through his hair, Gellion turned over in his bed and tried to clear his mind. Tenille and Veldon had been gone over a week dealing with the ramifications of the phoenix's attack in Maramor. Veldon had volunteered readily to accompany the journey, both for safety and to see Farra. Some of Gellion's tension melted at the thought of Veldon reuniting with his wife. Taking Veldon from Farra had been one of the hardest consequences for Gellion to face in those weeks stranded in Tala. The woman was spirited and independent, but Gellion knew how she adored Veldon. News of his death would have crushed her, whether or not she let it show. Gellion knew it was a wonderful thing that Veldon would get to bring news of his survival to Farra in person, he only hoped his little brother would still want to return to Tura afterward. It seemed wrong, somehow, discussing Eldian and fighting Kaelo and the phoenix without Veldon when he had been such a vital part of events these last months.

Still, it was with thin patience that Gellion, Valder, and Tornac had waited for Tenille and Veldon's return. Tornac had never told their mother of Eldian's last words and had asked Veldon not to mention anything about it on the trip to Maramor—a well meant omission that Gellion thought to be supremely stupid. If their father had told anyone about his plans, it would have been Tenille, but if she knew anything about the prior phoenix's downfall, why would she have said nothing about it, especially now? Only Tornac's reasoning that they should all be present for the interrogation had stopped Gellion from going to their mother the morning of her departure.

Noon today. They would know in a few hours.

Gellion groaned and pressed his face into his pillow. He couldn't turn off his thoughts. They chased each other through his exhausted brain until he was nearly asleep, then ripped him back to reality. He longed for the simple monotony of the work he had done in the forges. He longed to clear his mind and cool the emotions raging around his thoughts. Letting his memories consume him, he began to replay those last hours in the forges, remembering each snap of joining rock and rumble of reordered structure.

When Gellion awoke to Valder's knock on the door, he sat up with a start and pulled his hand away from the redstone in his pocket with a cool head.

"The elves are devastated." Tenille sat on the couch next to Gellion, staring into her cup of tea. "Of course, the elves of Tura were devastated as well, but it was still a gradual process here. The vierstone in Tura was destroyed over weeks. In Maramor, they lost everything in less than an hour—the city and the earrings all at once. They had hardly even heard of what happened in Tura when the phoenix came."

The floating platforms of Maramor were clear in Gellion's head. He imagined black lacing the paths and the pillars, elves wandering the city with bowed heads and broken spirits. It was all too easy to picture.

"Did you hear anything new from the Fieri?" Valder asked.

Tenille studied her tea. Next to her, Veldon's eyes turned away with the discomfort of bad news.

Hours before, Veldon had come to them in high spirits, brimming with fresh stories and renewed love. Gellion had smiled to see the glow in his brother, but could not deny his relief that Veldon had chosen to part with Farra once more. Apparently, the woman was running Maramor in the absence of Gellion's family and would not hear of leaving it, even to "follow her accident prone husband around the continent protecting him from his own selfless ambition." Veldon's eyes had sparkled when he relayed Farra's words.

Now, however, the joy had dampened in Veldon's face.

"What was the last you heard?" he said.

"Just that Kaelo was working his way through the Fieri lands the same as he did ours," said Valder.

"Messages from the Fieri have not been timely," said Gellion. "Or helpful for that matter. Of all the Kindom leaders, Cuvan is least amenable to working with Liera. His correspondences are brief and often belated."

Tenille nodded. "We heard everything from Auralia across the lake. Rone and Maramor are on much better terms than Telem Fier and Tura, though I would have thought this would change Cuvan's mind."

"What happened?" Tornac sat with a rigid back next to Valder.

"The Fieri mounted a colossal attack against the phoenix when it came to Telem Fier," Tenille said. "Scouts, archers, crossbows the size of this room. Nothing so much as phased the beast. It came as a shock to Cuvan, though I don't know why. He may not have been the Lord of Telem Fier during the Great War, but he was alive to see the power and devestation of the phoenix. Anyway, the Fieri lands are as devoid of vierstone as the Turi lands now. When I left Maramor, we had not yet received word from the Remsgri. Has Rhosti contacted you?"

"No," Gellion and Tornac said at the same time. They made eye contact for a moment, then looked away quickly.

"Why hasn't the Turi Council met again?" Valder said. "At this rate, Kaelo will have destroyed all the vierstone in Faeran within the month, yet we have only met twice since his descent on Tura and came to no decisions either time."

"Liera only called the latest meeting because I urged her to," said Tornac.

"I will go to her today," said Tenille with a sigh. "She will hate calling a meeting on my suggestion I am sure, but the Council needs to know about Telem Fier." She shook her head. "Though as for what we should do with that information, I do not know. The only way I can think to proceed is to meet the phoenix with as large a force of elves as we can—multiple Kindoms if possible—with whatever weapons we can bring together in so short a time. If we can separate Kaelo from the phoenix long enough to get that stone off him, it might give us a better chance to kill both him and the beast, though I still do not have much hope in the odds. It took us decades of attempts the last time. I cannot see how we can accomplish the same feat in a few weeks when we are so unprepared."

"That is why we asked you to come here as quickly as possible," Gellion said. "We have some—information. Well, not information exactly, more the vague possibility of a lead. Since you've been gone, we've been discussing it, and we hoped you might be able to help."

Tenille raised an eyebrow, and her mouth twitched into a very Valder-ish smile.

"Are you going to explain this 'information,' or ask me to guess it?"

Gellion's face relaxed, and he laughed weakly, but the laugh died in his throat at the thought of the pain he was about to ask her to remember.

"Father killed the last phoenix."

The break in Tenille's composure was slight.

"Do you think I have forgotten?" Tenille's voice was stiff.

"No," said Gellion. "We just ... we don't think it was luck. We think he knew what he was doing—that he had planned it long beforehand in secret."

The confusion on Tenille's face was so genuine, Gellion knew at once she did not know the answer to Eldian's last words.

"What makes you say that?" Tenille said.

"Because—" Gellion began.

"I was with him before he went into the tower," Tornac said.

Gellion slowly closed his mouth.

Tenille's face softened. "I know."

"He would not let me go into the tower with him—said he needed me to help distract the phoenix while he went up the tower—but I wouldn't do it. I said I would not leave him."

Gellion looked away from the pain in Tornac's face.

Just get to the words.

"Then he told me that he knew how to kill the phoenix."

Tenille's eyes widened. "What?"

"He told me to trust him, that he needed me to distract the beast so he could do whatever it was he planned. There was no time to ask questions or demand explanations. I did what he told me. I could not see what was happening on top of the tower. There was fire everywhere. I just remember the explosion. Rubble flew and ash rained and father ... father was dead."

Tenille stared at him, a sheen to her eyes. "Why did you never say anything about this?"

"I didn't think it mattered. The phoenix was dead. Everyone knew that our father killed it, and I did not know how he had done it any more than the rest of us." He sighed. "Not to say I didn't think about it. I obsessed over it, but I never found any hints as to what father could have discovered that the rest of us did not. It is a poor lead to follow even now, but ... but we had hoped you might have known something of what he did."

Tenille looked back to her tea, her eyes glazed in memory.

"Did he say anything to you at all about what he planned?" Gellion said when her silence became unbearable.

Tenille shook her head. Gellion closed his eyes and swallowed hard against his disappointment.

"But," Tenille said.

Gellion's eyes snapped open.

"He was distant in the weeks leading to that last battle. Months, really. He was always shut away in his workshop or our rooms, pouring over books and notes. I knew he was desperate to find the answer to end the war. Everyone was. He wasn't the only elf to turn to books and wild experiments to find the magic weapon that would kill the phoenix. But he never shared his research with me."

"Nothing at all?" Gellion tried to keep the desperation from his voice. "Not even a stray comment? Do you know the books he studied?"

"It was centuries ago, Gellion," Tenille said softly. "Sometimes I can hardly recall his face." Her voice cracked, and she cleared her throat. "I do not remember any comments that may have referred to his plans. I am sorry."

Gellion's body sagged into the couch.

"Did anything happen to spark this obsession?" Tornac said. "I don't remember him shutting himself away, but then those last months were so hectic."

And you hardly noticed anything after Vyra died.

"I don't know," Tenille said. "We had been in Maramor all those months—sometimes going north of the mountains or meeting with other leaders in Rone or Yavran. There was a battle he had helped lead in the Lay Hills that the phoenix was actually in. In those last decades, it did not grace many battles with its presence. I think it was the first time Eldian had faced the beast itself for some time. That may have been what sparked it."

"What happened in the battle?" Gellion said. "Did he get close to the phoenix? Did he try to fight it?"

Tenille shook her head. "I was not there. He told me about it after. I don't know that he mentioned any specifics."

The last flicker of hope still burning in Gellion's chest winked out.

"Did you look through his study?" Valder said, facing Tornac. "When you were trying to figure out what he did?"

Tornac opened his mouth, then closed it. "Yes, but not for some time after his death. By then, most of his books had been moved to the city archives and his desk had been reordered."

"Damn," said Valder.

"I did not even think to check while we were in Maramor." Veldon shook his head. "Do you think it is worth another visit? If father left anything behind of his plans, it would be there."

Tornac frowned. "Leaving Tura now seems a risk hardly worth taking. Liera's hold on the Council is slipping by the day, and if we only have a few weeks before Kaelo's goal is complete, it hardly leaves us time to get to Maramor and back, let alone act on any information we may or may not find there."

A knock sounded on the door, making all of them jump.

Veldon rose. With a backward glance at them all, he opened the door.

It was Reanan.

"Oh." Reanan looked around at the small gathering of elves in the sitting room. "I'm sorry, I didn't realize you were all—" His eyes locked on Gellion. "I was hoping to talk to Gellion."

Reanan looked as though he had been walking with purpose for some distance. His hair was disheveled and his eyes bright.

"Come in." Gellion stood.

Reanan bowed his head and walked through the door, closing it behind him. He glanced at Gellion's family, then back at Gellion, who smiled politely. With a nod, Reanan spoke.

"Did you—I mean to say—were you in the forges last night?"

Gellion felt Valder's attention turn to him like the heat of a flame blown in his direction. He ignored it.

"I was." Gellion tried to keep his face neutral.

"Did you do it?" Reanan said breathlessly. "All of it?"

Gellion nodded.

Reanan's eyes widened. "How?" he finally managed to say.

"What did you do?" A mischievous grin lit Valder's face. Next to him, Veldon's face was notably absent of grins. He narrowed his eyes at Gellion.

Gellion's mouth turned up.

"What did he do, indeed?" Reanan turned to Gellion's family. "It is entirely fixed. All the furnaces, the ground—in better repair than they have been since before the Great War, I would wager." He was shaking his head as he spoke, as though trying to make sense of the impossibility.

"Gellion, you didn't." Veldon was looking at Gellion as though he had snuck out and vandalized the Central Tower in the night. His eyes darted to Gellion's pocket, which Gellion's fingers had already begun to move toward.

"I did, actually," he said pleasantly.

Valder looked from Veldon to Gellion.

"Redstone?" he said.

Gellion produced the object in question and held it to the light.

"It was an experiment."

"You put the forges back together?" Tornac eyed the redstone. "Using that?"

Gellion nodded.

"Amazing." Reanan laughed. "Incredible! But of course, if it can destroy a city, why shouldn't it be able to build one just as well?" He clapped Gellion on the shoulder. "Do you know what this could mean? How we could use this to repair cities, build and craft like we never have before?"

Gellion's smile faltered. In all his hours of work the night before, this possibility had never occurred to him. For the first time, a measure of Veldon's suspicion of the stone crept into Gellion's conscience. He looked at Veldon, whose face was every bit as horrified as Gellion had expected it to be.

"We'll ... we'll see, Reanan," Gellion said. "I just wanted to repair the forges and learn something of the stone's abilities in case we are forced to use it against Kaelo."

Reanan's enthusiasm was not tempered. "Wait until Liera sees this." He beamed at Gellion. "And Alsena! She'll be thrilled."

The smile Gellion returned was devoid of its former pride.

Tenille offered Reanan tea, which the Master Builder refused with thanks.

"I really must be getting on. I just wanted to affirm my suspicions before anyone else saw the forges." He smiled at Gellion again in a way that reminded him forcibly of Dulon. Gellion winced.

Reanan left in the same whirlwind in which he had entered, looking for all the world as though a maniac was not presently flying a monstrous terror over the world, destroying the very essence of elven existence in his wake. His sudden absence left the room silent and tense.

Tornac cleared his throat. "You should go to Liera," he said to Tenille. "Plan for a meeting later this afternoon." His gaze wandered toward Gellion as he spoke, his expression bearing a remarkable resemblance to Liera's more recent regards of suspicion.

"I will go now," Tenille said.

Gellion returned to his seat. He picked up his cup of tea in one hand, while the other slipped the redstone back into his pocket. This meeting had not gone according to plan on any account. Knowing that their father had discovered how to defeat the phoenix was useless if they could not find out his secrets in the next week. Tornac was right. Tura needed them now, and chasing an ephemeral idea born centuries before would not stop Kaelo. The elves would have to discover their own way to stop the phoenix.

He took a sip of cool tea and watched his mother gather her dishes.

Veldon still stood facing the door, his brow furrowed, and his eyes laced with apprehension.

11

TO FIND A PHOENIX

Renyra nudged a mound of ash with her foot, sending a layer of the stuff scattering in the breeze like chaff. The ash was cool to the touch. Old. Yet its coating of the surrounding reeds suggested the phoenix had been here recently, else the breeze would have blown it away. Renyra sighed, then trudged through the burned reeds to the boat.

"We're still on the right path," she said. "They were here in the last couple of hours, I would guess. I say we just keep heading straight toward Riverseep." She sighed. "As straight as we can."

Traveling with a straight trajectory through shifting and twisting waterways was proving more trouble than it was worth. They would have been better off taking the Rale line to Riverseep and watching for the phoenix from there than attempting to track it through the riverlands by boat.

"Just please don't make us carry the stupid thing again." Caerlyn eyed the motor boat with distaste. Renyra did not blame her. Forcing their way through stiff reeds and slick stones with a boat on their shoulders was not Renyra's idea of fun, but it had saved them miles of detours.

"How far are we from the forest?" Raren shielded his eyes from the sun in the direction of Riverseep.

"We will reach the trees this evening, I think," said Firas. "Unless we have to carry the boat again." He nodded apologetically to Caerlyn. "Which I think we would all like to avoid."

"Keep the same direction, then?" Raren took his place next to the boat's motor and flipped a switch on its side.

"Yes." Renyra stepped back into the boat and moved to its prow. She liked to sit at the front to watch the horizon, though it was unlikely she would see the phoenix against the sky by daylight, not from the distance that likely separated them.

The phoenix could fly faster than the boat could wind through waterways, but the creature did leave signs of its passage. Anywhere it touched down, whether to rest, feed, or accommodate the elves with which it traveled, the bird left ash in its wake. The troupe always found the spaces cold and barren. More immediate indications of their target consisted of charred bird corpses floating in the water, or sodden trails of ash clinging to the reeds by the shore. Renyra followed these signs whenever she could, but they came few and far between, especially when Raren had to take the boat off course to keep to the water.

The easiest way they had found to track the phoenix was in the darkened skies of early morning or evening. From great distances, they could see what appeared to be a red star against the sky that flickered erratically and routinely changed its orientation to the horizon. This was when the troupe closed the most distance between themselves and their quarry, but it was only ever a few hours before the light of the phoenix would dip below their line of sight and leave them blind until morning.

"We'll never catch up to the phoenix like this," Renrya muttered.

"Riverseep will be easier," said Alura.

"Maybe."

Riverseep would offer protection from the phoenix's sharp eyes and would allow them to make use of Rale lines while tracking the phoenix's slower progress as it reigned its fire over villages, but they would have to climb trees to keep it in sight.

Even as Renyra had watched the phoenix's outline recede from her view outside Telem Fier, she had begun to realize the overambition of their endeavor.

On shaking legs, Renyra had forced herself to run to the horse she had tethered near the rocks—wild eyed, but blessedly still tied to the bush—and galloped it all the way to the northern walls of the city. The troupe had pulled Renyra into their boat—Firas had refused to get in the boat without her—then set off after the beast, though by then it was a distant form on the horizon. Renyra later reprimanded Firas for his stubbornness, but had to admit that an extra quarter of an hour's start would have offered them little advantage in their chase. That had become obvious within the hour.

Firas's hand trailed down Renyra's back. She relaxed against his touch, but was reminded acutely of her lack of vierstone by the *opaqueness* of the gesture. She could feel his hand, but nothing more. Without vierstone, the channel between them was closed. Would she ever feel him again?

"We have followed the phoenix's trail this far," Firas said. "And we will keep trying. If all else fails, we will go to Remsgraen and help Rhosti prepare his defense."

"What defense?" Renyra threw her hands in the air. "With everything Cuvan did to prepare Telem Fier, the phoenix was barely even phased by his attacks. Even the spears as thick as our arms were no use against it." She ran her hands over her hair. "I had hoped that Kyna would help us. I hoped she would have information we don't. But she wouldn't listen. Dammit Firas, I will track her down again and make her listen, even if I have to tie her up myself."

"I don't think convincing Kyna to join us will work."

Renyra looked behind her. It was not Firas who had spoken, but Alura.

"If she is using whatever power Kaelo possesses," Alura said, "it sounds as though she is helping him of her own free will."

Renyra gritted her teeth. "Then we will convince her to leave him."

"Look," Raren said. "I appreciate the idea of infiltrating enemy lines and converting one of them to our cause, but it's very possible that nothing we say or do can change Kyna's allegiance. And after what we saw in Telem Fier, these weapons," He waved a hand at the pile of supplies in the center of the boat. "Are useless against the phoenix."

"Unless we take the it by surprise," Renyra said for what felt like the thousandth time. "If we can slip a blade between its feathers before it has time to turn its fire on us—"

"I think we should use vierstone," Raren said.

The boat went silent as everyone turned to stare at Raren.

"What do you mean?" Firas said.

"A weapon made of vierstone," said Raren.

"Like the prophecy?" Caerlyn raised an eyebrow.

Raren shrugged. "Who cares if it was in a fake prophecy? For all we know, Kaelo was trying to divert our attention from the only way to defeat him by making it appear fake."

"But Liera tried to kill Kaelo with the vierstone sword," Renrya said. "Tornac said she tried to stab him through the chest with it, but his armor stopped it like it does everything else."

"Kaelo is not a phoenix," Alura said. "He could have made that armor specifically to thwart vierstone. But what if vierstone *can* pierce a phoenix?"

"Or," Raren said. "What if a phoenix can't reduce vierstone to ash, or melt it, like it does with other metals?"

Renyra's brow furrowed. She turned to Firas.

"Did elves ever try to attack the phoenix with vierstone in the war?"

Firas raised his eyebrows. "Not that I know of. No elf would have thought to use vierstone as a weapon. If you recall, we were wary of the idea ourselves when the prophecy called for it."

"With good reason," Caerlyn muttered.

"I do not like using vierstone to kill," Trali said. His brows were heavy over his eyes. "But, if it has not been done before, it is worth trying once."

Raren took Trali's seed of encouragement and ran with it.

"Exactly!" He was nodding, his eyes bright. "The phoenix came from vierstone ash, didn't it? Maybe that's the only way to kill it. Maybe that's even how Eldian killed it."

"Left!" Alura shouted.

Renyra jumped. Alura had sprung to the bench beside her brother and shifted the boat's rudder. The nose of the craft swung to the left side of a fork in the river.

"These speculations won't be much use if we end up in the Lay Hills." Alura smiled at Raren.

Raren grimaced, but placed his hand back on the motor and set his eyes to the river.

"It doesn't look like we're going to catch up with this thing before Riverseep, anyway," Raren said. "I just think it would be worth trying to get a vierstone dagger or something before we do."

"I can take us to towns south of Remsgraen," Trali said. "The elves there may help."

"Better get there before the phoenix does," said Caerlyn. "Or there won't be any vierstone left to turn into a weapon."

12

TEMPERS HOT AND COLD

Gellion sat with a straight back, trying to listen to the elves around the table without making eye contact with Tornac. It was a difficult game, especially when it was Tornac who was speaking. Even when Tornac was silent, however, Gellion's eyes had a tendency to drift to him of their own accord. He would find himself scrutinizing his elder brother, trying to guess his reactions, his thoughts, his emotions. It was not difficult to read him. Mostly Tornac cycled between solemnity and indignation regarding the topics being addressed. His brows would draw together. His eyes would light with fire. Lines would crease at his mouth.

Tornac's own eyes drew most often to Veldon. Only then would his features soften for a fleeting instant. Each time this happened, Gellion noticed a solid pressure within his chest, cool and persistent. He tried to identify the feeling, but could not place it. So, he both longed for and dreaded each pull of Tornac's eyes to the right, now more curious than anything at the effect it had on him.

"If the other Kindoms will not come to us, we must go to them." Tenille directed a flinty glare at Liera, who was staring pointedly at the table.

Tornac turned to face Liera, and his eyes passed over Gellion.

Gellion looked away a little too quickly. He scratched his ear to cover up the motion, then faced Liera.

"Why should we?" Liera said in an airy voice. "They will not cooperate with us. They blame us. They left us to our fate."

"They did not know of our fate until it was too late," Reanan said. "Can we truly blame them for wanting to stay and defend their own cities and people? I agree with Tenille. Sitting at this table and talking until we are blue in the face will only run down the clock until Kaelo has removed all the vierstone in Riure. If we are to counteract him, we must take action, and quickly."

Liera still flinched each time Kaelo's name was mentioned. Not for the first time, Gellion wondered if it was wise for her to lead the fight against her son.

"By doing what?" said Alos. "Traveling to another Great City and talking *there* until we are blue in the face? If a full defense at Telem Fier could not deter the phoenix, what hope have the other cities? We do not even know where the phoenix is."

Gellion sighed. No matter the century, there was always one Council member who found no greater joy than throwing knives into every idea and proposal of his peers without offering any better ones. Alos had long since designated himself as this elf.

"We do not need to track the phoenix," Gellion said. "We need to wait for it. It will not return to Tura, it has finished with Telem Fier, and if Kaelo is acting with any sense, he will go to Remsgraen next. Our path is obvious. We go to Morcanan."

Several nods met this statement, Tenille and Reanan among them.

Liera, however, looked daggers at Gellion.

"It is for Council members to decide where the Turi will go and what we will do there," she snapped.

Gellion stared at Liera with parted lips. Heat began to rise in his face, and he felt a retort building in his throat, but then the heat sank again into something cold and brooding. He pressed his lips together and leaned back against his chair without a word.

The stunned stillness that had followed Liera's words began to crack. Valder took an enraged breath, but Veldon's hand on his elbow silenced him. Veldon himself was watching Liera with cool calculation.

Tornac, to Gellion's surprise, was leaning toward the indignation spectrum of his two emotions.

"I hardly think—" Reanan began.

"It's alright," Gellion said. "The Lady of Tura is right. I am no longer on the Turi Council." He let his gaze pass over the Council members around the table. Most looked away. "I am, however, a member of the Kindom Council." He turned to Liera. There was a sort of wild fire in her eyes as she watched him. "Which gives me the right to voice my opinion in matters that affect all Kindoms."

"The Kindom Council!" Liera scoffed. "You are the representative of a city that lies in the sea with half its citizens dead and the other half refugees in *my* city."

Gellion could feel the color leaching from his face.

"You will forgive me," Liera said. "If I do not entirely trust your suggestions."

Cold fingers of anxiety and guilt were starting to reach up for Gellion. She was right, of course. Daro had been his fault. He had known no one would want to follow his lead after the disasters he had caused, but to bring this up in front of the entire Turi Council—to shame him before the leaders of his Kindom and his own family?

Gellion's cool anger drew him back from the edge. He forced himself to face Liera's faded eyes.

"If this Council refuses to heed the advice of those leaders whose mistakes have cost elven life," he said. "I believe there are few in this room left to make up the Turi Council." He raised his eyebrows at Liera pointedly and felt a simmering satisfaction when she blanched.

Every elf in the room lowered his or her head. They could all read the meaning behind Gellion's words. Liera had infamously led a massive siege against the phoenix in the Great War, the breaking of which had felled a terrible percentage of the elven army—an army of all four Kindoms.

"How dare—" Liera began.

"I am only offering my advice, Liera," Gellion said. "You all may do with it what you will. I do not pretend to possess the authority to lead the Turi to Morcanan myself, and I will remove myself from these meetings if you wish."

Liera narrowed her eyes, and for a moment, Gellion thought she actually would send him away, but then she glanced at the other Council members. Every one of them was looking at Liera as though she were a horse gone feral. A hint of panic passed behind the woman's eyes and Gellion again got the impression she was a hunted beast surrounded by predators. She blinked and the look was gone.

"There ... there will be no need for that," she said in a strained voice. "I was merely suggesting that matters involving the mobilization of this city be left to those whose knowledge of its current state of affairs is most—complete."

It was a weak argument. Brows furrowed around the table, and the looks of wariness remained despite Liera's attempted reason.

Gellion inclined his head to her, more for a show of grace than for any understanding of Liera's excuse.

"Traveling to Morcanan is the suggestion I would have made myself," Reanan said.

Liera's jaw tightened.

"I think it is the only option that remains to us if we intend to take any action," said Tornac. "And I, for one, will not be a part of inaction."

"Do we refer to only those on this Council going to Morcanan, or all the Turi?" asked Dorian.

"As many Turi as will come with us, I say," Reanan said. "If it is a fight we seek, we will need as great a number as possible." He cocked his head at Liera. "I am sure Miyela would welcome the aid."

Liera's frown deepened at Miyela's name.

"I will consider," she said at length.

"We do not have time to consider," said Tenille. "That much I think we have all agreed on. If we are to do anything to save what little vierstone remains, we must decide now and begin our preparations immediately. If we are to go to Morcanan, we must leave within the week."

Liera's papery skin flushed a delicate pink. She gave Tenille a long look, then let her gaze pass over the other Council members.

"We leave in a week, then."

The sun was reaching for the western horizon by the time Gellion stepped into the muggy heat. Excited conversation sounded behind him. The rest of the Council was beginning to trickle out of the tower. Gellion quickened his pace. He had practically run out of the meeting as soon as it ended. He had no intention of prolonging his social requirements this day.

Still, going to his rooms would mean exposing himself to the company of Valder and Veldon at the very least and leave him open to the attentions of his mother and any others who knew to find him there. He longed for the quiet solitude of his workshop in Daro.

Stepping onto a levit board, Gellion banked to the north, away from the center of the Public Quarter. He needed to do something with his hands. He needed to do something to focus his mind. There were plenty of preparations he could start on tonight—an overwhelming number of them. If preparing Daro for battle in a few weeks had been hectic, mobilizing a city a hundred times larger in less than half the time was so intimidating as to seem impossible, yet it was what the Council had decided to do. In a matter days, they would need to print notices, gather weapons, collect provisions, and assess the still broken Rale line out of the city. They would need lists: lists of supplies, lists of elves, lists of tasks, lists of lists. Gellion had no head for printing machines or Rale lines. The thought of packing food in a warehouse assaulted him with memories of Kyna. The weapons, then.

Gellion was almost to the Scholar Quarter. He tipped the nose of his levit board back to the northeast, turning onto the main road that split the center of Tura. In the last weeks, the city's lines and geography had come back to him as though he had never left. He moved through the streets with easy confidence, hardly paying attention to where his body led him. This was just as well, as his brain was still too stuffed and muddled from the meeting to sort out navigation.

Gellion still burned over Liera's treatment of him in the meeting. He flipped between rage and self disgust. Though he had managed to suppress it throughout the meeting, anxiety still reached its fingers through his chest. He could not blame a Kindom leader for passing off the suggestions of one who had so thoroughly condemned his own city —it was what he had expected—but his failures in Tala did not seem to fully explain Liera's vehemence toward Gellion. She had voted in favor of the Albaren alliance just as he had. Worse, she had not only condemned huge armies to slaughter in her past, but created the villain that now threatened their entire race.

The more Gellion thought about it, the more his self disgust gave way to fury. He did not regret his dignified response to the Liera in front of the Council, but he wished he had thought of all these invalidations of her accusation at the time. The rest of the Council, at least, did not seem swayed by Liera's hypocrisy. They had defended Gellion's opinions and ultimately chosen to act upon his suggestions. Gellion only hoped this time he was making the right ones. He clenched his fists and leaned forward, gliding faster along the ground.

The armory of Tura loomed ahead. The building was as close to the main gates of the city as possible while still remaining in the City Center, and ironically mirrored the House of Healing on the other side of the main road. It had probably been centuries since the contents of the armory received a survey of inventory, and hundreds of weapons had left the facility only a few months ago on a shipment to Daro. Fortunately—or unfortunately—swords, spears, halberds, and daggers would be of little use against a phoenix, so the inventory would be fairly brief. The Turi would bring bows, crossbows, and javelins mostly. Gellion held no delusions that these weapons would stop a phoenix, but they may provide enough distraction to enable their real goal—separating Kaelo from the phoenix and disarming him of his redstone.

Gellion flipped a switch inside the room, and silvery lights illuminated along the rows of the armory. He grabbed a leather bound ledger from a shelf and noticed his hands were unsteady. With a huff of frustration, he tried to push down the clawing hands of his subconscious, still coaxing him to descend into himself. He was being ridiculous, taking Liera's words to heart. She was obviously coming unhinged, and he had already established she was in no position to accuse him of anything. Still the hands reached for him.

Focus.

The smell of metal and dust was thick in the stale air. It was hot. No use cooling a building of this size that never saw use. Gellion started walking down the rows of weapons, searching for those built for ranged attack. Past several shelves of axes, he spotted the curved tips of bows and headed toward them.

A fine layer of dust coated the beautiful weapons. The bows ranged in size from small, heavily curved things to crescent shaped hunks of metal taller than Gellion. The ranks of bows stretched ominously into the distance, and for a fleeting instant, Gellion could see the ghost of elves behind each one of them, their faces flecked with sweat, ash, and blood. He squeezed his eyes closed and shook his head. Maybe coming to the armory had not been the best choice to calm his nerves.

With a tremulous sigh, Gellion opened his eyes and turned to a blank page in the ledger. He started to write. When he looked up to assess the bows again, however, his eye caught the tall spikes of halberds on the next aisle over. He looked from the towering weapons down to his unsteady writing in the ledger. It was no good writing out the inventory if no one could read it. Why not take a few moments to collect himself, then start the inventory with the javelins?

Gellion snapped the ledger closed and paced to the next aisle.

A shiver passed over his skin as he wrapped his hands around the cool metal of a halberd and hefted its weight. Yes. This is what he needed. Just a few minutes to balance his mind.

His stance widened, his body slipping into the stances of the A'vaeri like the embrace of a lover. He took a breath, let it out. The halberd tipped forward, then circled in front of his body, moving through his hands with the satisfying slap of skin on metal, before coming to rest under his arm on his other side. He shifted his feet again, performing a perfectly balanced half turn.

He moved through several more stances—slowly, so as not to hit the surrounding weapon racks. The tension in his mind began to bleed away. As Gellion's awareness centered upon his immediate surroundings, the tang of metal grew sharper in the air, the scuff of his boots more prominent. His muscles warmed, and his shoulders relaxed. He paused, taking a breath, and then went rigid when the scuff of shoes came again, this time in his stillness. His eyes flew open, and without thinking, he spun the halberd and moved into a defensive stance.

Breath catching in his throat, Gellion stared at Tornac, who had just rounded the corner into the aisle.

Tornac looked as stunned by the sudden meeting as Gellion, and as dismayed. He had taken a step back from Gellion's hostile greeting and was eyeing the tip of the halberd. Gellion's hands tightened on the weapon.

"Gellion," Tornac said slowly.

Gellion didn't move. "What are you doing here?" he said in a flat voice.

"I came to inventory the weapons."

"I was doing that."

Tornac's eyes moved again to the tip of the halberd.

"I can see that."

Gellion's hands tightened again. An unreasonable fury was building in his chest at the sight of his brother's face—so familiar, so cold.

"Gellion," Tornac said again.

The wariness in Tornac's voice reached something inside Gellion, and he blinked, seeing for the first time the merest hint of fear that showed in his brother's eyes. Letting out his breath, Gellion lifted the halberd's tip toward the ceiling, then straightened out of his crouch.

Tornac watched him as he put the halberd back in its rack.

"I will leave you to it, then," he said. "I can find other things to do." He started to walk past Gellion toward the entrance.

The cold anger that had been growing inside Gellion dropped like a lead weight, pulling downward in his chest so that his heartbeat sped up to counter it. The anger sent ripples of ice through his nerves and across his skin.

"Is that the limit, then?" He spoke softly and without thinking. He had been ignoring and avoiding his brother for so long it felt as though the words were coming from an outside source or a dream. "Is that the amount of time you can bear to stand in my presence without the buffer of others?"

Tornac's steps halted. He turned sideways and stared at Gellion.

"What?"

"Does my existence cause you so much pain?" Gellion said in an icy voice that cut him as much as he hoped it cut Tornac. "Do you think I have not noticed you carefully avoiding me since I came to Tura? You greeted our brothers with joy and relief, yet you have not spoken a word to me. Not one."

Tornac's brows lowered. "I have."

"You have talked to Gellion the Council member—the conspirator and informant. Not your brother!"

Gellion heard the heat in his voice and took a breath, allowing the sudden flare of emotion to cool once more. He would not give Tornac the satisfaction of his temper.

Tornac sighed. "You know it has never been simple for us, Gellion, but—"

"I don't know why I am surprised." Gellion went on as though Tornac had not spoken. "You made your feelings for me perfectly clear the last two hundred years. I suppose ignoring me is the best I could have hoped for."

Tornac gaped at him. "I ignored *you*?" He looked Gellion up and down, then shook his head with a snort of disgust and moved to walk away. Before he had taken two steps, however, he stopped again with stiff legs. He seemed to be fighting with his body, unsure which direction to face. Finally, he turned to Gellion once more, his expression a mirror of Gellion's anger.

"You have not changed at all in these two hundred years, Gellion. You are exactly the same as when you left Maramor."

Gellion narrowed his eyes. "And how is that?"

"Self centered and arrogant," Tornac snapped. "I had hoped that your time in Daro would have given you some perspective on leadership and responsibility, but clearly my hopes were in vain."

"You agree with Liera then? You think Daro was my fault—that I led all those elves to their deaths single handedly through my own selfish arrogance, and that I dragged our brothers along with me?"

For a moment, Gellion thought Tornac may actually deny the claim, but instead he closed his eyes and said, "Our brothers should not have been there in the first place."

"I didn't tell them to come to Daro!" Gellion shouted, the cold in his body giving way to heat once more. "I did not ask Valder to leave Maramor with me, nor did I ask Veldon to remain in Daro after the Kindom Council!"

"You didn't need to!" Tornac ran his hands over his face. "You have never understood the pull you have on people, Gellion—the natural leadership you posses. You are too centered on yourself to notice how you influence others. I could have told you that Valder would follow you out of Maramor before you even decided to leave. I am only shocked Veldon waited so long to join him. You brought our brothers to Daro and to battle as surely as if you had pulled them with ropes, and you did not even realize you were doing it."

Gellion's lip curled up in a snarl. "You insult them both," he said. "Valder and Veldon are as possessed of their own decisions as you or I, and probably more intelligent than us both. I never would have gotten out of Tala without them."

Gellion paused, then grimaced. "But of course, that's what you would have wanted—for Valder to go back to Faeran with Veldon and mother after the Council, leaving me to die on Tala as I should have. To be rid of me at last and still save our innocent brothers from my corruption."

Tornac's face went still. Opaque. His eyes searched Gellion's.

"That is what you think?" he said. "That I wish you had died?"

Chin raised, Gellion held his brother's stare. A hint of pain flickered behind Tornac's eyes, and Gellion had to fight not to look away.

"Then you are a fool as well as a selfish ass," Tornac said.

Gellion snorted.

"If I didn't care whether you lived or died," said Tornac, "why would I say these things to you? Why would I give a damn what you did?"

"Because you care how I affect the rest of our family."

Tornac turned his eyes to the ceiling. "You are my family! Riu above, Gellion—" He ran his hands through his hair and clasped them over the back of his neck. "I tried so hard. I have always tried so hard for you. But when it was I who needed you—" He closed his eyes and shook his head. His hands dropped to his sides and he looked at Gellion. "I only ever wanted you to get over yourself and live up to your potential. To use your talent and your brain to do something more than craft metal and impress others."

Gellion's eyes flashed, and he took a step toward Tornac, wishing he still had the halberd in his hands.

"I did more than you ever did after the war. While you were hidden away in Maramor, I helped rebuild Tura—our entire Kindom! I went on expeditions to find more vierstone for all the elves. I built Daro. I poured my soul into that city and all who lived in it, and if you don't think I *hate* myself for what happened to it—for the elves that died, for Kaelo, for our brothers—" His voice cracked, then faltered. He bowed his head and took several breaths, trying to recall the cold resolve he had felt before, but it had cracked, and the heat was rising into his face now. He could feel it burning him, melting him. He slowly lifted his head and glared at Tornac.

"If you do not think I blame myself more than you ever could, then you are the fool."

He walked passed Tornac, kicking the ledger he had left on the ground toward him.

Tornac did not speak as Gellion made his way to the armory entrance, and when Gellion allowed himself a single glance back before stepping out of sight, Tornac still stood with his back to Gellion, staring down at the ledger lying open at his feet.

Gellion slammed the door behind him, walked around the side of the building, and lowered himself to the ground against the wall. Away from the eyes of elves, he let the hands drag him down at last.

13

HUNTING AND HUNTED

While the trees of Riverseep Forest formed a permanent twilight beneath their canopies during the day, the night was so black Renyra could hardly make out the shape of the branches around her. Remsgraen was close enough that she could see its glow in the distance, and the illuminated lines of the Rale far below formed an eerie river between the trees, but here in the tops of the canopies, the world existed in suspended darkness, separated from the stars by a close but thick layer of leaves.

Despite the endless choice of trees, it had taken some time to find one with the right vantage point whose branches remained thick enough at the apex of its reach to support the weight of an elf, even a small one. Renyra pulled herself a few feet higher, then wrapped her arm around a sturdy branch and stood. Twigs scraped over her skin and snapped as her head broke the surface of the canopy. She gasped at the sudden blast of fresh air.

Rustling and snapping sounded a few feet away from her.

"Oh!" Alura said. "It's still so dark up here."

Clouds obscured any divine illumination they may have hoped for. The air was lighter than that in the forest, but it still held the heaviness of moisture.

"I think it's going to rain," Renyra said.

"Again?" Alura groaned.

Scout duty above the trees of Riverseep had become a regular and unpleasant job. Sometimes, the troupe would find a tree tall enough that a heavier elf could climb above the sea of trees to see the horizon, but mostly it was a job reserved for the small bodies of Renyra and Alura. Renyra loved climbing trees, and the beauty above their branches could be wondrous, but hours spent clinging to damp bark and squinting through misty rain was not her idea of fun. Fortunately, there was no mist above the forest tonight. Not yet, anyway.

Renyra adjusted her grip on her branch and tried to settle into a position that was sustainable, if not comfortable. She turned herself until the dim glow of Remsgraen fell to her left. The phoenix would come from the north, and it would come soon.

Tracking the phoenix through Riverseep had proved to be surprisingly easy. The Remsgri had laced the forest with Rale lines—large ones that ran through the bases of the trees, and levit paths that wound through the branches. Any given town was accessible within a day from any other location, and messages travelled rapidly. So, even with the delay of the troupe's first day in the forest, they had chased the news of the phoenix's progress and caught sight of the beast several times. Once, they had nearly managed to catch it by surprise as it rested in the branches of a tree, but Raren had slipped and snapped a branch—and let out a curse. The ensuing flurry of wings and fire had been enough to send them all scrambling down the trees and running for the nearest Rale path. Thereafter, they had been more careful. Did the phoenix know it was being pursued? Did Kaelo know? Would it make any difference if he did?

This would be the first time the troupe attempted to corner the phoenix again since the disaster two days ago. It was also their last chance. The phoenix would move on from Riverseep once it finished with Remsgraen.

"How long do you think it will take?" Alura said.

"An hour, maybe," said Renyra.

They had ridden the Rale ahead of the phoenix three hours before.

The beast made frequent stops to destroy vierstone, so it would likely lag behind them by at least an hour.

"I'll take the first quarter hour," Renyra said. She had managed to wedge her limbs into secure locations against the branches below her. She may as well stay for a while.

"Sure." Relief was plain in Alura's voice. "Just shout when you want me to come up."

More rustling announced Alura's departure. The rest of the troupe was in the branches just below them, though from up here, they seemed a world away.

It was not until Renyra's second shift nearly an hour later that a crimson star appeared above the trees. A fine mist was falling now, frosting Renyra's eyelashes so she had to wipe the moisture away to see clearly. The point of light grew bigger. Even in darkness and rain, the phoenix seemed unable to extinguish the glow of its feathers. For this, Renyra was grateful. She did not know how they would have come so close to the phoenix at night without the beacon of its body in the darkness.

Renyra crouched so one hand extended below the canopy, then knocked three times on the branch that held her weight. An affirmed sighting. Now she just had to wait and see if the phoenix disappeared below the trees. Surely it would not go on to attack Remsgraen so late? As far as Renyra knew, the phoenix had never attacked a city after dark.

Instincts flaring to life against conscious thought, Renyra lowered herself in the branches until she could just see the phoenix flying low over the trees. It was still miles off, but even in the camouflage of a forest at night, Renyra felt like a rabbit stalking a mountain cat—one that glowed in the dark and had the eyes of an eagle. She took a steadying breath and concentrated. She could not let her instincts get the better of her the next time she faced the beast. She was the hunter here, and the bird was her prey.

By the time the phoenix tucked its wings to dive below the trees, Renyra could almost make out the light of its eyes. Probably half a mile off. She let out a sigh of relief, then stared at the indistinct dip in the trees where the beast had disappeared, trying to orient and lock the location in her mind before dropping below the leaves.

"Half a mile northeast," she said. Automatically, her eyes searched for Firas among the shapes crouched in the trees. She couldn't make him out.

"Lead on," Raren said.

Renyra started to feel her way down the branches.

"Firas," she said into the darkness.

"I am here."

The voice was closer than Renyra had anticipated, and she nearly slipped. A hand caught her elbow.

"How can you see me?" Renyra said.

"I can't," Firas said. "I can—" he hesitated. "I know where you are."

Understanding spread over Renyra like the cool mist above her. She stiffened. Firas could sense her near him through the connection he still felt to her. A connection Renyra may never feel again. Tears stung her eyes. The rest of the troupe had managed to avoid the phoenix's destructive flames outside Telem Fier, but if this attempt on the phoenix did not succeed, Firas would lose his vierstone too. Would she still be able to love him years, decades, or centuries in the future without that connection? Would she still care?

Renyra swallowed the lump in her throat. "Do you have it?"

"Yes." Firas's voice was patient, as though he didn't mind answering the question several times a day—or a night.

"Are you sure you—"

"I am keeping it, love."

Renyra didn't respond. How could she explain to him that it was the touch of the dagger itself she craved, not the responsibility of stabbing the phoenix—though she wanted that too, if only to take its burden from Firas. She shook her head. She needed to focus on finding the phoenix. The dagger would be useless if they couldn't get close enough to the beast to use it.

The dagger was not forged like Kaelo's sword. It was a rough thing, hewn into the shape of a blade and chipped and filed like volcanic glass until its edges and point were sharp. It had not been easy to find a Remsgri willing to part with vierstone, let alone form it into a weapon. Trali had finally convinced a glassworker in a small town to help them after lengthy explanations and the warming influence of tropical wine.

The detour had cost them several days of tracking. She hoped the weapon would be worth it.

Firas's features became clearer as they neared the illuminated Rale path. Another two stories below them, the larger Rale line glowed brightly, but here in the branches, the track for levit boards curved smoothly around the trunk of their tree. Renyra stepped onto its surface with jittery legs. Half a mile was a short ways to travel by levit board, even through the trees. Whatever was about to happen with the phoenix, it would be over within the hour.

Six boards lay waiting at the tree's base. Renyra gravitated toward the one she had ridden from Remsgraen and stepped onto it. With the click of her heel, the board rose into the air.

"Ready?" She checked that her companions were all mounted and alert. A series of nods met her inquiry, and with a deep breath, Renyra leaned forward and glided into the night.

The white glow of the Rale path was far behind them by the time Renyra caught sight of what appeared to be burning embers in the branches of a tree. She halted her steps, watching the mottled red light with held breath. She listened.

There was still a good distance between the phoenix and the troupe, and through the still air, thick trunks, and dangling vines, there was little threat of the phoenix hearing them, let alone seeing them. Still, Renyra listened, trying to make out any hint of voices or creaking of branches. There was nothing.

"Is that it?" Raren's voice was barely more than a breath. The rest of the troupe had stopped when Renyra did, waiting for her signal.

"I think so," said Renyra. "It matches where I saw it dip below the trees, and I can't think of anything else in the forest that would make that color of light."

"Only a few of us should approach the tree," said Firas. "If it is stealth and surprise we seek, numbers will give us no advantage."

Renyra nodded, then realized no one could see the motion.

"I agree. Alura and I—"

"I will carry the dagger," Firas said.

"I never said you wouldn't." Renyra gritted her teeth. "I was *going* to say that Alura and I can tail you up the tree—offer support and extra eyes. We are the best at climbing trees and put the least weight on the branches. The phoenix won't hear us."

"And then if Firas succeeds, you get thrown out of the trees or accosted by Kaelo alone," said Raren. "If he fails, you fall with him or else face Kaelo anyway. Back up isn't going to help here."

"You want him to go up that tree alone?" Renyra said through her teeth. Raren never would have suggested the same were it his sister climbing up to a phoenix with a dagger.

"He is right," Firas said. "Whether or not I am able to stab the phoenix, I will need to descend to the forest floor as quickly as possible. We do not want to fight Kaelo in the trees, and I am sure it will come to a fight if we kill—or try to kill—his greatest weapon. The rest of you should wait below and prepare yourselves for whatever comes next, be it a fight, or running back to the Rale."

"I don't like it," Renyra said.

"Nor do I," said a smooth voice.

Renyra sucked in a breath. Adrenaline burst from her chest and through her body. No elf of their company had said those words. She jerked her head toward the voice.

Kyna took a step out of a patch of ferns behind them, her face illuminated by a sphere of light she held in her hands. Her eyes were locked on Renyra, and the expression behind them was not pleasant.

The troupe recoiled from Kyna as a unit, weapons glinting in the light of her lamp. Kyna did not flinch from the drawn blades. She did not take her eyes off Renyra.

"That was your plan?" she said in a low hiss. "To sneak up on the phoenix and stab it with a *dagger*? Are you really as naive as you act?"

The shock of Kyna's sudden arrival was wearing off. Renyra felt the adrenaline inside her change direction, fueling a growing heat in her chest. A warm presence moved beside her, and she felt Firas's fingers brush against her arm. Taking a breath, she tried to channel her emotions, then glanced at the ember light in the distant trees. It hadn't moved.

"Do they know we are here?" she said as calmly as she could manage.

A muscle twitched in Kyna's jaw as her eyes followed Renyra's glance.

"Not yet. But I will tell them if you don't turn back."

Caerlyn tried to step around Renyra. "You treacherous little—"

"No." Renyra threw an arm across Caerlyn's belly and pushed back against her. Firas tensed, his fingers closing over Renyra's arm.

"What?" Caerlyn glared at Renyra. "She will ruin everything! Unless you want to go back to Remsgraen and wait for that monster to kill us there—"

"It won't kill you." Kyna rolled her eyes. "If you haven't noticed in your ridiculous pursuit, it hasn't killed a single elf in all this time."

"Oh, so it's a tame monster, is it?" Caerlyn scoffed. "You know what, Renyra? I think she's right. We should just go back to Telem Fier and live our lives happily ever after because we know we won't be roasted in our beds at night."

Renyra ignored her. She was watching Kyna's face in the steady light of the lamp. It was the same face she had seen for weeks in Daro, and then in Tura, but there was something different about it now. Kyna had always borne a mask of blank indifference, never showing more than her words revealed. It was because of this, Renyra now knew, that the woman had fooled them all so successfully. But now that mask was cracked. The same fear Renyra had seen in the rocks outside Telem Fier lingered in Kyna's eyes, and there was an edge to her voice. Almost a desperation.

"Do you believe in what he does?" Renyra said. "Kaelo, and ... and the phoenix?"

"Yes," Kyna said. Her expression did not change.

Renyra's brows drew together. "You want to take all the vierstone from the world?"

The slightest hesitation. "Yes."

"Why?"

Kyna opened her mouth, closed it, then jerked her head as though fending off a swarm of gnats.

"I don't need to explain myself to you. You'll understand in time like everyone else. Just go back to Telem Fier, or to Tura, or to wherever the hell you want to live the rest of your life, and do not follow us again if you value your lives. He has noticed you already, and that is not a place you want to be."

"A place like you?"

"You don't know what you're talking about."

"So you've said before. Look. I don't know why you've done what you've done, or what Kaelo has said to persuade you into his plans, but I do know his actions have not been harmless. This phoenix may not have killed any elves yet, but can you say the same of Kaelo?"

Kyna's eyes flashed red. "You are just like the rest of them! You preach of love and forgiveness and justice and mercy, yet you withhold it for a centuries' old crime of an elf you never knew."

"I was not talking about what Kaelo did centuries ago," Renyra said. "I was talking about Daro! And Arvain! Those elves may not have been slaughtered by Kaelo's hand directly, but he killed them all the same."

"That was not supposed to happen," Kyna said.

Renyra blanched, understanding moving through her like cold honey. All this time, she had somehow convinced herself that Kaelo had approached Kyna after all that had happened in Tala. Visions of kidnapping and blackmail and threats in dark alleys had entered her imaginings, complete with a reluctant and terrified Kyna doing Kaelo's bidding even as he slowly poisoned her mind to his ideals. Maybe Renyra was as naive as Kyna accused—as they all assumed.

"You were a part of that too," Renyra whispered. "From the moment you came to Daro, you were working with him."

Kyna did not answer.

Renyra stared at Kyna with mounting horror.

"Daro. Aryn. Dulon—Gellion."

At the last name, Kyna flinched openly.

"It was necessary," she said, though her expression did not match the steel in her voice. "We did what we had to do for a better future."

Firas had flinched as hard as Kyna at Gellion's name and now took a step toward Kyna.

"You used him," he growled. "You used him and then you killed him."

Kyna jerked back from Firas's towering form as though he had slapped her. Her knuckles were white around her lantern.

"That wasn't my fault. It wasn't supposed to happen like that."

"Firas." Renyra placed a gentle hand on his shoulder. He remained coiled for a moment longer, then relaxed under her touch, though he did not retract his step. In the glare of Kyna's lamp, Renyra could see the fury boiling beneath Firas's eyes. And the pain. It was this that set fire to Renyra's own blood. Kaelo and Kyna had destroyed her home and friends, but they had also caused agonizing pain to Firas, and for that Renyra would not forgive so easily. She turned eyes hard as flint on Kyna.

"I wanted to help you. I thought that despite all you have done, there was some explanation that would redeem your actions. I wanted you to join us of your own free will and help us fight the elf that forced you to commit such terrible crimes. Now I see that no one forced you to do anything. You *chose* to destroy my home, to kill my friends."

Kyna's mask cracked further, revealing something very like pain. Renyra ignored it.

"And," she forced herself to continue, "you would condemn your own race."

"You don't understand," Kyna said in a hoarse voice. "You don't know what they did to him. What *it* did to him."

"What are you talking about?" Caerlyn said with an exasperated sigh.

"Vierstone isn't the savior you think it is. Daro was—" Kyna closed her eyes. "Daro had to happen. And Tura. We have to cleanse it all. Everything will be better when this is over, and if the elves would stop fighting—"

"What, you think we should line up quietly to be doused in phoenix flame, then say 'thank you' and go back to our lives?" This time it was Raren who spoke. His voice, so near behind Renyra, made her jump, but the next voice to speak shocked her still more.

"Kyna." Firas still stood a step ahead of Renyra. His body was tense, but his voice was low, almost gentle. "I don't know what Kaelo has told you about vierstone, but it is not true. You cannot understand what a world without vierstone will mean. Please. You must see what the phoenix is doing to the world—what Kaelo is doing. What will happen once the phoenix finishes this crusade? Will it fly to the mountains to lead a peaceful life the rest of its existence? You were not there when the last phoenix lived. They are treacherous, cunning, and hateful. This is a dangerous game Kaelo is playing, and losing could mean far worse even than a world without vierstone."

The fear had returned to Kyna's eyes, stronger than before. She glanced toward the distant glow of the beast in the trees.

"It—he knows what he is doing."

But Renyra could see the doubt behind Kyna's words.

"You don't trust the phoenix," she said.

Kyna jerked her head back to face Renrya, eyes narrowed. She looked as though she were about to deny Renyra's claim, but no sound escaped her mouth. Taking advantage of the hesitation, Renyra followed this new angle.

"Come with us, Kyna. Help us defeat it. You know the phoenix better than anyone—except maybe Kaelo. Whatever he's done to earn your trust, it can't be worth this." She let some of the heat still swelling in her chest show in her eyes. "There is nothing you can do to reverse what happened in Daro, but you can still stop this from ending in devestation. We might know a way to kill the phoenix."

For the space of three breaths, Kyna stood utterly motionless. She stared at Renyra as one stares at a mountain cat stalking toward her with hunger in its eyes and death on its bared teeth.

"No," she said at last. "You don't know how to kill it. You can't. There is nothing any of you can—" Kyna sucked in a breath as the swish of fern fronds brushing metal came from behind her. Another shape, a taller shape, stepped from the shadows, one side of his face faintly illuminated by Kyna's lamp. Kyna's eyes widened; her body went taut.

"Good evening." Kaelo's unsmiling eyes fixed on Renyra.

14

SMOKE IN THE TREES

Kaelo's words barely registered above the rushing and pounding that had suddenly filled Kyna's ears. She did not move. She did not look at him. She drew in a thin breath and watched the reactions of those in front of her. Weapons glinted in the light of her lamp again, but mostly the elves before her just stared at Kaelo with expressions ranging from shock to terror to anger. Normally, Kyna would have found it an interesting study to evaluate the emotions with each personality, if she was not so sure her own face was as disgustingly readable and predictable as the rest of them.

Her heart had stopped beating for a moment, she was sure. That must be why it was thrashing so hard against her chest now.

"I believe we have met, you and I," said Kaelo. Kyna risked a glance at her father and saw he was watching Renyra through narrow eyes. One side of his lips quirked upward in a humorless grimace. "In a manner of speaking," he added.

Renyra's face was not one of those projecting terror. Even the shock in her eyes had only been fleeting. She stared at Kaelo with a burning intensity and did not respond to his words. Slowly, deliberately, she reached behind her to disengage the javelin from her back. With the other hand, she brushed Firas's arm.

To Kyna's amazement, Firas retreated to the back of the group of elves, until the luminescence of his skin was barely detectable. Kyna watched him with nagging suspicion. Firas did not seem the type to leave his wife's side in danger as heated as this.

Kaelo raised an eyebrow at Renyra's drawn weapon, now poised in her hand at the ready. He passed a glance over the rest of the elves behind her.

"It seems you are acquainted with my daughter."

Renyra's brows twitched together in a moment of confusion, then her resolve broke as understanding dawned on her face. She stared at Kyna with wide eyes.

"Your *father*?" she croaked.

Kyna looked down. How long had her father been watching from the shadows? Had he heard their whole conversation? Her hesitation? She should have gone to him the moment she heard whispers in the night, the instant she abandoned her search for dry wood to investigate. But she hadn't. Why hadn't she?

"You want her to come with you," Kaelo said. It was not a question. His tone was flat, devoid of all emotion. When no one answered him, he went on. "Well?"

Molten lead dripped into Kyna's stomach as all eyes turned to her. She finally forced herself to look up at her father, who was watching her expectantly.

"Wh ... what?" she stammered.

"Do you want to go with them?"

Kyna opened her mouth, but only a choking sound came out. She shook her head, glancing between Renyra and Kaelo.

"I will not stop you." His words were casual, but Kyna could hear the ice behind them. "But I will not allow you to interfere with what we do here, or anywhere else. Leave with them and live your life elsewhere, or stay here and complete what you started."

It was no choice. The others would never leave peacefully. Even if she had wanted to help them, there was nothing Kyna could do in the face of their stubborn determination. They would fight. They would lose. Whatever answer they thought they had come up with to ensure the phoenix's demise would not work. There was only one answer, and no elf living knew it—none but her father and herself.

Kyna's nails bit into her palms. It was an answer she would not turn to. She could not. Killing that monstrous bird was not worth betraying her father—and herself. Besides, it was more complicated than that. Destroying the phoenix now and leaving their job half finished would mean plunging the elven race into chaos and grief. Renyra and her followers didn't understand what they strove to accomplish. It was for their own good that they fail.

They are nothing. You already betrayed them once, why should this be any harder?

But it was. Kyna had betrayed these elves for a fate that would change their race for the better, avenge her father, and fulfill her life's goal. That was something she could bear. But to leave them to their deaths as she stood and watched? Kyna bit down on the inside of her lip until she tasted metal.

"No." She composed her face, wiping the emotion from its every curve and line. In her voice, she put callous resolve. "I will not go with them. I will *never* go with them." She flashed her eyes at her father. "You *still* doubt my loyalty, after all I have done, after all the times I have chosen you." She flapped a hand at the frozen elves in front of her. "I was trying to get it into their thick heads that what they seek they cannot achieve. I was trying to make them turn back and stop their ridiculous assassination attempts before it kills them. I was obviously unsuccessful."

Kyna's skin crawled with the heat of the troupe's glares. She was sure Renyra's gaze alone would scorch a hole through her, but she forced herself to turn and meet their eyes head on. She was pleased when her expression remained impassive.

Kaelo considered Kyna with shrewd eyes, then nodded his acceptance. Kyna let out a breath. Her father did not speak at once. When he did, his voice was silken.

"And you?" He was looking at Renyra now. "Will you once more gamble your life—a life I have spared three times now—and the lives of your friends, on a fool's errand?"

For the first time since Kaelo had made his appearance, Renyra opened her mouth.

"I will not stop trying." The tip of her javelin shook, and her voice was quiet, yet those jewel bright eyes did not stray from Kaelo's stare. "As long as there is still a chance to end this black future you strive toward, I will follow you and the phoenix, and I will do all in my power to stop you."

Kaelo nodded slowly. "And you think you will succeed?"

Renyra's jaw tightened. She did not answer.

Kaelo raised his eyebrows. Then light blossomed through the trees. Kyna wheeled to face the phoenix, now blazing with yellow fire and flying through the trees, wings tight to its body. Its shriek would have raised the hair of a bald man. Before it reached them, the bird swooped close to the ground, talons outstretched, and a wordless cry echoed in the night.

"No!" Renyra shouted, her eyes round with terror.

The phoenix lifted into the air again, then glided to their small clearing, depositing an elf in a heap on the ground before landing. Firas leaped to his feet with the grace of a leopard, but the phoenix struck like a snake, hooking its wicked beak through the back of his shirt and lifting him off the ground once more. Firas cried out in pain. Kyna winced. The beast had probably gouged a good bit of flesh with that bite.

"Do it now!" Renyra lunged toward Kaelo with her javelin, the rest of her troupe close on her heels.

Many things happened at once.

Firas flailed in the phoenix's grip. Kaelo took one step back and drew his redstone sword, clashing it against Renyra's javelin and turning her weapon to ash in a matter of moments. Beside them, the phoenix let out a scream of rage, smashing Firas against the ground with a swivel of its neck and letting out a stream of blue fire that passed over his body and made a wall between the rest of the troupe and Kaelo.

Kyna had no time to react to any of this. She just stood with her arms tense at her sides and her lips parted.

The fire vanished. Kaelo pointed his sword at Renyra's heart, and the phoenix opened its mouth, swirling colors glowing at the back of its throat, but subdued for the moment.

"I would not come any closer if I were you," Kaelo said in a voice that suggested nothing more interesting had just happened than a casual conversation.

Raren, Alura, Caerlyn, and a dark elf Kyna did not recognize froze where they were, weapons clenched in fists and eyes turned to the unmoving form of Firas on the ground. Renyra's eyes flitted almost comically between the blade at her chest and her husband, but before she could do anything undoubtedly stupid, the phoenix stepped over Firas and dipped its neck close to the ground, hissing at her through a cloud of smoke.

Kaelo looked at Firas, then at the dagger lying next to his body. It reflected the phoenix's glow in strange, swirling patterns. Kaelo's eyebrows rose again.

"Vierstone?" He turned back to Renyra.

Renyra's cheeks were wet with tears.

"Let me go to him," she choked. "Please."

The expression on Kaelo's face could only be described as sad. He tilted his sword so the tip of it was even with Renyra's face, then used its edge to brush away a fresh tear spilling from her eye. He stared at the tear with a cocked head.

"This, child, is why I do what I do. Do you see?" He tilted the blade again so the tear rolled down its face. "You have spirit. Passion. Attachment. Traits I once admired. Traits I once possessed." He appraised Renyra once more and the sadness in his eyes was replaced by something harder. "Traits I have long since recognized for the weakness and bridge to pain that they are."

Renyra glared at him through her tears. "Traits born of vierstone?" she said. "Is that what you mean? Traits that give purpose and joy to life —that you would wipe from this world just so the rest of us can be as miserable as you?"

Kaelo snorted softly. "You think I seek to bring the rest of the elves the same pain I have endured? They may deserve it, but that is not my intention. In vierstone, Riu gave the elves fire, and with it, we have only consumed ourselves and burned all around us."

"And loved!" Renyra said. "And created, and lived!"

"Love?" Cruel lines etched over Kaelo's ivory skin. "There is no love. There is obsession, there is infatuation, there is lust—but not love. It is a concept that cannot exist within the flawed nature of the elves. Love requires trust and loyalty—things the elves can never truly possess."

"Just because love can fail does not mean it doesn't exist." Renyra drew herself up, closing the gap between herself and the sword. Kaelo lowered its tip to hover next to her throat.

"It cannot exist *here*," he said. "Why harbor a farce of the concept? Why endure this pain?" He looked from Renyra's head to her toes, then back to the anguish in her eyes. "Why not wait until we can experience it in its true form, rather than be repeatedly crushed by its imperfection upon Riure?"

"Maybe an imperfect glimmer is better than darkness," Renyra hissed through clenched teeth.

Kaelo's frown deepened.

"You are all drunk upon the influence of vierstone," he said. "A drunkard cannot contemplate his own drunkenness, nor understand what it means to be sober while he stumbles and slurs and craves more drink. Nor can you conceive of the freedom that is possible if you gave up that with which you are so infatuated and consumed. It rules your emotions. It rules your minds. It rules your very thoughts. You need someone outside its influence to show you how to escape."

"But they will not listen," said a voice.

Kyna flinched. From the twitch of her father's ears, she knew he had heard the phoenix too, though the rest of the elves showed no indication it had spoken to them.

"Do you see, now?" the phoenix said. "These elves will hear no reason. They will not stop until you are dead, or they are. Not unless you give them no way to rise against you."

Kaelo had not looked away from Renyra. He ground his jaw and stared into Renyra's shining eyes as though trying to extract her thoughts—her very nature.

Renyra may not have heard the phoenix, but she had clearly sensed the shift in Kaelo's attention. She tore her eyes away from him and looked toward Firas again, who still lay beneath the phoenix. It looked like his clothes were smoking.

The phoenix's rage rolled off of its body in palpable waves. Its talons bit deep into the soft forest floor and its throat was still glowing.

"Show them now," it said.

A strange hunger had come to Kaelo's eyes. His grip on his sword tightened, and its tip pressed against the soft skin at Renyra's throat. The Fieri's eyes darted back to him in panic, and she took a step back.

Kyna was fighting for breath now. Would he kill her? Renyra posed no threat to him now. None of them did. They never had.

Just leave them. Leave them and move on.

"Do it," the phoenix hissed, and a puff of flames rose from its nostrils. "Or I will."

Kaelo's lips twitched in a snarl.

"Remsgraen!" Kyna blurted.

Kaelo blinked.

"Go to Remsgraen now," she continued. "They won't be expecting it."

Brows drawn, Kaelo looked at her. His expression was almost dazed. The hand holding his blade lowered for just a moment, and Renyra jerked forward suddenly. Kyna saw a flash of silver going straight for her father's throat.

Before she knew what she was doing, Kyna reached for Renyra's arm, catching and twisting her wrist away from Kaelo's neck and pressing her other hand against her own thigh. A shocking cold spread from the stone at her wrist through her body, then into Renyra. Kyna projected fear and despair through the connection, forcing the emotions upon Renyra like pouring water down her throat. Then she shoved Renyra as hard as she could before Kaelo's sword came down. It grazed Kyna's arm, and she drew in a sharp breath of pain, stumbling into her father as she drew her arm back.

The phoenix was ablaze now, screeching into the night. It beat its wings twice, then flew straight toward them. Kyna felt hot talons wrap around her body and then she was in the air. She gasped as wind tore at her hair and clothing. The phoenix was ascending, faster and faster, and then, in a shower of leaves, twigs, and ashes—a shock of fresh air.

All was silent except the rush of air and the heavy beat of wings. Kyna grasped at the glassy scales of the phoenix's feet, not daring to speak or even to think. She could barely open her eyes against the wind and mist and the tangles of damp hair slashing her face, but through stolen squints and glances, she saw the glow of Remsgraen coming closer, rising to meet them.

———

The elves of Remsgraen had not been expecting a night attack, that much was obvious, but it was only a few minutes after the red fire began to fall upon their city that Kyna caught glimpses of armed elves moving in groups. She clung to the phoenix's talons as she watched the ashes of arrows raining below her.

This was not like Maramor, or any of the other countless towns over which Kyna had ridden the phoenix during a cleansing. In the darkness, the swirling lights and colors disoriented Kyna until she could not tell if the phoenix was flying upright, sideways, or vertically. She tried to focus on the splashes of red, because surely the fire would point down. The glowing blues and whites of Rale tracks and lamps came from all directions, blurred by the phoenix's speed and maneuvering, and the shouts and screams of elves mingled with the roar of flames and shrieks of the phoenix. Strange explosions dotted the myriad of sounds and lights. Kyna closed her eyes, but the lights flashing against her eyelids were no less dizzying, and the sounds and sensations surrounding her became all the more sharp for her blindness. So desperate was her mind to grasp something solid and real, the clear voice of the phoenix in her head came as a relief.

"Do it now," it said. "Release me. Lift the limits."

It took Kyna a moment to realize the phoenix was talking to her father. Did it mean for her to hear? Was it too distracted to narrow its thoughts?

"You saw what they are. It is as I told you, they will never listen to your reason. They will cling to their righteous beliefs and their hatred until you are dead. Until *we* are dead."

A pause.

"And these elves fight us harder even than the Fieri! Let me burn their city. Let me give them the consequence they deserve for their actions. Show them we will not stand for this retaliation, even retaliation done in ignorance and delusion."

No.

Kyna gripped the phoenix's scales so hard her fingers ached, though she doubted the beast even felt it. Was her father clasped in the phoenix's other talon, or was he on its back? She couldn't see anything but the swirling lights below. She wished she could see her father's face, hear his response. Surely he would not agree to this, even after what had just happened. He had promised.

Even as the phoenix whispered its poisonous words, it flew between the trees, spilling fire over the buildings and elves of Remsgraen and deflecting arrows and spears by flame and by its own glassy feathers. The explosions were getting louder and more frequent. What were they? The closest thing Kyna had ever heard to them was the cracking of stone in Daro when Kaelo had split the foundations of the city, or the ensuing pop of electrical lines and lamps. Concentrating on the sounds, Kyna began to see flares of light each time she heard an explosion. The phoenix swerved. It hissed.

"Let me." The beast's voice echoed in Kyna's mind again.

Kyna craned her neck through the phoenix's talons, trying to get a clearer view. Just then, the phoenix paused to hover for a moment, reigning its fire over a huge series of buildings stretching through the trees in the center of the city. A different light caught Kyna's eye. It was blue, like much of the city, but it was darker, almost purple, and brighter. Much brighter. Its intensity increased even as Kyna tried to focus her eyes on it, and through the rushing of flames and distant cries of elves, she heard a hum—a deep and ringing vibration that reached her teeth even as she dangled in the air.

An inexplicable panic seized Kyna's chest. She did not know what the glowing thing was, but she had no doubt it was nothing good—not for her.

"Look!" she shouted, aiming both voice and thoughts at the phoenix.

It was too late. Where the humming lights had been a moment before, the air exploded.

Kyna felt the impact through the phoenix's body—a shocking,

incomprehensibly powerful blow that seemed to shake Kyna's own body away from her consciousness. Then she was flying—first in a wild tumble of phoenix feathers and claws, then through nothing. Flailing and screaming, she dropped through shockingly thin air, the colors still streaking and swirling in what little of her vision hadn't blacked out. All sound seemed far away, or else padded, and Kyna wondered briefly if the screaming she heard was even coming from her own mouth. Maybe she fell silently and only thought of screaming, or maybe she had merely internalized the screams around her.

Then she hit soft ground in a rolling, skidding, twisting thud.

Silence enveloped her, like it had been trying to catch up to her as she fell and only now reached its target. She lay on spongy soil, and though she sensed movement around her, she could not seem to open her eyes. Or were they open? Was she blind now as well as deaf and paralyzed? Maybe she was simply dead.

Then sounds began to return again, far away at first. She blinked, and the blurred outline of lights and legs slowly came into focus. It was several more moments before Kyna could muster the strength to move. Toes and fingers alike responded to her cautious prodding, and when she arched her back experimentally, only an achy twinge fought back against her movement. In her relief, she barely repressed a bubble of hysterical laughter from coming up her throat.

The muted vibration of footfalls still surrounded her. As a semblance of sense returned to her mind, Kyna began to wonder why no one had come to her, if only to capture or kill her, but as she pushed herself off the ground, she saw she was hardly the only elf lying prone in the moss. The phoenix's crash landing seemed to have crushed several buildings and cracked off a few limbs the size of small trees. No one would have noticed her flying from the phoenix's talons in the chaotic explosion.

What had *happened*?

Kyna wheeled around, trying to find the phoenix. She bore no delusions that it was dead. No blast, no matter how powerful, could kill the phoenix. But her father possessed no such immortality. Where was he? And what in all of Riure had that explosion been?

She heard the phoenix before she saw it. Long and grating shrieks came from a thrashing mass on the ground fifty feet away. Kyna stood and squinted to see what was happening. Elves were shouting and converging on the beast. Why was it still on the ground? Could it be injured? She dodged around passing elves, trying to see if her father was down with the phoenix, or if he had been thrown as she had.

Then she saw the chains. Each link was as thick as her body; each section probably weighed as much as a small ship. Yet the chains flew through the air over the phoenix, ejected with loud pops from machines hidden by the elves crowding them. The chains flattened the phoenix to the ground, but no sooner did they meet its glowing feathers, they began to melt. The phoenix bucked and thrashed, tearing through the chains once they melted enough to weaken, but then a new set would fly through the air and pin the beast again. Kyna watched in horror. Surely the Remsgri knew what would happen when their chains ran out? The phoenix would melt through them until there were none left, and then its wrath would be beyond anything they had yet seen.

Kyna ran toward the phoenix with no plan in mind. She had to know if her father was with it. The phoenix would crush him if it kept up this thrashing show. Elves continued to block Kyna's way and obscure her vision. She cursed and shoved, hoping that the Remsgri's chains would hold long enough that she wouldn't be caught in the ensuing anger of the phoenix before it knew she was there.

It was no use. There were too many elves. Skin pressed on Kyna from all sides. She needed to see above the elves. With more shoving, and a bit more cursing, Kyna managed to extricate herself from the crowd surrounding the phoenix and ran to a pile of debris from a fallen building. She climbed the rubble, then turned to face the phoenix.

Her father was there. He stood next to the phoenix, sword raised. No one came near him. No one dared. Not with the phoenix so near.

Do something. Break the ground, cause an earthquake, destroy the chain machines. Do something.

But Kaelo did nothing. His eyes darted around, as though trying to find a solution to the predicament, but still he only stood.

A low rumbling caught Kyna's attention. It rose in pitch until it was a steady hum, and Kyna saw a new glow of indigo between two trees. She looked from the machine to the phoenix, and she understood. The

Remsgri did not need unlimited chains, they only needed to restrain the phoenix long enough that they could fire that cursed weapon straight at its head. It would not kill the phoenix, but it could very well kill her father. Kyna had to do something.

Leaping down from the rubble, Kyna fell to her knees and sank her hands into the ground, feeling the press of redstone against her wrist. She felt *into* the ground, trying to reach it, to command it, but she only felt disjointed flecks of metal and stone. Pressing her hands deeper, she intensified her draw on the redstone, but it was no good. The ground here was almost entirely leaf and animal matter. There wasn't enough stone. No wonder her father had made no move to defend himself using redstone, it was as good as useless in this mush.

Real panic was starting to creep up Kyna's spine. There was nothing she could do. She was weaponless, powerless.

The humming grew louder.

Kyna's eyes locked on the glowing instrument. Her mind raced for a fraction of a second, then she ran straight at it.

She ran until her feet met smooth metal, then she crouched, slamming her palm against the path that ran to the base of the tubular machine now humming so loudly she could feel it in the ground. She closed her eyes and concentrated. The path was longer than she would have liked, but not so long she couldn't extend her reach to the machine. A cold flush spread through her body from the redstone against her skin and she directed its current through her palm. She felt the path spread before her—a living thing waiting for her instruction. She ignored it, pushing the cold awareness further, until it enveloped the weapon.

The entire thing was metal—a huge body with two flat projections and magnets, lots of magnets. Kyna did not know how it worked, nor did she care. She concentrated on the housing of the thing, then squeezed her fist against the ground. Metal crumpled inward, magnets cracked and twisted. She forced the thing to break in every way she could think of.

There was a moment of gasps and shouts. A moment of hushed anticipation. Then, the world became nothing but light and sound once more.

The initial explosion of the weapon had been nothing—a candle compared to a forest fire, a puddle to a sea. Kyna dove away from the blast, throwing her arms over her head, and felt a rush of heat up her back. The phoenix's shrieks rose in pitch and volume. Kyna twisted and sat up, her ears ringing. The elves surrounding the phoenix were gone—thrown backward from the blast or else fled. The chains that remained on the beast's back oozed down its sides in molten rivulets, and the bird opened its wings in a shower of liquid fire.

Elves screamed. Arrows flew. Kyna ran.

Kaelo held out a hand to her as she approached and vaulted her onto the phoenix's back before swinging up behind her. Kyna hesitated for only a moment, thinking of the scalding metal that had been on the phoenix moments before, but she found its feathers clean and warm. Then the beast threw itself into the air, tossed its head back in a scream, and let fire pour from its beak. The fire was not crimson—at least, not only crimson. It was yellow—and orange and blue. Kyna gasped as the heat of the flames washed over her and knew this was no cleansing fire. The phoenix crashed through the trees and buildings, its wings crumpling buildings and felling more tree limbs. Smoke billowed from scorched leaves and bedding.

"Stop!" Kyna shouted uselessly. She felt her father's hands tight on her waist, but he said nothing. The phoenix did not stop.

Elves were running below them. Elves were screaming. The arrows had stopped.

Kyna held on to the phoenix and her father with all her limbs and closed her eyes against the tears that flowed down her face.

It could have been a few minutes or an hour before the wet slap of fresh air made her open her eyes. She did not look back until she was above the trees and all that remained to see was a hovering cloud of smoke dissipating in the misty night air.

15

BURNING

"Firas!" The word rasped through her throat, though she knew he couldn't hear her. Renyra clawed her way to him across torn moss, still fighting the manic fear that had possessed her moments before at Kyna's touch. There was light everywhere. The flashing reds and oranges of the phoenix still seemed to surround her, though the screeches of the beast were growing softer, distant. She shook her head, trying to clear both vision and mind. Why was there still fire? The moss was wet. The bird was gone. Wasn't it?

"Firas!" Renyra had come to him. She could see his pale skin against the ground.

It was so bright. Why was it so bright? Heat buffeted her face.

"Roll him over!" another voice shouted. Raren? Trali?

Just as Renyra reached for Firas, a set of hands grabbed him and wrenched him away from her. Renyra let out a wordless cry. Why were they taking him from her?

"Use the moss!"

The same set of hands started grabbing handfuls of damp greenery and throwing them on top of Firas.

"Stop!" Renrya yelled. "What are you doing? He's hurt!" She

grabbed the elf's arm and started pulling it away from her husband. Her love. Her life.

"He is on fire, Renrya!"

"Wh ... what?"

Trali ripped his arm out of Renyra's grasp and rolled Firas's body again.

"Stop!" Raren said. "It's out."

Pushing herself onto her hands and knees, Renrya stared in horror at the smoke and steam rising from her husband. She blinked against a wave of vertigo, thankful she was already on the ground. The blaze had been Firas. It was so dark now without the flames, she could hardly see him at all. Her eyes filled with fresh tears, and she crawled to his side. Trali did not try to stop her this time.

"Light," she croaked to no one in particular.

Trali fumbled in a pouch at his waist and brought out a handheld solar lamp. Its light was weak and white. It reflected off of Firas's skin like moonlight.

"Firas," Renyra whispered. "Firas."

He was lying on his back. From the front, it looked as though nothing had happened to him. His shirt was whole and unsinged, his face unmarred. Beautiful. Renyra ran a shaking hand from his temple to his neck. His eyes were closed, his long lashes curving over perfect cheek bones.

"Please." Her hand found the skin under his chin and pressed down. For the space of her own heartbeat, Renyra felt nothing, and she knew her life was over. Then, a warm throb of blood rose to meet her fingers. His pulse was feathery and rapid, but it was there. Renyra let out a breath that was a laugh, a sob, and a cry all at once. He was not dead. Not yet.

She placed her hands under his arm to roll him onto his stomach, but images of his body slapping the ground turned her stomach. Did he have broken bones? Would she hurt him further by moving him? But they could hardly leave him lying on his back in the middle of the forest. As gently as she could manage, Renyra pushed Firas over.

All heat drained from her face. A cold pain twisted in her chest, then moved down through her stomach, between her legs, and to her toes.

A few charred ribbons of blood-soaked cloth were all that remained of the back of Firas's shirt. Between his shoulder blades, a wide and straight gash ripped through his skin, exposing the lean muscle beneath. Dark blood coated his shoulders and ribs and ran down his spine in snaking rivulets. Any skin unobscured by blood showed shiny, mottled pink and red between peeling edges of skin charred black. Renyra retched into the moss.

A hand rubbed her back gently; another cupped her shoulder and pulled her away from her own sick. Renyra didn't know who it was that held her upright. She didn't care. She coughed and opened her mouth to speak, but her sobs were choking her more effectively than hands around her throat.

"Help," she managed to say before another painful breath forced its way through her teeth. "Help—him."

"Where did it go?" a voice said. "Is it gone?"

"It flew toward Remsgraen."

What did it matter where the damn bird had gone? Firas was dying *here*.

"Pleease," Renyra groaned.

"We're going to, honey. We're going to help him." Caerlyn's voice was low and sure. Renyra held onto it like a log in a raging river.

"Can you carry him, Trali?" said Caerlyn.

"I can," Trali replied. "The elves in Remsgraen can help him, though I think the phoenix is there now."

"It will be gone by the time we get there," said Caerlyn. "The beast never takes long in its work, even in a Great City. Let's get him to the Rale path."

Trali knelt next to Firas and turned him onto his back again. Renyra yelped in protest, the pain in her middle flaring again at the thought of Firas's ripped and burned back touching anything, but Caerlyn held her back.

"We have to move him to Remsgraen, Renyra," Caerlyn said in her ear. "Trali will be careful, but we cannot avoid hurting him if it saves his life. He can't feel anything now, anyway."

Renyra choked on another sob. She felt hands under her arms, then she was on her feet.

"Come on now, or do I need to carry you too?" There was a gentle smile in Caerlyn's voice.

Renyra felt the absurd urge to laugh, but she was afraid she wouldn't be able to stop if she started. Instead, she clenched her teeth harder.

Trali stood on powerful legs, lifting Firas in his arms, and started wading through the underbrush. Renyra took a shaking breath, scrubbed her eyes with the edges of her wraps, and followed him.

Boom.

Trali's raised foot hovered over the levit board.

"What was that?" Alura said.

All eyes turned to the lights of Remsgraen, still far too distant, yet blazing crimson. Now though, the red light faded away into the blues and whites of before.

"The gun," Trali said. He was staring over Firas's limp form into the trees, his eyes wide.

"The what?" Caerlyn said.

"A weapon the Remsgri created at the end of the war, though it was too late to use before the phoenix died. It sounds as though they have used it against this phoenix."

"Do you think it's dead?" Alura said.

"I do not know." Trali frowned. "The fire stopped."

"Come on!" Renyra shoved past Caerlyn, who had not strayed two feet from her side since they began their walk through the trees, and stepped onto a levit board. It had taken them longer to find a Rale path on the ground than the one they had come by in the trees. Trali may bear Firas's weight on the ground without undue effort, but to drag him up a tree was something else entirely. They were taking too long. Every moment wasted was another twist in Renyra's gut. She had regained much of the control of her legs, but tears still streamed in silent tracks down her cheeks, and the pain in her middle nearly made her double over every few steps.

"I don't care if the phoenix is still there when we arrive, we just have to *get* there." She clicked the levit board's lever and lifted off the metal track.

BOOM.

Renyra stepped backward with a gasp and nearly fell off her levit board. The ground rumbled. A flash like lightening lit the trees of Remsgraen.

"Was that the gun, too?" Raren said uncertainly.

"I ... I don't know," said Trali.

Then a rainbow of light flared; it grew.

Renyra's arms fell limp at her sides. Hair plastered to her face and cheeks with tears, she watched flames grow under the trees, not the crimson fire of the phoenix's foul breath, but orange and yellow—real and consuming.

"No!" Trali said.

"It's burning." Renyra's tears had run dry. She stared at Firas's only hope, burning as he had burned.

"Where can we go?" Caerlyn turned to Trali. "Where else can we go?"

Trali's face was anguished. His eyes were locked on his home, more lost to him than Tura or Telem Fier—as lost as Daro. Finally, he closed his eyes and shook his head, as though to wipe the memory from his mind.

"To the south," he said. "The nearest town to the south. The phoenix will have already been there. It should be safe."

"Take us." Caerlyn's words were harsh, but her face was pleading.

Trali nodded. He clicked his levit board into the air, then turned its nose away from Remsgraen.

They flew through the night once more.

Renyra followed as close to Trali's heels as she dared, her eyes transfixed on the silvery glow of Firas's hair in the lights of the Rale.

Dufar was a small town, though it clearly benefited from the close proximity of a Great City. Lifts ran up the trees, Rale paths formed a floating network within levels, and a clean beauty emanated from every building and path. It seemed the sort of place that would normally hold a sleepy peace, where days run into one another and each elf holds a comfortable camaraderie with every other elf in the town. Now, however, the atmosphere reminded Renyra of the ship ride from Daro-that-was to Tura—silent, grief stricken, angry.

Not that Renyra had ventured much into the town. For two days, she had remained in exactly the same place, staring at the same silver walls, the same fanned ceiling, and the same view out the curving glass that faced the forest. It was a nice view, but Renyra's eyes rarely drifted so far as to see it.

She stared at the side of Firas's face, always the same side, tracing its every curve and line. The tilt of his ear was so severe as to be nearly perpendicular to his jaw, a common trait among the Morcani. A soft fuzz of blonde hair was reaching over the top of his ear. He hadn't had time to cut the sides of his hair for weeks.

Tears blurred Renyra's vision. Lifting her chin, she tried to tilt them back into her eyes, but one drop welled and spilled over. She wiped it away with a huff of frustration. She was sick of tears. They did her no good, only serving to make her cheeks raw and her pride depreciated. She wished she could stop them. She couldn't.

"Has he woken again?"

Renyra did not turn to Caerlyn's voice. "No," she said.

She knew she should be grateful Firas had woken at all. If the phoenix's flames had not cauterized the edges of the gash in his back, he very well may have bled to death before they could get him to a healer. Unfortunately, the blisters and raw flesh left by those same flames were draining him of vitality at least as much as the wound between his shoulders. As if the burns and gouge in his back weren't enough, he had broken several ribs, a collar bone, and an arm, all on one side. Renyra cringed to imagine what would have happened had the phoenix smashed him on the stones of Tura rather than the soil of Riverseep.

For the few minutes of consciousness Firas had achieved last night, all he had done was groan in pain and choke down some water forced upon him by an obstinate Caerlyn. It was just as well he had not been coherent. Renyra had been no more able to form words in her very wet relief and anguish.

"It's for the best," Caerlyn said. "This way he heals without feeling the pain. His back looks better than it did yesterday."

That wasn't saying much. Renyra nodded absently.

"Come on," Caerlyn said. "The healer said he'll recover. He'll be back to his old self in a few weeks."

That was little comfort now. Though the incapacitating fear of Firas's death had lessened, the crushing anxiety of his pain was all the more acute. Renyra's tears were not of grief, but of anger. Anger at the phoenix. Anger at Kyna. Anger at Riu. And anger at Firas. She knew it was irrational, and looking at his fitfully sleeping face, she hated herself for feeling it, but Renyra could not help the deep-set anger that boiled beneath her skin and pressed against her ribs. Why did he have to take the dagger? Why did he have to be the one to go after the phoenix? And why had he let himself be caught? These grievances, at least, made a fraction of sense. It was the jealousy that perplexed and frustrated Renyra most.

She was jealous of Firas. She was jealous of his pain—physical, measurable pain. So much more would she rather be lying in a bed, bandaged and hurting, than enduring the agony of watching her love feel what she did not. To lie in self-absorbed anguish was so much easier than to feel that anguish second hand and have no power to stop it or take it for herself.

Even this, though, was not the worst thought Renyra had recognized within herself. Far more insidious was the relief she felt when she touched Firas. The relief that she did not wear vierstone. If the pain brought by the lingering presence of vierstone within her was enough to cause this kind of agony, she could not imagine how much worse it would be if she could truly feel Firas through vierstone's direct connection. For the first time since Kaelo had entered her life, a part of her understood—almost longed for—his goal. Was anything worth this kind of suffering? Was it possible that one could still love without vierstone, but be freed of the crippling consequences of empathy? But then Renyra would remember the phoenix and what it had done. She would remember the lengths to which Kaelo had already gone to follow his path, what it had cost her, and what centuries without vierstone had made Kaelo. Then Firas would shift and groan in his sleep and she would dissolve once more.

Back and forth, her resolve strengthened and wavered, broke and reformed.

And so the days passed.

Firas woke again. He woke more often and for longer periods of time.

Renyra stayed by his side night and day, holding his hand when the pain of his burns made him sick and trying to comfort him when he woke screaming, even as she screamed inside and could barely contain the anxiety that threatened to overwhelm her every moment of every hour.

Firas's wounds healed slowly and quickly. By the end of five days, he could walk for short periods of time and care for himself, but he wore bandages from his waist to his neck and gasped in pain with every movement.

It was the sixth day after the confrontation with Kaelo that Renyra found herself among the troupe in full, sipping fruit juice kindly forced upon them by the locals and sitting close enough to Firas that her thigh pressed against his. Her anxiety was still there and flared at odd moments, but it was better than it had been in days, and it was better when she was next to Firas.

"What's the point?" Renyra said. "It's not as though we can continue with our old plan. Even if by some miracle we managed to track the phoenix down again, we obviously don't possess the abilities or weapons to kill it. Morcanan is the only Great City left, and I doubt Miyela will be able to do any more than Rhosti to defend it."

No one had had the heart to discuss their future plans until today. Traveling had been out of the question with Firas bedridden, and no one wanted to split up the group. Raren had brought up the subject reluctantly.

"So you want to give up?" Raren said. "Stay here indefinitely, then try to get on with our lives?"

"Is that so bad?" Renyra said.

"It is not you," Firas said softly.

"He is right." Trali raised an eyebrow at Renyra and smiled. "You held more fire than any of us for this endeavor."

"That was before it almost killed us," Renyra said. "And then destroyed a Great City."

"That wasn't us," Raren said. "That was the gun. The Remsgri made the phoenix mad and then failed to kill it. That's what set the thing off, and it would have happened by daylight as well as night."

The stories of what had happened in Remsgraen had spread rapidly. A number of refugees from the city were staying in Dufar, and the accounts they told were as horrifying as they were depressing. The phoenix had survived a blow from a weapon that would have blasted a hole through any other animal of the same size. Remsgraen was nothing but blackened trees and the charred shells of buildings. Some neighborhoods on the outskirts of the city had escaped the inferno, saved by the damp of the night, but the scope of the damage was staggering. How could the elves stand against a creature that could survive any weapon and raze a Great City in half an hour? Renyra was only impressed that the elves had lasted two centuries against a similar foe. This phoenix must be stronger than the last.

Trali watched Raren with narrowed eyes. "It was not the fault of the Remsgri that our weapon failed as surely as the Fieri's weapons failed."

Raren's cheeks reddened. "I didn't mean—"

"The Remsgri suffered more loss than any other Kindom in the Great War," Trali said. "Our way of life makes us more vulnerable to the attack of one that wields fire. It took centuries to rebuild Remsgraen, and now—" He closed his eyes. When he opened them, they burned as emerald fire against his caramel skin. "We cannot leave this as it is. We cannot stay here and lick our wounds while the beast finishes its work elsewhere." He looked at Firas and bowed his head. "No offense, friend. You may lick your wounds without shame."

Firas's lips twitched in a grimace.

"I agree with you," Caerlyn said. "But the vierstone dagger didn't work. Recruiting Kyna obviously isn't an option. What else are we supposed to do?"

"Go to the last city," said Trali.

"What do you want to do in Morcanan?" Renyra said.

"We will tell their leader what we know—what we have seen. We know how not to kill the phoenix, yes? We know more of Kaelo and his daughter than most others—their plans and their desires. We have seen the phoenix attack two Great Cities. So we will offer our wisdom and we will stand with the elves for a last fight against our fate." Trali spoke as though this were the obvious and simple thing to do, as though any other options would be laughable.

Renyra sighed. A week ago, she would have been the first to stand behind Trali, but she felt she had aged four centuries in these last days. She told herself she wanted to stop Kaelo. She wanted to avenge Firas, but part of her longed for nothing more than to pick a city and start over, putting Daro, Tura, and all that had happened since behind them and get on with their lives as best they could without vierstone.

Caerlyn shrugged. "Why not?"

Renyra blinked and tried to remember what Caerlyn was agreeing to.

"I think it is a good plan." Alura nudged her brother, who nodded his agreement.

Right, going to Morcanan to talk to Miyela.

Renyra cringed. As if the task was not difficult enough already. Talking to tyrannical Miyela was less appealing even than their frustrating interactions with Cuvan. Would the Lady of Morcanan listen to anything they had to say? A group of elves with only one Morcani among them?

"It's already been a week since the phoenix left Riverseep," said Renyra. "How do we know the phoenix isn't already in Morcanan?"

"The phoenix must still get through the rest of the Morcani territory before it arrives in Morcanan," said Firas. "The Lay Hills and riverlands are no small area."

"And," said Trali, "the Rale line between Riverseep and Morcanan is straight and swift. If we leave here in the morning, we will be in Morcanan by night."

"But Firas can't travel across Faeran tomorrow morning!" Renyra said.

"I will." Firas laid his unbound hand on her thigh. "We are not walking across the continent. Riding the Rale is no different than sitting here."

"And once we're in Morcanan?" Renyra's voice was rising in pitch as she tried to suppress her panic. "Do you plan to fight when the phoenix comes? What if it destroys the city, like Remsgraen?"

"I will not fight," Firas said in the tone one uses to calm a spooked animal. "But nor will I stay here while my friends go to protect my own Kindom. Trali is right, love. We cannot give up until all hope is lost. I do not intend to."

All the fight drained out of Renyra. When Firas spoke so calmly, there was no convincing him out of his decisions. She placed her hand over his. After all this, would she lose him again in Morcanan? The possibility sucked all the air out off her lungs, and she squeezed his hand as tightly as she dared. But there was no other choice. If Firas would go to Morcanan, Renyra would not stay behind.

They would go to Morcanan. They would go to the last vierstone in Faeran, and they would defend it with what little remained to them. It was all they could do, and Renyra knew it was what they should do. She ignored the fears and protests fighting to form words on her tongue and nodded once, keeping her eyes lowered to hide the tears prickling behind them.

16

THE GATES OPEN

The markets of Tura hummed with anticipation. Not a conversation could be heard that did not pertain to the coming journey to Morcanan, phoenixes, or Remsgraen. Gellion longed to talk about anything else, but all other subjects seemed petty—irrelevant. He wanted to be moving, to start doing something, but amazingly, the Council had already finished almost all preparations for leaving Tura. There was just one glitch remaining—the Rale line out of Tura was still broken. Marching an army thousands strong all the way to Morcanan was completely implausible given their time constraint. If they couldn't move by Rale, there was no point to anything they had planned.

"Do you know what you're going to do when you face him?" Valder twirled a fork in his fingers, watching the sunlight glint off of its spokes.

Gellion shook his head.

"Winging it?" Valder raised an eyebrow. "I like it. Just like the phoenix."

Gellion groaned.

"Yeah, that one was bad," Valder said with an unapologetic smile.

"There's no use planning when I can't predict what may happen."

"But if something happens that you didn't predict, you are in a predicament once preventable by planning—even predictory and premature planning—with little possibility of panning out."

"Here's a plan for you, we'll just chuck you at Kaelo and let you talk to him. He'll surrender within five minutes to get you to stop."

"Or maybe he'll decide to switch his allegiance and help us." Valder shrugged. "It wouldn't be the first time my skills of speech performed such a miracle."

Gellion sighed. "You will never let that go."

"Nope."

A chuckle escaped Gellion. The sound surprised him.

"They'll get him off the phoenix somehow," Valder said. "We'll separate them."

"Then why hasn't anyone done it yet?"

"They haven't been trying to. Think about it. Kaelo's been to three Great Cities, none of which had the numbers we will bring to Morcanan. Tura was completely unprepared, and at Telem Fier, I can assure you everyone was aiming for the phoenix, trying to bring it down and kill it. Now we're aiming for the elf on its back."

"And Remsgraen? What Rhosti said?"

"Well they *did* knock Kaelo off the phoenix there didn't they? So it didn't work out so well. Morcanan isn't Remsgraen. Kaelo can't burn down a city of stone. He would be mad to attack Morcanan by force."

Gellion's stomach still twisted in knots every time he thought about Remsgraen. Over a hundred elves had died in the fire, thousands more injured. He had never been to the forest of Riverseep, but the Remsgri he had known in Daro had been some of the kindest elves he'd ever known. The thought of their Kindom in so much pain made him sick.

"We will get him separated," Valder said, clearly taking Gellion's worried silence for concern over his task. "You've figured out how to use the stone as well as Kaelo has. I'll bet you're more than a match for him."

"Oh yes, I've proven that so far," Gellion muttered.

Valder let out an exasperated sigh. "Just incapacitate him long enough to take his earring—or wherever he keeps his redstone." He frowned seriously. "Hope it's nowhere untoward."

Gellion was saved a response by spotting Veldon walking over the bridge toward them. Gellion raised a hand to him.

"Any news?" he said when Veldon reached their table.

Veldon nodded, taking a seat and grabbing a roll of bread from Valder's plate.

"Sixty miles," he said.

Valder let out a low whistle. "And he did it all from Tura?"

"He must have," Veldon said. "Kaelo couldn't have walked that far and back while he was finishing his work in Tura."

"He could have gone back with the phoenix after," said Valder.

"Does it matter how he did it?" said Gellion. "Let's just be glad it isn't more. Sixty miles is walkable with an army. Will we be able to bring enough Rale cars from the north?"

"Do we have a choice?" said Veldon. "It will be a close fit, I'm sure, but it beats walking five hundred miles."

"We're leaving tomorrow, then?" said Valder.

"I assume so," said Veldon. "It will still take a couple of days to walk to the working Rale line, which should give enough time to prepare cars from northern stations."

"Good," said Valder. "I don't think I could take another day of waiting—or another Council meeting." He rolled his eyes.

If the Turi Council had been unpleasant in the first weeks of Gellion's arrival, it was now downright miserable. Now that Liera had agreed to the assault at Morcanan, she was nearly hysteric in her desperation to plan every detail. Her hostility toward Gellion had not lessened in her obsession over the plan he had proposed, however. If anything, her fraying emotions only further revealed the depth of her suspicion of him—a suspicion he still did not understand.

Then there was Tornac. Gellion had not spoken to his brother since their confrontation in the armory. Tornac had become increasingly silent in the last few meetings, listening with a drawn brow and guarded expression. Gellion often caught Tornac watching him when he was not looking, though Gellion could hardly be annoyed by a behavior he himself had been guilty of in the weeks prior. Both in meetings and the company of his brothers, Gellion did his best to politely ignore Tornac.

Given that he and his brothers had more or less stopped gathering to discuss the enigma of their father, this was not a difficult task.

Though Gellion agreed their time was better spent focusing on Morcanan than their father's defeat of the last phoenix, Eldian's concealed intent bothered Gellion more than he liked to admit. He knew it was no good dwelling on something so far in the past. Even if they had the time and the luck to discover what their father had done, there was no telling if they would be able to emulate it, let alone succeed before all the vierstone was gone. No, it was his father's secrecy that chafed Gellion. Eldian had always been an honest man, always frank with his sons about everything from the running of Maramor, to his personal life, to life lessons. Why hadn't he confided in any of them about something so important? They could have helped him. They would have known what to do now. Eldian may not even have died.

Gellion let out a breath and ran a hand through his hair. He cringed as his fingers passed over his bare ear, and he felt the loss of his vierstone deep in the pit of his stomach.

"I'm going back to the apartment," he muttered.

He turned and set off for the bridge into the Public Quarter before his brothers could say anything more.

Not knowing what else to do, Gellion did set a path for the guest quarters, though considering he no longer owned any possessions, he certainly had no packing to see to. He just wanted silence. The constant talk about Morcanan was riling his nerves.

He watched the ground in front of him as he glided along the Rale path. The conversations around him became no more than incoherent buzz, and he let his instincts lead him where he wanted to go. So absorbed in his own musings was he that when Liera said his name, he nearly pitched forward off his levit board. Throwing his arms out to catch his balance, Gellion came to a halt and looked around to see where the voice had come from.

Liera stood on the side of the Rale path in front of him. The street was otherwise deserted, a wide path winding through the guest quarters just a block from Gellion's current apartments. How long had Liera been standing there? Gellion wrestled his face into a mask of composure, stepped off his levit board, and nodded to the Lady of Tura.

"Liera. What can I do for you?"

Liera's lip twitched up into something between a grimace and a snarl.

"I have been looking for you."

Gellion waited for her to go on. "Yes?" he said when she just continued to scrutinize him with that narrow eyed intensity he had grown used to these last weeks.

"We are leaving for Morcanan tomorrow," she said.

"So I heard."

"I do not want you to come with us."

Gellion stared at her. "What?"

"Do not come to Morcanan. Stay in Tura."

Gellion didn't know what to say. The thought of staying behind while his entire Kindom left was downright laughable. He was part of the plan. He had the redstone. For what reason could Liera possibly want him to remain in Tura? Gellion opened and closed his mouth twice before settling on, "Why?"

"I do not know what you intend to do in Morcanan, but I will not stand idly by and watch you do it." Liera spoke in a low hiss.

"What are you talking about?" Gellion shook his head, completely bewildered. "We already discussed what I'm going to do."

"Do you take me for an utter fool?" A dangerous light had come to Liera's eyes. Though she had to look up at Gellion, she stood with squared shoulders and an open stance—a commander confronting a soldier.

"Do I—what? Liera—"

"I was a fool. I will admit that. I allowed Kyna to take me in when I should have known better. But I will not allow you to do the same."

Gellion's jaw dropped. It took him a moment to find his voice again, in which time Liera had already prepared her next words.

"Liera—"

"Do you expect me to believe you found that redstone in a cave in the mountains? Did you really think anyone would find it plausible that you happened upon Kaelo's notes and plans while fighting your way across a human continent?"

Cold understanding was beginning to seep through Gellion's limbs.

"The humans remembered Kaelo. He influenced their very folklore and physical surroundings with his presence—they led us to him."

Liera scoffed. "No. He gave it to you. Don't deny it."

At a complete loss for words, Gellion stared at Liera, shaking his head.

"You have always sympathized with my son. You have always been in league with him. If it weren't for you, his corruption would have ended before the Great War."

Gellion snapped his jaw shut and clenched his fists.

"I voted against you to prevent an underhanded execution," he growled. "Not because I was in league with your son."

"And why is it you did not recognize him in Daro until after the city was destroyed? Why did you vote in favor of the alliance when it was so clearly against your nature?"

"You voted in favor of the alliance!"

"Why were you conveniently absent all those months while Kaelo and Kyna wrought their deceptions, only to show up afterward knowing all of Kaelo's past, methods, and plans, and carrying the very weapon he used to do it all?"

Blood was rushing in Gellion's ears. His heart was pounding against his chest. He tried desperately to think of a defense, but his throat had gone dry, and the roaring blood seemed to be disrupting his thoughts.

"You are in it with him," Liera said. "I know you are. I saw you with Kyna in Tura."

Gellion blanched.

Liera's eyes lit with triumph.

"I knew it. I know you were working with her, and I know you are working with him. Whatever you have been planning to do in Morcanan, I will not allow it. I will warn the Council. I will imprison you if I have to."

Panic was beginning to override Gellion's anger.

"Yes, I was with Kyna in Daro, but she tricked me. She was using me! Why would I have told you everything about Kaelo if I was working with him?"

"To plant false trails. To gain our trust. It matters not. It has not worked."

"Liera, this is madness! Everything I have said to the Council is true."

"I am not mad!" Liera thundered.

Gellion took a step back. Liera's hands were shaking, and the look in her eyes was murderous.

"I didn't say you were." Gellion lowered his voice. "I know you are only trying to protect the Turi, but I swear to you, I am no threat to them—to us."

Liera glared at him, her opinion clearly not swayed.

"You will not come to Morcanan," she said.

"I have to. I have to use the stone." Gellion had pulled the redstone from his pocket before he was aware he was doing it. "It is the crux of our entire plan!"

"It is the crux of *your* plan."

A cool resolve was flowing through Gellion. He closed his hand around the redstone and let it bleed away the raging emotions within him. There was nothing he could say to Liera to convince her of his loyalty. She was beyond reason, and had been since he arrived in Tura.

"I will go to Morcanan," Gellion said quietly. "I will go to Morcanan, and I will do all in my power to stop Kaelo and the phoenix. It is not my leadership that is a threat to the Turi, it is yours, and *I* will not allow *you* to condemn our entire race by your unfounded suspicions and paranoia."

Liera stared at him in outrage, then drew her brows over her eyes and opened her mouth.

"Go to the Council if you will," Gellion said before she could speak. "I am curious myself what they would have to say to your accusations."

Liera closed her mouth. The wild fire in her eyes turned to fear, and for a moment, Gellion felt pity for the woman. Her story was not so different from Gellion's own, but Gellion would not become this. He would not allow his fear and anger to enact hatred and callousness.

"I will see you tomorrow." Gellion stepped onto his levit board and urged it forward. Liera made no move to stop him, and he did not look back.

———————

Gellion got little sleep that night. As he watched moonlight begin to slant into his room, he counted the hours until the morning's departure.

Seven hours.

Six and a half.

Surely if no one had come to arrest him in his bed by now, he was safe. If his mother had not come to warn him, she did not know of any danger. Whether the Lady of Tura would make good on her threat to share her suspicions of Gellion with the Council, or on her intentions to prevent him from leaving the city, he could not be sure, but the uncertainty and fear that had shown plain in Liera's face as he glided past her gave him some measure of security.

Five hours.

Gellion had not told anyone about Liera's accusations. It was one of those occurrences so unpleasant that even reliving it in the hopes of receiving sympathy was more than he was willing to bear.

Clasping his arms about his middle, Gellion curled inward, trying to squeeze away the broiling heat and ice warring within him. Liera's suspicions were absurd. She had no proof whatsoever on which to base her claims. She was cracking in the head—he had already accepted that. Accusations from a madwoman should not concern him. Yet her reasoning was not entirely unsound.

From an outside perspective, Gellion *could* understand where Liera was coming from. He had been close to a known conspirator of Kaelo's in Daro, had been the one to identify Kaelo as the culprit of the city's crimes, and helped lead the elves out of the city. He had gone missing for weeks, presumed dead, then showed up just as Kaelo had succeeded in his plan, bearing information it seemed impossible he should know. Seen in this light, Gellion was surprised no one else on the Council had harbored any doubts of his loyalty—of course, only his family knew as much as Liera in regards to his past with Kaelo and his connection to Kyna in Daro.

Gellion sighed and turned over, stretching out his body beneath the sheets. There was nothing he could do about it now. He would show up in the morning as though nothing had happened between them and pray to Riu that Liera did not do anything stupid before the departure. Without his part in the plan, the Turi stood little hope of succeeding against Kaelo. They bore little enough hope with him.

The hours passed. Gellion tossed in his sheets, drifting into oblivion between thoughts and dreams.

When morning came at last, he was tense and sore. He pulled on a set of soft pants and a shirt, grabbed his small pack of clothing, ensured the redstone was secure in his pocket, and walked out of his bedroom to meet his brothers.

Elves stretched from the gates of Tura in a fan—forward, left, and right. They were not in ordered lines, but a jumbling mass of bodies moving forward. A few horses were scattered through the elves, carrying provisions for the two day hike that would precede a day long Rale trip to Morcanan. Gellion watched the procession from the gates, a line between his brow. Was it only months ago he had watched the first elven army in centuries march out of Daro? How had the world changed so completely in that time?

Unlike Dulon, Liera had given no parting speech for this departure. There was nothing to say. The elves knew what they were marching to and knew the stakes involved. There was nothing to do but get on with it and hope to Riu they did not arrive too late.

"Ready?"

Gellion turned to his mother's voice. She stood with Tornac outside the stairs that spiraled to the street below. Tornac looked a proper warrior in his close fitting, interlocking armor. Vyra's sword curved at his hip, and his hair was pulled back. Several brown strands blew gracefully about his face.

"The elves are almost out," Tornac said. "The gates will close soon."

A good portion of the city was remaining behind. It had simply not been feasible to mobilize even half the population of Tura in a week, and organizing Rale lines to transport hundreds of thousands of elves in a day was impossible in any time frame. The gates would be heavily guarded in the army's absence. Though the threat of the phoenix had passed from Tura, that beast was not the only concern of the city. Gellion had been unsurprised to learn that monstrous creatures had begun to converge upon Tura shortly after Kaelo's arrival, just like in Daro and in the Falspire Mountains. Kaelo's use of redstone seemed to draw the corrupted animals. Gellion was grateful that he and his brothers had arrived at the city in daylight weeks before.

Gellion followed his family down the stairs. He had chosen not to wear any armor. There was not enough of it left for all the elves anyway. If it was a fight with Kaelo he sought, he doubted it would come to combat with weapons. The weapons they carried were much smaller and less cumbersome—and much more powerful.

Less than a hundred of the army remained inside the walls of Tura. Gellion watched them flow through the gates, then followed behind. He stiffened when he reached the gates.

Liera stood tall and haughty in armor of deep grey and blue. A silver spear was attached between her shoulder blades and her shrewd eyes scanned the departing elves. When she caught sight of Gellion, she flinched.

No one had said anything to Gellion about Liera's suspicions, so he assumed she had done nothing to prevent him leaving, but he had expected her to be at the front of the army. Now that she could so easily bar his way out of the city, would she change her mind?

Gellion nodded to Liera, keeping his face carefully blank.

Liera kept her eyes locked on Gellion as he walked past. She watched him as though waiting for him to attack, but she made no move to stop him leaving the city. There was as much fear as anger in her eyes.

Letting his own gaze shift to the elves in front of him, Gellion stepped outside the gates. He held his breath for several heart beats, listening hard for any signs of pursuit, or for Liera to call out for him to stop.

A loud clank made Gellion jump, but he realized it was the gates closing. They were out of the city. Liera had let him pass. Gellion allowed himself a brief glance backward, and a shiver ran down his spine. Liera was still watching him, one hand at her side angled toward the butt of her spear.

Taking a deep breath, Gellion turned his back to her.

Veldon looked at him and raised an eyebrow, turning his eyes toward Liera.

"Everything ok?"

"Never better," Gellion said.

"That's the spirit," said Valder from beside Veldon.

Gellion's mouth turned up in a wry smile. He stood up straight and did his best to forget Liera stalking behind him. There were far more important things to worry about than the crazy mother of his enemy.

Just three more days. Three days until they arrived in Morcanan, until he came face to face with Kaelo and the phoenix once more. This time he would not be caught off guard. This time he would fight back, and he would have thousands of his kin behind him. This time he would not fail.

He clasped his hand about the redstone in his pocket and embraced the cool focus that bled through his body.

Three days.

17

BODIES OF STONE

The Terulian Mountains were impossibly high. Their peaks disappeared into a grey haze, and their bulk stretched from east to west as far as the eye could see. Kyna knew mountains. She had lived in them all her life. But the Falspires of her past seemed jagged hills compared to these. The phoenix could have been a lowly sparrow gliding over their vast sides.

Kyna took a breath and let it out slowly. This was only the second time the phoenix had left them alone in over a week. Since Remsgraen. Since everything had changed.

She waited until she could no longer make out the phoenix's shape among the trees, then turned to face her father. Kaelo wasn't looking at her. He was standing and staring, as he did more often than not these days. Kyna walked closer, a few steps at a time, until she was standing beside him. She followed his gaze.

Kaelo faced the mountains, not where the phoenix had flown, but further east. Toward Morcanan. His brow was furrowed, his eyes distant. Watching him out the side of her eye, Kyna tried to remember how things had been between them before the phoenix. Before Daro. Before even the Albaren and the Dierna. He had often made this face, thinking about what they planned, or of his life before exile, or of whatever else haunted the dark recesses of his mind. Throughout her life, Kyna had rarely wondered what her father must have been like before everyone and everything in his life betrayed him. He had been one of *them* then, and that was a time and identity Kaelo never spoke of. He had been remade in his years of exile. Nothing before that was worth remembering save to inform their future.

But now Kyna did wonder. Now she had lived among elves who had been alive when her father lived among them. Now she was beginning to see the veil that coated her father, setting him apart from everything around him.

Everything except the phoenix.

Kaelo glanced down at her.

Kyna blinked and looked forward, heart racing.

Come on, you coward, do it.

This may be her last chance. They would fly on Morcanan any day now, and after that—she had to know. She had to talk to him. The last time the phoenix had gone hunting, Kyna had not been able to summon the words. She was disgusted with herself. When had she become so spineless and emotional?

She looked out the corner of her eye and started when she saw her father was still looking at her. His eyes were unreadable. Opaque. But they were familiar, too. They were still her father's eyes, though they had darkened and hardened.

With a last steadying breath, Kyna spoke.

"Did you tell it to burn Remsgraen?"

Kaelo's face remained impassive. He regarded her, blinked slowly, then raised his head to resume his scrutiny of the eastern horizon.

"It was—necessary. What she did."

"Did you tell it to burn Remsgraen?" Kyna repeated.

Kaelo opened his mouth, but did not speak. He let out the breath he had taken, then clenched his teeth.

"You didn't." Kyna nodded to herself. She could not decide if the knowledge was comforting or terrifying.

Something in Kaelo's face darkened. His shoulders tensed.

"The Remsgri tried to kill us."

"They have all tried to kill us."

"They have never come close before."

Kyna's nails bit into her palms. "And Yavran? They had no magnetic weapons." She could still smell the smoke of the city in her hair.

Kaelo sighed. "They still fought us."

"Like every other city in all of Faeran, but we didn't destroy half their buildings and streets." Kyna flinched away from her father's expression. "I just—this isn't how—" She paused, trying to order her words in a way that would not sound accusing. "Do you really think this is necessary? We are almost done. Remsgraen was unfortunate, but what of the rest of the towns, and Morcanan? Can we not finish this without more blood and fire?"

Kaelo was silent a long time. His eyes wandered across the mountains.

"There is sacrifice in any war, Kyna," he said softly.

"This was not supposed to be a war."

"Yet the elves have made it one."

"A war has two sides—you can choose not to fight back."

"They leave us no choice. If it is war or failure, I will fight them."

Kyna bit off her next words. She glanced at the mountains. No sign of the phoenix yet. How much time did she have before it returned?

"And after Morcanan?" she said. "Do you still intend to send the phoenix back to ashes?"

If Kyna had never known her father to betray emotion, she would have sworn he flinched. The breach was so slight and quick that Kyna wasn't sure she had seen anything at all, but as Kaelo's silence lengthened once more, a cold shiver began to build along her spine.

"Father?"

"I will do what I said I would do," he said. His eyes flickered to the mountains.

Kyna stared at her father. For the first time, she noticed a new set of shadows under his eyes. The look within his eyes as he watched the mountains reminded her of something she could not quite place. Whatever it was, it raised the hair on her neck. *Could* her father do what he had promised? If the phoenix had attacked Remsgraen outside of his orders—was Kaelo losing control of the phoenix?

She shivered and grasped the redstone at her wrist. No. Her father had raised the phoenix and her father would send it back when the time came. It was not her place to interfere. In all likelihood, she couldn't if she wanted to. Knowledge of a thing was not the same as carrying it out. She did not know if she could end the phoenix if she tried, and if she failed—

A far off cry made both Kyna and her father jump. The outline of a bird appeared below the misted mountain peaks. Kaelo turned to Kyna with a sudden urgency.

"It is almost done." He looked full and intently into Kyna's face for the first time in weeks. "When the time comes, I will end this, and we will have changed the world. It will be over. Until then, you must trust me. Do you trust me?"

Do you *trust* me?

Kaelo had not questioned Kyna's loyalty aloud since Remsgraen, but she still felt the brush of his reservation when he spoke to her or looked at her. Trust was not a word her father ever used unless applied to the folly of the elves. Now he asked it of Kyna. Dare she give it, even to the man who had instilled in her a stalwart wariness, even loathing, of the concept?

A spark of green seemed to flare from the depths of Kaelo's eyes. For a moment, Kyna saw him as she had all her life. There was no phoenix behind his eyes. He was her father.

"Yes," she said.

The phoenix returned in a flurry of flames and wind. Kaelo's eyes lingered on Kyna a moment longer, then he walked toward the beast.

Kyna trusted her father—she wanted to trust him—but she would never trust the phoenix. She was not even sure if she trusted herself.

It is only the phoenix. All else remains as it always has been.

She still believed in her purpose. She had to. Vierstone was a power without which the world could be a simpler place. She had felt the anguish that afflicted the elves. She had seen the way it twisted their minds and ate away their souls—yet that was not all she had seen. Other memories punctured holes in her resolve. Warm memories. The echo of heady emotions she had heard about but never understood—emotions she thought she had understood until she felt them.

They had all led to pain. Grief. Guilt. Longing.

No. This was better. Her father was right.

She looked to her father with new determination, but it was the phoenix's eyes that drew her gaze. The beast scrutinized Kyna over Kaelo's head, its eyes unfathomable pools of flame.

Dropping her gaze, Kyna took a steadying breath and shook away the doubts creeping back into her mind.

It is only the phoenix.

She would not let it taint her resolve. She would trust her father.

The phoenix turned without warning. Kyna's arms flew around her father's waist, and her knees tightened against the bird's glassy sides. Why were they moving off course? The phoenix had cleansed only two towns today—small Morcani villages east of Yavran. Had her father asked it to land?

Kyna clenched her teeth as her stomach rose into her chest. She would never get used to landing. If all went according to plan, she wouldn't have to after another week.

The phoenix angled toward the mountains and glided up the slopes to a plateau of rock. Pebbles and shards of stone skidded over the ground as the bird landed with two huge flaps of its wings.

"Why are we stopping?" Kyna said into her father's ear.

"I don't know." Kaelo pulled away from Kyna and slid off the beast's back. Kyna followed suit.

"What is it?" Kaelo said to the phoenix.

The beast sat upright on its legs so its head towered above them. Kyna rolled her eyes. She hated when it did that.

"There is an army amassed outside the next town," it said calmly. "They must have been warned by the previous villages and await our arrival."

"And?" Kaelo said after a pause.

"And we have yet to discuss our change in circumstances."

"There is no change in circumstances," Kaelo said. "I have allowed you a freer reign over the Morcani resistance where necessary, and there have been no incidents. This town is no different."

"It is," the phoenix said. "Here is where we veer our course from the Great City."

Kaelo's dark brows sank over his eyes.

"We will circle back to Morcanan after the rest of the Morcani territory is cleansed, as we planned."

"First, we will discuss our change in circumstance."

Kaelo considered the phoenix from under the shadow of his brow.

"And what change is that?" he said.

The phoenix lowered itself sinuously, snaking its head down to better look into Kaelo's face.

"You said we would continue our previous discussion when faced a threat our methods could not surmount. That threat came in Remsgraen, and we broke free of your moral constraints to survive."

Kyna glared at the phoenix.

You *broke free. We could have survived without burning Remsgraen to the ground.*

"The Morcani resistance has proven as weak as the rest of the Kindoms," the phoenix continued. "But the elves grow more desperate with every cleansing. Morcanan's resistance will not be small. We cannot risk failure in this last city."

"Are you asking my permission to destroy Morcanan if it resists? You cannot. Remsgraen was a city of trees. Morcanan is a city of stone."

The phoenix ruffled its feathers with a series of metallic clicks. Light laced its throat. Kyna was not so sure the beast couldn't turn a city of stone to ash if it wanted to.

"The time has come to reevaluate our strategy," said the phoenix.

Kyna stiffened. *Our* strategy? The phoenix was supposed to be a tool, not an accomplice. It was supposed to follow orders, not make deals with its master. She looked to her father with wide eyes, but he only watched the phoenix with a raised eyebrow.

"The elves will fight us in Morcanan," the phoenix said. "More elves, I am sure, than we have faced thus far. The transport on this continent is fast, and word travels as quickly as I can fly. We must prepare ourselves for a final resistance and we must consider what comes next."

Kyna closed her eyes. She could feel her pulse fluttering in her throat. Had the phoenix heard any of her conversation with Kaelo about returning it to ash? Did it guess its fate?

"Nothing comes next," Kaelo said. "Morcanan is the end."

"And what if we have missed vierstone along the way?"

"You said you could sense the stone," Kaelo said in a low growl. "Are you saying now that you let vierstone slip through the cracks?"

"It is possible some elves evaded us," the phoenix said. "Avoided our path effectively enough to escape notice."

"What, then?" Kaelo said. Kyna jumped at his raised voice. "Explain yourself clearly, or let us be on with our day."

"The elves cannot be trusted," the phoenix said. "While they still resist this cleansing with their passion, we cannot trust that there is no vierstone present in Faeran. They will not leave you alone and accept you now that your goal is complete. Do you truly think they will change so quickly? They will continue to resist. They will track us and try to kill us. They will panic in the suddenness of this change we have wrought within their society. They may destroy each other as well as us in the chaos that ensues."

Kaelo was very still. His eyes reflected the mottled glow of the phoenix's gaze.

"We can guide them." The phoenix's voice was softer in Kyna's mind, almost a whisper. "We can provide them a structure on which to stand until they grow accustomed to the changes—a structure that can protect both us and them. It will give us the time to ensure there is no vierstone left hidden." The phoenix's voice faded on the last word, then disappeared from Kyna's mind, but somehow she was sure its words continued in Kaelo's mind.

The phoenix cocked its head.

"I do not seek retribution," Kaelo said in a hoarse whisper. He was pale, his shoulders tensed, as though he were fighting against invisible bonds.

Kyna stared at her father, then rounded on the phoenix. "No!"

The phoenix swiveled its head to fix an eye on her.

"This is not what we set out to do," Kyna said. "The elves will continue with their lives after this. We will disappear until things settle. The vierstone is gone. Morcanan ... Morcanan will be a fight, I am sure, but we will cause as little destruction as possible while still accomplishing our purpose. We just have to be more careful. Remsgraen caught us off guard."

Kaelo had turned to look at her, but there was uncertainty in his eyes.

"You do not understand the elves," the phoenix said to Kyna. "You did not grow up among them, and those you came to know these past months manipulated you and weakened your resolve." The phoenix spoke in a patronizing tone that set Kyna's teeth on edge.

"Enough," said Kaelo.

Kyna's retort died on her lips. She looked to her father. His eyes were fixed on the ground, clouded in thought. Finally, he looked up at the phoenix.

"What do you propose?"

The phoenix's feathers ruffled again, in pleasure this time, Kyna thought. The glow had faded from its throat.

"A force," it said. "Something to help us infiltrate Morcanan. You say half the city is inside the mountain. I do not know if my breath can penetrate so far. We will need help to ensure there is not vierstone hidden in the depths of the tunnels."

"An army," Kaelo said.

"Yes."

Kaelo shook his head. "The beasts and spirits you mean? We do not have time. There are not yet enough in the land to call them into an army."

"I do not need beasts."

A rising horror in Kyna's breast nearly made her cry out.

"Father, no! It means to make wights! Kill the elves to use against them!"

Kaelo's gaze snapped to the phoenix; fury was in his face.

"I do not need the bodies of elves," the phoenix said calmly. "I can make a force as easily returned to the earth as brought from it—an impartial force that can help us create our structure after Morcanan is cleansed and subdued. It is simple and efficient. No more elves need die than insist upon doing so."

Kaelo's expression cooled. His struggle seemed to be ebbing.

"We could march on Morcanan now," said the phoenix. "Take our army and catch the elves unawares. Afterward, we could cleanse the rest of the Morcani lands at our leisure, with little fear of resistance."

Kyna counted her heartbeats in the silence that followed. She tried to catch her father's eyes, to pull his thoughts away from the poisonous words of the phoenix, but his gaze did not stray from the bird's liquid eyes.

"Show me," he said.

"No," Kyna whispered. Neither the phoenix nor Kaelo paid her any attention.

The phoenix bowed its head, then rose onto its feet and spread its wings. Flames dripped from its feathers, and its throat broke into fiery light. Talons sinking into the stone, it arched its neck and opened its beak.

Red flames bathed the dark rocks on which they stood. Kyna leaped back with a gasp and squinted against the glaring light of the fire, trying to see within its depths. The stone was *bubbling*, like boiling water, only thicker. The rock glowed brighter as it morphed. Images of the phoenix forming within ashes flashed across Kyna's memory, and for a moment her heart rose into her throat. Was it raising another phoenix? Could it create an *army* of phoenixes? Kyna's horror subsided only slightly as the stone began to shape into something resembling an elf. The base of the pillar cracked into squat legs, and clumps of rock clustered and melded over each other to form biceps, then elbows, then forearms. Still the flames poured from the phoenix's mouth. Bits of stone began to slake off the roughly hewn body, narrowing hips, curving muscles, and revealing a neck which began to twist back and forth as the amorphous rock atop it shifted into something resembling a face.

Kyna could only stare, open mouthed. Whatever she had been expecting from the phoenix, this was certainly not it.

The flames ceased.

The sculpture remained luminescent for a few moments, then its light began to fade to the dark grey of basalt. The creature was not elven in form, exactly. It was shorter than Kyna and thicker in its limbs and torso. There was something wrong with the way its limbs bent, and its proportions were off. Its face, however, bore the obvious lines of a nose and mouth. Two dark spaces were gouged where eyes should be. The rocks that built the creature were not smooth. In the cracks between stones and bits of rubble, a red light glowed, like fresh magma showing beneath a crusted exterior.

Roughly hewn fingers bent. A club-like foot shifted. Then two pinpoints of crimson winked into existence in the gaping holes of the creature's eyes.

The phoenix folded its legs under itself and sat back, admiring its creation.

Kaelo's eyes roamed from the rock figure's distorted face to its feet. He looked as disturbed as Kyna felt, yet a sort of wonder shone in his eyes.

"It can move?" he said.

The creature turned its head to look at Kaelo, then took a step toward him. Kyna stifled a cry of warning, but Kaelo stood his ground, looking down at the thing with narrowed eyes as it came nearer.

"Do you control it?" he said.

"Entirely," said the phoenix.

"What is it?"

"A cherufin."

"Cherufin," Kaelo breathed. "They are legends."

"As were phoenixes," the phoenix said wryly.

The ghost of a smile was beginning to pull at Kaelo's mouth, his hesitation giving way to excitement.

"How many can you create?"

"As many as needed."

"Can they be killed?"

"With difficulty."

Kaelo raised a hand to the cherufin's head and trailed a finger down its face. His eyes grew distant, and his hand folded into a fist as it dropped away. The thing had not moved or blinked. Kyna doubted it could blink.

Kaelo stepped back. He looked from one monster to the other.

"No," Kyna whispered again. She could not find her voice. An army of these things? Controlled by a phoenix which was already slipping from her father's control? He wouldn't possibly agree to this. He could not allow it. "Father."

With a slow blink, Kaelo turned his head to face Kyna. His eyes followed the motion reluctantly. He looked at her, and there was pain in his eyes.

"Please," Kyna said.

"We cannot fail," he said softly.

Kyna shook her head, but she knew it was too late. Kaelo took a long breath, clasped a hand about the hilt of his sword, and turned to the phoenix.

"Do it."

The phoenix made a low sound in its throat that sounded like a purr.

"You will not regret it." It flexed its wings, rose once more to its feet, and lifted its head to the sky. In one bound, it was high in the air. With the snap of its wings, the phoenix soared over the rocky slope of the mountainside, circled in the air, and let forth a cloud of fire so immense, it could have covered half of Daro. Kyna flinched away, shielding her eyes from the onslaught of burning light. The sound of cracking, bubbling, grinding stone filled the air, and a wave of heat washed over Kyna. She lowered her arm from her face and stumbled backward on nerveless feet as the entire mountainside heaved and writhed before her eyes.

She looked at her father then, and saw grim determination in the set of his jaw. Crimson light painted his face and reflected in his eyes, and Kyna's skin went cold as she thought of Gellion's description of the phoenix's demonic lieutenants in the Great War.

Trust me, her father had said. She wanted to. She truly did.

Kyna took deep breaths and pressed her wrist against the redstone in her cuff. She tried to fall into its cool embrace, to counteract the heat of the phoenix's flames and the scalding fear growing in the pit of her stomach.

She watched the mountainside shape into a forest of statues. She watched glowing red eyes open in unison, dotting the rocky landscape like bloody stars reflected in the sea. She watched the cherufin break free of the ground and turn as one to face the mountains—to face their master—to face Morcanan.

Kyna closed her eyes, but she knew no amount of darkness would ever blot the scene from her memory.

PART II

18

MORCANAN

Morcanan was a city leached of color, though in the summer, snowless green pines skirted its walls, and clumps of mountain flowers forced their way into any patch of exposed soil the city offered—which wasn't much. Mostly the city was stone and metal softened by fur and wool. It was also a marvel of engineering. So great a marvel, that almost none of the engineering was visible. Only the power lines gave hint to the efficient functionality of the city. They hung gracefully in silvers, blacks, and whites from stone pillars carved in flowing shapes. Strung over the city in crossing lines and concave arches, they looked like weaving rivers that flowed through the air.

"I don't like being back here," Valder said as they walked out of a mountain.

Pine scented air blew against their faces, and Gellion breathed it deeply. He didn't mind Morcanan, but preferred to spend his mornings above ground.

"I know." Veldon's eyes shone with sad remembrance.

A weight settled on Gellion. His brothers had only ever been to Morcanan during the Great War. The city had been one giant war camp then—still severely damaged by the volcanic explosion that had started the war and militarized to the point that it hardly seemed a city. Gellion had returned to a fully repaired Morcanan after the war, when the city had hosted the second Kindom Council of the elves—exactly two hundred years ago. As far as Gellion could tell, Morcanan had not changed at all since then, but then, Great Cities rarely changed in so short a time, especially ones ruled over by Miyela.

Gellion fought the urge to look over his shoulder. He was not sure whether the Lady of Morcanan was following them out of the mountain or remaining in her lair.

Miyela had greeted the Turi Council members with the practical civility of an army commander. There had been no smiles or thanks for their aid, but Gellion had never expected any. Given all that had happened between Miyela, Liera, and the leaders of Daro months before, Gellion was only relieved Miyela had accepted their presence in her city at all. Gellion bore no love for the severe woman, and her treatment of Dulon still burned him, but the Turi's purpose was greater than one woman and her rankling superiority complex. Gellion was not doing this to help Miyela, or even to save Morcanan, but for the sake of their entire race.

"Still," said Veldon, "it feels amazing to be back in a city of vierstone. Did you feel it when we walked in?"

Valder nodded.

Gellion frowned. He had felt *something* upon entering the Great City, but he was not sure he would have called it pleasant. It had been more of a nagging pull he could not entirely throw off. Had it been vierstone? Gellion concentrated, trying to identify the feeling again. Yes, there was something, but its touch was so soft he could scarcely identify it.

"I just hope the vierstone's still here in a week." Valder looked at the sky as though expecting the phoenix to appear out of thin air any moment.

It was an expectation Gellion shared. The phoenix had not been seen since its attack on Yavran three days before. It was an eerie and inexplicable absence that felt unnervingly like the calm before a storm.

Just one more day and we will be ready for it.

The entirety of the Turi army was within the walls of Morcanan now, but it would take the remainder of the day to bring the preparations the Council had discussed this morning to fruition. Miyela's own soldiers had been in place for a week already. The Turi would supplement their ranks and extend the area of the city covered by weapons and watchful eyes. They would follow Miyela's plan of attack, but with the new tactic of trying to separate Kaelo from the phoenix. Though the Lady of Morcanan now knew about Kaelo's redstone, none but the Turi Council knew Gellion possessed the same weapon.

The anxiety Gellion felt when he turned his eyes to the sky was more personal than the fear of lost vierstone. Far more acute was his anticipation of a fight with Kaelo. Repairing forges, breaking rocks, and studying redstone were all well and good, but they were not the same as using it as a weapon with innocent elves on all sides. With the current of the stone in his body and a skilled enemy before him, would Gellion be able to focus his attacks on Kaelo, or would he bring down streets and buildings in his desperation? If it stopped Kaelo, was it worth collateral destruction?

"There! There!"

Gellion's body went rigid. His eyes widened and darted around, looking automatically to the sky, but he saw nothing, and the cry he had heard was not taken up by any other elves. Only when his panic subsided did Gellion realize the voice had been familiar. But it couldn't be. Here? In Morcanan?

"Gellion!"

Gellion's head swiveled toward the voice, and after a moment of stunned stillness, a broad grin stretched over his face.

A small, dark elf was frantically pushing her way through a group of annoyed Morcani. When no elves remained between her and Gellion, she launched herself at him, wrapping her arms around his neck. Gellion stumbled backward with the force of her body, but laughed and returned the embrace. Then, over Renyra's shoulder, he saw his best friend.

Firas was moving toward Gellion much more slowly than his wife, with careful steps and a stiff carriage. Always willowy, Firas was even thinner than usual, with sunken cheeks and bruised eyes. Still, his smile was as radiant as Gellion had ever seen it.

"I told you!" Renyra wheeled away from Gellion to face her husband. Her eyes were sparkling with tears. "I told you it was him!"

As Firas drew nearer, Renyra disengaged herself from Gellion. Stepping back, she noticed Valder and Veldon. Her smile grew still larger and she hugged each of them, too. Valder laughed in surprise. Veldon's cheeks stained pink.

"We saw the Turi come in," Renyra said. "I knew I saw you in front. Firas didn't believe me. I hardly believed it. But you're here! Sweet Riu." Renyra's breath was coming in short bursts. She looked rather dizzy.

Before Gellion could make any move to calm her, Firas was at her side, his hand against her back.

"Easy, love." He looked down at her with a gentle smile, then raised his gaze to Gellion.

Up close, Firas looked even worse. His pale skin bore a grayish tinge, and there were lines of pain around his eyes.

"I'm alright," Firas said, clearly seeing the concern in Gellion's face. "We had a run-in with the phoenix and I came off the worse for it." He held out a hand and his smile returned. "But by Riu it is good to see you."

Gellion clasped the hand, but made no move to shake it or embrace Firas as he would normally would have done. The man looked so fragile.

"A run-in?" Gellion said. "What did it do to you?"

"Burned him," Renyra said softly. Her excitement drained away at once, leaving a haunted look in her eyes. "His whole back. And it—" She clenched her jaw.

Firas moved his hand to her shoulder and squeezed.

"Most of the bones have healed." He looked back at Gellion with a grimace. "The burns are still a bit raw."

Gellion's stomach turned over. It couldn't have been more than a couple of weeks since Firas's injuries. Elves healed quickly—far more quickly than what Gellion had seen of the humans—but to have your whole back ravaged by phoenix fire? And the way he spoke of bones—

"Riu above, Firas," Gellion said.

Firas shrugged. "It could have been worse."

Gellion raised an eyebrow.

Firas chuckled, then his face softened.

"It is less pain than losing friends." His eyes roved over Gellion and his brothers. "A pain I no longer need endure."

"But *how*?" Renyra seemed in control of herself again, but her eyes were wide, and her cheeks glistened. "We waited in the mountains and the whole journey back to Daro. There were ships waiting for us at Daro, and we couldn't stall any longer. We thought … we were sure—" Tears welled in her eyes again.

"It's alright," Gellion said quickly. "We never went back to Daro. We were in Arvain for weeks, and—" Gellion paused and shook his head. "It is a story far too long to tell in the middle of a street. Where are you staying?" He knit his brow. "Why are you here?"

"Another long story." Renyra gave a weak smile.

"There you are!"

Renyra's smile vanished. She turned to look behind her, where a curvy elf with dark skin and a scowl was pushing through the crowds. Gellion recognized her as an elf from Daro, though he did not know her name.

"What are you thinking, sprinting off through crowds in a Great City when a phoenix could come down on us any moment?" she said.

Renyra's mouth twitched. "Sorry, Lyn."

"Oh, she's just worried about you." Another elf had walked up behind the dark woman—a Turi by the looks of him. He walked with a smooth grace and flashed a smile at Renyra.

Two other elves came behind him: a woman almost as small as Renyra, with cropped hair and delicate features, and a well muscled Remsgri with a thick bundle of braids spilling over his shoulder.

Gellion stared at the new arrivals. All of them seemed starkly out of place in the sea of fair hair and neutral colors surrounding them.

The Fieri woman noticed Gellion for the first time. Her brows rose.

"Oh, it's you."

"Renyra?" another new voice said from behind Gellion. He turned to see Tornac walking up to the group. Tornac looked from Renyra to the eclectic group of elves beside her with bemused recognition. "What are you all doing here?" he said.

Gellion's head was spinning. From the looks on Valder and Veldon's faces, they were as bewildered as he was.

"That seems to be the question, doesn't it?" Renyra said with a smile. She looked at Gellion and the younger of his brothers, then gestured to the elves beside her. "These are my friends. Caerlyn you may know from Daro. And this is Raren, his sister Alura, and Trali. We've been traveling together since everything that happened in Tura."

Gellion nodded, no less overwhelmed for knowing the names of the elves.

"And this is Gellion," Valder said. Gellion blinked, realizing that Renyra's friends had been watching him expectantly. Then, to his supreme annoyance, Valder went on. "Famed among the Councils of Daro and Tura." He grinned.

The Turi elf with his hair in a bun—Raren—smiled back.

"And you are?" he said.

"Valder." Valder appraised Raren with a spark in his eye.

"Famed for his self proclaimed wit and proficiency with tree branches," said Gellion.

Raren raised his eyebrows. "Is that so?"

Valder turned such a scathing glare on Gellion it made him laugh out loud. He couldn't remember the last time he had laughed as much as in these last few minutes. He felt strangely apart from himself—an actor stepping out of his role.

"And I am the long enduring brother of them both." Veldon rolled his eyes. "Veldon."

Renyra beamed, looking between the two groups with the nervous excitement of one introducing their significant other to their parents.

"Now, I think an explanation is in order." Gellion looked at Firas.

"On both parts," said Renrya.

"Then I say we find somewhere more suitable for conversation," Valder said. "Preferably somewhere with food."

Gellion had not expected to spend the evening in the company of friends, old or new. Part of him longed to pace the city, focusing on the fight to come, practicing with redstone and watching the skies with tense anticipation. Another part of him—the larger part—merely wanted to get away from Kyna's name, which was coming up far too much in this tale for his liking. But he stayed where he was, sitting in a dimly lit tavern with ordered tables and bare walls. He tried to attach the correct emotions to his face as Renyra and her friends explained all that had happened since they left Tura. Not confident of his success, he was grateful for the low lights and the plethora of elves at their table to distract attention from him.

Kyna was still with Kaelo. Gellion knew this should not surprise him. Where else did he expect her to have gone? Still, the confirmation made him uneasy. Was she on her way here now? Would she fly with her father over Morcanan, or wait in the safety of the mountains? What if he had to face them both?

A hand on Gellion's elbow made him start. He looked at Veldon, sitting next to him, whose eyes were round with concern. Gellion realized he had been gripping his mug with dangerous force and had probably been glaring at the table.

"Sorry," he muttered, blinking and relaxing his face.

"What are you thinking about?" Veldon said.

The conversation of the table had transitioned to the general and comparative storytelling that often occurs after more important matters have been softened by drink. The Remsgri elf, Trali, was narrating an embarrassing incident that had occurred between Raren and Caerlyn in a Sira show of the past. Caerlyn was scowling good naturedly at Trali, and Raren had the look of one trying a bit too hard to appear unconcerned. He kept glancing at Valder, who was laughing heartily at the tale.

Gellion had decided he liked Renyra and Firas's friends quite a bit, but just now he wished he could be alone with the two of them, or just with his brothers. He supposed the corner of the table with Veldon would have to do.

Bowing his head closer to Veldon, he said, "She might be with Kaelo when he ... when they—"

Veldon nodded. "I know. It does throw a sizable hitch into our planning."

Gellion's brows drew together. "What?"

"Kyna clearly has access to redstone as well," said Veldon, "and from what Renyra says, she knows how to use it. We may have to get the stone off both of them, in which case we are now outnumbered."

Gellion stared at Veldon for a moment, then cleared his throat.

"I know." He had not even considered this. "But what else can we do? We can warn the Council of the possibility, but I can't see how we can change our plans to account for it." He ran a hand through his hair. "Let's just hope Kyna doesn't fly into the city with the phoenix. If she does, we will just have to try our best to incapacitate them both. Either way, Kaelo is still my target."

"I think that is wise."

For a few moments, Gellion and Veldon were silent, listening to the stories and laughter around them. It was not until Gellion looked up at a particularly loud guffaw from Valder that his eyes met Tornac's. Tornac was watching Gellion pensively, his glass of amber liquid sitting motionless in his hand. Gellion lifted his eyebrows at his brother's sudden attention.

Tornac's avoidance these last weeks had taken on a different mood than that during Gellion's first weeks in Tura. The tense enmity between them had become more of an awkward tiptoeing around one another's glances and comments. Tornac's looks now seemed more confused than hostile, as though he were trying to read Gellion's thoughts, but couldn't quite make them out.

"What is it, Tornac?" Gellion said with a sigh. They were in the company of others, after all, why not try to bring out whatever was clearly weighing Tornac's mind?

Tornac showed no chagrin at being caught staring. He looked at Gellion a moment longer, his eyes flitted to Veldon, then he said, "You knew Kyna well?"

This brought Gellion up short. He felt blood rush to his face and looked automatically at Veldon, both to gauge his reaction to the question and to buy a moment of time away from Tornac's gaze. Veldon's eyes were wide. He shook his head in clear indication that he had said nothing to Tornac of Gellion and Kyna's relationship.

Tornac rolled his eyes. "Do not look for an informant unless it is with Kyna herself or your own reaction to her name. Each time she comes up in meetings or discussions your eyes turn down, and you never speak of her outside of formal situations, yet you clearly knew her."

Tornac's reasoning irked Gellion more than if Veldon or Valder had told him the whole story. Had Gellion been so obvious? And what had Kyna said to him?

"You obviously knew her well if she told you about me," Gellion muttered.

Tornac's lips curved into a grimace.

"Funny, that's exactly what I said to her about you. I was shocked you had mentioned my cursed name to any outside our family."

Gellion stared at the table, grinding his teeth.

"I am only curious." There was no jest or sullenness to Tornac's voice. He spoke softly, almost gently—a most uncharacteristic display of interest and empathy.

"She defended you against my temper. It surprised me."

Gellion's eyes snapped up.

"Well, not surprised me, exactly," Tornac amended. "I have told you that you inspire loyalty in others even where you do not intend, but the loyalty seemed at odds with Kyna's personality. I daresay she would have fought me over your honor if I had pressed the matter."

Gellion's mouth was hanging open, devoid of response. Kyna had spoken in his favor to his *brother* when she thought him dead? It didn't make sense. She had been using him all the time. She had brought about his supposed death with her treachery and plans. Had guilt driven her words? The possibility only incensed his anger.

"If ever I thought I knew Kyna well," Gellion said, "I was clearly a fool. She used me as thoroughly as she used the rest of the elves." He winced at the pain that sounded in his voice. Tornac's brows drew together.

"How so?" he said.

"Does it matter?"

"Yes."

Gellion stared at Tornac, then his eyes moved to the others at the table, still absorbed in their own conversations. Only Valder's gaze floated toward Gellion. He cocked his head. Gellion shook his head and Valder shrugged, turning back to Raren.

"Why?" said Gellion. "Do you want to embellish your list of reasons I am a failure as a brother and leader? Revel in my mistakes and my pain?"

"Gellion," Veldon said softly. His eyes were turned down.

"No," Tornac said. It was all he said. He sat patiently and took a sip of his drink.

Gellion let out a forceful breath. "Fine. She convinced me to go against my own judgment and follow the will of the elves I represented —to vote in favor of the Albaren alliance. She led us away from Kaelo's trail and helped us bolster the elves' support of the alliance while turning the Kindoms against each other and rousing suspicion in the wrong places. She gained my trust. She acted as though—"

He couldn't finish. He could never say those words to Tornac. She had acted as though she loved him—but had it entirely been an act? She could not have faked the emotions that had flowed between them in that brief moment of connection outside Nescari. He closed his eyes and shook his head. That moment would haunt him the rest of his life. It rose to the surface of his thoughts every time he convinced himself to hate Kyna. He could have misread the emotions—reflected his own feelings back to himself and convinced him they were hers.

Tornac seemed to have read the rest of Gellion's words on his face. He nodded slowly, as though confirming something to himself. Gellion could feel a snarl building in the back of his throat as heat flushed his skin once more. But Tornac's face held no satisfaction at Gellion's humiliation. There was something very close to sympathy in his eyes. This was worse than satisfaction.

"It doesn't matter what she was to me," Gellion said. "Now she is simply a possible complication in our plans for Morcanan's defense. Whatever Kyna and Kaelo once were in my life, they are now the elves' enemy—my enemy—and I intend to fight them both."

Tornac watched Gellion with a long intensity, then he lowered his eyes and nodded.

"I know you will," he said. The contemplative air had not left his expression, but he spoke no more, and eventually turned back toward the rest of their companions.

It was several minutes before Gellion met Veldon's eyes again.

"Damn," he said.

"Damn indeed," said Veldon. His mouth twitched into a smile. "To the world spiraling out of our control."

He lifted his mug and Gellion met the toast with his own glass. Taking a long pull on the fiery liquid, Gellion leaned back in his chair and let the heat suffuse his body.

The next two days were a confusing mesh of tension, boredom, and enjoyment, each directly dependent upon whose company Gellion was keeping. To his relief, the Turi Council had only gathered once more since their arrival in Morcanan, as Miyela had insisted upon being present for any such meeting, and her time was constrained enough as it was. Gellion didn't mind this in the least. The less time he had to spend beneath Liera's glower, the better.

Despite Miyela's increased patrols of the lands south and west of Morcanan, no one had seen any sign of the phoenix. Gellion was getting nervous, which meant boredom was his greatest enemy. He spent as much of his time as possible with his brothers or the sizable group of elves that had somehow become his companions in this faraway city. He sat most often with Firas, whose lingering physical pain made him as taciturn as Gellion. It felt good to sit next to Firas. He held a solid reassurance for Gellion—a stoicism that was both calming and familiar, without the forceful sympathy of Veldon or the volatile humor of Valder.

Often, as he sat with his friends, Gellion would find himself fingering the redstone in his pocket. It had become a nervous habit, one that grew worse as the wait for Kaelo lengthened. He had not told Firas, or Renyra, or any of their companions about the stone, adhering to the Council's strict opinion that the fewer elves knew of the substance, the better. Still, it felt like a lie, and hung a shadow over his time with them.

By the beginning of Gellion's third day in Morcanan, his impatience was escalating to near panic. Where was the phoenix? Had Kaelo learned of the resistance building in Morcanan? The longer the delay, the more prepared Gellion feared Kaelo would be for their fight.

At least he doesn't know you can match his weapon.

Gellion's grip tightened on the redstone. His anxiety eased—dampened. Yes, he had this weapon, at least.

The air was warming as the morning progressed, losing the bite of the mountains and slipping into the softness of a summer day. The scent of pine grew more heady, lending a spiciness to the air. He leaned back and closed his eyes, letting the sunlight fall over his skin.

Firas's voice was a pleasant white noise; he was talking to Renyra in low tones. Concentrating on this and the distant cry of birds, Gellion could almost convince himself he was back in Daro.

Gellion frowned.

The birdsong had ceased—suddenly and completely.

He opened his eyes, and his heartbeat leaped ahead of his thoughts. He could not explain the onset of this fear, except by the same instincts he had felt in Tura, right before the phoenix came.

He stood, roving the sky with his eyes.

"Gellion?" Firas said.

Gellion did not answer. His skin had gone cold.

It was close. He knew it.

"Raise the alert," he said calmly.

"What?" Valder was standing next to Gellion now, following his gaze. "Did you see it?"

Gellion shook his head. "Listen."

Valder knit his brows. "To what?"

"There are no birds, and I feel—I don't know, but everything is still. We need to raise the alert."

Without waiting for anyone's response, he began to run to the base of the mountain. He heard footsteps trailing behind him, but did not know to whom they belonged. No one called after him. He ran to the nearest Rale path, jumped onto a levit board, and leaned forward.

It could be nothing, but it was better to raise a false alarm than be taken unawares. He would go to the guard tower nearest the mountain —the tallest one. As he shot through the streets, Gellion kept his eyes on the sky as much as he dared. More than one shout of protest met his negligent speed, but he ignored them.

The guard tower. Get to the guard tower.

It didn't take long. Morcanan was smaller than Tura and half of it was inside the mountain. Gellion paused at the base of the tower and looked behind him to see Valder and Veldon on his heels. When they had caught up, he jumped onto the lift and kicked the lever to make it rise.

They kept their eyes to the sky.

"Have either of you seen anything?" Gellion said.

The lift was rising at a ponderous pace.

"No," said Veldon.

"I'm sure it's close," Gellion said. "But if we don't see it from the tower—"

The bells sounded.

Gellion jumped violently.

"Sounds like you were right," Valder said.

The lift clicked into place at the top of the tower, and Gellion ran to the nearest railing. He turned in a circle, tilting his head dizzily to catch sight of the phoenix.

He saw nothing.

"Riu above." Valder spoke in a whisper.

"What!?" Gellion said. "Where?"

Valder pointed, not at the sky, but at the mountainside.

Over the edge of a ridge, where the soil grew rocky and the trees thinned, the surface of the mountain seemed to be *moving*. Gellion squinted, trying to decipher the incomprehensible motion.

Were boulders rolling down the mountain? They were not moving fast enough to be falling rocks. It looked more like they were slowly rolling down the slope in a halting, swinging pattern.

A deep rumble began, then grew louder. The tower started to vibrate. It was not the shaking of an earthquake, but a steady, rhythmic buzzing of the stone around him.

"What is it?" Gellion said.

The rumbling grew louder still, and Gellion wheeled around to see a similar effect beginning on the other side of the mountain. Was this Kaelo? Was he trying to bring down the whole mountain on Morcanan? Could he?

"Cherufin!" said an unfamiliar voice. Gellion turned to see a

Morcani guard, who had just stepped down from the alarm bell that was now ringing steadily on its own. His eyes were wide.

"An army," he said.

The cold across Gellion's skin penetrated deeper to his core. He did not know what cherufin were, but the latter word was all too clear. Bearing the guard's description in mind, Gellion looked back at the mountainside. As the moving rocks came closer, he deciphered the shape of heads, then shoulders, then legs.

They were *creatures*—creatures made of stone—and there were hundreds of them in sight between the trees.

Below the guard tower, Morcanan was a hive of activity. Bells made an eerie chorus, interspersed with shouted orders and the clank of weapons. Gellion could see ranks forming in the streets, the tips of spears and bows lining the walls, and the slow turn of large machinery derived from the Great War, brought out from deep caverns in the mountain.

The rhythmic shaking of the ground was growing more powerful.

Gellion looked at his brothers. Their faces mirrored his own hopeless dispair. All of their plans had been for a phoenix and a single elf. The possibility of a second elf had worried Gellion, but an entire army of creatures Gellion knew nothing about? What chance did they have of stopping this?

Then, over the cacophony of bells and voices, a terrible shriek sounded, echoing off the mountains.

The phoenix soared upward over the mountain tops, trailing flames and smoke. It hovered in the air for a moment, facing Morcanan, then dived low over the marching creatures of stone, making straight for the city.

Gellion heard the first crunch of stone against the city walls.

19

ARMY OF STONE

Renyra stood frozen in the streets, her heart leaping into her throat. What was happening? What was that shaking? The phoenix had risen above the walls of Morcanan, but the bells had begun long before she saw the great bird.

Firas stepped closer to her. She could feel the warmth of him against her side. For a moment, she relished the comfort of his presence, then sudden panic shot through her.

"You can't be here!" she said to him. "Whatever this is, you have to get inside—go into the mountain." Her eyes darted to the main entrance to the caverns of Morcanan. It was too far for her liking, but by levit board, it would only take a few minutes.

A flicker of annoyance passed over Firas's drawn face.

"I will see what is happening," he said.

Renyra's brows lowered over her eyes.

"You promised. That's the only reason I agreed to come to this cursed city. You can't fight like that." She indicated the bandages still showing at the edges of his clothes.

"I will not fight," he said. "But nor will I hide underground."

The sharp crack of breaking stone rent the air.

Renyra went rigid, memories of breaking streets and crumbling buildings flashing in her mind. She spun to face the direction of the sound.

A web of cracks had split a section of the western city wall. Elves atop the breech were running to either side, aiming javelins and arrows on the other side of the wall.

Riu help us, what is out there?

Two more crashes came from the west, followed by another crack further north.

It's going to break into the city, whatever it is.

With a resounding crash, the wall caved in, raining thick slabs of stone. Renyra backed herself against Firas so she stood between him and whatever was about to come through the gates. She knew she should be dragging him through the streets toward the mountain, but her curiosity and terror were too great.

A beat of stillness. Then rocks began to pour through the wall. It was the only interpretation Renyra's mind could form at first. Through the dark debris of the stone wall came still darker rocks—nearly black and roughly hewn.

"What the—"

The rocks *jumped* through the gap, then stood. They *stood*.

Renyra's eyes widened in horror as she traced the elf-like shape of the stone monsters. Even their faces bore an abstract resemblance to noses and mouths, with holes gouged out of their heads that glowed like demonic eyes. The things carried no weapons, but Renyra scarcely imagined they needed them. They began to march forward, allowing room for more of them to climb through the breached wall.

"Let's go," Caerlyn said.

Renyra remained frozen. She watched as armored and armed elves started to shoot and throw weapons at the creatures, but arrows, javelins, and spears bounced and slid off the stone beings with metallic pings and scrapes. A Morcani with thick arms and legs threw himself at one of the monsters from the side, hacking at its neck with a two handed sword. The rock creature lifted a heavy hand and batted the sword away like it was a toy. It did not even look at the elf that had attacked it, but continued to walk forward.

"Renyra!" Caerlyn grabbed her arm. "Stop staring like an idiot and come with us!"

Renyra blinked. She turned to see Raren, Alura, and Trali turned halfway to the mountain, watching her anxiously. Firas was still next to her, but he now appeared much more willing to retreat up the city.

Renyra started to run. She kept one hand clasped tight to Firas's, ready to drop to a walk the moment he did, but Firas jogged along next to her without stopping. She winced at the pain the pace must be causing his back, but at least his long legs enabled him an easier stride.

A *whoosh* came from overhead, and Renyra ducked instinctively as a shadow covered her, but when she looked up, the phoenix was still far above the city. A few bolts soared upward toward it, but none came close to the bird, and those bolts that missed arched and came hurdling back down toward elves and buildings.

More cracks and smashes were coming from the northern sides of the city. So loud was the stone, the shouts of elves, and the clang of weapons, that it took a while for Renyra to realize the alarm bells had stopped sounding. She was grateful for that, at least. Every elf in the city was more than aware they were under threat by now.

The mountain loomed nearer, but so too did the rhythmic thud of stone feet. A pull at Renyra's hand told her Firas's strength was beginning to flag. Her mind darted between forcing him on and slowing their pace and finally decided that getting him to the mountain in a state of pained exhaustion was not worth the saved time. What if the rock creatures broke into the caverns? She slowed to a walk, watching her friends run on.

"We'll catch up!" she called.

Raren paused and looked back at her.

"Wait!" he called to the others.

"No," said Renrya. "Go on!"

"It's ... it's ok," Firas said through pained breaths. "Please. Keep going."

"Don't be stupid," Raren said. "I'm only going to the mountain because of you." He grinned. "Once you're safely tucked away, I intend to come out here and fight these—" his brow knit. "Things."

Renyra gasped as a large group of those 'things' stepped into the street just ahead of them. The beasts turned their steps north. Renyra looked behind her and saw another group marching with the same focus.

"They're going to the mountain," she said.

Arrows and javelins still fell harmlessly about the rock creatures. They seemed indestructible. How were the elves supposed to fight stone?

"Away!"

Renyra looked toward the booming voice and saw one of the massive crossbows, once aimed at the phoenix, pointed directly into the street. Without thinking, she grabbed Firas and ran sideways. She heard a click and the whoosh of a bolt, then exploding stone.

Raising her arms against the flying debris, Renyra peered under her elbow to see two of the rock creatures lying in pieces in the street. She thought she saw a faint wisp of red and green light rising from the remains like steam.

Spirits.

Renyra stared at the rock creatures with renewed horror. She traced the sign of the star across her body.

"Get out of the street," said Trali.

Renyra obeyed in a haze, stumbling beside Firas to shelter against a nearby building.

The creatures who had not been hit by the bolt carried on like nothing had happened, only moving against elves to slap away weapons, or occasionally knock them to the ground with a casual fist. Only when one elf came at the things with a mace did the creatures break their focus. The elf smashed his mace into a creature's head with all of his might, and the head broke free, crashing to the ground and crumbling into rocks. The rest of the body did not fall, however. It turned to face the elf, and raised a fist.

With a cry, the elf brought his mace down again, smashing off the creature's arm at the elbow. He did not get another strike. The creature brought its other hand around and hit the elf in the face so hard, he flew backward ten feet, landing on stone with a crack that made Renyra's gorge rise. Blood began to pool around the elf's head. He did not move again. The headless rock creature turned back to the mountain.

"Sweet Riu," Renyra whispered, clinging to Firas's arm.

More bolts flew, and soon all the crossbows in the city were aimed at the streets rather than the sky. Renyra stayed next to Firas, pressed against a building. She felt useless. But what could any of them do? She and her friends wore no armor, and they had only javelins and swords, which obviously made no more impression upon these creatures than upon the phoenix. It seemed the only way to stop one was to break it apart beyond use of its body.

Renyra had a sudden idea.

"Their legs!" she shouted. "Go for their legs, not their heads!"

Several elves turned to look at her, bewildered. Then Trali nodded and ran into the street.

"Wait!" Renyra yelled. This was not what she had had in mind.

Trali grabbed the mace dropped by the dead Morcani and ran up behind the nearest rock creature. The muscles of his shoulders bunched and stretched as he swung the weapon at the back of the thing's knees. The mace smashed through one of the legs. The creature stopped, teetered, swung its arms in slow motion, then fell sideways. Trali had leaped out of the way of the swinging arms and now backed up several steps as he watched.

Several rocks broke off of the creature when it fell. It made two attempts to push itself back upright, then collapsed in a heap, its light fading and its spirits fleeing.

Renrya grinned.

Trali stared back at her in amazement.

"They're animated by corrupted spirits!" she said. "As soon as their bodies are unusable, the spirits leave it."

But they had all the wrong weapons. It would take an elf as strong as Trali with a heavy and blunt weapon to take the legs off of these crea- tures. And there were so many of them.

Bolts still flew into the streets, one landing close enough to Trali that he stumbled from the impact.

"Come back!" Renyra screamed.

Trali glanced reluctantly at the creatures marching away from him, then ran back to the shelter of the building.

"It's too dangerous." Renyra huffed in frustration. "Even if we could spread the word, I doubt spears and swords could break off stone legs, and there aren't many blunt weapons around here. The bolts are more effective, anyway, if the Morcani have enough of them."

"But what are they doing?" Alura said, indicating the monsters still pouring into the streets. "They don't seem to care about killing elves unless they're threatened."

"Looks like they're going to the mountain," said Caerlyn.

"But why?"Alura glanced upward. "The phoenix hasn't even come close to the city yet."

Renyra shook her head, trying to make sense of it all, but a new sound of cracking stone broke into her thoughts. Her jaw dropped.

A rock body was flying into the air, as though yanked upward by its neck with an invisible rope. Half way through its arc, it fell back down with startling speed and force, crushing the creatures below it.

Another crack. Two more stone bodies flew through the air.

Renyra rose onto her toes, trying to see what was happening. Normally, she would have climbed onto Firas's shoulders, but that was obviously not an option with his still ravaged back.

"Trali! Let me onto your shoulders." She ran to him without waiting for an answer. As though by instinct, he lowered into a squat at her approach, extending one hand for her to take as she stepped onto his thigh and up to his shoulders. He wrapped his hands around the back of her calves and stood in a smooth motion as her second foot slid into position beside his neck.

Renyra towered above the crowds. She looked to where she had seen the rock creatures flying into the air.

She nearly fell off Trali's shoulders.

Crouched in the middle of the street, surrounded on all sides by marching monsters of stone, was Gellion. One of his hands lay flat against the street, and as the next creature approached him, a pillar of stone broke out of the ground right under its feet, sending it flying into the air.

Renyra's skin prickled. Her head spun, and she had to lean forward to grasp one of Trali's hands, which he had extended upon feeling her balance waver.

She couldn't understand it. Was her mind simply overexcited by the madness surrounding her? But no, she was sure of what she had seen. She would recognize Gellion anywhere, especially among a city of Morcani. The evidence of her eyes made no more sense of the situation. He had broken the street. He was wielding Kaelo's power.

Taking Trali's other hand, Renyra leaped off of his shoulders, landing with shaking legs on the ground in front of him.

"What is it?" Firas was at her side in an instant. "What's wrong?" he said when he saw her face.

Renyra swallowed and looked up at Firas with wide eyes.

"I don't think Gellion told us everything that happened to him the last few months," she said faintly.

20

CHAOS AND ORDER

Current was flowing through Gellion with a wild and buzzing energy. He could feel it pouring through his hand, saturating the stone around him. All he needed to do was direct his attention at one of the approaching cherufin, and the ground would rise at his bidding, sending the monstrous creature flailing into the air. Each time, Gellion sucked the rock pillars back into the street, leaving no trace of their fleeting existence.

Those cherufin that slipped through his attacks made no attempt to stop Gellion, they merely marched passed him as though he were an uninteresting statue in the middle of the street. Gellion growled in frustration. Between his attacks, he looked to the sky, trying to keep the phoenix in sight. The cursed beast was still circling above the range of weapons. What was Kaelo playing at? What dark task had he implanted in these creature's heads?

Another burst of current left Gellion's hand. His body felt cold and strangely distant, as though each use of redstone leached a part of him into the street he was commanding. Part of Gellion panicked at this, imploring him to stop, but the panic too, seemed distant. More apparent was the consuming energy of the current and the drive to make as big a scene as possible. The more destruction Gellion caused to Kaelo's army, the more likely Kaelo would turn his attention to what was happening below. The phoenix only needed to fly within range of the Remsgri weapon, hidden from sight just above the mountain gates. If they could just hit the thing once, separate Kaelo from his horrific steed for just a jew minutes—

Gellion forced the pillars of stone to push higher and faster. The cherufin began to break apart with the impact, chunks of stone flying in all directions. The progress was maddeningly slow. Gellion had tried to extend his current directly into the creatures, but something blocked him—a current already flowed in the things and had pushed back against his advances like an opposing magnet.

Come on, just look once. Just fly a bit lower.

The phoenix was circling around again, headed toward the mountain.

Gellion clenched his fingers against the street; they sank into the stone, sending cracks in all directions. Five more pillars exploded out of the ground; five more cherufin broke apart, incapacitating several more with their impact.

The phoenix turned and hovered. Was it facing him? Looking at him?

Three more pillars of stone.

A scream echoed off the mountain, not remotely birdlike, but clearly from the phoenix.

Gellion's hands clapped over his ears. His skin seemed to vibrate with the sound. Wrenching his eyes upward, Gellion watched the phoenix.

That's it. Come stop me.

But the phoenix did not move. Its cry cut off, leaving an eerie silence in its wake. Gellion lowered his hands from his ears. Then something hard wrapped around each of Gellion's arms, pulling them behind his back with iron force.

Gellion pulled forward and upward, trying to rip his arms free. He kicked and cursed at the cherufin flanking him, but his efforts did him as much good as fighting boulders.

The redstone. Reach the redstone.

But he had not been holding the stone when these hunks of rock grabbed him. The stone hung as a useless weight in Gellion's pocket, his hands firmly pinned behind his back. Then he remembered it would have done him no good anyway. These cherufin were not affected by it.

Gellion stopped struggling. His feet and arms ached dully with bruises from his struggle. Cherufin kept marching past him. His face burned with shame, sandwiched between these creatures that only came up to his shoulders, defenseless in their arms.

The phoenix still hovered high above, watching from a safe distance.

The cherufin holding Gellion began to walk toward the mountain, forcing him along between them. Gellion looked around wildly for his brothers, torn between his hope that they would free him of this restraint and his fear of them attempting a pointless and fatal rescue. All he could see around him, however, were cherufin. Over their heads, he could see elves resisting on the edges of the streets, but the cherufin had formed a sort of wall against the sides of the street, leading to the court that stretched before the gates of the mountain. No elves could get through.

The mountain gates loomed high overhead, shut tight against attack. The doors were not shut to protect any remaining elves in the mountain, but to protect the vierstone stored there.

Gellion looked to the opening in the mountain where the Remsgri weapon waited. It had been a close thing, transporting its bulk in pieces across Faeran and putting it together again in Morcanan before Kaelo's arrival. The weapon was the last of its kind—its twin having been destroyed beyond repair in Remsgraen. Gellion knew nothing of how the thing worked, but had heard accounts of its power from those Remsgri that had accompanied the weapon on the Rale.

It looked as though the cherufin were congregating outside the mountain gates. If the phoenix flew down to join them, it would pass right in the weapon's range. Of course, even if it worked, and both phoenix and rider fell separately to the court below, Gellion could not get to Kaelo while held between two rock monsters.

Gellion's guards halted at the edge of the court, turning him to face the inner expanse. It was empty. Cherufin were still coming from the surrounding streets, but they layered themselves against the outer rim of the court.

A series of metallic crunches and shouts made Gellion twist against the cherufin, looking for the source of the sounds.

His gut twisted.

The nearest crossbow, affixed to the edge of a flat roof, was being contorted and broken by a set of cherufin, the elf manning the weapon dragged away by the armpits. Only one other crossbow was in Gellion's limited sight, and it seemed to be undergoing the same fate.

Riu above, they're disarming the whole city without even trying.

His eyes darted again to the hidden weapon in the mountain, ensuring that their last defense was still unseen and ready.

The last bit of hope within Gellion drained down his body. He watched in numb defeat as cherufin scaled the walls of the mountain, their fists biting into its sides like the stone was made of of bread. They crawled with steady progress, unfazed by the rain of arrows aimed by the Remsgri defending their weapon.

It was over in a few minutes.

Gellion heard more crunching and tearing, the pounding of stone against hollow metal, and shouts of rage and terror as those elves fighting back were either restrained, sent running, or silenced.

As the cherufin crawled back down the mountain, Gellion saw the phoenix begin to lower itself between slow beats of its wings.

A flurry of movement in the court drew Gellion's eye, and he watched a path form between the thick layer of cherufin keeping elves out of the court. Two cherufin marched forward, an elf held firmly between them in the same manner as Gellion.

Miyela walked with dignity, her back as straight as her restrained arms would allow. Though her white clothing was ripped and dirtied and a trickle of blood ran down one side of her face, her chin was lifted above the horizon.

The cherufin marched the Lady of Morcanan to the middle of the court, then stopped.

Warm wind buffeted Gellion's face as the phoenix landed in front of Miyela.

Though the sight of the beast filled Gellion with rage and terror, he could not deny the mesmerizing beauty of its glistening feathers, its liquid eyes, and the flames streaming softly from its wings and tail even as it sat still on the ground.

Then two elves slid from its back.

It was a strange thing. Gellion had been wrapped in the lives and fate of both his mentor of old and Kyna for so long now that it had almost not occurred to him that he hadn't seen the latter for months and the former for centuries. The two had become so present and real in Gellion's waking thoughts that it was hard to accept that he had not been so present to either of them. Seeing this physical manifestation of them both caught him in the stomach like a stone fist.

Kyna came first, taking several steps away from the phoenix upon touching the ground. She looked exactly as Gellion remembered her—shining black hair, shapely limbs, and an angular face with a straight nose. The resemblance to her father was so obvious now, he wondered that he had never made the connection.

Heat flushed up Gellion's neck and spread over his face. He could not untangle the ball of writhing emotions within him. He wanted to hate the woman for all that she had done, for how she had used him, toyed with him, betrayed him. He wanted to hate her. He told himself he did hate her. Why, then, had his heart leaped for that first fleeting moment upon seeing her? Why did he not emanate cold fury at her presence?

Kyna's eyes darted around the court, then fixed on Miyela. Gellion tried to read Kyna's face, though with the distance separating them, it was difficult to make out anything behind her eyes. Then again, Gellion had never been able to discern Kyna's emotions. And yet—could he now? Was he projecting emotions upon Kyna's face, or were they written there in her eyes where before had been opaque indifference? Real or imagined, what Gellion now saw did not fit his memory of the woman. She looked afraid—cornered. Was it simply the family resemblance, or did she carry the same air of a hunted animal that her grandmother had possessed these last weeks in Tura?

What had she to be afraid of? She was about to accomplish the goal of her entire life.

Gellion's eyes turned to Kaelo.

So many years had passed since Gellion had seen the man outside of memory or dream. The picture of his face had become muddled and distorted in that time, yet now the details filled in as though they had never been obscured. Kaelo's hair hung loose to his shoulders, the same deep onyx as his daughter's. He stood with squared shoulders and a lifted chin, dressed from neck to feet in armor of liquid metal that matched his body's movements precisely. At his hip hung a sword, its blade obscured within a scabbard.

Gellion watched Kaelo with a pounding heart. Did he know Gellion was here? Did Kyna? Had it been they or the phoenix alone that had recognized and removed his threat to the cherufin?

Kaelo did not so much as glance toward Gellion, however, and Kyna now seemed to be staring at the ground just to the side of Miyela.

Slowly, Kaelo walked toward the Lady of Morcanan.

Only a sliver of the woman's face was visible to Gellion. From what he could see, she stared straight at Kaelo as he approached, her eyes hard.

Kaelo stopped a few paces in front of Miyela. For several moments, he just looked at her, as though expecting her to address him. She did not.

"Morcanan is mine," Kaelo said.

His voice carried through the court and shivered through Gellion's body—familiar, yet half remembered. It bore unquestioning authority, and it bore triumph.

"You have no weapons remaining to you," Kaelo continued, "and you have seen the effectiveness of your soldiers against my forces. Surrender now, allow me to go about my work without resistance, and no more elves need be harmed."

Miyela's expression did not change. She did not so much glare at Kaelo as impale him with her eyes.

"What do you want?" she said.

One of Kaelo's brows rose. "I want what you want. I want what you have striven for in your own Kindom—a world of order. A world untainted by the crushing pain derived from our own inadequacy."

"And you think this will achieve that?" Miyela's voice was calm, yet imbued with iron. "Destroying vierstone and taking cities?"

"Yes," Kaelo said simply.

"A godless world can have no order."

"The world is already godless." Some of the composure slipped from Kaelo's face. His lip twitched upward in a snarl. "Any attempt to pretend otherwise causes only grief and pain. The world we are about to inhabit will harbor no such delusions."

Kaelo composed his face into a mask of calm confidence. He looked around at the streets beyond the court.

"I did, however, make a mistake. I did not account for the time it would take for the hypocritical and defiant natures of the elves to change, nor did I expect the scale of ignorant resistance they would be willing to enact. If I complete my goal now and leave the Kindoms to wallow alone in the aftermath, chaos will ensue. I intend to correct my error."

Miyela's brows lowered, though Gellion could not tell if it was from confusion or defiance.

"Cede this city to me." Kaelo's voice rang louder and deeper than before. "After I have cleansed it of vierstone in peace, I will ensure it is run properly."

Miyela stared at Kaelo. "You're mad," she said, so softly Gellion could hardly hear it.

Kaelo ignored her. "Will you offer your surrender, or will you force me to take the city by other means?"

Gellion could hear the beat of his own pulse in the silence. He struggled to make sense of Kaelo's words. Surely he must have misunderstood. Kaelo had wanted to destroy vierstone. The prospect of this had been so terrible as to seem impossible, yet now the man planned to take it further, still? Did Kaelo really think he could take control of all the Kindoms—remake the whole of elven society with nothing but his will and a phoenix? It was impossible.

Miyela still had not answered. Slowly, her eyes broke away from Kaelo and moved to look about the court. Elves stood in haphazard ranks behind the cherufin, all watching the spectacle before them with frightened and confused expressions. Several elves were restrained, as Gellion and Miyela were.

Miyela turned her eyes back to Kaelo, and even from Gellion's awkward viewpoint, he could sense the fury and hatred in her eyes.

"Do you give me Morcanan?" Kaelo said.

Miyela took a slow breath and lifted her face with quiet dignity.

"Yes."

21

GRIEF

Relief mingled with dread. It was a sensation Kyna was growing accustomed to. She tried to hold her countenance in dispassionate control, but it was taking most of her concentration. Miyela had looked at Kyna as though she were a piece of scum on her boot. Kyna could hardly blame the woman. In Daro, Kyna had kept regular contact with Miyela, encouraging the uprising of the Morcani to undermine the cohesion between the Kindoms and goad the leaders of Daro into taking more immediate action. It had worked. Did Miyela now know she had been manipulated, or did she simply hate anyone in league with the man now ripping her Kindom from her grasp? It didn't really matter, Kyna supposed. She had long since labeled herself a public enemy of the elves —a role she had once accepted with indifference, even wry pleasure. Now, it only added to the crushing weight in her chest.

A corner of Kaelo's mouth had turned up at Miyela's surrender. He nodded to the Lady of Morcanan.

"Open the mountain," he said. "And order your people to drop their weapons."

Miyela called the orders. From her tone, one would never have guessed she spoke under duress.

A chorus of muttering and shouts met Miyela's words. Kyna allowed her gaze to sweep over the elves beyond the cherufin. All the shouts seemed to be coming from Turi interspersed in the crowds. The Morcani were grim faced, but crouched to lay their weapons upon the ground without complaint. Kyna looked to the hulking mountain gates, waiting for them to open, but before she heard the first gears turn, a voice called from behind Miyela.

"Kaelo!"

Kyna's breath froze in her lungs. A shock of electricity passed through her whole body. She was imagining it. How many times had she heard that voice in her dreams and haunted memories? Impossible. She shook her head.

Stop it. He's gone. He's gone.

A heavy silence had fallen over the court. The clang of weapons against the street ceased, and all muttering cut off in a moment. Slowly, reluctantly, hopefully, Kyna turned her head toward the voice.

The breath in her lungs shattered, its shards tearing through her body.

No. You're seeing things. You've finally gone mad and your eyes have followed suit.

But even as she blinked and told herself she was crazy, the image before Kyna remained steady and real.

Gellion.

He stood between two cherufin, his arms twisted behind his back. Strands of russet hair fell over his eyes, which were fixed on Kaelo.

It wasn't possible. He had never come back after the battle. He had not come to Tura on the ships. He had *died*. She was sure of it—had been sure of it. Yet Kyna knew her conviction carried no incontrovertible evidence. She had never seen Gellion in the last half of the battle. She had not seen him fall, nor spoken to any witnesses of his death as she had Dulon's.

As Kyna's mind fumbled with logic, a raging heat was rising up her throat. She had the absurd urge to laugh—to smile, to run to him. Before she had the idiocity to act on any of these traitorous impulses, however, Gellion's eyes turned to her.

All the emotions boiling within Kyna condensed into one.

Before Daro, Kyna had never felt grief. The foreign and terrible sensation had wormed its way into her veins only after Gellion's death, and it had eaten her away from the inside until even the touch of redstone had not drained it away entirely. Since rejoining her father, Kyna had done all in her power to forget the feeling. When that had not worked, she had used it as fuel to justify what they were trying to achieve. Yet the grief she had felt at Gellion's supposed death paled in comparison to what she now felt now as he looked at her.

There was no relief or joy in Gellion's face. He stared at Kyna with a cold dispassion. It was a familiar expression to Kyna, but not one she had ever seen on Gellion. He knew what she had done. And he hated her.

Something broke inside Kyna at this realization. She did not fall to the ground or cry, but stood as one paralyzed, falling within herself silently as the world went on without.

After another moment, Gellion looked back at Kaelo, disregarding Kyna as though she were of no more interest than the cherufin restraining him.

"What have you done?" Gellion said. The was no anger in his voice, only an undercurrent of pain.

Beside her, Kyna could feel the stillness of her father. She looked at him.

Kaelo was staring at Gellion, his posture rigid. There was shock in his face. A flicker of uncertainty. For a fleeting moment, a fragment of her father seemed to reappear behind the dark veil over Kaelo's eyes— that spark of green she still caught glimpses of at increasingly rare intervals. His lips parted, but he did not answer.

"I always thought there was more to you than any other elf." Gellion's voice was pitched for Kaelo alone. The pain in his eyes grew. "Even after all you did. I defended you. I clung to the man I had always admired above all. Yet now, you carry out this crusade from the back of a beast that devastated my family and Kindom. You hide behind the power of armies and demons, afraid to face the people you betray without your shields and armor."

Kaelo's eyes narrowed. He remained silent.

"Release me," Gellion said. "Face me. If you would destroy and imprison the elf who once called you master, do it with your own hand and by your own skill."

The uncertainty had been draining from Kaelo's face throughout Gellion's accusations, replaced by cold anger, but now that uncertainty returned as he regarded the elf before him.

A line formed between Kyna's brows as she watched her father. Months ago, upon hearing of Gellion's presence and position in Daro, Kaelo had been quiet for days. Even as he had outlined Kyna's manipulation of Gellion and the betrayal of his city, Kaelo had seemed regretful of the man's part in his plan. It was an emotion Kyna had never witnessed in her father, one she had viewed with both shock and confusion when first it came. That was, of course, before she knew of Gellion's connection to her father.

Now, Kaelo eyed Gellion with that same regret, yet it did not seem to possess as great a hold over him as it had before. Anger flickered behind his hesitation, and his lips thinned into a narrow line.

Then a scream of rage came from the other side of the court. Kyna whirled around, and her eyes widened in horror.

Liera, clothes torn and face bloody, was scrambling over the tops of several cherufin. Before the mindless creatures could react, she had launched herself into the court in front of them, scrambling upright on the stones. She ran directly at Kaelo.

Either due to the suddenness or the stupidity of Liera's crazed attack, neither Kaelo nor the phoenix immediately reacted to the Lady of Tura's advance. She did not appear to bear any weapons, and Kyna watched the woman with amazement as she approached her son in long legged strides.

Kaelo's eyes flashed, and he took a step backward, one hand twitching toward his sword hilt even as his knees bent as though to crouch to the stone. Sword or stone? Kaelo's moment of indecision gave Liera her chance. She slashed one hand forward, and Kyna saw a glint of metal. Liera did not aim for Kaelo's armored chest, or even the exposed throat just below his chin. She brought the knife down near the side of his face.

By reaction or luck, Kaelo ducked away from the blade just far enough that the knife left a long but thin streak of red from the bottom of his temple to the back of his jaw. As Liera stumbled forward, off balance from her attack, Kaelo regained his footing and leaped backward, drawing his crimson sword in a smooth motion. He stood with his feet apart in a steady stance, eyes and sword tip trained on his mother.

His expression was not one of fury, or even of surprise. Kaelo stared at Liera as though she had come at him with a strange and powerful weapon. His face was pallid.

The Lady of Tura seemed half insane, her eyes wild, and her appearance disarrayed in a way that suggested it was not merely a result of the recent fighting. Liera straightened, and a thin smile stretched over her face when she saw Kaelo's reaction.

Kyna had no idea what was happening. She was shocked by Liera's state, baffled as to why she had tried to attack the side of Kaelo's face, and still more confused by how seriously Kaelo seemed to be taking the failed attack. Before she could stop herself, she glanced back at Gellion. He looked furious.

So this is not part of a plan among the Turi.

But then Gellion's eyes widened in horror.

By the time Kyna turned her attention back to Liera, the woman was obscured by brilliant flame. Kyna cried out and jumped back from the inferno, nearly falling in her rush to get away from the blistering heat. There was a swirl of glistening wings and talons amid the flames, a screech and a scream, and then the fire receded.

Kyna stood in numb shock.

Where moments before had been her grandmother now lay a charred heap barely recognizable as a once living elf.

Smoke wafted past Kyna's face. She felt her insides heave.

Kyna clapped one hand to her mouth. The other she pressed desperately against her thigh, smashing the redstone into her wrist, but the terror now rising within Kyna could not be quelled by redstone. She needed to look away. She would throw up if she saw the horrifying wreckage any longer. She would throw up if she breathed.

With watering eyes and held breath, Kyna tore her eyes away from what had been Liera and looked up at her father.

Kaelo stood motionless. His feet were in the same wide stance, his sword still raised. His mouth was open, as though in a silent and frozen gasp, and he stared at the remains of his mother with wide eyes.

For a moment that seemed an eternity, all of Morcanan was silent.

Then the screaming began.

Every elf within sight of what had just occurred broke from the restraint that had held them while Kaelo spoke with Miyela. The uproar was incredible and spread outward from the court rapidly. Previously dropped weapons reappeared in hands, and elves began wild attempts to scramble over the cherufin as Liera had.

Kyna looked around in growing fear, expecting the elves to break through into the court any moment. She did not fear for her own safety —with the phoenix near her, no elf would be able to touch her—but if they provoked the phoenix further—Kyna's eyes flickered to Liera's remains, and she fought another surge of vomit.

The phoenix ruffled its feathers. Its throat glowed with fiery light, and it let out a beastial growl.

Stop, she pleaded to the rushing elves. *Someone has to stop them.*

She looked to her father for guidance, but Kaelo hardly seemed to have realized what was happening around him. He still stared at Liera.

"Father!"

Kaelo blinked. He raised his head. The sight around him seemed to surprise him, and he straightened from his crouch, turning to Miyela.

"Stop them or the city will fall in chaos." His voice seemed hoarse and distant—frayed.

Miyela's eyes were blazing. In Daro, the woman had made it no secret she disliked Liera, but to see the woman burned to death right in front of her by her enemy was obviously not something Miyela appreciated.

"You murderer," she growled.

"Stop them," Kaelo said again.

Miyela snarled and hissed through her teeth, but a moment later, she shouted, "Morcani, drop your weapons! You received my orders. They have not changed." Her words barely carried past the tumult of voices and weapons, but those Morcani nearest immediately grew still, and the effect rippled outward until three quarters of the elves were once more silent and subdued, though with murderous expressions. Only the Turi still fought.

The surrender of their comrades seemed to have no effect on the Turi whose leader had just been killed. They continued to fight against the cherufin, who stood stalwartly against the elves' wrath.

"Stop!" Miyela cried again. This time her voice carried much further, but the Turi paid it no heed.

The phoenix shrieked once more, and the cherufin turned on the elves.

The creatures did not touch those Morcani who had dropped their weapons, but actively fought the Turi. Heavy fists fell on bodies, weapons bent and snapped, and cries of fury mingled with cries of pain.

No.

Kyna sucked in a breath and took a step backward toward the mountain.

No, no, no.

"Father," she said.

Kaelo watched the mounting destruction with his arms at his sides.

"Father, please."

Kaelo did not look at her. He only shook his head. His expression was turned inward, almost dazed.

"They would ruin it," he whispered. "They would ruin it all. It is their choice."

"Retreat!" The familiar voice stabbed at Kyna's hollow insides. "Elves of Tura! Fall back! Out of the city!"

Gellion shouted as he fought against the cherufin restraining him. He bucked and twisted in their iron grip, swinging himself up against their arms to kick backward at their chests and heads. It did no good. His arms remained twisted behind his back, and the cherufin did not so much as flinch at his frenzied attacks.

Finally, Gellion gave up his efforts, going still between his captors.

"Turi!" he yelled. "Do not fight! Retreat!"

A hand grasped Kyna's arm.

"We must get off the ground," Kaelo said.

Kyna did not take her eyes off Gellion. He watched the chaos around him with furious frustration. Had he helped lead the Turi to

Morcanan expecting a last battle with the phoenix? Had he planned to confront his old mentor, maybe even her? A stab of pain ripped through Kyna's middle. Had he come to kill her? Imprison her? She did not know which would be worse.

The pressure on Kyna's arm increased.

"We must get off the ground," her father said again.

But at that moment, one of the cherufin next to Gellion collapsed.

Kyna pulled back against her father, her brows pulling together. The creature had not released its grip on Gellion, and Gellion cried out in pain as his left arm jerked down away from him.

The cherufin flailed its free arm, as though trying to pull itself up by something, then the entire body simply broke apart.

Kyna's mouth fell open.

A burly Remsgri elf stepped over the wreckage of the cherufin and swung a heavy mace at the legs of the creature still holding Gellion. It, too, fell in a mass of rock once its legs were a ruin.

Gellion staggered out of the rubble, clutching his left shoulder. The Remsgri elf steadied him and helped him get to clear ground. Then Gellion's eyes locked on Kyna and her father, flitting between the two of them with calculated intensity.

Kyna could not move under his gaze. Her mouth was still stupidly open, and she forgot all about her father's hand tightening on her arm. There was a grim determination in Gellion's face—that same cold dispassion she had seen earlier. Kyna shivered.

For a moment, the battle around her faded, leaving only the man behind her and the man before her, each connected by a past too distant for Kyna to comprehend, each with a painful stake in her soul. What would Gellion do now? Come at them with his friend's mace? Surely he was not as dimwitted as that? An overwhelming desire to run to Gellion washed through Kyna, and her eyes stung with tears of both longing and shame. Gellion would probably kill her before she got to him, if her father didn't stop her first.

Fortunately, the decision was made for her. Kyna felt herself jerked backward by her arm, and an instant later, a flurry of metallic feathers enveloped her. The sounds of battle returned to her ears—screams of fear, rage, and pain.

"Stop this!" she screamed. "Tell the phoenix to call them off!"

Her father did not answer.

"You can still cleanse the city without this!"

Her feet were somehow off the ground now, and without knowing exactly how she had come to be there, she was straddling the phoenix's slick body, one of her father's arms wrapped tightly around her middle.

A crack of stone sounded to Kyna's left, and the phoenix screamed in fury, careening sideways before righting itself and soaring straight upward. Kyna gasped and fell against the bird's neck. Her father held her steady, though she felt her insides attempting to drop through her feet.

When the phoenix snapped its wings to its sides and flattened its flight once more, Kyna looked down at the courtyard. A large pillar of stone stood in its center, Gellion standing next to it with his head tilted to the sky. Had her father raised the pillar to separate them from Gellion's wrath?

Around Gellion, cherufin streamed toward the mountain gates, which were beginning to open. The cherufin marched through the widening gap, and Gellion's diminutive form began to move away from the court into the streets leading out of the city.

The phoenix swooped closer to the buildings below, and Kyna's vision was obscured by crimson flame.

2 2

FIGHT OR FLIGHT

It was far more confusing than the battle at Arvain. Renyra was surrounded by elves and an army of possessed rocks, yet the majority of them did not fight. Fair haired elves stood motionless beside the streets, weapons at their feet. Some of them had gone inside buildings, but most stood in the chaos around them, facing the mountain. Renyra saw tears glistening on some of their faces, but more held expressions of grim resolve. The Morcani's leader had chosen their fate, and they would accept it until circumstances changed. They would not fight.

Part of Renyra saw the wisdom of Miyela's surrender, but the complete inaction of the Morcani stoked her anger as she struggled past them, dodging around marching rock creatures and trying to follow the Turi out of the city.

She did not know where Trali had gone and was having trouble keeping track of Alura, Raren, and Caerlyn. Firas she kept clasped to her hand, not allowing so much as a foot of space between them.

They stumbled through the streets, Firas's weight pulling her back as his remaining strength drained away. She hated herself for continuing to drag him on, but what other option did they have? If the Turi escaped the city without them, they would be trapped in Morcanan, and from the sound of Miyela's surrender, passage out of the city would not be a simple matter of catching the next Rale. So, with tears blurring her eyes, she pulled Firas harder.

Some of the Turi still fought, though more and more were turning and running as they realized the futility of their struggle. Those that attacked the rock creatures were invariably crushed, unless they managed to incapacitate one severely enough that its spirit fled. It seemed few elves had caught on to this strategy, however—that, or there simply were not enough suitable weapons for the task.

Raren and Alura ran in front of Renyra, occasionally glancing back at her and slowing their pace with obvious frustration.

"Here!" Caerlyn's voice called from behind Renyra. She appeared on the other side of Firas and took his arm.

Renyra smiled at her gratefully and moved her grip from Firas's hand to his elbow, though that appendage was even with her ear. Caerlyn, at least, might offer Firas some actual support.

"Where is Trali?" Renyra said.

"I don't know," said Caerlyn. "He ran off with that cursed mace. I hope he isn't getting himself killed with it. He can't fight all of these things by himself."

Renyra's eyes widened.

"Oh, I'm sure he's alright," Caerlyn said, looking guilty at the panic she had caused Renyra.

The air shimmered, then turned red.

Renyra screamed, throwing one arm over her head by instinct. She stumbled as the world careened and her mind spun. Then the flames were gone. She could see the torrent moving up the street in front of her.

"I really hate that," Renyra said.

"The gates!" a voice called from the streets behind Renyra. "Get to the gates!"

"Is that Gellion?" said Renyra.

"Sounded like it," said Caerlyn.

A glimmer of hope rose in Renyra's chest. Gellion had broken free, then. Somehow she felt more assured of their escape with him leading the charge behind her.

Stone cracked. Renyra flinched. He was still doing it. Renyra would be having a talk with Gellion after this, but if his secret got them out of Morcanan, she was not about to confront him now.

The sounds of snapping stone grew closer, and Gellion continued to shout orders and encouragement to the Turi. His cries were taken up by several elves, who ran down side streets to spread the message: To the gates. Get out of the city. Retreat to Tura and regroup to fight another day.

Firas tripped. He would have fallen to his knees if Caerlyn hadn't held him up, but the motion pulled at his back and he yelped in pain. The sound ripped through Renyra's insides.

"Just a little further," she said to him. "We just have to get through the gates, then you can rest, I promise. I'm sorry. I'm so sorry." She tried to make her voice soothing, but it sounded more like sobs.

Firas did not answer, but allowed himself to be dragged forward once more. They didn't run now. Elves passed them on both sides.

"Trali!"

The Remsgri spun around and his face brightened to see them.

"Ah, there you are!" he said. He took a leaping stride forward and brought his mace into the knees of a passing rock creature, bringing the weapon around for a backhanded swing at its head as it fell.

"We are *retreating*, Trali," Caerlyn said. "Drop that thing and help us with Firas."

"I too am retreating," said Trali. "I am just taking out enemies as I do it."

Raren and Alura had dropped back to walk beside Renyra.

"I can do it." Raren put a hand on Renyra's shoulder, reaching for Firas. Renyra's hands tightened on Firas's arm.

"It's alright," Raren said gently. "I've got him. You follow behind."

Reluctantly, Renrya let Raren slip into her place.

She jumped as the ground to her right cracked and sank into a pit. A rock creature fell into the gap, and its head and arms broke off upon hitting the edge of the pit. Then the ground snapped back together so fast Renyra hardly processed what had happened as the decapitated monster launched a few feet into the air and fell back to the street. Red and green vapor leached from the cracks of its broken body.

A flash of dark red hair bounced passed them. Gellion was running,

Veldon and Valder at his heels. Stone broke and creatures fell in a wake ahead of him. Renyra stared in disbelief. Gellion did not seem to be touching the ground with his hands as she had seen Kaelo and Kyna do. He carried no weapons and held one arm tightly against his body as he ran. How was Gellion doing it?

Gellion took a flying leap over two crumbled rock creatures, and Renyra almost laughed as his legs bent and exposed his feet. They were bare. As he touched down, cracks extended out from where his feet fell, and a pillar of stone broke upward under a creature twenty feet away from him.

A shout of pain pulled Renyra's attention from Gellion.

"Trali!" Alura had stopped in her tracks, her hands over her mouth.

Renyra went cold. Trali had fallen to the ground, his mace dropped several paces to the side. A rock creature stood over him and was raising a fist to finish its attack.

Raren dropped his hold on Firas and dove for the mace. Renyra stepped forward to steady Firas as he swayed, and watched with terror as Raren swung the weapon at the creature's legs with all the might he could muster.

It only made contact with one leg. The creature fell sideways, and Alura just managed to pull Trali's legs out of the way before it crashed to the ground. Raren scrambled to his feet and brought the mace down on the thing's other leg over and over until it crumbled beneath his blows and the spirits rose from the monster.

Alura was at Trali's side, cradling his head.

"Is he—" Renyra could not finish the question.

"He's breathing," Alura said. "But it got him in the head."

"Get him off the road," Raren panted, moving to help his sister with Trali's weight.

There were still rock creatures marching through the streets, and fleeing elves did not look where their feet fell as they ran to the gates of Morcanan. Renyra and Caerlyn helped Firas off the street, dodging through bodies, both flesh and stone.

Renyra looked desperately at the gates. They were close. Close enough that a running elf would reach them in about a minute. But carrying Trali and dragging Firas?

The terrible cry of the phoenix echoed through the city. The rock creatures paused in the street, then turned on the spot and started marching toward the gates.

"No," Renyra said.

"What?" said Caerlyn, looking up from her inspection of Trali.

"They're going to the gates. Those creatures. The phoenix is sending them there."

Raren stood, craning his neck to try and see the gates better.

"The Turi are still running out of it. Looks like Gellion's there now, getting elves through and fighting any monsters that try to prevent it. You're right though, more of the rock monsters are converging on him."

"We have to get to the gates," Renyra said. "We have to get out." She looked between Firas and Trali desperately. Firas was slumped against the side of a building. His eyes were open, but clouded with exhaustion and pain. Trali was still out cold, one side of his face slick with blood.

"I ... I can help Alura with Firas. You two." She looked to Caerlyn and Raren. "Do you think you can handle Trali? Drag him?"

Caerlyn nodded, though she looked far from confident.

They took to the streets once more, now moving even slower than before. Renyra kept her eyes fixed on the gates. They were beginning to close.

Riu save us. Hold the gates. Please.

Renrya wanted to scream from their agonizing pace.

The gates stopped moving.

Renyra could hear grinding stone.

"What's happening?" She rose onto the balls of her feet, but could not see the base of the gates.

"Gellion's stopped the gates from closing," said Raren. "The Turi are still running out, though not many of them are left. He's fighting rock monsters too, though. They're trying to get to him now. I doubt he can hold the gates much longer."

Come on. Just a little longer.

"Can you jog with him?" Renyra said to Raren and Caerlyn.

The two picked up their feet into a lurching jog. Renyra and Alura matched their pace, Firas staggering between them.

A deafening crash came from the gates, and half a dozen rock creatures flew through the air.

It happened again.

The gates shuddered, cracked, then started to close once more.

Renyra just made out a flash of red hair whipping through the center of the stone slabs, then the gates smashed closed.

Renyra stopped.

She watched the gates, waiting for them to break, to open again. They didn't.

"Are there other gates?" Renyra said to no one in particular.

"Not like this one." Firas spoke in a hoarse whisper. "There are smaller entrances—along the walls."

"Looks like those monsters have formed a perimeter around the city, though." Caerlyn nodded to the walls to either side of the gates.

She was right. The rock creatures had formed a line along the city walls. They were guarding the openings they had made to break into the city.

The adrenaline leached out of Renyra, leaving cold emptiness in its wake. There was no way out. The Turi were gone.

Slowly, she turned back to face Morcanan. In the distance, the phoenix flew over the Great City, pouring its crimson flames over stark buildings and motionless elves.

JUDGMENT

It felt strange to sit on a bed again, even one as thin and sparse as this. Furs were piled on the floor where Kyna had pushed them away. She wanted to feel the cool, musty air against her skin. She wanted to feel the solidity of the stone walls, the heavy essence surrounding her that bespoke of thick rock and soil—a blanket of earth between her and the world.

She took a deep breath, relishing the familiar scents. With closed eyes, she could imagine the mountains around her were not the Terulians, but the Falspires. Her thoughts extended outward, to the slopes of crops leading to the quiet town of Suri Ranta. Beyond, the glassy sound glittered between mountain peaks, teeming with fish and boats. And spirits.

Kyna's arms tightened around her knees. The spirits had always unnerved her. They were insidious things, worming their way into animals and plants, water and fire, stone and wind. They had infused everything in those mountains. Taking a deep breath, Kyna rested her head against her arms. In truth, she could not recall anything endearing about her home in Tala, except that it had been hers—it had been predictable, sensible. She longed for it simply because it was something less complicated than Daro or Tura or Morcanan. It was something that did not cause her an agony she had never known could exist.

Fear rose in Kyna's throat. She swallowed it down. To think of the last days was to relive them. She would not. She could not.

Yet the memories crept into her mind like mist. Gellion's look of callous contempt. Liera's crazed eyes and shocking death. An army of monsters breaking the weapons and bones of elves.

Kyna squeezed her eyes closed. Of all these images, it was Gellion's face that latched most often to her unattended thoughts. He was alive. He was real. What, then, did that mean of the grief Kyna had battled all these months? Was that real, or was it now meaningless? She sighed and opened her eyes. What did it matter? The anguish consuming Kyna was so complete, fed by so many different sources, that no one cause seemed important enough to consider on its own. Even the strength of her anguish had faded in light of its constant presence. She was learning to live with it, though her mind was undoubtedly cracking under the strain.

Her hand strayed to the small lump of stone concealed in her pocket, and a new thrill of panic shot through her body. It had been madness, what she had done. Even now she could not fully explain her actions. She had simply had to do something. She had had to retaliate in some small way. Her lips twitched into a smile, and she shook her head at the insanity she was sure was stealing over her. At least it was an insanity apart from whatever now dwelled within her father.

The smile vanished. She pulled her hand away from the stone.

She had stayed in her room too long. It was surely well past dawn now, and her father would be expecting her. With a shuddering sigh, Kyna wiped her hands over her face and stood to dress.

The caverns of Morcanan were not cheery, but they bore a sort of comfort in the soft glow of their lamps. Kyna made her way to the central chamber of the caverns with ease. It had only been two days since her arrival in the strange city, but the paths within the mountain were as meticulously organized as those without and were marked at the corners by different colored lamps.

The central chamber was tall and wide, with pinpoints of light streaking down from silvery holes in the ceiling above. At its center, Kaelo paced.

The pacing had only begun last night. Before that, her father had spent the last days nearly comatose, staring at various floors or walls with a heavy brow and stormy eyes. He had roused himself to confront Miyela on a few occasions, but had otherwise remained silent and brooding. Kyna wondered if he spoke with the phoenix during these times. The bird, too, was in the chamber. Kyna watched it warily as it fanned its wings. It's fiery eyes locked on her as she stepped into the space.

The phoenix had not deigned to speak to Kyna since their arrival in Morcanan. Kyna was not one to complain about this, but she did wonder what the beast might be whispering to her father without her knowledge. Kyna looked at the phoenix with a burning hatred. No more did she harbor any illusions as to the nature of the monster her father had raised. The beast was conniving, manipulative, and cruel. It had twisted her father's ambitions into something terrible—something she was beginning to fear neither she nor her father had the power to stop.

But you could. You could run to the phoenix right now and try to destroy it.

Would her father stop her? Would he go so far as to kill her rather than let her destroy his precious and twisted creation? Her heart raced at the thought of it. She couldn't. The phoenix would kill her before she could kill it, she was sure. Then none but her father would possess the knowledge necessary to end this. But what good was knowledge if the possessor never used it?

To pass it on to those who will.

But pass it on to whom? Every elf in Riure hated her. She sympathized with the feeling.

Her father had not noticed her arrival. Since the scene in the court, she had hardly spoken to him. She didn't know what to say. It had been obvious by her father's reaction that Liera's death had not come by his command, nor would he have had time to stop its execution, but somehow Kyna still blamed him for the gruesome death. Kaelo had not called off the cherufin or the phoenix after his mother's murder, nor had he attempted to punish or exert control over the phoenix after Morcanan was conquered.

Only a few days ago, Kaelo had told Kyna to trust him, but that trust was growing so thin, Kyna did not know how much longer she could hold to it without falling with her father into whatever pit of madness the phoenix had created in his mind.

Kaelo did not halt the stride of his pacing until the scuff of Kyna's feet was close enough to break through his thoughts. He rounded on her with black eyes and a half a snarl. Kyna took a step back, her heart lurching.

"Oh," he said when he saw her. Then he began to walk again, as though she had not interrupted.

Kyna watched her father with rising alarm. His steps landed with focused force, and his eyes scanned the ground before him, his jaw working. His hand occasionally rose to the thin cut along the side of his face, as though itching at it. Kyna puckered her brow at the motion, thinking again of her father's strange reaction to Liera's attack. Something had deeply disturbed him about it. Was it his fear that had urged the phoenix to kill Liera? Was that fear part of his current state? Her father had always been a man of few words and dark moods, but he had never been erratic or neurotic. Kyna could no longer predict his reactions or his moods.

"I was waiting for you," he said, not looking at her. "We are leaving this morning."

"Leaving?"

"You will stay here."

Oh. That 'we.'

"Miyela has been compliant so far, and the cherufin will remain with orders, but they are not adaptable without the phoenix here. You will stay and ensure Morcanan remains under control until we return. No elves are to leave. If things get out of hand, break the Rale line."

Kyna stared at her father. When her silence stretched, Kaelo stopped his pacing at last and faced her.

"You have questions?" Kaelo spoke as a commander to a soldier.

"I—where are you going?"

"To cleanse the rest of the Morcani lands."

"Oh." Kyna had almost forgotten that vierstone still remained in the lands south of Morcanan. The slight lifting in her chest that accompanied the realization horrified her, and guilt stole through her veins. For weeks she had convinced herself that she was still loyal to both her father and his cause. She had hoped that confirming her fears about the phoenix would put to rest the other doubts creeping within her mind, that by placing all the blame of her reservations upon the corrupted beast, the resolve of her true purpose would shine bright once more. It did not. Her hand strayed to the lump in her pocket. The rash theft had been a retaliation against the atrocities of the phoenix—the rebellion of a child—but now she was beginning to fear her own underlying motivations. She closed her hands into fists.

"And then?"

Kaelo's face was hard, yet his eyes did not bear the same resolve as he turned them to the floor.

"Then we go to Tura."

A heaviness settled over Kyna, pressing down on her lungs and dropping into her shoulders. It was as she had feared, then. The phoenix would not stop until all of Faeran was under its control, and it would take a greater fool than Kyna to think the monster would give up that power once won.

This wasn't supposed to happen. The phoenix was supposed to follow his orders—a dumb beast to be destroyed once its purpose was fulfilled.

"Father." Kyna's voice was barely a whisper. She looked up at him, pleading, begging some part of him to come back to her—to end the terror they had unleashed.

Kaelo raised his eyes.

The trace of confidence in Kaelo's face that Kyna had been clinging to these last weeks was now absent. He was a man overpowered by his own creation, and he knew it. He accepted it.

It was that acceptance that snapped something in Kyna. A sudden blaze of heat lit up along her spine and laced through her body. Her father would not fight. He would not destroy the phoenix as he had promised, but would ride its power beyond his own ambitions. He would pursue not revolution, but total control. He would pursue vengeance.

The last of Kyna's trust and hope shattered. Her father was lost. What, then, was she?

"It killed your mother." Kyna glared at her father. His flinch was barely noticeable, but its presence drove Kyna on. "It *murdered* your own blood. It killed hundreds of elves out there, and it did it without your permission."

A purring growl emitted from the other side of the chamber. Kyna did not let her eyes move toward the sound.

Kaelo was utterly still. He looked down at Kyna with a wooden expression, though Kyna could sense the cold anger rising within him.

"She knew, Kyna," Kaelo said. "Liera *knew*. Do you not understand? In her moment of chance, she did not try to kill me, but to take my power. How can we know what other elves she has told?"

Kyna's eyes moved to the healing cut on her father's face. Just beyond the dried and darkened blood, a brighter spot of crimson shone against the skin of his ear.

She knew.

Redstone. Liera had known something of redstone and tried to cut it away from her son. But how? How could the elves possibly know? What more had they learned since Kyna's departure?

Kaelo's voice softened to a deadly whisper.

"My mother spent her life hating me. She led elves to death and to hypocrisy with her selfish pride, and she would have destroyed you and me, even if it meant seizing the same power against which she fought— even if it meant condemning her whole people."

Kyna shook her head. That Liera may have known of the power of redstone did nothing to change what the phoenix had done to her, or what Kaelo had allowed thereafter.

"The same people you pursued and killed after her death," Kyna said.

Kaelo's control cracked. His eyes flashed, and he took a jerking step toward Kyna.

"They would have destroyed us! They were possessed of the same righteous passion as their foolish leader!"

"And so they deserved to die?" Kyna spoke as calmly as she could manage, though her treacherous voice quavered. "Does life mean so little to you now that you give yourself the right to dictate it by your own judgment?"

"My judgment," Kaelo hissed, "is the only judgment untainted by the poison that flows through the veins of those I seek to change."

"The only one?"

Kaelo's eyes moved over Kyna, as though remembering for the first time who she was.

"Do I not possess the same soundness of judgment?" Kyna said. "The same pure soul untainted by that which you call poison?"

Kaelo narrowed his eyes. "You did," he said.

Kyna ignored the past tense. "Then hear my judgment." She did her best to stand tall, ignoring the more sensible side of herself screaming at her to keep her mouth shut. "The phoenix has overstepped its bounds. It has twisted the goal we strove to achieve my entire life, and it has corrupted your thoughts and actions. You have forgotten your purpose —or at least the purpose you shared with me—and are now committing the same heartless acts for which you were once condemned with no regard for their consequences, so long as they further your goals. You have broken your word."

Kyna waited for fire to come. She waited to join Liera as a stinking corpse of meat and bone. To her surprise, she found she no longer cared. Her life's goal was now ashes in her mouth. What did it matter? She wondered vaguely if her father would still bow to his phoenix after it destroyed her.

But no fire came. The phoenix remained silent, watching the exchange between father and daughter with calculating eyes.

Kaelo stared at Kyna as though she had just pushed a knife through his gut. He nodded to himself slowly, and something seemed to confirm in his eyes.

"My word," he said softly. His mouth turned up in a humorless smile. "Never have I lied to you, Kyna. I have spoken nothing but truth to any elf I have ever known. It is they, not I, who have all broken the trust of both tongue and kinship." He closed his eyes, and his smile twisted into a grimace. Then he raised his head and looked at Kyna. "Go, then."

Kyna went rigid. "What?"

"Go." Kaelo's voice was cold and flat. He looked at Kyna in the same way she had seen him look at Liera each time she denounced him. "Against my better judgment, I trusted you. I broke my own rule. It was my fault. Tainted by vierstone or not, trust is a foolish exercise reserved for the naive." He shook his head, and his words softened, turning inward. "I will not wait for your betrayal to ruin all I have worked for."

Kyna's breath came shallow and quick. She looked between her father and the phoenix. Being murdered by the phoenix's own rashness was one thing, but to be burned under her father's command? He wouldn't. He couldn't.

Kaelo was still shaking his head, his jaw working. He glanced at her, but did not seem able to hold her gaze.

"Get out of Morcanan," he said at last. The words were low and toneless. "Leave the city and do with your life as you see fit."

Kyna did not move at once. She felt numb. Empty. There was so much more she wanted to say to him, but her mouth had gone dry, and the words in her mind would not come into order.

Her father had made his choice. There was nothing more she could do. She waited until he looked at her once more and forced him to hold her gaze.

Then she turned and walked away.

Her steps were measured and calm, though it took all of her effort not to collapse or run. Still she waited for the fire to come.

"Wait."

Kyna stopped.

"Leave the stone."

For a moment, Kyna's heart stood still. The stone. He knew. How —she let out a bitter snort as she forced rationalization upon her panic. The redstone.

She wrapped her hand around the cuff at her wrist, running her fingers along its smooth leather. How often had she resorted to this motion through her trials in Daro and in Tura? Once, she had even ripped the redstone from her wrist in a fit of rage and grief. Without it, she was useless, powerless, nothing. Gritting her teeth, she undid the clasp and let both cuff and stone fall to the ground.

Taking a slow breath, she forced back the tears threatening to break through her control and resumed her steady stride. She counted the rhythm of each step all the way through the caverns and out into the court. It was not until the buildings closed around her, hiding her from the mountain, that she began to run.

As she ran, she plunged her hand into her pocket, grasping the stone —the other stone—within her bare grip. Her grief sharpened. Her sense of betrayal and her anguish flared as burning heat through her body, but so too did her resolve strengthen. She could not have stayed with them. She could not have borne the burden of her guilt and fear much longer. She could not have kept the stone hidden.

Elves stared at her as she tore through the streets. Did any recognize her? Kyna did not meet any eyes, keeping her blurring gaze trained on the gates of the city. Before she reached them, the cry of the phoenix filled the air, and Kyna looked back to see the bird rising against the mountain.

The cherufin opened the gate, and she stumbled through, falling to her knees at last as the gate ground closed behind her. Another cry sounded, and a shadow fell over her.

The phoenix swooped low enough that the flames trailing from its tail nearly brushed Kyna. She doubled over, shielding her head with her arms.

When she finally looked up again, the phoenix was a silhouette in the distance. She watched the shape until it disappeared beyond the hills.

Kyna drew the smooth stone from her pocket. Light shimmered off of its surface, and her fingertips warmed where they touched it. She relished the pain that warmth opened within her. She greeted her grief with bitter satisfaction. It was all she had left to hold on to. At least she knew now the phoenix had lied about one thing. It could not sense vierstone.

Pocketing the stone, Kyna stood on shaking legs and began to walk, not bothering to wipe away the tears coursing down her cheeks.

2 4

TO LEAD A KINDOM

The flowers were as big as Gellion's head. Even from the edge of the river, he could see the swirls of color on their petals. Orange and red. Could the Council not have picked any other color? The fanning petals looked like frozen flames in the reflection of the sun. The water around them was stained crimson by the dying light. Gellion grimaced and turned away. Elves lined the river to either side of him. No voices broke the rhythm of the wind and water around him. Even the birds were silent. For that at least, Gellion was grateful. The brash calls would only intensify the morbidity of the scene.

Gellion's insides still twisted when he thought of the scene before the mountain of Morcanan, but far worse than his disgust and his fury was his relief.

"Come on," said Veldon. His hand rested on Gellion's uninjured shoulder, guiding him away from the river. The flowers had all passed them now. The elves were free to go.

Gellion followed his brother away from the Orhiri River. Valder and Tornac walked behind them. For once, Valder's expression matched his eldest brother's. His jaw was set, and his eyes burned in brooding anger. It was the same anger that ran like a current through the Turi—hot and powerful. So why did it not touch Gellion?

Gellion and his brothers walked past the Central Tower, its shadow casting a long stain over the Public Quarter. Veldon was leading them to the apartments they still shared in the guest quarters. Gellion didn't know what they would do shut up in their rooms the rest of the evening. It was far too early to attempt sleep, but he had no better ideas. Undoubtedly, Veldon wanted to talk. Veldon had attempted conversation through the whole journey back from Morcanan, but no one had been in the mood for discussion. The entire army had been silent through the days of their return. The silence would have to break soon. There was a Council meeting at first light in the morning, to be followed by the election of a new leader. Gellion had never witnessed the forced election of a leader during times of hardship. It was a different protocol entirely from the usual election process. A new Lord or Lady of Tura would have to be selected by the end of the morning, nominated by those already on the Council and approved by the Turi army—those elves whose lives would be most closely tied to the identity of their new leader.

Gellion did need to talk with his brothers before any of this happened. If only he had decided what to say.

The apartment was in sight when Tornac put a hand to Gellion's elbow and pulled him back. Gellion stiffened at the touch and turned to face Tornac.

"Could we talk a moment?" Tornac said.

Gellion glanced at Valder and Veldon, who had paused and were looking at their older brothers curiously.

"I—" Gellion tried to think of an excuse to refuse and hoped for a moment that Valder or Veldon would speak up, but neither option came to his rescue. "Alright," he said.

Valder and Veldon moved on toward the apartment, exchanging a look as they turned their heads.

Tornac stood in the middle of the street, looking profoundly uncomfortable.

"Shall we walk?" he said after several beats of silence.

Gellion nodded and stepped beside Tornac, watching the ground as they passed the apartment.

"I have been meaning to talk to you," Tornac said.

Gellion waited for him to continue. He did not.

"Well, now you are," Gellion said.

Tornac let out a soft snort. "Not very well." He shook his head and stopped again, as though deciding that walking and speaking at the same time was too difficult. He looked at Gellion.

"You handled yourself well in Morcanan." His eyes were as serious as Gellion had ever seen them without a fire of anger or scorn behind them. "You handled the Turi well after Liera's death."

Gellion blinked in surprise. Of all the scenarios he had been imagining when Tornac asked to talk to him, compliments had not entered into a single one of them.

"Thank you." Gellion spoke the words as almost a question with an edge bordering on sarcasm.

"I'm serious, Gellion." Tornac waited until Gellion met his eyes again. "I was wrong when I said you hadn't changed since I last saw you. You have."

Gellion's expression did not soften. "Or maybe you never truly knew me before."

Tornac's lips thinned. He opened his mouth to speak, then shut it again and took a breath.

"What I am trying to say," he said. "Is I am sorry for the blame I placed on you. I am sorry for holding you responsible for Valder and Veldon and for assuming you acted in rash bravado taking the elves to battle. I just could not believe you would willingly lead elves back into war after having lived through what we did. It was beyond my ability to reason. I know that you got through the Great War relatively unscathed, but—"

"Excuse me?" Gellion stared at Tornac in stark disbelief. So great was his shock, he did not even immediately summon the rage he knew Tornac's words should incite. "*Unscathed?*"

"I am not saying it was easy for you. And father—" He shook his head and looked away. "But it did not affect you like it affected the rest of us, Gellion. While we drowned in fear and stress and sorrow, you seemed to float above it, laughing and joking and taking everything in stride. And afterward, you could not even see how you held us together. You left us."

When Tornac raised his eyes to Gellion, they were glossed with pain. "I had just lost the love of my life. I had just lost Vyra, and then father, and then you left me to sink in my grief alone. And you never looked back."

A cool numbness stole through Gellion's body. Tornac's interpretation of Gellion's experience in the war was so false and warped he wanted to laugh with bitter mirth, but the sinking of his stomach at Tornac's final words stole away the desire. He did not know how to respond. There was too much—too many words, too much disparity between their worlds and minds and memories.

"You are wrong," Gellion finally said. He spoke in a low voice—controlled and even. "If you think the war did not affect me, then my outward illusion was far more effective than that within myself." He looked straight at Tornac, and for once, he tried to strip away the mask over his inward struggle, to lay bear his pain and his grief and his anxiety in the depths of his eyes. "It destroyed me, Tornac. It *destroyed* me. I watched all of your pain and wondered that mine was so much sharper, so much heavier and piercing and hot. It would have pulled me under—it would have broken me. So I did all in my power to push it away. I *couldn't* stay in Maramor after that war after all I had seen in that city, all I had lost. I could not live in a place of ghosts and see my own memories and nightmares reflected back at me in the faces of those I had shared them with every day of the rest of my life. I couldn't look back."

Tornac had been staring at Gellion with an expression that was as unreadable as it was out of place on his face. He looked as though Gellion had just explained to him that the phoenix was truly a caring and benevolent being, only misunderstood.

"You never said anything to me," Tornac said. "To any of us. Why?"

"To acknowledge it would have been to accept it. It would have drowned me."

Tornac frowned, then nodded. "It did drown me," he said softly.

"I didn't know."

Tornac nodded again.

Gellion's lips quirked into a grimace. "I thought you would all be better without me. Turns out my leaving only imposed my poor fortune onto the elven race as a whole."

Tornac moved his head slowly from side to side, a line between his brows.

"No," he said. "The disasters Kaelo has wrought do not lay at your feet. They would have happened whether or not you were in Daro." He looked at Gellion thoughtfully. "I think your leaving Maramor may be what holds the elves together." He raised his eyebrows. "If what I saw in Morcanan is any indication."

Gellion snorted, but he could feel a pull in his chest at Tornac's words. He wanted them to be true. He wanted it so badly that it did not seem possible it could ever come to fruition.

Tornac's lips parted, then he smiled. It was a humorless smile that turned into a humorless laugh.

"By Riu, Gellion, in all this time—we just might be as similar as Valder and Veldon."

Gellion's lips curved into a grimace. "Only their similarities attract while ours quite obviously repel."

Tornac's own grimace softened. "Only if we let them." He raised an eyebrow.

Gellion nodded and wondered for a moment what the two of them could have been together in all those centuries of unspoken resentment and misconstrued assumptions. Then he set the thought aside. He would never know, and it did not matter.

"Shall we go back to the apartment?" Gellion said. "I believe we have some matters to discuss."

Tornac nodded with a sudden solemnity that was not quite serious in its intensity.

Gellion smiled and turned back the way they had come, Tornac following behind.

The apartment was exactly as they had left it a week before. Gellion could not explain why this was strange, as no elf would have been here to disturb anything, but it seemed unfitting that so much had changed in his world while Tura went on exactly as before. He expected the same would have been true if Daro had still been there to greet him after the battle at Arvain, but that Great City, at least, had fallen with the rest of his world.

"Tea?" Veldon was waiting at the kitchen table with a steaming pot, four glasses, and Valder.

Gellion and Tornac walked to the table and sat. Veldon poured steaming liquid into each of their cups, then sat back with his brows drawn over his eyes. He and Valder were both looking between Gellion and Tornac as though trying to read the content of their discussion upon their faces. Gellion kept his own face carefully neutral. He felt strange. To say he and Tornac had reconciled their differences and would now be as close as Valder and Veldon was an exaggeration bordering on laughable falsehood, but something had clearly changed between them. Still, something told him it was a change best left between himself and Tornac.

Gellion took a breath, then wrapped one hand around his cup. He shifted in his chair, wincing at the pain still throbbing dully in his left shoulder. He had taken the sling off this morning, but he could tell it would be several days before he had full use of the appendage again.

"Well?" Gellion said when the silence stretched to a minute.

Veldon blinked and took a tentative sip of his tea. "I, for one, have been trying to have this discussion for days. I assumed that if I began it, I would be promptly silenced once more." The twinkle in his eye belied the stiffness of his words.

"You have our permission," Gellion said.

Veldon smiled. "Alright then. What is the plan? How do we oppose Kaelo when he comes to Tura?"

Gellion felt a stab of foreboding at Veldon's words. His discussion with Tornac now seemed a small and inconsequential thing as the weight of their situation fell upon him once more.

"Are you saying we should fight him?" Gellion said.

Veldon raised his eyebrows. "You would have us surrender?"

"He has already destroyed all the vierstone in Riure," Gellion said. "What more is there to fight for?"

Veldon's eyes flashed. "You know there is worse to come. This is no longer about vierstone alone."

"You saw what he can do with those cherufin." Gellion tried to keep his voice calm, but an edge of anger touched it nonetheless. "Nor am I convinced he wouldn't let the phoenix turn loose on the city if we resisted hard enough. Our chances against him were precarious enough when it was us against an elf and a phoenix. Even with redstone, I cannot fight an entire army."

"That's why we make sure it's not an army you are fighting," Veldon said.

Gellion looked at Veldon and shook his head.

"I already tried to challenge Kaelo by himself. He won't accept, nor do I blame him. His power is absolute with his phoenix and army. He will not duel me merely to preserve his honor."

"He never answered you, actually," said Valder. "You were —interrupted."

Gellion flinched. Liera's charge had been untimely and foolish. She had ruined everything and lost her life for it. The woman's gruesome death had horrified Gellion, yet now, the only grief he could manage to summon was for his lost chance against Kaelo. Liera had been mad. She had nearly thrown Gellion in prison for treason against the elves when he was the only hope of their victory.

She was still the Lady of Tura.

Gellion had known Liera since he was a child. She had always been shrewd, but she had shown him kindness and led the elves as well as she could through the war. Shouldn't he feel regret at her death? Pain at the loss of an elven life? Yet the terrible and familiar pull of grief and horror Gellion had just admitted to Tornac was not where it should be—where it had always been. Even picturing Kyna's face caused him more pain than imagining Liera's death. Gellion tentatively reached toward the pit of despair that had consumed him following Dulon's death, but found nothing. He frowned and pictured the Lord of Daro's face. Dulon's smiling countenance appeared, his hair falling artfully over his face before he tossed it away. The face dissolved into a blood stained memory, yet Gellion only felt cool anger toward the events that had led to his friend's death.

As for Kyna—Gellion tried to close his mind to her, but it was like trying to cover a stain the size of a room with only his hands. That he had reacted to Kyna's presence with anything but contempt and hatred was unacceptable, a betrayal of his body. That must be it. Treachery and betrayal did not lessen one's physical attraction. Gellion had simply reacted to the base feelings he had once borne for the woman. Why, then, had the feelings not faded upon his return to Tura? Why did his confusion remain? He had heard Kyna's pleas to her father as he pulled her to the phoenix. She had begged him to call off the cherufin. But had she tried to stop Liera's death? Had her pleas done any good for the elves? Getting cold feet after seeing the more gruesome results of one's decisions was not proof of bravery or a change of heart.

"What would it accomplish if Gellion did duel Kaelo?" Tornac said.

Gellion pulled himself back to the conversation with considerable effort.

"That phoenix is as autonomous as an elf," Tornac said. "At least Kaelo can be reasoned with. Take him out of the equation and we're left with the same demonic enemy as in the Great War."

"What do you suggest, then?" Valder's voice held an edge of annoyance.

Tornac ran a hand through his hair and closed his eyes.

"Maybe we could incapacitate him? Capture him? If he holds power over the phoenix, we could force him to subdue it."

Gellion nodded.

"What about the cherufin?" said Veldon. "If we manage to capture Kaelo, they'll swarm us."

"I can deal with them," said Gellion.

"Maybe." Veldon did not look convinced. "I think it's a plan we will have to consider, but I still think we are going about this the wrong way. The Remsgri had it right. Target the phoenix, not its master. Kaelo we can handle on his own." He nodded toward Gellion. "But I'm just not convinced we can get at the phoenix through Kaelo, not unless his control over it is directly tied to his redstone. It's still worth separating Kaelo from the stone, but—" He shook his head. "I keep coming back to father."

"We don't have time to solve a mystery right now," Gellion said. "Kaelo could be here any day."

"We may not have time to solve a mystery, but we must solve one nonetheless." Veldon's tone was hard. "Even if we do not pursue the same path as father, we must use our heads to defeat this enemy. The proof that force alone will not work is extensive and absolute."

"Then let us use our heads." Tornac leaned forward over the table, his tea pushed to the side. "What do we know of this phoenix? We know how it was made—more or less. We know what it is capable of."

"It's made of vierstone ash," said Gellion. "Using this." He pulled the redstone from his pocket and threw it on the table.

"So," said Valder. "The phoenix is made of vierstone?"

"Not necessarily," said Veldon. "We do not know the extent of redstone's power. If it can destroy vierstone, maybe it can turn it into something else."

"Life?" Tornac's brows knit. "How can any stone create life from another stone, even if one of them is vierstone?"

Veldon frowned. "Do you think the phoenix is really alive?"

Tornac raised his eyebrows. "As opposed to what?"

"I don't know. But I'm not convinced those cherufin are living creatures." He shook his head. "I've studied vierstone for a while, Tornac. There is a reason we call it lifestone. We say Kaelo kills vierstone when he turns it black, and I think that term is correct. The stone does have a sort of life to it."

Gellion took in a sharp breath. He stared at the crimson rock on the table.

"What?" Valder said.

They were all watching Gellion, but he was not ready to speak yet. His mind was still working, trying to piece together possibilities. The phoenix had risen from the ash of vierstone, but it seemed impossible that it should now be made of the stuff. How would it destroy vierstone with its breath, or raise stone creatures? It was possible that the phoenix was simply possessed of a demonic magic unknown to the elves, but was there another possibility?

"Redstone," he said. "We say it is almost identical to vierstone in its appearance, its touch, its feel, except that its current—its life—runs in the opposite direction. It has it too, that life you speak of." He nodded to Veldon. "It's somehow linked to vierstone. What if the phoenix is *made* of redstone?"

Gellion's brothers stared at him, then each of their eyes lowered to the stone on the table.

"Could it be so obvious?" A smile pulled at Valder's lips.

"What?" said Tornac.

"Well, the phoenix is *red*. It's flames are red too, when it destroys vierstone."

Veldon's eyes were round. "If the entire creature were made of redstone, could Kaelo control it by touching it?" He looked to Gellion.

"I have no idea," Gellion admitted. "This rock," he pointed at the stone on the table, "is hardly comparable to a phoenix. It is possible, though."

"But the phoenix in the Great War could speak," said Tornac. "And it had no master to control it."

"It's master was Olcon, wasn't it?" Valder grimaced, but the sarcasm in his face was unsure. The elves would never be able to prove or disprove their theory that the demonic bird had been raised by the devil himself. It seemed the stuff of silly legend and superstition, but any elf who had faced the beast or its armies of corrupted spirits and animated dead would not scoff at the possibility.

"So what if it is made of redstone?" said Gellion. "How does that help us?"

"Well, maybe *you* could control it," said Veldon. "The phoenix, I mean. Or any of us for that matter, though you have the most experience manipulating that stone." He glanced distastefully at the rock on the table.

"But I can't affect the redstone itself," said Gellion. "I use it to control other things. It's a tool. You can't cut a sword with its own blade."

Veldon's eyes clouded in thought. He rested his chin on a fist.

"But you can cut a sword with another sword. When I craft—" he paused and pain crossed his face. "When I *crafted* vierstone, I did not solely use the influence of the vierstone that I was crafting. I still felt the warmth and energy of the stone in my earring when working with vierstone in my hands. Vierstone behaved more like rock, metal, or stone depending upon how I worked it. Although, I think it was more than simply behaving more like one substance over another. I think the vierstone took on the *role* of whatever substance I wished it to emulate. I was able to influence vierstone using the understanding gained by vierstone. Does that make sense?"

Valder was staring at Veldon with an open mouth. Tornac's brows were almost touching. Gellion did not try to comprehend the nuances of Veldon's description. He focused on its meaning.

"So what you're saying is," he said. "I should be able to exert control over the phoenix so long as I have an external bit of what it's made of?"

Veldon shrugged. "I don't know. The phoenix is alive in at least some sense. We have no way of knowing what sort of control you would have over its mind, even if all of these theories are right. But it's all I can think of, and we're running out of options."

Memory and emotion were slow to come back to Gellion when he woke the next morning. He stared at the ceiling of his room and waited for the events and discussions of the day before to roll over him. A funeral. Lives and relationships altered. His thoughts moved to the day at hand, and he rose with a dragging reluctance to prepare for the Council meeting. Whatever else came of the meeting, they would end the day with a new Lord or Lady of Tura. Gellion found he didn't much care who the elf was. The Council would act as a collective unit against Kaelo either way. What did it matter who stood at their head? Still, Gellion was curious to see who would be chosen. The options were limited to say the least.

Alos had taken a stone fist to the head in the fighting at Morcanan. He had never regained consciousness, and died shortly after the elves' arrival in Tura. The man's death had not particularly upset Gellion, but his passing was another blow to the Turi. That was two members of the Council gone, and Dorian sent home with his injuries. Dorian would recover, but it would come too late. The Turi only had days before they faced the same ultimatum as Morcanan, and they could not be leaderless and broken.

By the time Gellion left the apartments, the morning's first illumination cast a cool glow over the city. Gellion's family trailed behind him.

They walked in silence. Gellion could practically hear the buzz of thoughts surrounding him. He ignored them and focused on his own thoughts with such intensity that he nearly ran into a solid wall of elves when he rounded the corner leading to the Central Tower.

Gellion looked up in shock and gaped at the scene before him. There were ranks of elves. Hundreds of them. Elves lined the pavement leading to the Central Tower. Elves surrounded the building on three sides and spilled into the streets leading to the city's center. They all faced the white pillar in patient anticipation. Amid the bodies, Gellion saw the points of weapons and the sheen of armor. The Turi army awaited the acceptance or rejection of their new leader.

A subtle chill rippled under Gellion's skin. He had thought the election would be a quiet affair—private, with later representation from the army to confirm or reject the Council's choice. But this—the election would be almost immediate, then, and it would be very public.

It took several minutes for Gellion and his family to shoulder their way to the entrance of the Central Tower. They pushed through the doors and made their way to the lifts leading to the main meeting room.

Reanan was already there when they arrived. He turned pained eyes on Gellion, but smiled weakly in greeting.

Gellion glanced at the empty chairs.

"Saethir?" he asked.

"Coming soon." Reanan watched Gellion's brothers and mother fill the seats nearest him.

Gellion nodded.

"And—" He trailed off. That was it. There were no other elves left on the Turi Council. He thought dully that they would have to invite more members of the city's council for the next meeting. If there was a next meeting.

"It would seem your family now makes up the majority of our Kindom's leadership." Reanan's mouth twitched.

Gellion snorted without humor, but felt uncomfortable as he lowered himself into a chair. It did seem absurd, his family meeting with two other elves to dictate the fate of the Turi. It was more than absurd. It was terrifying.

The door swung open, emitting a flustered and panting Saethir.

Gellion watched him without interest. The man was quite unremarkable as Council Members went. His representation on the Council was more a matter of courtesy to the Turi countryside than an asset to important decisions.

Not so different from your role in Daro.

Gellion had never expected to make any decisions more influential than trade agreements in the isolated city. His position in Tura prior to sailing to Daro had been a job of restoration, of rebuilding a nation ravaged by war and grief and making plans to move forward and inspire hope. He had been good at it. He had enjoyed it. This was something entirely different.

"Well," Reanan said. "Shall we begin?"

"How many did we lose?" Saethir said.

An uncomfortable stillness settled over the table.

Gellion exchanged a look with Reanan. It had been difficult to accurately count those the Turi had lost in the fighting at Morcanan. There had been no opportunity to recover bodies. Reanan nodded to him.

"Over fifty," Gellion said. "A small number compared to the size of our army, but far more than we should have lost. We were unprepared. We cannot let that happen again."

"You think Kaelo will bring those monsters to Tura?" said Saethir.

"Why wouldn't he?" said Valder. "They worked well the first time."

"But how would he bring them here?" said Reanan.

"I don't think he needs to transport them," said Gellion. "He can just make more once he gets here. It was less than a week between Kaelo's last sighting in the Lay Hills and his attack on Morcanan. It clearly doesn't take the phoenix long to create and move large numbers of cherufin. Even if Kaelo doesn't come with any cherufin, we face the same threat we have these last months. If you haven't noticed, we haven't done too well against Kaelo and his phoenix even without the cherufin."

"But you haven't really faced him yet," said Veldon. "We cannot know our chances. As you say, we were unprepared every other time we have tried to fight Kaelo. This time, we know what we might face, and we have a way of combating it."

"You think we should fight?" Saethir had gone pale. "Even Miyela saw the wisdom in surrendering rather than condemning her people to destruction."

"Like we said," Valder barely concealed his annoyance. "Miyela was taken off guard—all of us were. This time, we can prepare for an attack by an army. We can—"

"Saethir has a point." Reanan's voice was soft, but it cut through Valder's like a sword. "We cannot keep the cherufin out of our walls. Morcanan was evidence of that. Even prepared, I do not think we could take on a full assault by the creatures. They are too difficult to kill."

"You think we should give up?" Tenille said. "You would have us bow to a demon and condemn our people to slavery?"

"That is not what I said," said Reanan. "I said that we can't win a lengthy fight against the phoenix and an army. Once we elect a new leader, we must convince Kaelo to meet with them and come up with a hell of a good plan to trap him as he negotiates. We take his redstone. Then we either break his control over the phoenix, or we use that control to our advantage."

Gellion glanced at his brothers. Reanan's words were straying close to their own theories of the phoenix and its relationship to Kaelo. Valder opened his mouth, but Gellion silenced him with a slight shake of the head. He wanted to think more about their speculations before making any decisions based upon them.

"Which brings us," said Reanan, "to the real purpose of this meeting." He looked between them all wearily. "None could fail to notice the audience we have awaiting our decision outside. To further our plans, we must first elect a leader."

Gellion looked between the four remaining members of the Turi Council. Reanan seemed the obvious choice. Tornac and Tenille were too invested in Maramor, though they may accept the appointment if it was only temporary. Saethir—well.

"Reanan?" Gellion inclined his head at the Master Builder. The man would make a good leader. He had a sound head and good judgment, and Riu knew they would need the guidance of a good Builder if they made it through this disaster.

Reanan raised an eyebrow. "Yes?"

Gellion paused, taken aback.

"You," he said. "I mean … I am nominating you. I suppose." His voice grew more unsure as Reanan's expression did not change. The elf's eyebrow had continued to rise up his forehead.

"Very well, I have been nominated." Reanan turned his gaze to the rest of the Council. "I, in turn, would like to make a nomination."

Gellion knit his brows and followed the man's look, trying to see who he would nominate. Slowly, Gellion drew back in his chair. Everyone's eyes were on him—some amused, some intense.

"What—" Gellion stared at them all, then turned back to Reanan. Reanan looked at him with a smug smile.

The realization slammed into Gellion. He laughed.

"Me?" he said. "No. I'm not even on the Council."

"You were," said Reanan.

Gellion's laughter faded.

"Yes, *were* being the operative word. It's been centuries since the Turi elected me for anything." The only effect his words had on those around him was a conversion of more expressions to amusement. What was wrong with them? Was this a joke?

"You aren't serious." Gellion watched the faces of the Council Members with narrowed eyes, looking for any break of composure. There was none. Blood rushed in his ears, and cold goosebumps rose over his arms. He couldn't. It was wrong. He wasn't on the Turi Council. He had failed Daro. He didn't *want* it.

"I am entirely serious." Reanan's smile disappeared. "Whether or not you are the best choice for Lord of Tura, Gellion—and I personally believe you are a good one—you are the best elf to face Kaelo. You are the only elf, in fact. You know him as none of us do. He owes you his life. And you possess the one weapon that has any chance of stopping him."

All the moisture had gone from Gellion's mouth. He gaped at Reanan, unable to form any words to set on his dry tongue.

Owes you his life.

Did Kaelo owe Gellion his life? He supposed so, but that had not stopped the man from destroying Daro, or turning his army against the Turi in Morcanan. Kaelo may not have attacked Gellion with his own hand when he had the chance, but he had left Gellion to die on more than one occasion. He would never listen to Gellion. Would he even agree to fight him?

"The Turi will not accept me as their leader," Gellion said hoarsely. "They don't even know of the weapon that I possess. To them, I am the man who let Kaelo live. I am the man who led Daro to its destruction. I am—"

"You are the man who got them out of Morcanan alive." Tornac said. "And you are the strongest leader on this Council."

Gellion's head was shaking back and forth.

"They won't," Gellion said. "They won't follow me. I can't—" He looked to his mother, pleading for her to agree with him, to say that Reanan was a more prudent choice. She watched him with a carefully blank expression, her hands folded on the table in front of her.

"You think they will not?" Reanan stood. "Come, then."

"Wh ... what?" Gellion's head swiveled to follow Reanan as he walked to the door. "Come where?" But the sinking of his heart through his stomach told him exactly where Reanan wanted him to 'come.'

"Come with me," Reanan said.

The others were following Reanan now, casting sideways glances at Gellion. Gellion leaped to his feet and caught Veldon's arm as he walked by. His youngest brother looked up at him nervously.

"Did you know about this?" Gellion demanded.

"I—well. Mother mentioned that she and Reanan had discussed this —and Tornac, too. But she only told me last night."

"There was plenty of time to tell me since last night," Gellion said through his teeth.

Veldon gave him a small smile.

"I honestly feared you wouldn't come if I told you their intentions." Gellion glared at him.

"Oh come on." Valder came to his side and slapped him on the back. "Your moping won't help the situation. Just see how they react." He raised an eyebrow. "It may surprise you."

Seething, Gellion followed his brothers and the Council out of the room. Reanan took them around the curving hallway that led to the other side of the building—the side that faced the Public Quarter of the city. Gellion's head was spinning. Should he just go back? Sit in the meeting room and refuse to move until they all agreed to drop the ridiculous notion that he should be—he couldn't even use the words to describe himself. He was no Lord of anything.

Reanan walked to glass doors that led onto a shallow terrace. Gellion's breath caught in his throat as he heard the familiar sound of muted conversation rising from the streets beyond. Visions of a shouting crowd in Tradira threatened to turn his vision black. It was happening again. He was to be paraded in front of a crowd once more, his judgment resting upon their reactions.

"This is how it is always done," Tenille said, her voice gentle. She lay a hand on Gellion's shoulder. "It is a public conferral of transition in power.

"What?" said Gellion. "Blindsiding and ganging up on the chosen leader and forcing him before half the elves of Tura with no chance to prepare?"

"No one blindsided you, Gellion. Did you honestly not think you would be a candidate for the position?"

He hadn't. Never had the thought even occurred to him. It was insane.

"A candidate?" Gellion scoffed. "You entertained the possibilities of no other *candidates*, mother. And what were you doing meeting with the rest of the Council without me?"

The smile that spread over Tenille's face was twice as smug as Reanan's earlier expression.

"I met with all the active members of the Council, Gellion. You yourself pointed out—quite vehemently—that you are not, in fact, on the official Council." She cocked an eyebrow. "Yet."

It took Gellion several breaths to think of a retort.

"Maybe those having secret meetings and making important decisions should be the ones elected as Lord of Tura." It sounded even more pathetic when he said it aloud.

"Maybe those with the potential to lead their people out of war should not throw tantrums to their mothers." There was a hint of a smile in Tornac's voice. He looked at Gellion as he passed. Gellion very nearly tried to hit the smile off of his face.

"He has a point dear." Tenille smiled innocently at Gellion.

Gellion growled deep in his throat, then walked out onto the terrace.

From this height, the elves that filled the court below seemed to have tripled in number. The glint of metal shone in the rising sun.

Panic began to gnaw Gellion's insides. They would never accept his nomination. He would have to step down in humiliation to make way for Reanan, who should have been the nomination in the first place. Why were they putting him through this? Gellion was no commander. He had played at the role in the Great War and then again in Daro, but he had been a failure in every attempt. He had not defeated the phoenix of the Great War. He had allowed his father to die without even knowing the secret that had saved them all. He had led the elves of Daro to a slaughter based upon his own naivety. Lord of Tura? He bit his lip to stop his teeth from chattering.

"Elves of Tura." Reanan's voice rang in the space, and the elves two stories below quieted at once. "You know why you are here. The leader this Kindom has known for most of your lives is gone—destroyed by our enemy. By her own son." Angry hisses coalesced in the crowd, rising up in the air like steam. "In times such as these," Reanan continued. "We must choose those who lead us out of usual convention. We must make decisions quickly, based upon core judgment of character, merit, and valor."

The little blood remaining in Gellion's face drained away.

"The Council has chosen a candidate for your approval." Reanan paused and let his gaze sweep over the crowd. Gellion winced as Dulon's visage momentarily overlay Reanan's.

Why couldn't this be you, old friend?

Reanan opened his arm toward Gellion and nodded for him to step up to the terrace railing. Gellion swallowed, then took a step forward.

"Do you accept Gellion," Reanan said to the court, "to take command of this city and this Kindom?"

Gellion went rigid. Reanan was no Dulon. No pomp and circumstance. No flourishing speeches. Not even explanations, reasoning, or justification. A simple question.

"Ai!"

Gellion jumped at the word, spoken in resounding and solemn unison from the crowd below.

"You will willingly follow him," Reanan said, "and trust his judgment in all matters to do his best for you and your Kindom?"

"Ai!"

Gellion's heart, once hammering against his chest, was now positively thrashing against his sternum. Did he have no say in this?

Reanan turned to Gellion.

Tell him no. Back away. Beg him to take on the title himself.

Gellion could feel the terror in his own eyes, but so too could he see the confidence in Reanan's. The man trusted him without question. The army below him trusted him. Despite all he had done, they would follow him. It was too much. He did not deserve it. He began to shake his head. A hand fell on his shoulder.

Tornac turned Gellion to face him. His eyes were hard and burning.

"There is no leadership without the possibility of failure, brother, but a true leader does not let the fear of inadequacy stop him from bringing hope and resilience to his people. You have already led them, Gellion. Do it now, with intention, and we may just have a chance in this war."

Gellion's shoulders fell.

"Well?" Reanan said.

Slowly, Gellion turned back to the waiting army below. Hundreds of faces looked up at him. Their lives would be bound to his words. His decisions would mean slavery or freedom. He could turn them over to Kaelo, or he could be the hero that liberated them from a lifetime of despair. But they had already lost. Even if he defeated Kaelo and the phoenix now, what would life be without vierstone?

Gellion closed his eyes. There was nothing he could do about that now. It was done. All he could do was make the next right decision as it came along. He could make those decisions mean something.

And he wanted to. Despite the sorrow and terror his choices had wrought these last months, he still wanted to make them. He still wanted to try to get them right.

He nodded once.

Reanan returned the gesture. "The Lord of Tura!" he shouted into the morning.

There was no answering 'Ai!' this time, nor were there cheers of joy or welcome. The elves of the army began to beat their spears against the stone court, the rhythm rising in volume and tempo until the crack of metal on stone seemed to fill the city.

Heads appeared in windows. Bodies appeared in doorways. Gellion watched as civilians began to join the numbers of the army in the court. Every face looked up to the terrace outlined against the alabaster tower. They looked upon their last hope, their new leader. They looked upon the Lord of Tura.

25

THE MAKING OF HEROES

The phoenix's shadow fell on the street—a silent stain over stone and walls. Renyra flinched, but the shadow moved on, streaking toward the southern gates of Morcanan. Dully, Renyra watched the bird's form disappear beyond the walls. It was leaving the city. Part of her wondered why, but her curiosity was quickly consumed by her previous thoughts. She kept walking.

The walls of Morcanan were thick and unyielding. Where the rock monsters had broken through, Renyra could see the stone was as thick as her body. Maybe even as thick as Trali's body. A thrill of anger coursed through Renyra. She frowned and sped her steps.

The breaches in the wall were heavily guarded by stone sentinels. Rock watched by rock. Renyra gave the monsters a wide berth, though they never moved to attack her. The things had piled crumbled stone between the gaps in the wall in a messy attempt at repair. It would have been easy to climb up and over the piled rocks. There weren't too many guards at each site. If Renyra and her friends could crush the legs of enough of the rock creatures quickly, they may have a chance at slipping out of the city before any of the patrolling creatures came by. It was a possibility that Renyra would have considered, if she hadn't seen Trali nearly crushed by one of the things. She doubted if she or Alura would have the weight or strength to break a finger off one of the monsters, and neither Firas nor Trali would be swinging weapons for some time. The thought of Raren and Caerlyn trying to take on four creatures alone was not one Renyra was willing to entertain.

Why do I even care if we escape?

The vierstone was gone. Kaelo had won. The elves had failed.

Even if she did escape Morcanan, the rest of Faeran would look just like it within a few months. What was the point? Still, Renyra made her way toward the mountain, scanning the walls for any points of weakness. She couldn't help herself.

The walls of the city ended where they met the mountains. Renyra looked up with a scowl. The face of the incline was nearly vertical and sheer as glass. The elves had rebuilt Morcanan in the Great War. Every inch of the city was designed to keep monsters out. It was just as effective at keeping captives inside.

I will not remain in Morcanan of all places while the world crumbles around me.

It was a place she had never wanted to live in the best of times.

All hope may have bled from Renyra in these last days, but a stubborn anger had now taken its place. Riu had abandoned them to this terror. He had allowed the elves' strongest connection to him to be destroyed. This was worse than the Great War. This was defeat.

But Gellion—

Gellion stood in the darkness of Renyra's thoughts, an annoying glimmer of light that would not wink out. Rankled as she was that Gellion had not confided in her, Renyra could not help but draw hope from his unexplained power. Somehow, Gellion had figured out what enabled Kaelo's control of stone and learned to manifest the power himself. Of course, his abilities had done little good stopping Kaelo in Morcanan. They had barely allowed Gellion to escape with his Kindom.

It's still more than you managed.

Renyra sighed and turned away from the walls. Another useless scouting mission.

She began to walk toward the mountain entrance, but her feet dragged as she neared it. The dim caverns within dampened her moods further, and the room her troupe shared felt more like a sick room than a refuge. It still caused Renyra physical pain to be near Firas and his injuries, but the pain turned to anxiety when she was away from him. She preferred the pain.

A stout Morcani elf with shorn hair walked out of the mountain gate. He eyed Renyra suspiciously as he passed. Renyra narrowed her eyes at him as she walked into the mountain.

All in all, she had not found herself the subject of as many stares and judgments as she would have imagined in Morcanan. Those stares she did receive were mostly looks of interest or curiosity. A Fieri elf in colorful wraps was bound to stand out in a society of subdued fashion and washed palettes. Renyra wondered if the curiosity would turn to aversion in time, as the novelty of her appearance wore off. Hopefully she would never find out.

She counted hallways and turns as she walked, glancing at the numbers carved above doors. Thirty-seven. One more turn and two doors should do it.

There. Forty-three.

Renyra's hand hovered over the door handle. She took a breath and walked in.

The atmosphere was as heavy as when she had left; it fell against Renyra like an over fluffed pillow. There were two square beds in the room and a couch along the far wall. Trali lay on the couch in a pose so dramatic she was sure he had put it on theatrically. The others in the room were less flamboyant in their bearing. Alura huddled next to her brother, her arms wrapped around her knees. Caerlyn was sitting on the edge of one of the beds, staring absently into a nearby fireplace. Firas sat propped up on the other bed. He alone smiled as Renyra entered the room.

It was a weak smile, but Renyra had to admit Firas looked far better than he had after the attack on Morcanan. His eyes had brightened, and his skin had lost most of its grey hue. She crossed the room to him in two strides and crawled onto the bed.

"How are you?" She leaned back against the wall next to him and let her fingers trail down the bare skin of his forearm. The touch brought her a thrill of pleasure, but the sensation was only skin deep. She could feel no echo of his pain, or of his love. She wanted to grab his arm, to squeeze as tightly as she could until she forced their connection to return. Instead, she pulled her hand away.

"Spectacular." Firas's smile widened.

Renyra narrowed her eyes. "Really?"

"On my honor," Firas said seriously. He chuckled at her expression. "Truly, I do feel better. I can even lean back against the wall." He pressed himself further into his pillows, and though Renyra scrutinized his face, she caught no hint of a grimace.

"Good," Renyra said. "But that doesn't mean you should start rubbing your back against everything you see to test if it hurts or not."

"Of course not." His face went serious again.

"I, for one," Trali said from his couch. "Feel ready to smash more legs." He pulled himself up from his sprawled position. "The rocks deserve punishment for what they did to my hair."

Renyra smiled. The healers had shaved the hair around Trali's head wound in order to clean and stitch it. This had meant sawing off several of his thick braids. The Remsgri had not been pleased upon waking. Aside from bruised pride, however, Trali seemed to have born no lasting damage from the injury. That did not mean his friends allowed him to test the limits of his returning strength.

"I'm not sure you could aim well enough to find their legs," Renyra said. "Last time you turned too quickly, you fell against a wall—if I remember correctly."

Trali let out a booming laugh. "The rocks are large targets. I could manage to hit something."

The echo of Trali's voice fell away in the heaviness of the room. Caerlyn and Alura had not broken their blank stares since Renyra came inside. Even Raren seemed in no mood to laugh with Trali. His eyes lifted to Renyra.

"Did you find anything?" he asked.

Renyra shook her head. "Still guarded as heavily as before. We would have to get through three or four of those monsters if we tried for one of the breaches—that's assuming no others came to help. Any doors or stairs to the top of the wall are watched as well—not that we could get down on the other side of those walls even if we got to the top. It's too far of a drop. The mountain is no use climbing, either."

Raren let out a long breath. "So we live in Morcanan now?"

Renyra did not answer. Was this her life now? Sitting in an underground chamber, staring morosely into fires and at walls? Life without vierstone was terrible enough to imagine, but would freedom be taken from her too?

The anger flared in her chest. The passion for which Kaelo had mocked her was still inside her, at least for now. She would use it as long as it was there.

"Firas, are there any other ways out of this city?" she said.

"What's the point?" Caerlyn said before Firas could answer. She did not take her eyes off the fire. "Where would we go if we escaped? It's over. We can't fight the phoenix anymore."

It was the same argument that had been plaguing Renyra's thoughts for days. She ground her teeth against its pull.

"We go to Tura," she said. "We find Gellion. He knows something he didn't tell us about, Caerlyn. I saw him breaking stone just as Kaelo does. With him, the Turi defense might stand a chance. If we can get to Tura before the phoenix—"

"We would do what?" Caerlyn tore her eyes away from the fire. Despite her words, her expression was not one of defiance. She shook her head sadly. "Even if Gellion has discovered something he can use against Kaelo, we would hardly be a help to him. We tried to help Miyela, but our information was clearly useless. We only made Remsgraen's destruction worse by pissing off the phoenix before it flew there. We don't possess anything special, Renyra. We aren't warriors, or wielders of inexplicable magic. We just get in the way, trying to be heroes when we're not."

No one spoke. Renyra waited for someone to contradict Caerlyn, to come up with some defense or reasoning to prove her words false. None came.

Renyra could sense the same dark chasm of hopelessness within herself as she saw in Caerlyn's eyes. It drew her, tried to sink her into its depths. Maybe Caerlyn was right. Renyra's involvement in everything that had happened since that first earthquake in Daro had been based upon nothing but her own determination to insert herself into the action. Never had she possessed any skills, knowledge, or divine purpose to justify that determination. Had she simply wanted to play the hero? Throw herself into a role that was never meant for her? Everything she had tried had failed. Daro had fallen. Kaelo had evaded her feeble attempts at capture and assassination without even trying. She had *helped* lead the elves into the trap that had raised a phoenix. Her foolish insistence that Kyna could be swayed back to their side had ended in nothing but disaster and heartbreak. Renyra was no hero. She never had been.

But still, the embers of a fire burned in her chest.

Renyra acknowledged her failure, but it only fueled her anger. If she stopped now, she would have done nothing for the elves but speed their fall. If she stopped now, she would forever be a failure. She narrowed her eyes at Caerlyn, holding her stare until the woman met her gaze.

"Heroes," Renyra said, "are not made by their success or their skill. Heroes are made by their resilience. I am not saying we can do anything to stop this phoenix, or that we can offer Gellion, or the Turi, or the elves as a whole, anything more or different than the nearest elf we meet on the street. I don't think we can. But if we let that stop us, we will never be more than we are now. We may not be saviors. We may even be failures. But I refuse to be apathetic cowards who watch the world fall without lifting a finger to stop it."

Caerlyn flinched. She dropped her eyes.

Beside her, Renyra could see Firas nodding, his eyes fixed on the bed.

"So," Raren said. "What do we do?"

"We get out of here," said Renyra. "And we keep trying." She turned to Firas. "Are there any other ways out of this city?" she asked again.

Firas was still looking down, his brows furrowed in thought. "There used to be tunnels through the mountains leading off of the main city caverns. Most led to the north, into the Terulian Mountains. I would guess those either collapsed during the war, or fell out of repair after it. There was at least one tunnel that led to the edges of the Wildwood, though. The Morcani withstood many sieges here during the war, some lasting months at a time, or even years. We conducted trade with the other Kindoms through the Wildwood, using Ciel as a port on its eastern edge. The Wildwood was dangerous during the war, but it was not under the phoenix's control. The tunnels didn't come out too far from Morcanan—there wasn't time to make them longer."

"So they're still there?" Renyra said excitedly.

"I assume so, though I never used them myself."

"Do you think you can find them?" Alura had unwound her arms from her knees and was sitting up, her eyes more alert than Renyra had seen them in days.

"We could try." Firas did not look confident. "I don't think we would meet any resistance by looking, anyway. I have not seen cherufin inside the mountain since they looted the vierstone." He turned to Renyra. "Have you?"

Renyra cocked her head. "Cherufin?"

Firas nodded. "The rock creatures."

"You've seen these things before?" Renyra's eyes widened.

"No. They are a part of Morcani legend, though—creatures of stone, animated by flame and terra spirits. I assume that is what these are, though there is no way to be sure. It is only a legend and a name."

"Oh." Renyra frowned. "Well, no. I haven't seen them inside the mountain gates."

"Good," said Firas. "We will need all the time we can get. I suggest we find some lamps."

It was nearly nightfall by the time Renyra found herself in a halo of silvery lamplight. A bag of scavenged supplies hung from her shoulder, and she watched Firas's every step for signs of fatigue. He looked much better than he had since the phoenix's initial attack, but she still wished he did not have to travel so soon after their latest skirmish.

"I didn't like the central caverns," Caerlyn muttered from behind Renrya. "But these feel more like the burrows of monstrous rodents."

Ahead, Firas chuckled. "These halls are not used much anymore. Morcanan used to house far more elves than it does these days. The builders excavated this area during the war to create more space during sieges."

"There are rooms behind these doors?" Alura eyed the stark planks of wood cut into the stone on either side of them.

"Yes," said Firas.

"I'm guessing they are no palace suites," said Raren.

"You guess correctly." Firas smiled, but there was a lingering melancholy to his eyes.

Had he come to this part of Morcanan during the Great War? Could he have even weathered a siege in one of the gloomy spaces they now passed? Renyra turned her eyes to the floor. It was overwhelming, at times, to think how much more life Firas had lived than she. The time they had spent together made up the merest fraction of the time Firas had spent on Riure, yet it made up nearly half of Renyra's life.

"What do we look for?" Trali said. He trailed a hand along the rough wall—a gesture that seemed so casual, Renyra suspected he was using it for balance. His footsteps were steady, though, and his demeanor as cheerful as ever.

"A seam," said Firas.

"What?" said Caerlyn.

"In the wall. We may be able to see the lever mechanism from this side as well. At least that is how the doors leading to the northern tunnels worked. I never went in the eastern tunnels."

"Why do they need doors?" Renyra felt a flicker of nerves.

"The northern tunnels led all the way through the mountains. These tunnels abut the Wildwood. Unsavory creatures inhabit both places. Doors on both sides were an extra precaution worth taking."

"As long as we can find them," said Raren.

"I don't think it will be too hard to recognize an entrance when we see it," Firas said. "I just don't know where it is, and these tunnels could take a few hours to navigate in their entirety."

"I hope by 'their entirety' means you know how to get us back out of here if we don't find any tunnels," Caerlyn said.

Firas's mouth twitched upward. He didn't answer.

An hour passed, then two. Renyra's feet were beginning to hurt, and the javelin at her back clanged against her calves every few steps. She was grateful to have found the weapon among Morcanan's stores, but it was made for an elf far taller than herself.

Renyra had been shocked at how easy it was to obtain weapons and supplies within an occupied city. Of course, the overseers of the city's occupation had left that morning, and most weapons were useless against the hulking stone guards they had left in charge. She was sure neither Kaelo nor Kyna nor the phoenix knew there were any other ways out of Morcanan on this side of the Terulian Mountains.

"Ha!" Firas said.

Renyra planted her feet, sliding a bit on the dusty stone. Firas had stopped in front of her and was holding his lamp toward a wall to their left. Renyra saw nothing. It looked like a perfectly blank wall, but then Firas stepped forward and slid his hand behind a panel she had not been able to see from her angle. A metallic click sounded, followed by grinding, and a final, resonant clap of rock. The outline of a door appeared in the wall and swung inward at a touch on smooth hinges. Renyra's mouth fell open.

"Got it." Firas grinned.

"You say this hasn't been used in centuries?" Raren ran a hand over the side of the door, his face skeptical.

"I doubt it." Firas's grin twisted in amusement at Raren's expression. "For all the Turi's skill in architecture and artwork, you really do not know how to engineer anything more complex than a metalworking tool. Those hinges won't rust, nor will the mechanisms in the latch deteriorate over time."

Renyra hid a smile at her husband's excitement. In Daro, he had been a shipwright, the sole engineer among a crew of Turi and Fieri artisans. Those artisans had built beautiful ships, with shining sides and artistic lines. It had been Firas that made the ships functional. Always a humble man, the joy Firas took in a job well engineered made Renyra smile.

"Yes, yes, it is a work of miracles, this door," said Trali. "Now may we go through it?"

Renyra's amusement melted away, leaving cold reality in its place. They were not in Morcanan sightseeing. Though the discovery of a way out brought Renyra relief, it only made possible the infinitely harder tasks that awaited them beyond. It would have been far easier to agree with Caerlyn, to stay shut away in their grief and depression while they left the happenings in the world to others, but Renyra had made her decision and brought her friends with her. She would see it through.

Taking a deep breath, Renyra lifted her lantern above her head and stepped past Firas, leading the way into the blackness beyond.

LIGHTS IN THE TREES

The ground was wet. The trees were wet too, and so were her clothes. Strangely, Kyna did not mind. It seemed fitting, lying here in the cool, damp darkness, surrounded by her own misery. It was satisfying. Sitting on a sunlit slope in her current mood would only have annoyed her.

Just as fitting, but far more annoying, was the hardness of the ground. How could something so wet remain so unyielding? Kyna flipped over again, laying her head on a soggy pile of pine needles. She smiled wryly. Isn't this what she had wanted all those months in Daro and in Tura—to be alone in the mountains with everything done and behind her?

You got your wish.

Kyna curled her knees to her ribs. The heat of Tura didn't seem so bad just now. When she had imagined the coolness of mountains, she had imagined herself dry, or at least with a fire to return to at the end of the day. With a shiver, Kyna opened her eyes. The forest wasn't much lighter than the inside of her eyelids. She lay facing the heart of the Wildwood. It had seemed wrong, somehow, to turn her back to the oppressive forest. The thickening trees held a kind of presence, one that did not seem benevolent. Still, Kyna had deemed it better to shelter beneath a canopy than to find a place to sleep in the open. At the time.

Eyes glowed in the distance. At least Kyna thought they were eyes. Pinpricks of light appeared and disappeared in the deep black beneath the trees. Kyna flinched as an eerie cry echoed through the space. A bird of some sort?

Just stay still until morning.

But then what? If a day of wandering the hills and forest east of Morcanan had not brought her inspiration, another day of the same hardly seemed likely to bring any brilliant revelations. For hours, she had wallowed beneath the weight of her own hopelessness. Then, she had obsessed over what to do next. Now she lay in numbed stillness.

There was nothing for her. Nowhere to go. No one to go to. She was exiled from Morcanan and would find no welcome reception from the elves within even if she snuck back in. If she went to Tura, she would be imprisoned or killed on sight. The most obvious course of action was to build a home for herself in the Terulian Mountains, as her father had in the Falspires, but without redstone, she was useless at stonework. She was useless at everything.

The bird cry came again, long and high.

Maybe if she started walking again, some creature would come eat her. It could be a quick death—even relatively painless, depending on the ferocity of the animal.

If only the phoenix had done it.

A fresh wave of pain coursed through Kyna's body. Hot tears built behind her eyes. Her every endeavor had succeeded. She had done exactly as she was meant to do, as she had always planned to do. Were things truly so different now than she had envisioned? Cleansing the Great Cities had taken more force than she had imagined, but only Remsgraen had sustained major damages. All in all, very few elves had died in their efforts, and as for the cherufin, they were only a temporary measure. Had Kyna overreacted to her father? Had she ruined every-thing over her own cold feet?

The tears turned to sobs. Kyna raked her fingers through her hair and turned her face into the pine needles. They pricked her skin and stuck to her running nose. She wanted to hit something. She wanted to fight something. She wanted to fall into nothing and never feel again. But there was no redstone lashed to her wrist. There was no escape. There was only the vierstone. She cursed at the retched object, but could not summon the will to throw it away from her body. Stealing the vierstone now seemed an utterly stupid thing to have done. Surely these emotions would kill her. Maybe that was the fate she deserved.

The hours dragged by. Sleep came to Kyna in fleeting brushes, but would not take hold of her. She bore her stubborn consciousness with grim acceptance. The sounds of the forest grew increasingly disturbing as the night deepened, and Kyna did not dare open her eyes to see what fate may creep upon her. She tried to tune out the sounds until they echoed as a distant background to her uneasy waking dreams.

"No. No that's east. See?"

Kyna's body jerked. Her head whipped toward the sound.

The faintest hint of rustling was coming from somewhere toward the mountains. Kyna sat up, listening. She heard another voice, this one lower. She could not make out the words.

Elves? Here? At this hour?

Kyna scrubbed at her face with a damp sleeve, wiping away pine needles and snot. Should she move? Would the elves hear her? What if they were hunters? As welcome as death had seemed moments ago, taking a hunter's arrow to the back was not a comforting prospect. Slowly, Kyna stood. She stepped closer to the tree under which she had been sheltering and peered around its edge toward the voices. There were lights in the distance, silver ones, much larger than the pinpricks she had taken for eyes earlier. They bobbed and swayed in a mesmerizing dance.

Lamps. Hunters didn't carry lamps.

Kyna started to back away, relying on the pine needles to soften her steps. Hunters or not, there wasn't an elf in Faeran who would be happy to encounter her in the woods at night. Unless these elves didn't know who she was.

Kyna stopped her retreat. What if she stumbled across the elves, muddy and exhausted, pleading for help? They couldn't be from Morcanan, whoever they were. They couldn't have gotten out of the city. Maybe they could take her to a nearby village where no one would know her.

The voices were coming nearer. Kyna stood, immobilized by her desire to both run from and approach these nightwalkers.

As she focused all of her attention on the approaching elves, another sound raised the hair on the back of Kyna's neck. It was not the murmuring of voices, or the haunting cry of a bird, but a low, gravelly growl, and it was right behind her.

Kyna forced herself to turn slowly.

Two oval glimmers hovered level with her face several paces away. In the nearing lamplight, they gleamed crimson and silver, and Kyna could make out a huge and hulking outline around them. The beast snorted, then growled again. Kyna tried to back away, but her legs had turned to jelly. She had nothing. No weapon, no redstone, not even a stick.

Suddenly, choosing to spend the night at the mercy of woodland monsters seemed a much stupider idea than risking elves on an open road.

A scream was building in Kyna's throat, but she was sure the outburst would only provoke whatever monster stood before her. She bit down on her tongue and forced her feet to start moving. She managed two shuffling steps, then the pair of eyes rose twelve feet into the air, and a roar ripped through the still night.

Kyna screamed as the eyes lunged toward her.

MY ENEMY'S ENEMY

The scream nearly stopped Renyra's heart. She recoiled backward, tripping over Firas and landing in Raren's arms.

"What the—" Caerlyn stepped in front of the group, holding up a lamp in one hand and a dagger in the other.

Renyra scrambled back to her feet, squinting against the lamplight. The throaty roar preceding the scream had frozen them all in their tracks, but that scream had sounded like no animal. Was there an elf out here? Renyra's fingers squeezed around the shaft of her javelin. Her heartbeat pumped in her ears.

"I don't see—" Firas did not finish his sentence.

At that moment, a dark shape came hurtling out of the darkness.

Renyra was sure she would have run the shadow through on sight had she been in Caerlyn's place. Fortunately, Caerlyn seemed to ascertain that the shape was an elf before the others and dropped her dagger to her side as the figure stumbled past them. Loose hair caught the light of the lamps, and Renyra saw the heavy flap of fabric around the elf's body.

"Wait!" Firas said. "What's wrong?" Firas reached for the fleeing figure, but they ripped their arm away from him, recoiling so violently they fell backward onto the ground. The swinging lamplight bathed a pale face.

Renyra's mouth fell open.

"There!" Raren pointed a sword into the darkness. A heavy thudding sent vibrations through the ground, growing nearer with each repetition. Another resonant roar sounded.

Renyra did not look toward the roar. She could not seem to move her eyes. Sprawled on the ground, soaking wet and smeared with mud and pine needs, was Kyna. Her eyes were wide with terror and darted between Firas and the thudding darkness.

Raren's shout finally broke Renyra's stare. She wheeled around to see scarlet eyes higher than her head emerging from a sheet of blackness, accompanied by gleaming black teeth. Raren slashed at the monster with his sword, slicing through part of a massive muzzle. He twisted out of the way as the beast barreled past him, unfazed by the cut.

The closest thing to which Renyra could compare the thing was a bear, but it was as complete a comparison as a fluffy puppy to a demonic wolf. The bear was as tall as a horse—twice as wide and covered in matted slabs of black hair.

The troupe scattered to make way for the beast. It thundered past and disappeared outside the halo of their lamps. Renyra spun around wildly, trying to make out where the thing was, but the lamplight morphed and flickered in dizzying jerks, and the bear was black as the night closing in around them. The footfalls came again. Renyra spun toward the sound, and her eyes locked on Firas. He was standing with his back to Kyna, a spear raised toward the beast making its second pass.

Panic surged through Renyra. Images of the bear exploding from the darkness and landing on Firas painted the air in front of her—images of his beautiful skin torn to shreds once more, of his face, still and blank. She sprang in front of him, knocking his spear away and crouching with her javelin. A snarl ripped through her throat. Let the bear come. She would tear it apart or die trying before it touched Firas.

Claws scratched pine needles. The thud of heavy feet stopped. Renyra still could not see the monster, but these cues were enough. Renyra had hunted animals most of her life. She had hunted animals like this outside Daro. She lunged. It was a low lunge—a crouching leap from the ground up. The bear would not expect its prey to move first, nor would it anticipate an attack from below. The beast's hulking presence soared above her. It had leaped at the same moment as she, its teeth snapping at Firas.

Renyra thrust upward with her javelin, heaving her weight against its shaft and pushing its tip as deep into matted hair and thick skin as she could. Grunting with the effort, she felt the give of muscle and the jerk of bone. Then she was ripped off her feet.

The beast's momentum pulled her forward. She held on to the javelin, twisting the weapon's tip as her feet scrambled along the ground. She felt her body whip to one side, then the other. With each movement, it felt like her head dislodged more completely from her neck. The bear was trying to shake her off. It had stopped running. If it started clawing at her—

Renyra let go of the javelin and rolled across wet pine needles. Distantly, she could hear shouts and thuds and roars, but her head was spinning, and she could not seem to orient which direction was ground, lamplight, or darkness.

"Again!" called a deep voice.

More roaring.

"I'm trying!" Caerlyn's voice.

"Use this!"

Renyra pushed herself onto all fours, shaking her head. A hand fell onto her shoulder.

"Are you alright? Renyra!" The frantic voice was closer than the others and more familiar. Renyra raised her head to see Firas, whole and well, eyes wide in concern.

"I'm fine." Renyra shook her head again. It was beginning to clear, but she could tell her neck would be sore by morning.

A strangled, wet roar made her turn her head sharply, and she winced in pain. Trali had taken up Renyra's javelin, still lodged in the space between the bear's throat and chest. Raren and Caerlyn stood to either side of the bear, bloodied weapons raised, but they stood still, staring open mouthed at the scene before them. Perched atop the beast's back, Alura held the pommel of her slender sword, now sunk to the hilt between the bear's shoulder blades. Her knees hugged the bear's ample sides, and she looked for all Riure as though she routinely rode bears with a sword for a saddle horn. She stood, drew her sword neatly from the beast's body, and leaped to the ground.

The horror was beginning to fade from Raren's face, replaced by a ridiculous grin. He slapped his sister on the back, laughing.

"Way to make neat work of our hack job."

Renyra, though relieved, could find no smile within herself. As soon as she had assured herself that her troupe was unharmed, her eyes moved to the woman still huddled on the ground at the edge of the lamplight. With Firas's help, Renyra stood. Her head swam for a moment, then she nodded to Firas and walked toward Kyna. The troupe fell silent as they watched her progress.

Kyna was not looking at Renyra. She sat with her legs sprawled before her, leaning back on her hands and staring at the bear's corpse. Her face was ashen.

The silence deepened. The growing tension seemed to break through Kyna's trance, and she slowly turned her head to Renyra, her eyes following with delay. Renyra saw the same fear in the woman's eyes as she had their last few meetings, but now it was colored by something else.

"I'm sorry," Kyna said in barely more than a whisper.

Anger flared within Renyra, urging her tongue to give voice to the scathing remarks running through her head. Sorry? Sorry for what? For bringing a raving monster into their midst, nearly killing them? Or did Kyna mean something larger? Sorry for the destruction in Morcanan? Sorry for almost killing Firas in Remsgraen? Sorry for betraying the elves to a madman and a demon and condemning the world?

Instead, Renyra said, "What are you doing here?"

Kyna looked away. "I was sleeping."

Renyra knit her brows. Well that was not the response she had expected. She exchanged a glance with Firas, now beside her. The rest of the troupe was gathered several paces back, their expressions ranging from cold hostility to confusion.

"What?" Renyra said.

Kyna took a breath, then tilted her face up to look Renyra in the eye. "I left him."

Renyra did not know how to respond. So, Kyna had finally come to see the truth of her father. Well, it was a little late for that. A changed heart would not help the elves now. The anger flared once more in Renyra's chest, but it was punctuated by a stab of pity—even a tinge of respect. There was a sheen of tears in Kyna's eyes. She was ragged, wet, and dirty, stranded alone in exile from a life of which Renyra couldn't begin to imagine. In Kyna's face, Renyra recognized the same loss of hope that threatened to drag her under every moment, yet there was still a touch of iron in the set of Kyna's expression.

Still, Renyra couldn't let go of the resentment burning in her core. The woman was the reason she had nearly lost Firas. She was the reason there was no vierstone left in the world. She was the reason Renyra had lost everything.

Kyna did not drop her eyes from Renyra's gaze this time. She made no further attempts at explanation or supplication, but waited with a raised chin for her judgment to fall.

It was not Renyra who spoke first.

"About time." Caerlyn stepped beside Renyra and snorted in derision, then held out a hand for Kyna to take. She glanced at Renyra and raised an eyebrow.

Renyra hesitated, longing to knock Caerlyn's hand away and leave Kyna in the dirt. She ground her teeth together, swallowed the last of her burning words, and nodded.

Shock had replaced all other emotion in Kyna's eyes. She stared at the proffered hand as though expecting it to smite her.

"Would you rather us leave you here?" Caerlyn's eyebrows rose further, and she nodded to the dead bear.

Kyna blinked, then cautiously lifted a grimy hand to place in Caerlyn's. When she was on her feet, she looked at Renyra again. Renyra tried to summon a smile, even just a twitch of the lips, but it was like trying to move fingers numb with cold. She turned her back on Kyna, taking Firas by the hand and leading the way into the night once more. She did not turn to watch who followed.

The escape from Morcanan was turning out to be much less exciting than Renyra had envisioned. Finding the tunnel had been satisfying, and the bear attack was certainly something she would not soon forget, but the endless hours of walking and waiting were already beginning to wear on her. The day was colorless and flat. There was no breeze, no definition to the clouds, and no temperature worth noticing. Renyra's feet ached, and she wished they had been able to take horses with them, though she was sure the rest of the troupe would not have shared her enthusiasm for the quicker mode of transport.

"I hope it's not broken." Alura's eyes followed the Rale line to their right. It was sleek and shining against the craggy grass and cut a straight line through the hills. It was also empty, and had been all day.

"There wouldn't be any Rales going into or out of Morcanan either way, would there?" said Raren. "I'm sure the station at Morcanan is locked down, and any towns south of it would surely have heard what happened by now."

"Maybe." Alura did not look convinced.

A sliver of worry was growing in Renyra. If all the Morcani Rale lines were locked down or broken, the troupe would have little hope of getting to Tura at all, let alone before anything important happened there. It would take weeks to get to Tura on foot, and that would mean packing serious supplies. Renyra was not keen to spend any more time in the open wilderness than was necessary. Bears, demon dogs, and lind-worms had been bad enough. She hardly wanted to imagine what other creatures had come crawling from the shadows.

Renyra glanced at Kyna. The woman had hardly spoken since the night before. Her presence smothered any conversation that would normally have occupied a ponderous journey. Did Kyna know why these monsters were populating the land? It was a question Renyra had wondered about for some time. Similar creatures had made up armies during the Great War, bound to the original phoenix's bidding. Were these animals related to Kaelo's phoenix in the same way? But the animals had begun plaguing Daro and Tura long before Kaelo raised the phoenix.

Questions pressed against Renyra's lips—scores of them, ranging in tone from scathing to demanding to curious. She swallowed them all.

Kyna owed them far more than answers. She owed them explanations, apologies, a way to reverse all that had been done and account for her actions. Yet Renyra could not bring herself to say a word to the woman she had tried so hard to befriend. Kyna had used up all of her chances and had only come running to them with her tail between her legs after her involvement had spiraled out of her control. Renyra would not send the woman away—the information she possessed was far too valuable for that—but she did not have to be sociable to the traitor.

"How far is it to the nearest city?" Renyra asked Firas again.

"I expect we will reach one by the evening." Firas's voice was tired. His few days of rest in Morcanan had done him good, but walking half the night and sleeping for only a few hours on hard ground had hardly vitalized him further. "This plan assumes, of course that Kaelo has not yet taken control of the cities we come to." He glanced at Kyna and raised an eyebrow.

Kyna dropped her eyes to her feet.

"Do you really not know any more of his plans?" Caerlyn said.

Renyra's attention sharpened. It was not the first time Caerlyn had asked Kyna about her father, but Kyna had made it clear she was in no mood to discuss the man. Still, Renyra was eager for any clues at all as to what Kyna knew of Kaelo and the phoenix.

"I don't know their itinerary to the hour," Kyna muttered. At Caerlyn's raised eyebrows, she let out a breath and said, "I know they will make their way through the Morcani lands and then go to Tura."

"To take it as they took Morcanan?" Renyra said.

Kyna nodded.

"And then they'll go to Telem Fier?" Renyra said. "What then?"

"I don't know anymore," Kyna said. "I don't know what the phoenix is capable of, or what it will coerce my father into doing."

"And you couldn't discover a way to find out or stop them before you left them?" Renyra snapped. She was losing her grip on forced civility.

"There was nothing I could do," Kyna said. There was defiance in her voice, yet it was tempered by the unmistakable pitch of desperation. Renyra's scowl softened at the shame she saw hidden beneath Kyna's stony eyes.

"I wanted to—" Kyna trailed off. Her eyes went distant. "Only my father has the power to stop this now."

"Well that's a real comfort," Raren said. "I'm sure he'll put things right for us any day."

Kyna's shoulders stiffened. She stared straight ahead as she walked. Clearly she had used up her allowance of speech for the morning.

Renyra let out a slow stream of air through her nose.

"Hopefully Gellion will be more useful than you," she muttered.

Kyna stumbled to a stop and stared back at Renyra.

"Gellion?" She mouthed the name, barely giving voice to it.

"That's where we're going," Renyra said, not looking at Kyna. "To Tura. Gellion knows—" Renyra's eyes snapped to Kyna. "You!"

Kyna's brows rose. The rest of the troupe had stopped to watch the confrontation.

"You did it too!" Renyra could have smacked herself for being so stupid. All this time, they had been on their way to Tura to join the one elf who knew Kaelo's secret to controlling stone, but Gellion was not the only elf Renyra had seen use the inexplicable magic. Her fuming anger at the cursed woman had wiped the memory clear out of her head.

"Did what?" Kyna's eyes moved uncertainly to the other elves before settling back on Renyra.

"You broke the stones outside Telem Fier. You know how to do whatever it is Kaelo does too."

"What do you mean, 'too?'" Kyna said slowly.

Renyra shook her head impatiently. "I saw Gellion do it in Morcanan. That's why we're going to him. But you know how, too. I've seen you do it!"

Kyna's mouth was hanging open. "That's impossible," she whispered. "He can't have—" Her brows drew together, then her eyes widened, as though remembering something.

"It doesn't matter how he knows, it matters that *you* know!" Renyra took a step toward Kyna, and though the woman was a good head taller than Renyra, she backed away.

"Yes. I know." Kyna took another step back.

Renyra realized she had drawn the javelin from her back and was pointing it at the woman. Reluctantly, she lowered its point.

"But I can't do it now," Kyna said. "He took—" She looked around at them all. "I can't do it now."

Renyra narrowed her eyes.

"Why? What did he take?" Renyra could see indecision in Kyna's eyes. She tightened her grip on the javelin. "What did he take?" she said again, lowering her voice to a growl.

Kyna paused a moment longer. Her eyes hardened. She took a breath.

"My redstone."

Renyra stared at Kyna, uncomprehending. She read the same confusion on the faces of her troupe.

"Your what?" Raren said.

"The opposite of vierstone," Kyna continued. Each word seemed to cause her effort. "Its mirror, its reverse."

Silence.

Renyra's javelin hung slack in her grip. She tried to make sense of Kyna's words. The *opposite* of vierstone? Her mind began racing through the implications and possibilities. She shuddered.

"But if Gellion has it—" Kyna's eyes went wide. "I can't imagine how he could have it, unless he has always had it—unless he found it first, or his father—but why not use it until now? It would have changed everything." She shook her head. "He can't have it." Kyna's conversation had clearly steered to a one-sided discussion. She hardly seemed aware of the elves around her.

Raren broke through her mutterings.

"Where the hell did Kaelo find the reverse of vierstone?"

Kyna's eyes snapped up, and her external musings broke off. Pain showed in her eyes, and her voice dropped to a near whisper.

"In Maramor."

2 8

MASTERS OF STONE

T wo days.

It was more time than Gellion had hoped for, but it was not enough. Would any amount of time be enough? Certainly two days had not made Gellion feel any better suited to the ridiculous title now lashed to his name. Then again, these two days may prove to be the only days he ever possessed it.

The gates of the city stood wide open. Gellion stared through them. A road spilled from the mouth of Tura, racing through the rolling landscape toward towns and farmland. The grass spreading to either side of the road was a soft yellow, its color leached by the force of summer. The weeks were entering autumn now, but it would still be months before the air of Tura shed its dregs of heat. What would the Great City look like by then?

It is up to you.

Gellion grimaced.

He stood alone on an expanse of stone—smooth and whole. The black sickness that tainted every surface of Tura was not visible from standing height. Seen from a distance, Tura had not changed at all since Kaelo's arrival, yet the city was a shell of its former self. Would the same be said of Tura's inhabitants in a few decades? What would his family be like after years or even centuries without the touch of vierstone? Or would it even matter? Would the elves live under oppression so complete and pain so acute that an absence of vierstone would be a blessing?

The edges of the redstone bit into Gellion's palm. He squeezed harder.

Finally, the merest echo of vibrations reached Gellion's feet. He had been waiting for it, but confirmation of his approaching fate still sent shivers down his spine. He shaded his eyes and looked to the horizon. The cherufin were not yet visible, not from ground level.

Gellion had known of the cherufin's approach for hours, thanks to his scouts. Now all he could do was wait—wait and worry.

Never had Gellion known a best case scenario to be so dismal or so improbable. The battle he now fought was to preserve the last remnants of a broken race, but there would be no rebuilding of what had already been lost. Would it be better to die now, in a last fruitless fight against their enemy, than go on for centuries as broken shadows in a world devoid of hope?

The outline of wings materialized in the sky, distant at first, indistinguishable from an eagle.

"Be ready!" Coren shouted from the top of the wall. The Master of Sport stood at the head of a line of archers. None had their weapons drawn. They would wait until Gellion's orders.

Gellion glanced around, watching the elves gathered in the streets shift their feet and their weapons in agitation. Several elves craned their heads over their companions in attempt to see out the gate. The Turi Council had insisted that the army be present for Gellion's meeting with Kaelo, though they were more a symbolic audience than a guard. If the dragging Council meetings these last two days had resulted in any agreement, it was that a battle between elves and cherufin should be avoided at all costs. There would be nowhere for the elves to run this time, should things come to a fight, and Gellion was determined that no more elves would die under his command. It was a foolish resolve.

The cherufin were visible now. En masse, they looked like a broken wall moving steadily across the landscape. Gellion's eyes darted to the gate mechanisms. His every instinct screamed at him to close the gates against this approaching foe, but he ignored the prompting. The cherufin would get into the city one way or another. He may as well keep Tura's walls intact.

Gellion counted his breaths as the shape, then colors, then piercing eyes of the phoenix came into focus. It flew ahead of its army, a rippling flame brighter than the daylight. He watched death fly to him across golden grass.

The beat of the phoenix's wings sent a hurricane of hot air through the courtyard. Gellion kept his feet rooted to the stone and squinted against the dry wind. Around him, elves hissed and muttered. A few even let out cries of fear or anger. Gellion ignored them. He knew the elves would not strike without his say. The knowledge was heady, yet it gave Gellion a sense of security he had not possessed in Morcanan, or even outside Arvain. The events of those catastrophes lay on his conscience, yet neither situation had been under his direct control. This time there were no other Lords or commanders to whom he must accede. Tura would triumph or fall by his words and his actions, but they were his to make.

The phoenix landed inside the gates in a burst of swirling flame and metallic feathers. It let out a shriek before folding its shimmering wings to its body, then took in the scene before it with rolling eyes and a swiveling neck. The thing's movements were not as jerky or frantic as those of a normal bird; it moved with eerie control and deliberateness, its eyes possessed of an intelligence entirely out of place in its avian head.

"Be still," Gellion said to the surrounding elves. He pitched his voice to carry, but did not shout. He could feel the elves' agitation growing around him. Several of the wall-mounted archers had begun to draw their bows. Gellion could hardly blame them. The phoenix's proximity was sending bursts of fear through his own nerves and muscles, but he would not allow the fear to take over. He couldn't.

A molten eye the size of Gellion's head swiveled to focus on him.

"You command these elves, now?"

The voice nearly broke Gellion's composure. He took a sharp breath and stepped back, his eyes searching for the source of the words, though the less excitable portion of his mind already knew from whence they came. The voice was slithering and sharp—seductive. If Gellion had to place a gender to its sound, he would say it was that of a woman, though it was unlike any woman he had ever heard. The sound of it made his skin crawl, yet he found himself wanting to hear it again.

Gellion cleared his throat and put his feet back together.

"I am," he said.

The phoenix's feathers ruffled, and a glow rippled from its throat down its chest.

"You have opened your gates to surrender?" the phoenix said, its tone colored by a smile, though the beast's face remained expressionless.

"I have opened the gates to speak," Gellion said. "But not to you."

Light rippled down the phoenix's throat again, but this time, its feathers remained plastered to its body. Gellion wished he could read the creature's body language. It swiveled its neck again, and this time, the motion revealed a face behind its head.

Kaelo stared down at Gellion.

If Gellion had thought that seeing Kaelo a week before would have softened the blow of his presence now, he was woefully mistaken. The familiar face sent an electric current ripping through Gellion's body, leaden with memory and power. Gellion said nothing, willing his own face to mimic the hard dispassion of his old mentor. He waited in a silence that pressed against his ears. The next move was Kaelo's.

Slowly, not taking his eyes off Gellion, Kaelo slid from the phoenix's back. His feet hardly made a sound as they landed on stone. Each step he took toward Gellion was deliberate and measured, as though Kaelo were testing his own reactions. As he moved, Gellion's eyes drew to the man's armor. It shifted like liquid with his movements, glinting in the sunlight in shades of black, red, and gold. Woven metal.

Gellion felt the shadow of an old anger wash over him at the sight of the material. It seemed a petty thing now, the loss of his crafting master-piece before a now meaningless competition, yet the theft still rankled him. His tunic, patterned off the teachings of Kaelo himself, had rendered Kaelo nearly invisible as he systematically terrorized Daro. The tunic had lent an infuriating ease to a task the man would undoubtedly have accomplished anyway.

He couldn't have waited one more day to take the damn thing?

Gellion forced his mind back to the present. This was the last thing he should be worrying about right now. The tunic was probably thrown out somewhere. Kaelo clearly had no use for stealth any longer.

Kaelo stopped an arm's length away from Gellion. Gellion drew his eyes from the man's attire to his face, and as his gaze locked with Kaelo's, the world around him seemed to dissolve.

He was a child again. The face in front of him was harder than that of dreams and memory, the expression unrecognizable, but the lines of Kaelo's face and jaw were exactly as they had been so many centuries ago. Gellion saw the man not in woven armor, but simple cloth, his dark hair bound at the nape of his neck to keep it away from molten metal and intricate tool work. There was still laughter hidden in that face, and a slow patience to his bearing. A deep burn of longing welled within Gellion's chest at the memory. A life of beauty, simplicity, and honest work. A time before any phoenixes had come to taint the land. A time before the power of Kaelo's anger had brought about the unthinkable and condemned the elves to the terror they now faced.

"Lord of Tura." Kaelo's voice broke the illusion. He was looking at Gellion with sharp and reading eyes.

Gellion blinked, hoping his face had not shown his emotional breech. Still not trusting his voice, he inclined his head, never breaking eye contact.

Had Kaelo's eyes always been so dark? Gellion could see the man's mind working fast behind the opaque spheres of jade and onyx. There was uncertainty there, almost—a line formed between Gellion's brows as he looked closer at his old mentor. Kaelo's face was not as composed as it had seemed in Morcanan. There were dark shadows under his eyes, and his skin had begun to take on a hue reminiscent of Liera in her final weeks. His eyes were intense, but not with the cold purpose and anger Gellion had expected. They were almost desperate.

Kaelo nodded his head, his eyes unfocusing and his expression turning inward. As his head moved, a glint of light caught Gellion's attention—a speck of color beneath dark locks of hair. Gellion nearly gasped. Fastened to Kaelo's ear, just as every elf in all Riure, was an earring, though instead of emerald, it was deep crimson. The stone shone like a drop of blood against Kaelo's skin.

The man was too absorbed in his own thoughts to notice Gellion's stare. A corner of his mouth quirked up.

"I should have expected no other, I suppose." He nodded to himself, then raised his head. Gellion forced his gaze away from the redstone earring. His hand itched to grab the knife at his belt, to act as rashly as Liera and separate Kaelo from his weapon here and now.

Not yet.

The desperation in Kaelo's eyes was better concealed now, though once seen, Gellion could still catch traces of it. This was no tyrannical dictator confident in his own power. The realization was not comforting, but it bolstered Gellion's words with new strength.

"You have come to take Tura, then," he said. "As you did Morcanan? Demand my surrender and cooperation to rule under your hand?"

Kaelo raised his eyebrows. His crooked smile had faded.

"Yes."

"And if I refuse?'

"Why would you?"

Gellion paused. This was not the response he had been expecting.

"Why?" Gellion said incredulously. "Why would I resist domination by a monster that means to enslave us? That made my life a living hell for two centuries and killed my friends and family?" Gellion did not raise his voice. There was no raging heat of fury in his blood, only a cold and heavy anger. He looked pointedly at the phoenix perched behind Kaelo. Flame and smoke wafted off of the monster's body. Its liquid gaze was trained on Gellion. Gellion looked back at Kaelo with narrowed eyes.

"Why would I refuse the orders of a man who destroyed my life and livelihood? Who betrayed every elf in Riure?"

"I betrayed no one," Kaelo said. "I have only reacted to the blind hatred and violence of a race that condemned me for far less. But this is not about me. I have done this world the greatest service since its broken creation. You, of all elves, should understand what I do. If you would listen, rather than fight, you would not need to surrender. You could join me. You could help. You could lead."

Gellion tried to maintain the force of his glare, but he could feel it slipping. Something in Kaelo's words grated on him. Drew him.

"You have seen the power of anger, Gellion. You have experienced its betrayal."

Gellion flinched. He saw images of a body lying broken among rosebushes, heard the scream of a woman.

"You know the pain of love, the pain of loss. In your eyes, I see the same fear that once possessed me." Kaelo cocked his head. "Do you know what happened when I acted against that fear—when I chose to pursue passion in spite of it?"

Gellion stood as one entranced. He remembered. Kaelo had transformed when he fell in love with Arela, but the joy of that transformation had only made what came next all the worse.

"It destroyed me." Kaelo spoke through clenched teeth, his voice pitched for only Gellion's ears. "As it has nearly destroyed you. As it destroys every elf who strays too close to a thing too powerful and marred for this world."

A slow panic was building within Gellion. He remembered the deep despair, the bottomless chasm that inexorably drew him closer. He remembered it, but he did not see or feel it. He hadn't for weeks. His hand strayed to the stone in his pocket.

"You no longer know me, Kaelo," he said, trying to control the tremor threatening to overtake his voice. "How can you claim to know my experience and pain?"

But then another face flashed in Gellion's mind. He closed his eyes. Though they had only known each other a few months, Kyna knew as much of Gellion's mind as his own brothers. She knew what had happened in Tradira. She knew the extent of his struggles, his temper, his fear. Had her betrayal run deeper even than a secured alliance? Had she been not only a spy among the elves, but a spy upon himself to her father?

"I can see it in your eyes," Kaelo said. "I can hear it in your voice. I knew you once, and a man's nature does not change with years."

"This is why you destroyed vierstone?" Gellion said. "To dull the pain of life?"

Kaelo snorted softly. "Poetically put."

"Then what is this?" Gellion gestured to the phoenix, to the army of demons now close enough to see their glowing eyes. "The vierstone is gone, Kaelo. What more do you have to gain from this? Why does this abomination still answer to you?"

The fear that flashed in Kaelo's eyes was fleeting and powerful. He glanced sideways, as though sensing the eyes of the phoenix behind him.

In that moment, Gellion saw everything.

His insides turned to ice. He looked between Kaelo and the phoenix with a growing dread. Kaelo was no longer the master of the phoenix. He was its slave. The weapon he had created to achieve his purpose had developed its own ambition, and its own hand.

"You fool," Gellion whispered. "In all those centuries of research and planning, you never considered the nature of the beast you sought to raise? You assumed that stone pierced through your ear would give you control, but you were wrong, weren't you?"

Kaelo paled. His eyes flickered again to the phoenix. A steadier fear was beginning to stain his expression, no longer restrained by his will.

"Where did you find it?" Kaelo said.

"In the mountains," said Gellion. "In your cave."

If Kaelo had been white before, he now turned nearly blue. His eyes flashed in shock and anger.

"How—"

"I know everything, Kaelo," Gellion said before he could finish. "The Albaren, the Dierna, the tunic," he spat. "I know what all you have done and how you did it, and I intend to stop you."

Kaelo's mouth was frozen open in a snarl. He shook his head.

"You cannot stop this," he said. "There is nothing you can do." The nearly undetectable tremor in those words was more frightening to Gellion than any amount of threat or conviction could have been.

A low growl sounded, and Gellion looked to the phoenix. It had ruffled all of its feathers, and its throat was glowing with a steady light.

"There is nothing you can do," Kaelo said again, more forcefully this time. His eyes were wide and intense, and one hand strayed toward the phoenix as though trying to keep it at bay. "You cannot fight this. If you refuse to surrender, you will leave us no choice but to react with force. You have seen the wisdom in my purpose. What is more, I see that you have experienced it."

His look was too knowing for Gellion to question or object.

Gellion did know. He had carried redstone for weeks now. He could not remember the last time he had exploded in fiery rage or descended into consuming despair. He felt—control. And he liked it.

"You can save the lives of your people in more ways than one," Kaelo said. "There is no need to perpetuate the strife now riven through the Kindoms."

Gellion's hand closed around the redstone in his pocket. Its current spread up his arm—cool and dissonant. He tried to remember the plan he had agreed to with the Council. What was he supposed to do now?

Fight. You're supposed to fight.

But how? Gellion's mind was moving faster than he could comprehend. The dagger at his hip. The stone in his hand. Kaelo. The phoenix.

The phoenix.

His mind snapped back to focus, but the remembrance of his task was tainted by a new and sudden fear. Gellion had thought Kaelo controlled the phoenix with redstone, but now Gellion questioned whether Kaelo had any control over the beast at all. Was the monster even made of redstone?

Kaelo was watching him, waiting. Gellion suddenly became aware of the hundreds of elves gathered on the streets, roofs, and walls. Their orders were to wait in silence. They trusted him, though none of them knew his plan or his intentions. The details of those particulars were blurring even to Gellion. Kaelo's eyes were those of a father waiting either to praise or disown his son. Gellion felt a child again under that gaze.

No! Focus.

Whether or not Kaelo's destruction of vierstone was founded, the continued existence of the phoenix was not. That was his job now, destroying the phoenix. This was about more than Gellion. His decisions were no longer his own.

Gellion's hand tightened on the redstone in his pocket. He shifted his focus to his feet, where his bare skin met the street beneath the cover of his soulless shoes. He concentrated. Current flowed through him and into the street, extending toward the phoenix.

The familiar sense of heady power consumed him. The street would answer to his command. He could collapse the city, entrap Kaelo and the phoenix in a tomb of stone—except they could use the power too, and that was not his goal. Not yet. He reached the current further and then—

It was like grabbing onto a speeding Rale line. Gellion felt the current from the stone in his hand rip through his body and across the expanse of street, joining with the current within the phoenix like a stream feeding into a raging river. Gellion staggered. He had never been electrocuted, but he imagined it must be very much like this. He felt frozen in place. The city seemed to fade around him. All that existed was his body, the street, and the phoenix. Nothing else could be so alive, so powerful, so *real*. Yet even so, Gellion's sense of the phoenix was distant compared to that of the street. It was as though he were looking at the beast through fogged glass. He could see a vast shape—moving and complex beyond comprehension—but he could not yet sense its entirety.

Closer. Get closer.

He took a step, then his legs swept out from under him.

Gellion hit the street hard. The current snapped. Gellion blinked and shook his head, trying to regain his senses. A shadow fell across him.

"What are you doing?" Kaelo stood over Gellion, his crimson sword drawn. Anger twisted his face, yet he glanced between Gellion and the phoenix with an air of uncertainty.

The corners of Gellion's lips twitched upward. The phoenix was no simple rock, but there was now little doubt in Gellion's mind that it was somehow made of redstone. He felt a supreme satisfaction in the affirmation of his theory, but now what could he do about it? He knew that to even test the last bit of his plan, he would have to get closer to the phoenix. He would have to touch it.

Gellion shook his head from side to side as though dazed. Leaning against one elbow, he shifted so that his hand could again reach into his pocket. Intense relief filled Gellion as he felt the smooth surface of the redstone. It was still there. Gellion did not look at Kaelo or the phoenix.

If they had any time to react, he would be a pile of ashes before he could take two steps.

He took a breath, then, relying on the sheer stupidity of his next action to baffle his enemies into unreactivity, he sprang to his feet and charged the phoenix.

With every step, Gellion sent shocks of current into the street. Behind him, he heard the crack of stone and a grunt. Ahead, the air shimmered in a wall of crimson feathers. The ground fell away beneath the phoenix. Gellion dodged a jet of flame and dove for one of the phoenix's flapping wings before the beast could extricate itself from the pit he had created.

Gellion's hand clasped over slick feathers. He pulled on the energy of the stone in his hand. The electrifying current seized him once more, only this time, he was submerged in it. He no longer felt the solidity of his own body. He was nothing but a vessel, and beyond that vessel, Gellion could see the phoenix. The current vitalized the beast—fed it, controlled it, *made* it. Blood and organs were molten stone, bones were shaped glass, everything about the beast hummed with the current of life, though only at this intensity could Gellion feel the sheer wrongness of that hum.

Yet in all that he sensed, Gellion found no hint of a mind or spirit. He felt icy anger, but no thoughts behind the emotion. How could he control what he could not sense? Was the beast's mind separate from the redstone? There was only the current—the constant, powerful, never ending current that seemed to rip Gellion away from himself. It was like being in the vierstone quarry during the earthquake. The laws of physics, of life, did not matter here. The frequency was wrong. It was opposite.

If Gellion had retained any sense of his body, he would have shouted. Drenched in the current of redstone, the answer was so obvious he could not believe it hadn't occurred to him before. Veldon was right. The current in Gellion's pocket was the same as that in the phoenix, but it was separate too. Gellion may not be able to use the stone to control the phoenix's mind or alter its behavior, but he could alter the current. He could *stop* the current.

The cold anger enveloping Gellion dissipated, replaced by triumph.

"You will not do it." The phoenix's cool voice filled Gellion's mind. "I see your soul."

Gellion froze. He could feel the phoenix's death in his fingertips.

Stop the current.

That was all he had to do. Just stop the current.

"Even if you did, it would not matter," the phoenix said. "I told Eldian I would rise again, and so I would beyond this, whether tomorrow or in a thousand years. You cannot destroy me. My destruction is my life. Put off my reign for a time, but it will come back more terrible than before."

Just do it. Just stop the current.

The phoenix was lying. It was only trying to save itself.

How, then, does it know about your father?

What did it matter? The elves would fight the beast again if it rose once more. Now they had the answer. Gellion could end this war before it began. Still he hesitated.

The phoenix's satisfied amusement hummed through its body, then the current rushed into Gellion. Mind numbing terror engulfed his mind. There was nothing else in the world. The pit he had evaded for weeks loomed wide and deep before him, and the current pushed him closer to the edge with each pulse. What had he been thinking? He couldn't defeat the phoenix. He could do *nothing*. He was pathetic, a fraud, a mouse beneath the talons of an eagle the size of the world itself.

Gellion opened his eyes to profound stillness. The current that had consumed his existence was gone as suddenly as it had come. He could feel the terror like an aftertaste, but he could no longer understand why he had felt it. It took a moment for his eyes to readjust to his surroundings, and even as he registered the flat of the sword extending away from his throat, he felt the prick of its point against his skin and heard the chaos of shouts around him.

Kaelo stood over him once more, only this time his expression was contorted by cold fury. The knuckles of his hand were white around the sword's hilt, and there was murder in his eyes.

Gellion fought to regain his wits.

"I saved your life!" he said, ignoring the jab of pain as the sword bit into the first layer of his skin.

Kaelo flinched, but his hand remained steady.

"I trusted you even after you left me in Tura without a word of explanation," Gellion said. "After everything you did."

Kaelo's nostrils flared. Behind him, Gellion could see swirling reds and oranges. The elven shouts had turned to screams.

"But in the end, you too betrayed me." Kaelo spoke so softly Gellion could hardly make out the words. "Just like all the others." For a moment, the pain in his eyes overshadowed all else, and Gellion felt the beginnings of pity for the man Kaelo had once been.

Then the hardness returned to Kaelo's face.

"This is your decision then?" He gestured around him. The elves had drawn their weapons and were starting to fight the encroaching army of cherufin. The phoenix hovered above the scene, its mouth hanging ominously open, as though awaiting the signal to douse all those below it in flame.

"You will watch your people fall rather than forsake your self-righteous pride?"

Gellion watched elves crushed beneath stone fists. He listened to the sounds of rage, terror, and pain saturating the air. He had failed. He could not protect them. More out of instinct than defiance, Gellion reached his hand into his pocket. His fingers met cold stone. Lifeless stone. The redstone was dead.

"No more of that, now," Kaelo said silkily.

Gellion was weaponless. Powerless.

"Surrender," Kaelo said. "Call off the Turi, Gellion, or you will leave me no choice but to destroy this city as it deserves."

Gellion's heart was beating in his ears, muffling the sounds of battle. There was no choice. He would not lead his entire city to slaughter—not again.

Clenching his fists, Gellion bowed his head.

A shriek cut through the tumult of shouts. The sounds of crashing rock subsided.

Gellion raised his head to see the cherufin frozen in place and the phoenix hovering with a closed beak. The elves paused, stumbled, hesitated.

"Drop your weapons," Gellion said in a voice that carried through the streets. "It is over."

Kaelo waited until he saw Gellion's orders carried out, then nodded and lowered the tip of his sword to the ground.

"Clean this up and reorganize as you see fit," he said. "We will meet tonight to discuss the future of this city."

The phoenix landed next to Kaelo, and he mounted it in a single bound. The beast lifted off the ground in a buffet of wings. Gellion could have sworn he heard its laughter in his head as it flew toward the city's center.

Gellion's brothers were upon him the moment the beast's shadow left the courtyard.

"Gellion!" Veldon's eyes roved Gellion's body. "Riu above, are you hurt? What happened?"

Valder and Tornac flanked Veldon, blocking a frantic Tenille, who was grabbing at their shoulders to get through.

Gellion sat on the ground, feeling more like a child than he had even under Kaelo's gaze. He could have killed the phoenix. He could have ended it. He had hesitated, and he had failed.

"What did he say?" Tenille pushed through her sons and kneeled next to Gellion. Her eyes were rimmed with red.

"He will meet with me tonight." Gellion gritted his teeth and sat up straighter. A firm resolve was forming in his mind, fed by the last possibility of hope he could imagine. "But I do not intend to be here to keep the appointment." His eyes turned to his brothers. "Our time ran out. Now we reset the clock to a new end."

Gellion's brothers stared at him as though fearing for his sanity.

Gellion pushed himself to his feet and looked toward the retreating form of the phoenix.

"Now we go to Maramor."

PART III

2 9

WEAPONS OF THE PAST

The clouds over Tura formed swollen towers. They were the deep blues and greys of an ocean storm—an autumn storm. Kaelo had told Kyna stories of the Semestrial Sea, how its calm and glassy waters turned violent before the leaves began to change in the mountains and proved impassible until the first buds began to break six months later. It looked as though no ships would be leaving the shores of Faeran any time soon. Kyna grimaced. What reason had they to leave anyway? Daro was gone. There would be no more trade voyages or expeditions to find vierstone. There was no escaping the terrors now ruling over the land.

Kyna's feet ached. She could not say she missed the phoenix's company, but flying had certainly been less exhausting than walking. The Rale line was still broken for over a day's walk north of Tura. At least they had managed to slip out of the Morcani lands on one of the machines. Kyna had to admit she liked the smooth and constrained track of the Rale line far more than the levit boards and lifts of the cities, though the cars had been shockingly crowded with elves. Where were they all going? All the cities would be the same in a few weeks. There would be no escaping by Rale.

"How do we know if he's been here?" Raren said.

The gates of Tura were closed, but whether to keep enemies out or elves in, there was no way of knowing. There was no damage to the city walls as far as Kyna could see. Either her father had not yet arrived, or the city had been turned over without violence.

"There are no guards on the walls," Firas said.

"So," Renrya said. "You think we're too late?"

"I think we should get a better look," said Firas. "Carefully."

Kyna took a deep breath, trying to break up the tightness in her chest. The prospect of seeing Gellion again was enough to freeze her blood, but to do so while sneaking beneath the conquest of her father—

"We can go to the river entrance," Caerlyn said. "We'll be able to see if it's guarded from outside the walls. If it's not, we can slip through and get a better look."

Kyna sighed. The Orhiri River rushed into Tura a good five miles west of the main city gate. Her feet throbbed, and the force of her heartbeat was growing exhausting. She just wanted to get this over with.

Renyra set off along the outside of the city walls, as much bounce to her step as when they had stepped off the Rale line. Even Firas and Trali seemed in better shape than Kyna after the day's hike.

Bloody Sira performers.

The clouds were blowing closer to land now. Kyna could feel the air turning ahead of the storm. She had stayed in Tura long enough to know that most sea storms never reached the city, but this one seemed in no mood to stop before the sea cliffs. Distant grass and shrubs were beginning to bend against the wind, but the city walls blocked the worst of the gusts. Still, the temperature was dropping. This would be no warm summer rain.

By the time the Orhiri River was in sight, fat drops of water had begun to fall from the sky. Kyna did her best to ignore the unpleasant splashes and narrowed her eyes toward the gap in the walls ahead. Hunks of rock still littered the water where her father had feigned an attempt to stop their escape from Tura weeks before. Kyna grimaced. The troupe had thought her so clever for getting them out of the city unscathed. They had thought their mission a grand and Riu-inspired attempt to save Tura with vierstone and warn the other Kindoms of what may come. They had all been fools, but perhaps none so much as Kyna herself.

"Damn," said Raren. "I think I see one of those cherufin inside the walls."

Kyna's heart jerked. Her eyes followed Raren's pointed finger. It was difficult to distinguish the figure of stone against a stone wall, but once pointed out, Kyna could see the outline of a head and shoulders. These cherufin looked different than those the phoenix had raised in the Terulian Mountains. Those cherufin had been dark and course, made of basalt and granite with molten eyes and ligaments. These were a lighter grey, marbled with tan. They were no less imposing.

"We're too late." Renyra hissed between her teeth.

Firas laid a hand on her shoulder.

"We are too late to confront Kaelo here, but we can still find Gellion. That is our true goal, remember?"

Renyra grimaced.

"The city looks to be intact," said Alura. "That must mean the Turi surrendered."

"I wonder who did it though," said Raren. "With Liera gone." He turned his eyes down.

Kyna flinched at the memory. She could still smell the charred smoke every time she thought of it.

"How are we supposed to find Gellion if we can't get inside?" said Caerlyn.

"It looks to me like there is only one cherufin," said Trali. "We could wait until dark and slip past it—swim."

The thought of submerging herself in water made Kyna shudder. The raindrops were coming faster now, and she could feel her clothes beginning to dampen. Much more of this, and a dip in the river wouldn't make a difference anyway, she supposed.

"Tura isn't as defensible as Morcanan," said Raren. "We could probably walk to the cliffs and slip past the wall there."

"We would still have to get across the river," said Alura.

Kyna opened her mouth, then closed it. Even after days spent back with Renyra and the troupe, she felt uncomfortable speaking to them. It was as though she had been acting the part of a different person when she had known them before, and now entered their ranks as a stranger.

At least she had come with valuable information. Information they may not even be able to act upon if they couldn't find Gellion.

Her mind reeled with the possibility she still could not accept. Could Gellion have redstone in his possession? It seemed impossible, yet the entire troupe claimed to have seen him perform feats only a bearer of redstone could achieve. And then there had been the pillar of stone in Morcanan. Kyna had assumed her father had created it, but could it have instead been an attack by Gellion's own hand?

"What is it?" said Firas.

Kyna blinked, realizing after several moments that the willowy Morcani was talking to her.

"I—well. I don't think it makes sense for us all to go into the city, not if it's under guard. We don't know if the phoenix is still here, and my ... my father can recognize any of us. If we could just slip one person past the walls, they would have a better chance at getting through unseen. They could go find Gellion and bring him to us, or at least relay our message."

Firas gave her a considering look, then nodded. "A good plan."

"I'll go," Renyra said immediately.

Firas looked as though he regretted agreeing to the plan already.

"Actually," Kyna said carefully. "I think it would be better if Alura went, or Raren. They are Turi and will draw less attention. They're also a lot less likely to be recognized if my father is still in the city." Kyna did her best to endure Renyra's withering look. She could hardly blame the little Fieri for her suspicion and disdain, but the constant glares and silence were beginning to wear on Kyna. What more did the woman expect her to do? She had already apologized and offered her help.

"Makes sense to me," said Raren. He glanced at his sister, obviously as reluctant to send her into the hostile city alone as Firas was to send Renyra.

With a calm smile, Alura said, "I'll be back as soon as I can. Wait for me by the cliffs. I think they are a safer return route than swimming upriver." With that, the woman dropped her satchel at Raren's feet, took two steps toward the river, and dove gracefully into its depths.

The weak sunlight was doing little to dry Kyna's clothes. She gnawed on a strip of dried venison and tried to concentrate on more pleasant things. They had stopped walking. Finally. The storm had passed. Finally. She had food, even if it was rubbery and tedious. These things, along with the fact that Renyra hadn't glared at her in over an hour, almost made up for the rest of this situation—Kyna was exhausted and damp, surrounded by elves who eyed her like she was a dangerous criminal, and if all went to plan, Gellion would be here any moment. Kyna's stomach lurched, and she lowered the venison from her lips.

What would he do when he saw her? Would Alura warn him she was here? Would he scorn her as Renyra had? Refuse to listen to or travel with her? Or would he simply run her through with a halberd?

More than once, Kyna had considered simply walking away. She had gotten safely out of Morcani lands, and she had passed on the key to the phoenix's destruction to elves who might be able to make use of the information. For what reason should she wait around to confront Gellion? What further use could she be? Maybe she should go find a mountain village in Ard Gael, where she had once told Gellion she was from. Elves in the country probably wouldn't recognize her. She could start a new life. Let other elves deal with the problems she had set loose in the world.

Still, Kyna remained stretched out in the newly revealed sun, her back against the thick walls of Tura. She stared at the edge of the sea cliffs, only a stone's throw away. A shiver passed along her spine. How close were they to the place? Everything that had happened—Daro, the vierstone, the phoenix, her existence—came from a moment in time, centuries ago, on these very sea cliffs. Had her father revisited the site during those weeks they had spent in Tura? Could he still see blood soaking into the golden grass? Kyna closed her eyes. It had all made so much sense. Everything her father had done had been justified. Everything they had worked for had been so clear. How had it all twisted into something so terrible?

"There," Raren said in an urgent whisper.

Kyna's eyes flew open. Her head snapped toward the end of the wall, where stone crumbled away to a sheer drop below. An elf was crawling sideways along the rocks. Kyna's breath froze in her chest, then she recognized the cropped hair of Alura.

Rising to her feet, Kyna followed the other troupe members toward Alura. Kyna thought she could hear the scuff of another elf behind the woman. Raren helped Alura onto solid ground, and another hand appeared against the stone. Kyna felt a jolt of electricity pass through her as the setting sun caught a flash of auburn hair.

Kyna's legs tensed to run. It wasn't too late. She could get away before he got to his feet.

Then the elf's face came into view.

It wasn't Gellion. It was his mother.

Trali came up behind Raren and offered a large hand to Tenille, who took it with a polite smile. Kyna stared at Gellion's mother, her heart seeming to drop to her feet. Gellion must be dead. Or imprisoned. Why else would Alura have returned with one of Gellion's family but not the man himself? Kyna's knees turned to jelly, and she grasped the wall with one hand. Had her father done it? Had he turned on his old student— the one elf who had not turned on him in his centuries of exile?

Alura and Tenille brushed off their clothes and walked away from the cliffs, Raren and Trali on their heels. Tenille looked serious, but not upset. Kyna remembered the shadowed and hollow look of the woman's face during those first Turi Council meetings, when she had thought three of her sons dead. This was not the same woman. But if Gellion wasn't dead, why was he unable to come himself?

Tenille's eyes locked on Kyna. The rage that flashed behind them was so akin to Gellion's that Kyna had the insane urge to laugh. She stopped herself.

A thick silence fell. Everyone looked between Tenille and Kyna. Tenille's expression was not so much hostile as murderous, but when she spoke, it was in a controlled monotone.

"Explain."

Kyna's lips parted, but no sound came out. Explain what? How much had Alura told Tenille? Kyna swallowed and opened her mouth again, but it was a different question that came to her lips.

"Where is Gellion?"

Tenille raised an eyebrow. Her face practically screamed, "You have the nerve to ask about my son after all you did?" The woman remained silent.

Next to Tenille, Alura nodded at Kyna encouragingly to go on.

So Kyna spoke.

She began by trying to explain redstone, but she had hardly uttered a sentence before Tenille interrupted.

"I know about redstone. Go on."

Tenille was not a forgiving audience. She questioned Kyna with snappish responses, asking for a full explanation of Kaelo's plan and what Kyna knew of the phoenix. Kyna spoke quickly, glossing over as many details as she could in the interest of time. It was not Tenille who needed to know these things, it was Gellion.

"So what does it mean?" Tenille said when Kyna had finished. "What is the point of coming to Tura with this story?"

"Redstone is the key," said Kyna. "It's the only way to destroy the phoenix, and she," Kyna nodded to Renyra, "is under the impression that Gellion has some."

"You do not have any?" Tenille said.

Kyna looked away. "Not anymore."

"Why didn't you use it when you had the chance? When you were close to the phoenix?"

"I don't know the details of how to do it," Kyna said. "I have never had an affinity for the stone like my father. Besides, he and the phoenix together would have been able to stop me."

Tenille looked thoroughly unconvinced by this explanation. She maintained a narrowed gaze on Kyna. Kyna raised her eyes to meet Tenille's.

"And I was afraid," she said. "I was a coward."

This seemed to satisfy Tenille more.

"Alright, and why should I believe this—everything about the redstone?"

"Why would I make it up?"

Tenille's eyebrows rose to her hairline.

"Would this be the first time you have invented an elaborate story to further your father's aims?"

Kyna closed her mouth and took a deep breath.

"This is different. Everything I have told you is true, as far as my knowledge goes. Now please, where is Gellion? Does he have redstone?"

Tenille eyed Kyna a moment longer, then turned her gaze to the rest of the troupe.

"Yes," she said. "Gellion has redstone, and from what you describe, I think he already tried to use it against the phoenix."

Kyna's mouth fell open. "What?" She still burned to know how Gellion had come upon the redstone in the first place, but this new information wiped all else from her mind. Gellion had redstone—he knew how to use it—he had tried already what Kyna had been too afraid to do herself.

"He rushed the phoenix and touched it with his hand," said Tenille. "I do not know what happened then, but Kaelo threw Gellion off the phoenix before he could do anything. Gellion would explain nothing afterward. There was little time. Gellion had surrendered the city and wanted to escape before Kaelo came for him."

Firas's eyes snapped up. "You said *Gellion* surrendered the city?" he said. "What do you mean?"

Tenille's eyes softened when she looked at Firas.

"He was named Lord of Tura before Kaelo's arrival."

Everyone stared at Tenille in stunned silence, then Caerlyn let out a laugh.

"Well, I guess if anyone deserves the title at this point, he does."

"But what do you mean escape?" Renyra's eyes were wide and worried. "You mean he is gone?"

Tenille nodded. "He hid with his brothers until nightfall, then slipped up the river."

Raren laughed. "Well, looks like we're embarking on another midnight river escape. At least we're well practiced, though I suppose Tornac was familiar with the tactic too."

"But why?" said Renyra, ignoring Raren. "Where are they going?"

"To Maramor," Tenille said. "They think that my husband knew something more of the phoenix than he let on in the last weeks of his life. They think he knew of a different way to destroy the phoenix. They are going to try to find out."

Kyna went rigid. All eyes but Tenille's were resting on her. Following their gazes, Tenille knit her brows.

"What?" she said.

"They won't find anything there," Kyna said softly.

Based upon Gellion's shocking knowledge of redstone, she had begun to assume that Tenille already knew this part of the story. It was clear she did not. Kyna hesitated, then took a breath. There was no use hiding the information from his wife, she supposed, but it seemed wrong somehow, coming from an outsider. Tenille would find out eventually anyway, when Kyna told Gellion. If she ever found him.

"Because my father already did," she said.

Tenille's eyes were burning pools of emerald.

"Found—what." She pronounced each word separately.

"My father learned to create redstone from vierstone," Kyna said. "But he was not the first to discover redstone. He found it. In Maramor."

Tenille went pale.

Kyna went on. "Eldian was the first elf to discover redstone. Redstone *is* what he used to destroy the phoenix."

CONVERGENCE

The Archives of Maramor were not large. Most of the important documents of the Turi resided in Tura. The books and scrolls surrounding Gellion were manuals of metalwork, stonework, or glasswork. There were tomes on architecture and art, the natural history of Ard Gael, and personal musings of elves who had called Maramor home over the centuries. Not one of them was of any use to Gellion.

The dull eyes of Gellion's brothers reflected the hopelessness seeping into his own bones. Only Farra still flipped through pages with any conviction. Gellion watched the woman. She was fierce in her study of the pages before her. Gellion liked Farra, but the force of her personality had frequently clashed with his own in the final years of the war when she had joined their family. Still, he could not deny how happy she made Veldon. Some of the worry that had creased Veldon's face these last weeks melted away each time he sat next to her. His brow was furrowed as he half heartedly skimmed a page of notes, but he was sitting so close to Farra that their arms touched, and a corner of his mouth curved upward each time she huffed in frustration or snapped the cover of another book closed.

After the productive week spent searching Kaelo's notes and books in the Falspire Mountains, Gellion had expected their search of

Maramor to uncover Eldian's secret quickly and efficiently. Surely Tornac had overlooked some hidden compartment in their father's study or glossed over a vital tome that he had not thought relevant at the time. Surely a meticulous and desperate search by five dedicated elves would uncover Eldian's secret in a matter of days.

There was nothing.

Gellion had not even found a mention of the phoenix in all the words he had skimmed these last three days. His heart had lurched when he finally found sheets of paper bearing his father's handwriting, but the notes had been about vierstone—interesting enough in their content, but nothing to do with the phoenix.

They were running out of books to search. There were no papers, scrolls, or hidden crevices yet to be uncovered. As the hours dragged by, Gellion found himself closer and closer to admitting that his father had taken his secret to the grave.

"This is useless." Valder pushed away the last of the books yet to be searched. They were natural history books. "None of these are going to give us any clues about father. We got lucky in Suri Ranta. That entire library was dedicated to Kaelo's cause. But this?" He gestured at the Archives.

Veldon was nodding. Tornac was scowling at his hands. Farra continued to read.

"I think he is right," Veldon said softly. "I do think it was worth coming here—trying. But I do not think another month would give us the answers we seek. There are none to discover." He looked at Gellion with searching eyes. It was an expression Gellion had endured often these last days.

Gellion had rushed his brothers out of Tura with little explanation of what had happened with the phoenix. In the chaos following Kaelo's arrival, it had been easy enough to find a boat and hide it away until night-fall, then zip past the cherufin stationed to either side of the river. Ever since, Gellion's brothers had questioned him relentlessly, but something had prevented Gellion from telling them what had really happened when he touched the phoenix. He had told them that the phoenix was indeed made of redstone, but that he had been unable to control it. He had left out the detail that he could have destroyed the phoenix. The moment of hesitation that had cost the elves an end to their terror shamed Gellion to his core, but it was fear that truly held Gellion's tongue. The phoenix's final words played in his mind over and over—*I will rise again ... I told Eldian.*

So his father had known the phoenix would rise again before he died. Had he only learned the fact right before his death? Had he died knowing he had unknowingly condemned the elves by hiding the key to his victory? And *how* in all of Riure had he done it?

"Gellion," Veldon said. "Do you have ... are you sure you didn't—" He looked afraid to continue, and Gellion felt a moment of guilt. "What happened when you touched the phoenix? If you learned anything at all, or even suspect something." He shook his head. "We are out of options here."

Everyone was looking at Gellion. Even Farra raised her eyes from her book.

Gellion fingered the redstone in his pocket. The shame of his failure prickled along his skin. Even if using redstone against the phoenix was the only possible way to destroy it, even if that destruction would only last a few years or centuries, Gellion no longer had the means to carry out the act. His redstone was black—as dead and lifeless as all the vierstone he had watched destroyed these last months. This too he had kept to himself. What was the point of telling his brothers how to kill the phoenix if the only weapon left to them was in the possession of their enemy? There had to be another way. His father had to have found another way.

"Gellion?" It was Valder who spoke this time. His face was serious, his eyes as searching.

Then the door to the archives opened. Gellion let out a breath.

"My lord," said a voice.

Gellion cringed at the honorific. The Lord of Tura, shut away in a damn library hundreds of miles from the city he had surrendered to their enemy.

Some Lord.

Sighing, Gellion turned to see an elf he did not recognize standing in front of him.

The elf inclined his head, then said, "There are elves here to see you. Elves from Tura."

Cold fear seeped into Gellion's skin. Elves from Tura? Had something happened to the city? To his mother? He had known it was foolish to send his mother to meet Kaelo in his stead. Had Reanan and Saethir come to tell him that she was dead, and the city destroyed for the abandonment of its leader?

"Let them in," said Gellion.

"Gellion!"

The familiar voice sent a shock of adrenaline through his body. Renyra had stepped into the room with a huge smile on her face. Behind her was Firas. Gellion stared at his friends with wide eyes. The tension fell from his shoulders, and he felt an answering grin stretching across his face. He had feared the worst for his friends after the disaster at Morcanan, yet in the strange fog that had descended over him, he had hardly seemed capable of mourning their potential loss as he had following the battle at Arvain. But here they stood, alive and well.

"How in Riu's name did you get here?" Gellion stepped forward, catching Renyra's hug with a stumble and clasping Firas's hand. The man's grip seemed firmer than it had in Morcanan, and his face was less drawn.

"It was not easy," Firas said with a chuckle.

More figures were moving in the doorway. Gellion looked past Firas to see Caerlyn, along with the bulky Remsgri elf and a few more indistinct shapes behind them.

"You brought the whole troupe I see?" Gellion stepped back to allow all the newcomers to file into the Archives. Despite the high ceilings, the room suddenly felt cramped with the influx of bodies and emotions.

The smile faded from Renyra's face. "We have to talk to you." She glanced behind Gellion. "All of you."

"What has happened?" Tornac was standing now, his brow furrowed in concern.

The last of the newcomers were walking into the room. At first, Gellion only registered the dark heads of Turi and passed them off as the other members of the troupe he had recently met, but then his memory nudged him. Hadn't there been only two Turi among Renyra's troupe?

"A lot has happened." Renyra cast a furtive glance behind her, then turned her eyes on Gellion. She looked just as Veldon had before he asked Gellion about the phoenix—wary, afraid.

"What—" Gellion began.

"Just hear us out." Firas's expression was as cautious as Renyra's, and Gellion felt himself growing annoyed. What were they hiding?

"All of us," Firas said.

The third Turi stepped into the light, and Gellion turned to face her.

The impact was not immediate or forceful. Gellion's recognition came as a slow spread. His mind caught up with his eyes in halting steps as he took in the familiar gloss of hair, the straight nose, the jeweled eyes. Perhaps it was the expression sitting within those eyes that gave him pause—an expression so disjointed with this otherwise flawless manifestation of his memories that he could not at first reconcile the two. But as her image remained—this impossible specter—the reality of the woman before Gellion began to seep into his being with the thick stickiness of cold molasses.

Kyna stood with her eyes lifted to Gellion. The opaque mask of haughtiness and irony Gellion had come to know in her face was absent, replaced by a disconcerting clarity. He could see her wariness, her fear, her sorrow. As strange as these emotions were on her face, stranger still was how—well, *normal* Kyna looked. In her achingly familiar countenance, Gellion could detect no hint of the changes his newfound knowledge of her past and identity should have wrought. Kyna looked just as she had as they strolled through the sun dappled streets of Daro, as they sparred with wooden staves, as they drew close on a breezy night in Albarad.

A spark of heat penetrated Gellion's sluggish encasing. He began to emerge from the fog of his brain and found his shock was melting away. Beneath that shock was something much less comprehensible, and much more frightening.

Without so much as a blink or a nod, Gellion moved his eyes from Kyna to Firas. No sound had permeated the still air of the Archives since

Kyna's arrival, save the initial intakes of breath from Gellion's brothers. Gellion trained his gaze solely on Firas. His best friend. The man who had brought this terrible ghost back to Gellion.

Firas glanced from Gellion to Kyna and shifted his feet. Gellion waited.

"She left him, Gellion," Firas said. "She left her father. She came to us, and she wants to help."

Gellion did not react. He did not trust himself even to raise an eyebrow, lest the tangle of emotions pressing against his ribs rip free. He had not felt this way for weeks, months even. Still, the writhing mass within him was more akin to churning magma than licking fire. It would not overwhelm him without warning, not all at once.

Gellion turned his head back to Kyna. The same emotions still pulsed behind her eyes, but she seemed incapable of giving voice to any of them. She stood silent and wide-eyed, as though awaiting the fall of a sword.

"Why?" Gellion's lips hardly parted to utter the word, yet Kyna flinched as though his voice had reached across the distance between them and hit her.

"Why—" she began.

The sound of her voice weakened Gellion's hold over the bubbling anger now rising in his throat.

"Why," he said, "do you want to help us? For what reason, after all this time, have you decided that your loyalties are better placed elsewhere? What did it finally take?"

Kyna opened her mouth, but Gellion did not allow her to answer.

"It could not have been seeing the last of the vierstone turn black. That was always your plan, was it not? Nor do I expect it had anything to do with guilt over the elves you manipulated and betrayed. Guilt never was an emotion of which you proved yourself capable. Was it," he said with an arched eyebrow, "simply the completion of your personal goal? You have no further need of the phoenix now that vierstone is gone. Or was it perhaps *you* who proved yourself of no further use to the phoenix and your father?"

Pain had been growing in Kyna's eyes throughout his accusations and broke over her face at Gellion's last question, but the pain was colored by the beginnings of anger. The anger fed Gellion's own. He went on.

"Or," he said in a lower tone, "was it watching the mother of your father burned to ash a few steps away? Seeing an army of demons raised against an entire race?"

"None of that was supposed to happen," Kyna said. Her voice was unsteady, shaken by the weight of emotions Gellion had never known her to feel. He raised his eyebrows.

"No? Did the phoenix not live up to your expectations? Did you think it would be different from the beast that tried to destroy the elves for two hundred years? Your father has lost control of it. I saw it in his face. He is now as much a slave to the monster as the rest of us will be, should we lose the war it is sure to wage, and *you* helped create it."

The rage flowing beneath Gellion's skin was cold and steady. It hummed in satisfaction at the agony in Kyna's eyes. So what if she regretted what she had done? She had still done it. She had still condemned the elves to a life of unfeeling brutality. She had still used them, used him, betrayed him.

Kyna had looked away from him. She took a slow breath, then looked up at him with an expression that was somehow both broken and defiant.

"Do you remember your father?" she said softly.

Gellion bristled.

"Do you remember what you thought of him?" Kyna continued. "What you felt for him? Did you trust him—his words, his opinions, his decisions?"

She paused. Gellion did not respond.

"And if he was the only elf you had ever known?" Kyna said. "His the only words, opinions, and decisions you had ever known? What would you have done? What would you have done differently than me?"

Gellion's mouth, open in half a snarl ready to retort, slowly closed.

"Would you have run away from your father—the only elf, let alone family—you had ever known, to lead a life of solitude and danger in the mountains of a hostile and human continent? Would you have intrinsically rebelled against the purpose given to your life—rejected the only view of the world you had ever known?" Her face twisted into an ironic smile. "Surely *you* would have had the courage to destroy the phoenix with your own hand, a step away from your father, when you did not know if your attempt would even work."

Gellion flinched.

"Surely you would have had the courage to leave both phoenix and father, after all you had seen and all you had lived, condemning yourself to exile and hatred."

Gellion stared at Kyna, bereft of speech. His righteous anger was ebbing, a squirming discomfort taking its place. He held onto the anger with a desperate and painful grip.

"My existence was to serve a purpose," Kyna said. "My existence was to be an example. That is why I *live*. Why Kaelo fathered me." Her voice broke. She cleared her throat. "I abandoned the purposes of my existence. I abandoned them for the sake of elves that hate and mistrust me."

Gellion nearly turned his eyes away from her then, but forced himself to hold her gaze.

"I am not calling myself a hero, Gellion. I know what I am. I know what I have done, and I know the pain it has caused you. You have the right to be angry with me. You may even have the right to hate me. But you do not have the right to judge me." A sheen of tears brightened her eyes, but her stance remained firm.

Every further retort Gellion had been preparing died in his throat. His anger for the woman still weighed against his bones like lead. Whatever her justifications, it was Kyna who had made Daro's fall possible—Kyna who had enabled Dulon's death—Kyna who had caused Gellion more pain, anxiety, and shame than he had known since the Great War. Yet Gellion's attention returned again to her eyes. The strength that showed behind her tears was too much for Gellion not to admire. Deeper still than the strength was sorrow, regret. A shadow of the same regret pulled at Gellion's chest. After all this woman had done to him, after all he had learned of her truth and her past, Gellion found with a surge of longing and self disgust that part of him still loved her.

Grinding his teeth, Gellion looked away from Kyna. Renyra was staring at the floor, her brow furrowed. Beside her, Firas was watching Gellion with an expression that said "Well, will you listen?" Gellion moved his gaze to his brothers. Tornac watched Kyna with obvious hostility, but there was reservation in the intensity of his stare. Valder and Veldon were both looking at Gellion. Gellion tried to read their eyes for some hint of what to do. If Kyna was telling the truth, he would be a fool to deny her help. Had he and his brothers not just exhausted the last of their own hopes? Yet there still remained a part of Gellion—the part most hurt by her betrayal—that insisted this was another trap. Another part urged Gellion to simply throw Kyna out of Maramor out of spite.

Predictably, Veldon exuded sympathy, though for Gellion or for Kyna, Gellion could not be sure. Valder was more reserved in his encouragement, but gave a small shrug and a nod.

Taking a slow breath, Gellion squared his shoulders to Kyna, looked her in the eye, and nodded once. Then he walked back to the seat he had abandoned, turned it to face Kyna, and lowered himself into it.

He waited.

A DAUGHTER'S TALE

Gellion said nothing. He just sat there, staring at her. Waiting.

Kyna wished her heart would stop attempting to burst itself against her sternum. More embarrassing were the tears shimmering over her eyes. She knew Gellion had seen them.

Say something.

He had nodded. What did that mean? That he would accept her help? That he forgave her? Kyna was not so naive as to believe the latter. She would settle for the first. But where to begin? There was so much ... so much.

Every eye in the room was fixed on Kyna. She felt the weight of their expectancy, their hostility. Kyna glanced nervously at Firas, who raised an eyebrow and motioned for her to speak.

"Well?" Gellion said.

Kyna nearly jumped at his voice. It was so perfectly the same as in all of her memories. Just like his face—his face that had always showed everything. Now it was still and blank.

Gellion raised his eyebrows. His arms were crossed over his chest.

"Explain," he said. "Everything."

Everything.

Kyna took a long breath, nodded to herself, and began.

"I was born among humans, raised in the Falspires next to their villages, though I don't remember my mother and only saw humans from a distance after I left the village. There was only my father. He raised me. He told me stories. At first the stories were about the elves: their customs, their cities, their history. I was fascinated by them and wanted to know more—why they were so far away, why we didn't live with them.

"My father told me the elves were broken, that it was our job to fix them, but we had to stay away from them until the time was right. I accepted his explanation. I enjoyed the solitude of the mountains and longed for no more company than my own, but my curiosity grew with the years. Whenever my father spoke of the elves, a shadow crossed his face. His stories were touched by a darkness I could not place or explain. Eventually, when I was fully grown, he told me everything. He told me his story."

Kyna stopped. Raren and Trali had appeared on either side of her, carrying stacked chairs. Raren shrugged.

"Sounds like it's going to be a long story," he said. "We may as well sit for it." He placed one chair behind Kyna, then moved on to give one to his sister.

Still shaky, Kyna lowered herself awkwardly onto the edge of the chair and took advantage of the momentary reprieve to observe her audience. Gellion and his brothers had blinked and shaken themselves at Raren's interruption as though emerging from sleep. The diversion of Gellion's attention had been like a snapped cord—Kyna had not noticed the intensity of its pull until it was gone. Now it returned in full. At least his expression was no longer laden with contempt and cold fury—it was hungry. The knuckles of his clasped hands were white. He opened his mouth, then seemed to realize who he was about to talk to and closed it. After several more moments of grinding his jaw, he opened his mouth again.

"You know what happened, then?" he said. "In Tura? What really happened?"

Kyna nodded.

For a moment, Gellion's anger seemed to vanish. His eyes widened, and his posture slackened, though his hands still remained in a tight ball.

Kyna saw him then as he must have been centuries ago—a young and unmentioned apprentice in her father's story, watching from without as his mentor was accused of and banished for murder, never knowing the truth of what had happened.

The truth was not Kyna's to tell. Her father had told no one—not Liera, not the Council, not his apprentice. No one but Kyna. She had not intended to tell this part of her father's story, yet now she found herself wanting to justify him, if not to all of these elves, then to Gellion —to the one who had not turned against his mentor. Not until he had raised a phoenix.

The room had settled again. Everyone was watching Kyna.

"My father had a wife. Arela," Kyna said. "For her, he gave himself over to a love he had never allowed himself to feel before. It consumed him, and spread the heat of his passion to everything else in his life."

Gellion nodded. He had lowered his eyes, lost in unseen images of his own memories.

"They were happy together for years, but long before my father had married Arela, his own mentor had loved her. Bardan had known Arela since childhood. He and my father hadn't been on good terms for decades. He never told me why. But out of spite, jealousy, or something more, Bardan tried to take Arela from Kaelo. My father wouldn't tell me the details of Bardan's treachery, or anything about Arela, but a time came when Bardan openly professed his love of Arela, claiming that she had always felt the same for him, and that Kaelo had coerced her into marriage. It was a lie, but the rumor spread. It broke something in my father."

Kyna paused, remembering the look in his eyes the first time he had told her this story. It was the first time Kyna had ever seen a shadow of the feelings her father had sworn he left behind. It had frightened her.

"His rage and pain were all consuming. Stronger than anything he had ever felt. He accused Bardan of slander before Tura's Council, and demanded the man be forced to take back his heinous words and leave the city, but there was no real backing to support the exile, and Bardan was a respected metalworker of the city. The Council's refusal only deepened my father's shame and anger. He couldn't bear it. He challenged Bardan. The two would fight to first blood, the loser to bow his head and leave Tura. It was an old ritual practiced by the elves of the countryside and banned in the Great Cities, but Bardan accepted.

"My father met him on the sea cliffs of Tura. Blood was drawn quickly in their duel, but neither relented. Stoked by fury and desperation, the fight grew vicious. Then Arela showed up. Someone must have seen my father and Bardan leaving the city together, or maybe she saw them herself and followed. My father turned to her call, and in his moment of distraction, Bardan knocked the knife from his hand. He attacked my father. Kaelo fought back, trying to fend Bardan off with his bare hands, though he had little chance against the blade. I don't know if Bardan meant to kill Kaelo or not, but before his knife could cause any serious harm, my father felt Bardan's body jerk—saw his eyes go wide. He scrambled out from under Bardan and saw Arela standing behind the man, her face white with horror. My father's knife was in her hand, dripping blood.

"Arela started backing away from the unforgivable crime she had committed, shaking her head. But she was too close to the cliff. She stumbled. My father watched her fall." Kyna bit her lip, deciding whether to include the last part. She took a breath. "Arela had been pregnant."

Kyna's ears rang in the silence. Several jaws hung open. Every eye was round and horrified, trained on her. Except Gellion. He stared at the ground. His face was pale, and his jaw was working again. He looked almost angry.

"So, he ... he didn't kill either of them?" Renyra's eyes glistened.

"So he says," said Tornac. "How do we know this account is the truth?"

"It is the truth," Kyna said flatly.

"Then why did he say nothing?" said Tornac. "Why did he allow himself to be exiled and shunned rather than tell the truth?"

"Because of Arela," said Renyra in a broken whisper. "He loved her. She would have been condemned as a murderer, her memory disparaged forever."

Kyna looked away from Renyra's anguished sympathy.

"Liera never asked my father what happened," she said. "She looked on him with shame and disgust—with hatred. Her son had publicly caused the death of two elves, but only she knew he had also killed his unborn child. To her, it was an act entirely unforgivable, no matter the story behind it.

"My father left Tura, consumed by pain and anger. He was unravelling, drowning beneath the weight of his agony. He wandered through Faeran over the years, never settling in one place. Eventually, he started to hear about the discovery of vierstone. He heard how the stone's touch gave elves their skill in crafting, how its presence in the Great Cities gave elves their very capacity to connect to one another. It gave him the first hope he had felt since his exile. He thought the touch of vierstone could give him control over his emotions—heal the wounds in him and steady his unraveling mind. He returned to Tura."

Kyna looked at Gellion. "You know what happened there."

Gellion blinked, his eyes staying closed a moment too long.

"Yes," he said. "I know."

"He left Tura without vierstone and carrying a betrayal far greater than banishment," Kyna said. "By then, he had spent over a century away from the Great Cities. His grief had cooled, replaced by a cold anger. He latched onto it. It was easier to bear than the pain that had threatened to burn away his soul. Still, he obsessed over vierstone. I think his desire for it began to change then. He still longed for a release from his pain, but as the skills of the elves grew around him under the influence of vierstone, he began to brood over what he could have achieved through its touch."

Eyes glassy, Gellion was nodding again.

"He decided to take vierstone for himself, but when he finally managed to steal some, its touch unleashed within him an agony beyond all he had experienced. Every bit of pain, fear, grief, and love from his past crashed into him; every repressed thought, feeling, and memory flooded his soul. He could not bear its touch. The stone that had formed the last of his hope tore him apart. It betrayed him."

"He lived in despair for some time after that. He tried to touch the stone again and again, but each time brought new waves of anguish. The Great War unfolded around him. He ignored it. His obsession with vierstone grew. As elves studied the substance, he snuck into cities and read their work. He began to keep notes of his own. If he could understand the stone, maybe he could find a way to use it. It wasn't until the end of the war that his research bore any fruit. In Maramor, he found what he was looking for."

Kyna paused, watching Gellion and his brothers as her words sank in. Telling Tenille had been uncomfortable enough.

"Kaelo came to Maramor?" Gellion said. "After the war?"

"The city was a mess," Kyna said. "It presented the perfect opportunity to raid the Archives. Eldian was well known by then as a vierstone master, and my father had yet to read his writing. Eldian's—absence made it easy to go through his books and notes." Kyna paused, but Gellion and his brothers looked more shocked than angry.

"And what did he find?" Tornac said. "I searched our father's study after the war. There were a few tomes on vierstone, but nothing I hadn't read before."

"That's because my father took them," Kyna said softly. "He took the notes Eldian had written in the months before the end of the war, and he took the redstone."

Tornac's face went slack. Veldon's eyes widened in slow realization, then closed. Valder just looked confused.

It was Gellion's reaction Kyna waited for. He alone did not look surprised by Kyna's revelation. Like Veldon, he closed his eyes, but in something more like pained acceptance.

"He did use it, then," Gellion said.

"He discovered it," Kyna said.

Gellion's eyes opened. "What?"

"My father found his notes. Eldian had dislodged one of the phoenix's feathers in a battle. The phoenix is made of redstone. Eldian studied it until he understood it and took extensive notes on its properties."

"Why did he never say anything?" Valder said. "He knew of this *months* before he used it? Why would he tell no one of his plans?"

"He feared it," Kyna said. "He wrote of the stone's power, but also of the effects he feared it wrought in its user. It was those very effects that first drew my father to the stone, before he understood its full potential."

"And what are its effects?" Veldon's big eyes were watching Kyna with knowing intensity. He glanced at Gellion once, then waited for Kyna's explanation.

"Where vierstone creates connection and understanding between elves and the elements, redstone enables control. Control of stone, metal, glass, and to an extent, control of other elves."

Veldon's eyes widened. "What do you mean?" he said.

"Eldian said vierstone formed a channel of emotion between two elves," said Kyna. "With redstone, one elf can influence the emotions of another elf. Force fear upon them, for example, or a sense of peace, or insecurity."

Kyna shifted in her chair, carefully keeping her eyes averted from Gellion and Renyra. Both had been victims of these particular manipulations on more than one occasion.

"Eldian feared redstone would not only sever the bonds between elves, but relieve its user of those emotions that linked them with the world. To Eldian, this meant a life of deadened isolation. To my father, it meant a life without pain—a life freed of the chains wrought by the greatest weaknesses of the elven race. It changed everything.

"My father took the redstone, a store of vierstone, and Eldian's notes, then he left. Seeds of ideas were sprouting in his mind, but he needed time to sort through them and make his plans. He sailed to Tala, stowed away on a ship sent to find vierstone. The ship landed near the Falspires, and he created a home for himself in the mountains, far from the prying eyes of elves. There he studied redstone until he learned to create the substance himself."

"Create it?" Gellion knit his brows. "How?"

"I don't understand it, really." Kyna shrugged. "Eldian discovered the technique. That's how he made a weapon to use against the phoenix. Redstone can be used on vierstone somehow to create more of itself. Anyway, my father experimented with redstone as obsessively as he had researched vierstone. He learned to destroy vierstone—to stop its current entirely—to kill it. That's when his plan took shape." Kyna paused. "Beyond that, I think you know most of what happened."

Uncomfortably, she remembered the story Tenille had told the troupe after Kyna had explained Eldian's discovery of redstone. They had talked long on that breezy cliffside—an exchange of stories as painful as they were enlightening.

"You saw the cave," Kyna said softly. "You read his notes."

That Gellion had stood in her abandoned home brought her an odd mixture of jealousy, shame, and exhilaration. What had he thought of her when he discovered the secrets of her past from stories and clues? How much had he guessed?

Gellion's jaw dropped.

"Your mother told me," Kyna added. This explanation only seemed to cause Gellion further alarm.

"There weren't any notes about redstone, though," Valder said with a frown.

Kyna nodded. "He burned them after he had learned all he could. He didn't want any other elves to learn the secret." A precaution that had clearly not worked.

"But—" Veldon spoke carefully, looking at Kyna with a strange mixture of concern and curiosity. "What about you?"

A prickling warmth spread up Kyna's face, and she turned her eyes away from Veldon. This part she had not told Tenille, or any of the troupe. The truth of Arela's death may have been her father's secret to tell, but the reason for Kyna's birth was as much her own as anyone's. This only made it more difficult.

"As I said," Kyna said, still looking at the ground. "I was an example. An experiment. My father used to tell me that I was a gift—to him and to the elves. No other elf's loyalty could be ensured, and my father couldn't infiltrate the elves alone. I was to be his partner, his spy, and his proof that an elf raised without vierstone would grow up stronger, better, untainted by pain and weakness. He told me how elves crushed themselves with self-wrought anxiety, grief, and pain—how elves fell to depression over concern for one another, how imperfect trust and love shattered the souls of those foolish enough to embrace them. I was strong. I never knew fear, pain, or grief. They could not touch me. I never cared about anything so much that its loss could break me. I never wanted to. I had seen what it did to my father."

A steady pressure was building in Kyna's chest. Every vow she had sworn to herself and her father had fallen to ashes when she came to

Daro, when she met Gellion. She had given in to the weakness, and it had crushed her, just as her father had always warned.

"So he," Valder said. "Kaelo I mean. He—" Valder looked distinctly uncomfortable. "He lay with a human girl so that he could—take you?"

Kyna did not answer at once. The urge to defend her father rose in her again. Centuries of pain, anger, and betrayal had twisted her father's mind. Redstone had changed him. No elf would ever have agreed to join him in his endeavors, and his purpose was greater than the life of one human. He had caused the girl no true harm. It had been for a greater good.

"Yes," Kyna said simply.

Valder hid his disgust poorly, but had the decency to look away. Veldon looked startlingly as though he were about to walk to Kyna and give her a hug.

"He really believes it, doesn't he?" Gellion said. "That this is all for the good of the elves?"

Kyna nodded.

"Revenge had nothing to do with it?" Tornac said.

"You don't think he deserved some measure of revenge?" Kyna said. "The Turi left him for dead and worse. They abandoned him for a single crime they didn't even understand. My father did believe in what he did, but if revenge came as a side benefit, he was not wont to complain."

"So what's happening now?" Gellion pitched his voice loud enough to silence any retorts by his brother. "The phoenix twisted Kaelo's ideals and goals and is taking matters into its own hands?"

"It would seem so," said Kyna.

"And you have come to help us how?" Gellion's clipped tone was not lost on Kyna. Her story may have distracted him, but it had clearly not curbed his suspicion or his anger.

"I came to tell you about redstone and your father," said Kyna. "To make you understand. Whatever my father has done, and for whatever reasons, the phoenix is our enemy now. Using redstone against it is the only way to stop it." She sighed. "Though from the suspicions your mother shared, it sounds as though you already figured that out. Still, you can stop trying to find other ways to do it. There are none. You just have to find another opportunity to face the phoenix with redstone."

Gellion looked as though Kyna had just told him the world was condemned. Shifting in his chair, he passed his gaze from Kyna to his brothers before looking at the floor.

"There will not be another opportunity," Gellion said. "The phoenix destroyed my redstone." He pulled a lump of black rock from his pocket, then looked at Kyna with dead eyes.

"If you don't have any redstone, the last of it is with Kaelo and the phoenix."

Kyna slumped back in her chair.

CYCLES OF LIFE AND DEATH

A burning lump was moving up Renyra's throat. She stared at the black stone in Gellion's hand. Had it all been for nothing? Escaping Morcanan, traveling across Riure, sneaking into Tura, escaping to Maramor. She had thought they finally had the answer, that they would be able to help Gellion in a last heroic attempt to defeat the phoenix and its master. But what had it all been for if their only weapon was useless?

"Why didn't you tell us sooner?" Tornac said.

Gellion was still looking at Kyna. "I had hoped we would find another way." He nodded to indicate the Archives around them. "Here. But it's now clear we will not."

Firas leaned forward in his chair. "Kyna, are you sure there is no other redstone we can find? Could Kaelo have left pieces of it behind?"

Kyna shook her head slowly. "I don't think so. He has always been careful with it—in Riure anyway. To have another elf discover it would have been disastrous." She glanced at Gellion. "I can't imagine he meant to leave that piece in the Falspires. Unless you found any other pieces in the cave?"

"No," Valder said. "We combed the place." He rubbed a hand over his face.

The cold despair that always seemed just beneath Renyra's skin these days began to pull at her once more. Her head was still reeling with the weight of Kyna's story. She felt sick. The battle at Arvain, the destruction of Daro—it had all come as a shock, but her own suffering now seemed nothing compared to what she had heard today.

So much tragedy.

Gellion and his family had lost their father, only to learn that he had discovered and inadvertently handed Kaelo the weapons now pointed at every one of them. Kyna's entire life had been a twisted experiment and bond of servitude. And Kaelo—Renyra shuddered. She didn't think she would ever erase the images of Kyna's description of that cliffside. What sort of world allowed these things to happen?

The three pointed star stretched across Renyra's hand as she clenched her fist. If all of these things could happen with vierstone in the world, maybe Kaelo's cleansing had not been so terrible after all. Maybe feeling the tragedy less was the best option.

No. Stop.

The despair pulled harder. Renyra resisted. That could not be the answer. She had vowed she would not stop trying, that she would not stop looking for hope, no matter what happened. It was a vow she intended to keep, even if it drove her to madness. Or death.

"Then we just have to find a way to take it from him," Raren said.

Renyra resurfaced. Raren sat with his legs crossed and one arm draped over the back of his chair.

"If we were planning to sneak up on the phoenix with redstone anyway, adding a theft to the equation shouldn't make much difference." He nodded to Kyna. "You may even be able to talk some sense into your father."

"You don't think I've tried that?" Kyna glared at Raren. "Why do you think he threw me out of Morcanan?"

"A lot has happened since Morcanan," Gellion said. "I think Kaelo may be more amenable to persuasion now, if you could get him away from the phoenix."

Kyna's brows lowered. "What do you mean?"

"I confronted Kaelo when he came to Tura," said Gellion. "He's breaking. He's lost control of the phoenix, and he's afraid."

"Then why doesn't he destroy it?" Valder said. "He has redstone. Why not just finish the thing off himself while he's riding it?"

Everyone looked to Kyna.

"That was his intention," Kyna said. "In the beginning. When the vierstone was gone, he was supposed to unmake the phoenix. He told me he would. He told me to trust him." She paused, bit her lip, then went on. "My father may fear the phoenix, but I think a part of him still believes in what he's doing and knows the phoenix enables its completion. The phoenix speaks to him—manipulates him and gets in his head. I think he fears destroying it as much as he fears living under its influence."

"Nor is destroying the phoenix as simple as destroying vierstone," Gellion said. "The phoenix may be made of redstone, but it is far more complex than a rock. It is powerful—overwhelming. The moment I directed redstone's current toward the beast, its own current nearly brought me to my knees. It was a battle of will as much as it was of power. The phoenix destroyed my redstone when I failed to destroy it first. I ... I hesitated." His face darkened, and he opened his mouth to continue, then clenched his jaw shut, dropping his eyes.

"What happened?" Veldon said.

Gellion did not answer. Veldon sighed.

"The time for secrets has passed, Gellion," he said. "This is our last chance. If we manage to get more redstone, we need to know what we're up against and what the stakes are."

Renyra watched Gellion with a cocked head. Was he ashamed? Embarrassed by his failure? When he looked up, however, his brows were drawn together in anger.

"Fine," Gellion said. "If you all want to know the full extent of our hopelessness, I will not deny it to you. There was more than one reason I was so desperate to find another weapon to use against the phoenix. Even if we had redstone—" He shook his head and ran a hand through his hair. "The phoenix spoke to me when I was about to destroy it. It told me that it could not be destroyed—not really. 'My destruction is my life,' it said." He allowed his gaze to slip between every elf in attendance. Renrya felt a chill creep up her spine when its heavy weight fell upon her.

"It is a part of its existence, don't you see?" Gellion said. "If we use redstone against the phoenix, it will go away—for a time. But it will rise again from the ashes. It will come back, again and again, and from what I have seen of this phoenix, it will be more powerful each time."

All the heat left Renyra's body. Hope was slipping through her fingers.

"How do you know that what the phoenix said is true?" said a dark haired woman sitting between Veldon and Valder. "Maybe it was only trying to make you hesitate."

"I thought of that," said Gellion. "But ... but the phoenix mentioned my father."

The woman's eyebrows rose. Gellion's brothers leaned forward.

"What did it say?" said Valder.

"That it told our father it would rise again." Gellion shook his head. "It doesn't matter what it said, it matters that it knew our father—that it remembered him. It is the same phoenix. The beast that Kaelo raised is the same one that terrorized us for two hundred years, and destroying it with redstone will only delay its terror for another few centuries, or millennia, or decades."

Renyra looked down at her lap. Even victory would not last. Was temporary peace better than none at all? They knew more of the phoenix now than any living elf had before. What if they used the time after its death to prepare, to research, to tell scholars and vierstone masters and leaders all they knew? It didn't seem enough. It didn't seem right. There had to be another answer. Riu would not leave the elves to this fate without a way out. He couldn't.

Renyra closed her eyes as she thought, blocking out all else around her.

Decades. Centuries. It was a cycle. A cycle of life. A cycle of death. It reminded her of the infernal insects that came back to pester her crops year after year. She grimaced. Were the elves to be a crop of fruit trees, eaten away by each cycle of leaf chippers until there was no longer enough foliage to live by? At least Renyra knew how to deal with leaf chippers. Break the little beasts' life cycle and their numbers would drop low enough to keep under control. If only a phoenix were so easy.

Renyra frowned. A phoenix was hardly comparable to an annoying insect, but could there be some way to use the same principle against it?

Break the cycle.

But how did one break the life cycle of a demonic bird wrought of vierstone's antithesis?

"What are you saying?" Tornac said. "That we should give up? Stop all attempts to end this nightmare just because it might come again?"

"That's not what I said," Gellion said. "But what is our alternative? Fight with blood and tears until we secure a peace lasting enough to partially rebuild, then fight again when the evil rises once more? Last time the phoenix was terrible beyond measure, but look at what it has done this time—it can produce different kinds of flame, each with its own devastating effect. It can raise monsters out of the stone itself rather than creating them slowly from living creatures. It's power grows with each resurrection. If we allow this cycle to continue, the phoenix will eventually destroy us."

"What if we found a way to destroy the last of the redstone after killing the phoenix?" said Caerlyn. "With no redstone or vierstone left, there would be no way to raise the phoenix again, right?"

A thoughtful silence followed Caerlyn's logic.

"It's a plausible theory," Gellion said. "But how can we trust the phoenix will not find another way? The first phoenix rose in vastly different circumstances. It could come a third time in a way we have not yet considered. Without redstone, we would have no hope of defeating the thing a third time."

Memories, words, and ideas were fighting each other for purchase in Renyra's mind. This whole conversation was wrong. The whole scenario was wrong. It reminded her of the discussions of the Turi Council over Kaelo's false prophecy. They had planned to use vierstone to destroy another elf—to use lifestone to end a life. It had seemed the only option at the time, even an answer provided by Riu, yet it had always felt wrong. And it had been wrong. Renyra's instincts had been right. Death had never been the answer. Vierstone had never been the answer—not as a weapon. What, then? What was the alternative?

"Redstone can't be the answer." Renyra finally gave voice to the confusing tangle of thoughts still crowding her head. She needed to discuss them, say them aloud. "It's not right. The stone itself isn't right." She looked to Kyna. "You say this stone controls elements and emotions with callous force. It drains us of those emotions that give us any sense of connection to other souls. It gives life to the evil of the phoenix, yet we want to use that same evil to keep the phoenix at bay? We are using the very substance of the phoenix's existence to perpetuate its cycle."

"But there is no—" Kyna began.

"There has to be another way," Renyra said with more confidence than she felt. She jumped to her feet and started to pace.

"Gellion already said the phoenix can't be destroyed. Not really. What if we aren't meant to destroy the phoenix at all? The phoenix rises, lives, destroys, dies, and rises again. If we are to be free of its threat, we must break the cycle."

Renyra looked from one incredulous face to another.

"How?" Firas's expression at least was more curious than frightened for her sanity. "How do we break the cycle without destroying the phoenix?"

Renyra resisted the urge to shout that she didn't know. She had to keep thinking—keep talking.

"We can't destroy it without bringing it back. We can't let it live and destroy us." What else was there? Life. Death. "We ... we change it." Her feet slowed to a stop. "We turn it into something else—reshape it."

"That still sounds to me like a feat that would require redstone," Valder said.

"I—well. Maybe," Renrya admitted. "But we wouldn't be using it to destroy. We would be using it to make something better—like forcing good out of a bad situation."

"You tried something similar." Veldon turned to Gellion. "When you faced the phoenix, you tried to control it—to change its behavior."

Gellion nodded. "But that was its mind I sought to control. I couldn't feel it's mind, only its body. Still, I suspect changing any substantial aspect of the phoenix would require a level of control we can't attain."

"But what if you could do it without *controlling* the bird?" Renyra knew she was grasping at straws now. She couldn't stop herself. "Maybe you could do something to its current, or change it physically in some other way—make it into something that is still alive but not the same."

"It's possible," Gellion said doubtfully. "But it's not something we could experiment with before facing the phoenix itself. As I said, even a moment of hesitation can mean failure when it comes to destroying the phoenix. If I paused to find a way to alter the creature first, we may lose any chance we had if it doesn't work."

"Besides," said Trali. "We would then find ourselves in the same position as we were ten minutes ago, yes?" He chuckled. "We still need to take redstone out from under the nose of our enemy's greatest ally. Maybe we should make that plan first?"

"It is a good idea and an important concept." Firas nodded to Renyra. "And not one I think we should forget. Still, it is unknown—untested—and therefore a risk. We must treat it as such. When the time comes, we must weigh the importance of a sure end and the possibility of a better outcome. Trali is right, however. The very existence of that decision rests upon our success in obtaining redstone."

"I think we should focus on killing the thing, personally," Caerlyn said with an apologetic shrug to Renyra. "If we succeed, we'll probably have centuries to keep theorizing ways to end the phoenix once and for all. Time is not on our side now—it could be later."

It was the same rationale that Renyra had thought to herself only minutes before, yet now it grated against her. What about what Gellion had said about the phoenix's power increasing with each resurrection? But Firas was right. It was a risk. Did they dare take such risks when so much was at stake? How many lives may be lost while they sorted through puzzles that may not even form a picture? Perhaps allowing centuries for vierstone masters and scholars to expand upon her thought was the more prudent choice. Save lives now. Plan for next time if you survived.

Renyra bowed her head in consent.

"So," Raren looked to Kyna. "Our task remains the same. We go to your father armed with either persuasion or theft." He raised an eyebrow. "One does not readily supply an opportunity for the other should our first choice prove ineffective."

"I don't think we will have much of a choice," Gellion said before

Kyna could respond. "Either we find Kaelo alone or we must face the phoenix—possibly in the midst of an army. The situation will dictate our methods. First we must get ourselves into the situation. We go to Kaelo."

"Telem Fier." Renyra said the name with a mixture of excitement and dread. Telem Fier was the last Great City outside Kaelo's control. Based upon his dealings with Morcanan, Kaelo would set his sights to the Fieri as soon as he was satisfied with Tura's ruling.

"Telem Fier," Gellion agreed.

"But he could be there any day," Renyra said. "He could be there already."

Gellion raised his eyebrows. "Then I suggest we leave soon."

33

A CROWD OF ELVES

Cold water dripped from Gellion's arm, replenished by a new spray with each pulse of the boat. The temperatures of the mountain gorges did not warrant bare arms, let alone wet ones, but skin dried faster than cloth, and Gellion was determined to arrive in Rone with dry clothes. So he clung to the edge of the boat and shivered, doing his best not to look over his shoulder.

The boat was crammed full of elves—too many elves. Farra had remained behind to preside over Maramor, but that still left eleven of them in a boat meant for half a dozen. Even in the mass of bodies, Gellion knew exactly where Kyna was. He could feel her eyes on him. He ignored her.

With any luck, they would all be in Telem Fier by mid afternoon, and Gellion could more easily distance himself from company he would rather avoid.

"You look comfortable." Valder had twisted backward to look at Gellion.

"Extremely." Gellion kept his eyes forward.

"Actually, you rather look like you are about to break the side of the boat with your bare hands."

"Plunging head first into an icy river seems the preferable option in the current situation."

Valder rolled his eyes. "Ever the drama."

Gellion's grip on the boat tightened.

"Drama? Why in Riu's name would I be dramatic right now?" He saturated the words with as much sarcasm as he could.

Valder's smile did not reach his eyes. His gaze slid from Gellion to the back of the boat.

"Have you talked to her at all?"

Gellion's stomach swooped as the boat took a dive over a rock. The sensation sent a burst of adrenaline through his limbs, which did not subside when the boat steadied.

"No," he said.

"She's been staring at you for hours."

"I know."

"Has she tried to talk to you?"

"I haven't given her the chance."

Valder nodded, then he glanced at Gellion furtively.

Gellion gritted his teeth and kept his eyes trained on the passing cliffside, gleaming with moisture in what weak sunlight reached it. Valder glanced at him again.

With a long sigh, Gellion said, "What is it, Valder?"

"That was some story she told."

"Yep." It was with effort that Gellion kept his face blank, staring straight ahead. It had been half a day since Kyna's arrival and every mind numbing revelation that had come with it. Gellion had hardly had time to think at all in the whirlwind of preparations that had followed the discussion in the Archives, but skimming over the water with nothing to look at but rocks had already given him more time than he liked to dwell on what he had learned. It was overwhelming. It was disturbing. It was a relief and a devastating blow.

Gellion had been right in his initial judgment of Kaelo. The man had never even committed the murders for which he was exiled. Had Liera had her way with Kaelo's trial decades later, the Council would have murdered an innocent man. But while the truth of Kaelo's past innocence lifted some of Gellion's guilt over his own decisions, it made him feel still worse over his own actions. Kaelo had never killed an elf before coming to Daro. The deaths he had caused thereafter had been the actions of a man torn apart by centuries of tragedy, exile, and corruption. Gellion had caused the death of a human man out of sheer temper—the accident of a moment. The incident had been rigged by the Albaren nobles, but it had been Gellion's temper that made it succeed. It had been frightening enough for Gellion to realize he might be turning into his mentor, but to realize he had instead been following his own path of destruction was somehow worse.

"Father—" Valder looked down into the water streaking past.

A new punch of pain made Gellion suck in a breath. His father was a subject over which he had not yet allowed himself to dwell. He did not want to talk about it now, but the look of grief on Valder's face softened his reluctance.

"He did what he could to save the elves," Gellion said. "The same as we were planning to do. It's hardly his fault Kaelo found out about his discovery before any other elf."

"Yeah." Valder did not look up. "I just wish he had said something."

Gellion didn't answer. He could see why his father had kept his discovery a secret. Hadn't Gellion insisted the Turi Council do the same when he had brought redstone from Tala? But to keep it from his own family—

"He probably thought no one would ever need to know about redstone, with the phoenix gone," Valder said. His eyes were distant and misty a moment longer, then snapped back to their usual brightness. "Ah well. Nothing to be done for it. We know now."

Gellion let out a soft snort. He would never understand his brother's ability to bounce back from grief and sorrow on the turn of a heel, but in Gellion's current state of mind, he was coming to find the quality endearing rather than annoying.

Valder's face relaxed into a smile at Gellion's break in composure.

"I think you should talk to her, you know."

Gellion's expression hardened in an instant.

"I know what she did to you," Valder said. "But I've also seen the way she looks at you. She may not beg for your forgiveness, but she wants it."

The wall of the gorge was beginning to recede from the boat. Its surface was becoming rougher, less sheer. Gellion watched the progress for several breaths before he answered.

"Why should I give her what she wants? Can she give me what I want? Can she bring Dulon back to life, raise Daro out of the sea, or remake all the vierstone in Riure? Can she—" Gellion bit down on the words.

Even to Valder, he would never admit to his true anger with Kyna. She had used him, yes, but if she had done so with callous indifference, he could have forgiven her. But she had not. She had opened herself to Gellion, and she had forced him to do the same. Worse even than this, she had loved him. He had seen it that night, when her distraction had allowed the current of Gellion's vierstone to breach the gap between them for a single moment. She must not have had redstone on her then, or at least had not been touching it. It had been a moment of pure, unrestrained emotion. It had been wonderful, intoxicating, freeing— and it had broken him.

No heartbreaking life story could change what Kyna had done. She had lied, coerced, and caused death and destruction. She had helped raise a phoenix and cleansed the world of lifestone. She had betrayed the elves, yes, but her sin went deeper than that. She had loved Gellion, and betrayed him anyway. She had betrayed him after he loved her.

And still she pulled him. Her very presence seemed to heighten Gellion's senses and dull his sense. In moments of her nearness in Maramor, he had almost thought he could feel an echo of vierstone reaching its touch over his skin. The memory of that feeling disturbed him more than he cared to admit.

"Look." Valder held up his palms. "I'm only saying that I think you should talk to her—without an audience of a dozen other elves. For your own sake if not for hers." He raised his eyebrows. "You haven't exactly been a ray of sunshine without her."

Gellion muttered a string of incomprehensible words, including several insults implying what Valder could do with various metal-working tools.

"Ah, you prove me wrong!" Valder grinned. Gellion took a swipe at the side of his head.

Ducking, Valder laughed, then nodded toward the expanding water in front of them. The current was slowing. The gorge had widened and shallowed, and in the distance, Gellion could make out the hazy outline of a golden shore.

"Plenty of time to talk on a Rale ride." Valder winked at Gellion. His duck did not come fast enough this time.

<hr>

Rone was a buzz of activity, but not of the organized variety. Elves walked with brisk steps and glanced around with wide eyes. Gellion weaved between milling bodies, trying not to step on the hem of colorful wraps or run full-on into any rushing Fieri. He felt like a giant among the elves of Rone, and more than a little obvious with his bright hair. Still, his constant need of evasive maneuvers seemed to prove that very few Fieri were taking any notice of him.

"Where are they all going?" Veldon side-stepped a woman who had shoved past him at a trot, holding a clunking bag in her arms. She did not look up.

"No idea." Gellion tried to see past the milling elves in the direction they seemed to be flowing, but could not make out any obvious attractions. A tug on his sleeve made him look down. Renyra was looking up at him.

"The whole city is like an angry anthill." She took hold of his wrist and began to walk with the flow of traffic. "I couldn't find Auralia anywhere. I say we just get on the first Rale we can fit on and get to Telem Fier as quickly as possible."

"What do you mean the next one we can fit on?" Gellion said. His only experience on the massive Rale lines of Faeran had been the recent journey between Tura and Morcanan. A full army had packed the cars, but there had hardly been any other elves using them.

Renyra pointed ahead.

Squinting, Gellion looked again in the direction they were walking. He still saw nothing worthy of these crowds and agitation, but could now make out the shining metal of Rale cars. The crowds were converging on them. Gellion groaned.

"They're all getting on the Rale lines? But why? Is this normal for Rone?"

"Not at all," said Renyra. She had begun to jog, closing the distance between them and Firas ahead.

Gellion glanced behind him. His brothers were on his tail, Kyna and Caerlyn taking up the rear. He looked away as Kyna's eyes rose to meet his.

"It seems Telem Fier is a popular destination today," Renyra said.

The frantic attitude enveloping the city was setting Gellion's nerves on edge. He was already overwhelmed and riddled with anxiety over the madness of what they were going to Telem Fier to do. The last thing he needed was the company of a thousand frazzled elves complicating their travel. What in Riu's name were they all going to Telem Fier for? Surely they knew Kaelo would be flying to the Great City any day.

"Here!"

Gellion whipped his head around to see Firas standing near the entrance of a filling Rale car. It was one of two or three with the door still open, and it was filling fast. Gellion ran, trusting that his companions would be able to keep up. In three strides he was there, leaping into the car and backing up to make way for Renyra, then his brothers, then Kyna and Caerlyn. Scanning the car, Gellion spotted Raren, Alura, and Trali standing along a wall. Trali was waving to Gellion, pointing toward a string of seats further down the car. Gellion pushed his way toward him.

The Rale was hot. Even so far north in the grasslands, the early autumn sun was intense, and the cooling system of the Rale was struggling to overcome the uncharacteristic mass of bodies. Gellion heard the smooth sliding of metal and a clank. The door had closed. Hardly twenty seconds later, Gellion found himself grasping at the back of a chair as the momentum of the Rale pulled him backward. Twisting himself around the chair, he sat in it, Raren on one side and Firas on the other. At least he wouldn't have to talk to Kyna.

"Switch with me."

Before Gellion could register what was happening, let alone protest, Gellion found himself pulled to his feet and nudged aside. With the Rale's mounting speed, Gellion stumbled forward and hardly had time to see Valder sitting in what had been his chair before grasping at the very annoyed elves around him in order to stay on his feet. Valder winked at Gellion, then turned with a smile to Raren.

A sick certainty filled Gellion's gut. Muttering apologies to the elves around him, Gellion braced his feet and stood up straight, looking for the seat Valder had vacated. He saw it, just a few chairs down from where he had nearly fallen on his face. To one side sat a Fieri elf Gellion did not know. To the other sat Kyna.

Blood colored Kyna's cheeks when she saw Gellion. Her eyes darted to the empty chair, then to the filled seats around her.

Gellion considered walking away. He could find a place to stand, or threaten Valder with another punch to the head if he didn't give his seat back. Even sitting down right where he stood with his back to Kyna seemed a more pleasant option than being trapped next to her for an entire afternoon.

Kyna stood. "I'll just—" She took a step away from her chair.

"Don't be stupid," Gellion muttered. He walked to the empty chair without looking at Kyna and sat down.

Slowly, Kyna lowered herself back into her chair.

Gellion took a long breath, then crossed his arms and stared straight forward, resting his glare heavily on Valder. Valder was paying Gellion no mind, however. He was fully engrossed in what seemed an animated conversation with Raren.

The minutes stretched, long and painful. It was a four hour trip to Telem Fier. Hardly any of the elves around Gellion were talking, yet the silence to his right was louder than those few conversations that carried over the rush of the Rale. Gellion did his best to ignore it. As far as he was concerned, everything there was between himself and Kyna was her doing, not his. She could suffer in strained silence as long as she wanted. He couldn't care less if she ever talked to him again.

The pull came from her again.

Only in his stillness did Gellion sense it—that strange sensation like a breeze over his skin. No. Not a breeze. It was less substantial upon his skin, yet more noticeable within his being. It seemed to pass *through* him.

Gellion narrowed his eyes and cast Kyna a sideways glance. The jerk of her own eyes told him she had been looking at him, but now she stared out the far window of the car. Gellion shook his head to clear it. No doubt it was simply his mind playing tricks on him—his body betraying him with an attraction he could not heed. Leaning back, he set his gaze to the windows.

The sky was bright and milky, clouds smeared over blue like thin paint. The sight was astonishingly normal. In all the battles in which Gellion had fought, in all the wild and terrifying situations he had been in, it always struck him how indifferent the sky was. The sun shone, clouds moved, rain fell. The weather had no concern for the affairs below its domain. It treated each day with the same arrogant disregard as the last. It was frustrating, and it was comforting.

Kyna shifted in her chair. Gellion felt the change in her weight and the altered pressure of the air. His attention had just come back to the prickling of his arm when the Rale swung into a turn and Kyna's bare skin touched his.

Gellion nearly jumped out of his chair.

That was no trick of his mind, nor was it a breeze, or even a pull. A current had passed between Kyna and himself—clear and strong. He wheeled to face her.

"What was that?" he demanded.

"What was what?" Kyna said.

He looked down at her arm—at her hands. One was in her pocket.

"You have it," he said. Ice was trickling down Gellion's back. Had he really trusted her? Even for a moment? "You have redstone. With you. Now."

Kyna stiffened. "What are you talking about?"

"I felt it."

"I don't have redstone, Gellion."

"Don't lie to me," Gellion said through his teeth. "I felt the current." He narrowed his eyes. "What game are you playing?"

Color touched Kyna's cheeks. Gellion could not tell if it was from indignation or shame.

"I am not lying," she said. "After all I told you in Maramor, do you really think I'm leading you into a trap? Lying to you about redstone?"

Her insistence only strengthened Gellion's determination. Kyna was hiding something. Whether or not she remained a traitor, secrets still hovered about the woman like static to cloth. Gellion was tired of getting shocked.

He grabbed Kyna's wrist.

The first thing he felt was the heat of her skin—a jolt of electricity ran through him that had nothing to do with any stone. He shoved aside the reaction and focused on the current he had felt before, buzzing beneath her skin. It was familiar, yet shadowed, its intricacies veiled from his senses even though he knew its essence in his bones. As Kyna struggled to pull her hand back from Gellion's grip, the current flared and lapped against him, carrying the unmistakable flavor of emotions. He could not decipher them precisely, only sense their presence and their inclinations.

He let go and stared at Kyna. He couldn't make himself say the word. He dared not give heed to the brush of recognition he had felt through Kyna's touch. But as shock lay bare on Gellion's face, the defiance in Kyna's own faded away. She looked down.

"It isn't redstone," Gellion said.

"No." Kyna drew her fist from her pocket and into her lap. Her other hand clasped around it.

"Kyna." Gellion's suspicion was growing stronger.

Kyna's eyes darted around. None of the elves nearest them seemed to have caught the tension between them. Every gaze was aimed toward windows or other elves. Kyna brought her fist closer to her person and looked up at Gellion. Without averting her gaze, she opened her hand.

A small stone lay in the center of her palm. Gellion's breath caught in his throat.

Vierstone.

Gellion's voice eluded him. Questions packed his mind, and emotions tumbled through his body, but all were suppressed by the sheer force of his shock.

"I took it," Kyna said. She closed her fist again.

Gellion blinked.

Vierstone.

It was not all gone. It still existed. And it was within his reach. His fingers twitched in response, though as strong as his desire was to reach for the stone, so too rose in him the desire to fling it as far from him as he could.

"Why?" Gellion said.

Kyna turned her head upward to regard him. Taking a breath, she opened her mouth, then let out the breath and closed her lips again. She looked down at the back of her hand.

"I don't know," she said. "I saw it there, in the pile of vierstone the cherufin had dragged out of Morcanan. I ..." She moved her head side to side. "I had never touched it before." These last words were barely a whisper, more a confession than an explanation.

Gellion felt the bite of his temper fade. Shrunk back against her chair with her head bowed, Kyna looked so small. She was so young. Gellion had not known how young until he connected her with Heleena's story of the faery child, but even then he had not considered the implications. Though not a child, Kyna was still less than a century old. At that age, Gellion had still been an apprentice metalworker, studying under a new master just a few decades after Kaelo's banishment.

"Never?" Gellion said. "Not even in Daro?"

"I was afraid to touch it. I was afraid it would taint me." A half smile twisted up her face. "Turns out it tainted me even without my touching it." Her gaze slid to Gellion, and the smile faded, replaced by a deep sadness.

"What do you mean?" Gellion said stiffly. It was becoming more difficult to maintain his mask of cold indifference.

"I thought you were a fool."

Gellion snorted.

"Just as all the other elves," she said. "I thought vierstone had weakened you to the point of near madness, drowning you in your own emotions until you could barely control them or bear their weight."

Cold crept over Gellion's skin. Even as his temper rose at Kyna's opinion of him, he cringed from the accuracy of her words. He could feel the phantom tug of his grief, his fear, his despair, his anger. Always a step away. Always waiting for him to step too far.

"But over time," Kyna said. "I began to sense the same tendencies, the same reactions, in myself. It disgusted me. I pulled away and turned to my redstone more and more often. I thought you were going to drag me under with you." The sadness in her eyes deepened. "And a part of me wanted it. That was what scared me the most."

Now that his awareness was wakened, Gellion could practically feel the emotions rolling off of Kyna. It was distracting and more than a little disconcerting. Even without his own vierstone, it was like Kyna's was reaching for him through the air, carrying her essence with it. Never had Gellion been more aware of how unreadable Kyna had been in Daro. He thought of the rare moments of authenticity he had seen of Kyna in that city. Those moments had both thrilled and confused him and had always been fleeting. Then had come the last one. The single moment of utter clarity when his skin had touched hers under a star-flecked sky among whispers of scrubland.

Gellion turned away from Kyna. He could not look at the pain in her face. So what if she had been afraid? That didn't change what she had done to him. It only meant her fear had been stronger than her love.

"I thought I had killed you," Kyna said. "After you didn't return from Arvain."

"Wasn't that the plan?"

"No."

The force of Kyna's response made Gellion turn his head. Kyna's eyes were tight with pain.

"The battle wasn't meant to turn out like that," she said. "The Albaren weren't supposed to betray you. It should have been a simple distraction, two armies played off one another." Her words were coming fast now, like she was afraid Gellion would stop her before she could finish. "Father wrote to the commander of the Albaren. He told them lies about the Dierna—staged raids on the Albaren border and whispered rumors of their treachery. He told them too of the strength and technology of the elves and convinced them that the elves would be a threat to the Albaren if they remained in Tala. He promised to bring the elves back to where they had come from if the Albaren could get them out of Daro, and he told them how to bribe the elves."

Kyna sucked in a ragged breath, then continued. "The Albaren weren't supposed to be a threat to the elves. I went to the Dierna and warned them of the Albaren's attack so they would be evenly matched, but the Dierna response was stronger than we had bargained for, as was the Albaren's greed and fear."

Gellion stared at her. He felt himself pulled between fury at the complexity of the role Kyna had played in Daro's downfall and a strange relief that her plans had gone awry. But that was ridiculous. Why should Gellion think any better of Kyna just because the worst parts of the last months had been *accidental* results of her actions?

"I thought I had killed you," Kyna said again, this time in a hoarse whisper. "And that was when I knew the extent of the taint within me. I fought against it, but it dragged me under. I was losing control, falling into the stories my father had told me all my life." A single tear spilled over her eye. "I wanted to destroy what was causing my anguish. I wanted to escape. I understood then what drove my father, better than I ever had before."

Gellion felt heat leaking into his cheeks. Was he the reason Kyna had remained on Kaelo's side? Had grief he thought her incapable of feeling driven her to raise the phoenix? The twisting of their paths made Gellion's head ache. Had he been given the chance in the weeks following his father's death—when grief ate him from the inside, and the world was crashing around him—would he not have done anything he could to make the pain stop?

I wouldn't have resurrected the phoenix.

But what if he had never known the phoenix in the Great War, as Kyna had not? She had seen so little of the world—so little of life. She may have been physically mature when she stepped into Daro for the first time, but had she been so different from a child in experience?

'What would you have done?'

The words echoed in Gellion's mind, not for the first time since Kyna had uttered them that morning.

"But I was wrong." Kyna was staring at her pocketed hand again. "I saw the grief vierstone wrought in the world. I felt it. But I saw what else it did, too." She looked up to where Firas sat with his arm around Renyra. The little Fieri was talking in a never ending stream, and Firas was chuckling, his eyes sparkling as he watched her face.

"I still think you are a fool," Kyna said. The crooked smile she gave Gellion made his heart stutter. "But I am a bigger one." The edge of her smile drooped, and Gellion caught a fresh light of pain in her eyes. "I am sorry."

Gellion looked away. How could she have chosen vierstone after all of this? How could she bear its touch when her father could not? He tried to imagine a life having never touched lifestone. It sounded empty. Lonely. But was an empty and lonely life in fact better than one filled with the agony of pain and loss?

There was no doubt in Gellion's mind that he wanted to kill the phoenix—it was a demonic monster set on enslaving the elven race—but the grief he had once felt at Kaelo's successful eradication of vierstone was fading; so too was his confidence in the plan they had made this morning.

The whole thing was absurd. At dawn, Gellion had planned for another fruitless day combing the Maramor Archives for an answer he now knew had never existed. Within the space of a few hours, he had made a plan with elves he never thought to see again and planned to execute their desperate last attempt within twenty-four hours.

"Will you try to talk to him?" Gellion said.

Kyna clasped her hands tighter in her lap.

"If there's time, I can try, but I'm not convinced we will be able to find my father without the phoenix." She looked down. "Or that I'll be able to change his mind about anything," she muttered.

Gellion ignored the last bit.

"He was on his own in Tura after I surrendered the city to him," he said. "I saw the phoenix flying patrols without a rider. There might be time to find him after Cuvan surrenders, if not before."

"Maybe." Kyna stared at her hands. She opened her mouth. Closed it. Glanced at him. With a sudden breath, she said, "I want you to take it." She thrust her fist toward him.

Gellion recoiled as though the hand held a dagger.

"What?"

"If I am to go looking for my father," she said. "I don't want to have it with me. What if he senses it? What if he touches me as you did, or the phoenix comes upon me unawares with its cleansing flame? I don't—" She paused and lowered her hand. "I want it to stay safe."

Gellion's pulse throbbed in his throat. His palms prickled with sweat.

Stop being ridiculous.

He should be overjoyed by the prospect of carrying vierstone again. Any elf in Faeran would take his place in an instant. Why then did his hand shake as he extended it toward Kyna? He lay the back of his hand on his thigh to still the motion.

Kyna lay her hand over his. Gellion took in a sharp breath when the warm bit of stone landed against his palm. His anxiety spiked. His heartbeat raced to a new tempo. The lingering presence of Kyna's hand on his skin sent waves of exhilaration through his body. Holding his breath, Gellion slipped the stone into his pocket and let go of it.

The instant relief he sought did not come. The sudden rush of senses was slow to dull, and incomplete. There was a renewed and lingering sharpness to Gellion's emotions.

Clearing his throat, he clasped his hands in his lap and returned his gaze to the far windows.

The rest of the ride passed with considerably less pain than Gellion had anticipated. Long silences stretched between sparse and careful conversations with Kyna, but they were not charged with the same awkward tension as before. More than once, Gellion found his chest lifting with the same enjoyment he had once felt for every word he had managed to ring out of this confusing and inconsistent woman. It should not be so easy to forget all this woman had done. He should have more control than this. Yet each time he heard her voice, his body betrayed him. He wanted to hear her speak. He wanted to watch the subtlety of her expressions, study the gleam of her hair and the shape of her eyes. She was achingly familiar and yet a stranger—the costume of her hidden role fallen away.

When the low skyline of Telem Fier at last curved into view beyond the Rale's windows, the atmosphere in the car rose to a new life. Elves stood to get a better look and began speaking rapidly to their neighbors. Excitement. Anger. Fear. All were palpable in the hushed and raised voices.

Gellion stood, trying to get a clearer view, but the Rale turned its nose toward the Great City before he could see anything. Was the phoenix there already, visible from the Rale? Had they arrived too late to head off the initial confrontation? Gellion craned his neck to the side, trying to use his un-Fieri-like height to his advantage, but to no avail. Finally, the Rale curved again, south this time, and Gellion turned toward the glass behind him to see an unblemished view of Telem Fier and the swaths of fields before it.

He nearly fell back into his chair. It was not the phoenix causing the excitement, it was elves. Hundreds of them. Thousands. Before the walls of Telem Fier stretched ranks of elves. The bright wraps of the Fieri cast a rainbow in the glaring sun, but within the vivid tapestry were blocks of greys and whites and strips of brown. Morcani. Remsgri. Were some of the colors the silks of Turi?

Gellion stared with a slack jaw. Where had they all come from? How had he not heard of such a mass movement of elves across the continent? Elves jostled around Gellion to get a better view behind him. Suddenly the presence of all the elves on the Rale made sense. They had known. These elves had been traveling to stand with their kin.

A hand clasped Gellion's sleeve, and he looked down to see Kyna pressed against him. Surrounding elves were pushing her into him, and she had grasped his shirt to keep from falling. Catching Gellion's eye, she quickly let go and grabbed for the back of her chair instead. She looked out the window with wide eyes.

"Did you know about this?" she shouted over the tumult.

Gellion could only shake his head.

The look Kyna returned was laden with fear.

"I don't think Cuvan plans to surrender," she said.

Cold washed through Gellion's body as shock turned to horror, for these elves had surely not congregated to greet their new master, the phoenix. He closed his eyes. The Fieri would not surrender. The elves would fight a battle they could not win against an enemy they did not understand, because that is what they had always done. It was what they had to do. There was pride in Gellion at the brave resilience of his people, but so too was there fury at their stubbornness.

They would ruin everything. There would be no seeking out Kaelo following a peaceful surrender, no sneaking up on the phoenix as it revelled in its victory. If they did not find a way to confront Kaelo and the phoenix before Cuvan started this battle, elves could die by the thousands.

"What do we do?" There was panic in Kyna's eyes, and Gellion knew she had come to the same conclusions he had.

Gellion set his jaw, trying to summon a resolve that wasn't there.

"We try to stop this before it begins," he said.

The Rale began to slow. Kyna on his shirt tail, Gellion pushed his way toward the exit.

3 4

PHOENIX DESCENDS

The air was heavy—heavy with breath, heavy with presence, heavy with emotion. Elves pressed against Kyna on all sides, each an unknown body, an unknown mind. How many of them would be left after this foolish show of rebellion?

In front of her, Gellion stopped. Kyna ran into his back, and three more elves ran into her, exclaiming in annoyance. She resisted the urge to snap back at them that it wasn't her fault. It was, really. None of these elves would be here if it wasn't for her.

"Firas!" Gellion waved an arm, rising onto the balls of his feet. The gesture was hardly needed. Gellion already towered over the surrounding Fieri. He and Firas were two pillars among the crowds. The edge of Gellion's shirt stretched in Kyna's fingers. The sensation sent an odd thrill through her. Even in the midst of the chaos surrounding them, she could detect Gellion's scent, close to her, touching her. She closed her eyes and squeezed her fist tighter around the fabric.

"Come over here," Firas called.

Opening her eyes, Kyna watched Firas move out of the current of elves flowing from the Rale. Gellion's shirt jerked to the side, and Kyna followed.

"Riu above," Gellion said when they reached a patch of unoccupied grass. "Did you know anything about this?"

Renyra and her troupe gathered beside Firas. Behind them filed Gellion's brothers.

"No," said Firas. "But there were a lot of elves traveling on the Rale out of Morcani lands the last few days. We assumed they were simply creating as much distance between themselves and Morcanan as possible, but maybe—" His gaze fell to the north, where a mass of fair elves in plain clothes stood tall and straight.

Gellion turned to face his brothers, then stiffened, looking down at Kyna. With a jolt of horror, Kyna realized she was still holding onto him. Heat rushed through her body. She dropped her hand and her eyes.

"But how did they all get here so quickly?" said Alura.

"Or at all?" said Raren. "The other Great Cities are locked down."

"Not all of them," Renyra said. "Remsgraen was half destroyed, but not controlled. The rest of these elves must be from the country—from outside the Great Cities."

"But how did they know to come here?" said Trali.

"How did we know?" Valder shrugged. "It's the last Great City still standing free. Looks like we weren't the only elves set on making a final attempt at freedom before this turns into a war."

"Yes," Gellion said. "Only *we* actually have a plan that might work, and this resistance could ruin everything. You realize we'll never get the phoenix alone before Cuvan starts something? Kaelo may not even bother to meet with Cuvan when he sees this." Gellion threw his hand in a violent gesture encompassing the standing army. "He may just attack. If that's the case, we'll have as much chance of getting up close to the phoenix as Cuvan has of saving Telem Fier."

Renyra looked desperately from Gellion to the distant walls of the city.

"What if we go to Cuvan," she said. "Explain what we're trying to do and convince him to give us some time before attacking?"

Caerlyn snorted. "He'd be thrilled to see us again."

"I can't imagine Cuvan would allow an attack without meeting with Kaelo first," said Veldon, though there was a question in his voice, and he looked at Renyra and Caerlyn for reassurance.

"I don't know." Renyra shook her head. "I would have guessed he would surrender the city rather than risk the lives of his people. Clearly I was wrong. I don't know what he might do."

The voices surrounding Kyna seemed to be coming from a distance. She could barely hold onto the meaning of the conversations bouncing from one elf to the next. It was all too much. Everything was so wrong. There was never supposed to have been a battle in Faeran. There were never supposed to be any deaths at all. Daro had changed that.

Guilt rose in Kyna's chest, accompanied by the pain that had begun afflicting her whenever she thought of the atrocities brought on by her father's grand schemes. The destruction caused by their plans had been unfortunate, but necessary—part of a greater good. When had things changed? When had unfortunate turned to monstrous, necessity to ambition?

In Remsgraen.

Kyna's skin grew hot at the memory. The attack on Remsgraen was the first time the phoenix had followed its own will rather than her father's. Had it already been poisoning his mind before then? Had it always possessed its own malignant autonomy and simply bided its time until it could act with her father's support?

Kyna should have done more. She should have acted sooner.

A gaping absence beside her pulled Kyna back to the present. Gellion was no longer standing next to her. She looked around wildly and saw him walking toward Telem Fier, the rest of their company moving to follow him. Renyra lingered where she was, watching Kyna with a raised eyebrow. Ducking her head, Kyna turned to follow Gellion, stung by the ease with which he had left her standing alone.

What had she expected? Gellion's acceptance of her presence was far more than Kyna had dared hope for. She should be thrilled by his partial forgiveness, however grudging it came and on whatever terms. The mere fact of his continued existence should be enough for her after all she had gone through these last months.

It was not enough.

Every time Kyna looked at Gellion, her chest burned with a blistering heat more painful even than the grief she had felt over his death. She could hardly bear it, yet neither could she keep away from him. The emotions roiling within her were maddening. Vierstone's influence still lingered beneath her skin.

"Are you—alright?" Renyra's voice came as a halting mutter. She was watching Kyna out the side of her eyes as they walked toward the gates of Telem Fier.

Kyna hardly knew how to answer the question. Would anything be alright ever again? She shrugged, then let her eyes wander away, hoping Renyra would let the matter drop.

The woman looked back at the city, took a few more steps, then said, "Thank you."

Kyna's steps faltered. She turned to look at Renyra. There was no hint of a smile on the woman's face, now. She was looking at Kyna with those round, clear eyes, and for the first time since Kyna had rejoined the troupe, there was no hostility in them.

"Thank you for helping us," Renyra said. "For telling us your story —his story. I could see it was difficult for you."

Here was the Renyra that had perplexed and infuriated Kyna in Tura. After enduring the usually cheerful Fieri's cold judgment, Kyna had found herself longing for the painfully sympathetic and optimistic woman from whom she had fled with such disgust. Now, as hot blood prickled under her cheeks, she began to miss being ignored.

"I—it was a long time ago." Kyna concentrated on Firas's back ahead of her and noticed with a jolt that Gellion was now walking beside him. Further on, Caerlyn seemed to be leading the group. Gellion's head was turned sideways, talking to his friend. Kyna drank in the lines of his profile, the waves of his hair glinting copper in the sunlight. The burning in her chest returned with new force. Gellion glanced back at her, and she dropped her eyes.

"Maybe for your father," Renyra said. "But it is not so long for you."

Kyna blinked, trying to remember what Renyra was referring to.

"Did he love you?" Renyra said suddenly.

Only the forward flow of the elves around her kept Kyna from stopping in the middle of the path. Instead, her steps faltered, and a passing Fieri knocked into her shoulder. Kyna recovered herself with as much grace as she could manage, pushing several strands of hair back from her face. She jerked her head up to look at Gellion. Were his shoulders stiffer than before? Was he closer?

"Did ... did who—" Kyna's voice came out with a humiliating crack. She cleared her throat and fought to regain her composure.

"Your father," said Renyra.

"Oh." Relief cooled the heat rising in Kyna's body, but a different weight settled over her.

"I mean," said Renyra. "Can he still ... *can* he love?" Her voice grew softer with each word.

Kyna did not respond at once. It was a question she had not considered often in her life in the Falspires, but one that had crept upon her these last months. She was not sure she knew the answer.

"I don't know," she said. "I think he can still feel love, in a way but —" She looked at the ground. "It is a selfish love—an obsessive love. He loved me because I was fulfilling his ambition, because I was the only one he could trust."

"I'm sorry," Renyra said. "I can't imagine." She looked over the heads of the elves around them, her eyes misted as though attempting to imagine anyway.

Kyna's ears burned with sudden heat. What was the point of bringing up things like this? To what end did Renyra want to share in Kyna's pain, forcing Kyna herself to relive it in the process? Kyna lengthened her stride and set more force to her steps, but was brought up short by a looming presence she had not noticed was so close to her.

She managed to stop herself before running headlong into Gellion's back—again—but came close enough to brush his shirt. Gellion arched his back at her touch and tilted his head over his shoulder. His eyes met hers, and Kyna's skin caught fire.

She bowed her head and stormed away from them all—Gellion, Firas, Renyra. She could feel the weight of their eyes on her back as she fled, but did not slow her pace until she was nearly level with Caerlyn.

The gates of Telem Fier were close now. A sliver of activity was visible beyond the opening at their center—just large enough to let in a few elves standing abreast. Taking a deep breath, Kyna followed Caerlyn through the gap.

If the streets of Rone had been a hectic mess, Telem Fier was near chaos, though pockets of order kept traffic moving. Kyna took deep breaths and tried to focus on her own body, her own steps. She would not let herself think about Gellion walking behind her.

Forget him.

In all likelihood, none of these problems would matter at all by the end of this confrontation, or battle, or whatever disaster awaited them. Even if they miraculously succeeded in destroying the phoenix, Kyna would probably be thrown out of elven society for the role she had played in its near destruction. As for her father—no. Kyna would not think about that now. Her hand snaked into her pocket, but met only cloth. After a jolt of panic, Kyna remembered that Gellion now held the vierstone. She tightened her fist and huffed out a breath. It wouldn't have assuaged her anxiety anyway.

Even after a week with the substance, Kyna had found herself reaching for the stone with the expectation of a cool release of her emotions, but vierstone was not redstone. It was no cool dampening that had met her touch, but a tingling heat that reached into her fingers and spread in pulsing waves through her skin and body. It did not subdue her fears—some of them even burned to a hotter intensity. All the same, the sensation was usually accompanied by an incongruous sense of comfort. She found herself longing for it now, and her eyes strayed to Gellion.

He followed on Caerlyn's heels. The woman was stopping elves in the street, talking to them in rapid bursts and shaking her head in frustration. Though Kyna could hardly hear her own thoughts in the tumult of voices around her, she caught Cuvan's name on Caerlyn's lips. Could they possibly locate the Lord of Telem Fier in this madness?

A deep and resonant horn sounded. The vibrations sank through Kyna's bones. The city fell silent.

Caerlyn stopped and turned to face the city walls.

"What does it mean?" said Kyna

Caerlyn only shook her head, but the look on her face told Kyna the horn was no announcement for dinner or prayers.

Lines of elves ran in tight formations onto the city walls. Shouts of fear and anger rose above the din of moving feet and rushed voices. Some elves ran toward the gates, some toward the city's center, others into the nearest buildings. Kyna turned her head back and forth, searching for some sign of danger. A low grinding sound brought her attention to the gates. They were closing.

Raren, Alura, and Veldon had gathered around them now, the others piled in layers beyond them. Kyna scanned the sky above the city walls, but saw nothing.

Then she heard it.

Heavy and rhythmic rushes of air.

Kyna's throat seemed to be swelling shut. She couldn't move. The phoenix had incited nothing but dread in her since she had watched it cleanse its first city, yet she had always been on its side, however grudgingly. Now the beast took on a whole new level of terror. Would it hesitate to kill her if given the chance? Would her father let it? Could he stop it?

The wing beats came closer, then a shuddering call cut through the noise of the city. It was not the phoenix's usual intimidating shriek, but an ominous announcement of presence.

Caerlyn started to run.

Snapping out of her trance, Kyna followed. The woman was heading toward the taller buildings at the northern end of the city. Kyna did not ask where they were going. It took all of her energy to keep up with Caerlyn in the twisting and crowded streets. She looked up as often as she could without falling over, and after sprinting the length of two streets, the distant sounds of the phoenix manifested into a glittering and streaming body of fire and glass. The phoenix glided low over buildings, unconcerned by the possibility of arrows or javelins. None came. At least the elves had learned something from their previous encounters with the monster.

Caerlyn ran faster, and Kyna gasped for air as she pushed her legs to their limits. The phoenix was angling toward the same buildings on which Caerlyn had set her sights. They wouldn't get there in time. It was too far, and the phoenix wasn't hindered by winding streets—or legs.

With a graceful swoop and a billow of flames, the phoenix disappeared below a line of buildings.

By the time Caerlyn began to slow, Kyna could feel sweat soaking the back of her shirt. Every breath hurt, yet she could not seem to get enough of them. When she finally had enough control over herself to look up, her heart sank into her stomach. The plumes and arching neck of the phoenix rose above an impenetrable mass of elves. Kyna couldn't even see her father.

"Damn!" Caerlyn stamped her foot and swung her gaze from side to side, clearly trying to find an alternate route, but there was none. Elves had packed every street surrounding the confrontation.

"No!" Renyra said. She spun toward Firas. "Can you see anything? Hear anything?"

Firas craned his neck and narrowed his eyes. "I can see Cuvan— maybe Kaelo? But I cannot hear anything."

"What if the phoenix attacks right now?" Renyra said. "We'll never be able to get to it."

No one offered an answer. All they could do was wait to see what happened.

They did not have to wait long.

The phoenix let out a long cry and launched itself into the air. Elves gasped and ducked as it flew over them. It was headed out of the city.

What are they doing? What did Cuvan say?

Kyna didn't think. She ran.

Elves were everywhere. Buildings were everywhere. Kyna barreled through the elves and cursed at the buildings, not caring if the others were behind her. She had to follow the phoenix out of the city. She had to see where it landed. Whatever her father had decided with Cuvan, she had to find him before the cherufin came and a battle began.

Whether by luck or sheer force of will, Kyna came to one of the city's smaller gates when she reached the outer walls. This one was wooden, and it stood open.

Knocking over two elves in her haste, she barreled through the gate, keeping her eyes trained on the retreating form of the phoenix. It screamed as it flew over the armies, long and grating cries that made

Kyna's teeth vibrate. Below the soaring monster, the elven armies moved in agitation, ducking or raising weapons.

Where would it land? What would it do?

Kyna's muscles tensed, ready to spring her forward. Her foot barely left the ground before stopping mid air. A deep tremor had shaken up through her shoes and into her bones. A familiar tremor, distant and vast.

No.

The phoenix fanned its wings in a swirling cloud of flames, stopping its forward momentum and lifting itself higher into the air.

"Kyna!" Gellion's voice fell in time with another call from the phoenix, and Kyna jumped violently. She glanced sideways to see Gellion striding through the gate, his face red and his eyes blazing. Valder and Veldon trailed behind him.

"What the hell was that?" Gellion said as he neared her. "You—" His voice fell away. He looked down at the rumbling ground.

"It's calling its army," Kyna said. "We've run out of time."

The rest of the troupe was steadily filling in the space behind Gellion. They all stared at the phoenix, hovering above the army like a fallen sun.

When Gellion raised his head, he looked again like the man Kyna had known in Daro, his emotions burning behind his eyes with such fervor she could almost feel them in the air. She felt her own emotions rising through her, as if to meet his.

"Then we will meet him in battle," Gellion said.

His broad shoulders pulled away from his neck. Travel-worn, without armor or banner or army, he looked more like a Lord among the elves than Liera or Dulon ever had.

It was a task nearly laughable—finding Kaelo alone in a battle of thousands of elves, let alone getting redstone off of him and using it against the phoenix—yet looking at the emerald inferno of Gellion's eyes, Kyna could not find it in herself to doubt him.

She nodded. "We will meet him in battle."

Gellion was standing close to her. Their eyes met. Kyna could sense the depth of his feeling in the air between them and felt her own energy buzz through her body in response. For a moment, Gellion looked at her without a trace of hostility or disgust. For a moment, she saw in him the same passion from which she had once fled. For a moment, their past didn't seem to matter in the face of what lay before them.

"Ahem."

Kyna turned to see Valder watching them. Next to him, Tornac looked between Gellion and Kyna with a look all too knowing for Kyna's comfort.

Blood rushed to Kyna's face. She stepped backward, only now realizing how close she had been standing to Gellion and how long the silence between them had stretched.

"If we are about to join a battle," said Valder. "We may want to make a plan before *that* gets to us." He nodded toward the eastern horizon.

The rumbling of the ground had become notably heavier. Heart skipping with alarm, Kyna spun around. Beyond the colorful mass of elves and blazing glare of the phoenix, a solid wall had appeared on the golden plains. Cherufin by the thousands marched with indifferent force toward Telem Fier, and the elves' only hope hovered a thousand feet above their heads, mounted on the back of a demon. With her back to Gellion and her mind sobered, the impossibility of their success fell upon Kyna once more like a fist of stone.

RAISE THE MONSTERS UP AGAIN

"So many," Renyra whispered.

Her hand had found Firas's and twined through his long fingers. The warmth was comforting, but never had Renyra so longed for the exchange of emotion of which she was now deprived. This was like holding the hand of a gloved stranger. She squeezed his hand harder.

The cherufin were without end, stretching north to south. Where had they all come from? How had the phoenix created so many so quickly?

They can be as infinite as the stone beneath our feet.

The realization nearly brought Renyra to her knees. The elves could not win this fight. The phoenix would only raise more of these demons for each one that fell. Bringing down the phoenix was the only way to survive this.

The cries that had rippled through the elven army upon the phoenix's flight had now resolved into clipped orders and calls of response. The morphing masses of bodies were aligning into organized rows.

"So, what's the plan, my lord?" Valder said to Gellion.

Gellion narrowed his eyes at the honorific, but turned his attention back to the approaching enemy. They were almost to the elven lines now.

"We get to Kaelo," he said.

"Right," Valder said. "Simple."

Gellion shook his head. "There is no other option. If Cuvan will not surrender, we either find a way to destroy the phoenix in the midst of this battle, or we run now and try for a new opportunity after it is over." His eyes turned hard as flint. "Would you like to wait and see what is left for us to save then?"

The humor left Valder's face. "I didn't say we should run. I'm only saying that getting redstone off Kaelo has more or less been our continually failing plan since the start of this. What if he never leaves the phoenix's back?"

"We make him."

"How?"

Gellion ran a hand through his hair.

"I don't know." His voice was heavy with frustration, and his eyes darted back and forth across the battlefield as though looking for answers. "If the phoenix flies low enough—"

"We cannot predict what the phoenix will do," said Tornac. "We cannot predict anything about this battle. Our plans have failed every time we try to guess Kaelo's game."

Renyra snorted. Tornac looked at her.

"Sorry," she said. "Just—yes. You're right."

Tornac's lips twitched.

"So you suggest we throw ourselves into a battle with 'getting to Kaelo' as our only goal?" Valder said.

"I suggest we stay together and build our plan as the situation evolves," said Tornac.

Valder shrugged. "I like it."

A resounding clash ripped through the air and shook the ground. All eyes turned to the front lines of the elven army. The cherufin had infiltrated the elves, and this time they were not marching passively to their destination. Stone fists swung, bashed, and punched. Metal weapons sent off sparks upon meeting stone flesh. Soon the air was as full of elven screams as of clashing rock and metal.

Renyra's stomach churned. Her limbs seemed to seize up. The terror that gripped her body now was worse even than that upon the rolling hills of Diernas. Then, at least, she had understood something of the battle before her. Then they had been facing a living, breathing, defeatable enemy. Then there had not been a phoenix.

The beast now called its triumph and began circling the battlefield, though it still kept a dizzying distance from the ground. What if it never came down?

The elves were charging forward now, condensing where they met the cherufin.

Renyra looked at Gellion. He wore the same hard expression as before. His eyes flickered between the battle and the phoenix. Finally, he turned to Tornac.

"You're right. We will look for any opportunity to get at Kaelo—catching his attention, separating him from the phoenix—any means we can think of, but we don't have the power to force this battle to our advantage. We will use what we're given. In the mean time, try to stay together. Protect each other."

Renyra's palms were slicked with the sweat of cold fear, and her heart pounded a rushing cadence against her ribs, but so too did she feel pride. She was doing something. She would not stand by and watch the world rise or fall from her corner of hopeless security. She would fight with her kin, her friends, and her love.

Gellion disengaged the halberd from his back and held it in front of him. Renyra gave Firas's hand a last squeeze before pulling the club from her hip. She eyed the weapon with distaste and had no confidence that she bore the strength to wield it against a cherufin, but it would still do her more good than a javelin against this enemy.

"Shall we?" Gellion looked around at all of them, meeting each pair of eyes with a confident, if slightly manic, gleam.

Then they were running. Renyra followed on Gellion's heels.

They closed the gap between themselves and the phoenix with frantic yet halting progress as they pushed through and dodged around hundreds of elves trying to converge in the same direction. Groups of Fieri remained close to the walls of the city in a defensive stance, but the majority of the army seemed possessed by a desperation to push against the enemy with as much force and haste as possible. Did they know the hopelessness of their charge? Was this desperation some twisted product of lost hope, or did they truly believe their sheer force of will could prevail where logic could not?

Renyra's view of the front lines of the battle had receded as taller elves crowded in front of her, but she could hear the screams and crunches growing louder. She clung to Firas's shirt and kept her eyes fixed on Gellion's back, occasionally glancing around to see that the members of her troupe and Gellion's brothers still occupied the space immediately around her.

Gellion stopped.

The phoenix was still ahead of them and far overhead, hovering with blazing strokes of its wings and facing its oncoming army, but Gellion was looking straight ahead.

His eyes widened in horror just before a cacophony of new sounds reached Renyra's ears.

Inhuman screams. Growls. Bellows. Roars.

The hair on the back of Renyra's neck stood straight up as visions of black toothed wolves, lizards, and lindworms flashed before her eyes.

"What is it?" she shouted at Gellion. Even on the balls of her feet she could not see the cause of his fear. The horrible sounds grew louder.

Gellion lowered his halberd and took a step back. All color had fled his face.

"What?" Renyra half screamed.

Firas's hands braced around Renyra's waist and hoisted her upward.

The cherufin were close now, the brutality of their attacks much more gruesome at close proximity, but even the horror of the cherufin paled in comparison to what was now sprinting through their numbers.

Wild cats—spotted, striped, and brindled—charged toward the elves at breathtaking speed, weaving between the cherufin's legs and leaping over their heads with astonishing strength and agility. The predators spat and screamed their fury and bloodlust through red gums and black teeth. Snarling dogs snapped at their heels, followed by what looked to be a massive herd of buval. No more were the eyes of the cow-like buval gentle, but wild and rolling with red glares. They tossed their heads and shook their horns with shuddering bellows so unlike their usual soft calls that Renyra would have never recognized the beasts had she not seen them with her own eyes.

"Sweet Riu," she whispered.

Firas lowered her to the ground. She held his hand to steady herself. How far had the phoenix extended the reach of its corruption to bring all of these monsters to Telem Fier? She almost laughed at her previous fear of corrupted reptiles, worms, and mangy dogs. The beasts of the grasslands could be dangerous in their own right, but possessed of vicious and powerful spirits?

It was too much. The animals. The cherufin. The monsters and the fear. Cuvan had been a fool to enable this battle. He had condemned them all.

They had to get out of this. She looked to Gellion, who seemed to be emerging from his own trance of horror. His eyes darted around him and locked on her pleading stare. He opened his mouth, but then the chaos hit them like a thrashing, screaming wall.

A cat galloped within a foot of Renyra's legs, its thick tail slapping into her knees. Another roared and snapped at an elf to her right before gurgling and squirming beneath a spear thrust through its neck.

Fur and stone surrounded them, and above it all rang the chilling cries of the phoenix.

Renyra's club hung useless in her nerveless fingers, and Firas's incoherent shouts fell muffled on her ears. The ground was vibrating with the footfalls of the cherufin. Renyra could see their glowing eyes amid the tumult now. Blinking and shaking her head, she tried to regain control over her body. The world around her seemed to be moving in a slow and distant dance. This was surely the end. This was a battle they could not dream of winning.

Not unless we can get to Kaelo.

Renyra felt one of her arms jerk sideways and looked down, sure that she would find the appendage ripped from her body, but it was only Firas trying to drag her catatonic form. She shook her head and forced her legs to move with his urging.

To the right, an elf's ribs splintered with an audible crack as a cherufin punched both its fists into his middle. Renyra winced. A wild dog jumped over the cherufin and finished the elf with a swift bite to the throat. Renrya gagged.

"Back to the walls!"

She recognized Gellion's voice and saw the tip of his halberd rise against the sky. It was streaked with red.

Hand in hand with Firas, Renyra ran.

The distance to the walls seemed infinitely further than their brief struggle to the heart of the battle. Fighting enveloped them and chased on their heels. Cries of pain and rage mingled with guttural growls and the wordless smashing of stone against metal and bone. Renyra struck sideways with her club whenever she caught sight of fur or teeth or rock.

Would they try to get back inside the city? Would they hide and wait for another opportunity to corner Kaelo and the phoenix? It seemed a cowardly thing to do, yet they were possibly the only elves alive who knew how to end the phoenix's terror, even if it was only temporary. Surely the eventual termination of this monster was more important than the help of a dozen elves against an unconquerable army of demons?

It was not until they were once more surrounded by Fieri defenders that the sounds of pain and death fell behind them. Air was rasping through Renyra's throat in wheezes.

Gellion ran straight at the wall, but did not turn toward the main gates when he reached it. A sweeping glance over his shoulder must have shown him an adequately complete company, and he waved an arm as he took off to the right.

Renyra tried to count her friends, but it was impossible to keep track of them all as they wove through soldiers. Had they all made it back? Her stomach turned over.

Don't think about that now.

The small gate through which they had originally come loomed ahead. Gellion was leading them back into the city.

The relief that seized Renyra shamed her.

Gellion ran through the opening and up a flight of stairs to the left. Renyra took the steps two at a time to keep up with Firas's long stride. He lifted her hand with each leap.

Finally, Gellion stopped.

Renyra leaned against the wall's parapet, gasping for air. For several moments, she focused only on the immediacy of her own body, then of Firas's.

"Are you alright?" She squeezed his hand before releasing it. Her muscles were sore from the strength of her grasp.

"Yes," said Firas. His back was to the battlefield, his eyes roving over each member of their company as they filed onto the wall.

Gellion stood with all three of his brothers. Caerlyn and Kyna had collapsed against the wall on the other side of Firas.

"The others," Renyra said in a high voice. She stepped away from the wall to look down the stairs. "Where are the others?"

For the space of three breaths, no one spoke or moved. The sounds of battle seemed to mute. Had Renyra run past the deaths of those who had been as brothers and sister to her for over a decade?

The scuff of leather on stone came from the bottom of the stairs and Renyra jumped.

Hot relief washed through her body. Trali was coming up the stairs.

"Thank Riu," Caerlyn muttered.

Renyra opened her mouth to repeat the praise, but stopped. Something was wrong. Trali was moving slowly, with one arm twisted back behind him. He took two more steps, then shifted to the side. Raren was behind him.

The big Remsgri had a hand clasped around Raren's arm and seemed to be guiding him up the stairs. Raren stumbled after him as though in a daze. His skin bore a green tinge, and his eyes were wide and empty, shifting from one point in space to another; they were brimming with tears.

The fear that gripped Renyra was entirely unlike that which had possessed her on the battlefield, yet it froze her limbs and numbed her mind just the same. She stepped back as Trali reached the top of the stairs and took Raren to the parapet. Raren gripped the stone with white knuckles and leaned out over the side. He looked like he was going to be sick. Trali wrapped a hand in the back of his shirt to keep him from going over the edge.

"What happened?" Firas said.

Gellion and his brothers had come closer and were watching Raren with mingled expressions of confusion and sympathy. Valder was nearly as pale as Raren himself.

Raren only shook his head.

One hand still braced in Raren's shirt, Trali bowed his head and turned to face them.

"Alura—she is gone."

Some part of Renyra had known this from the moment she saw Raren's face, yet the words stabbed through her like daggers of fire. Alura. The most kindhearted among them. Her friend. Gone.

"Are you sure?" Renyra's voice cracked on the last word. The shock was too new for tears, yet she could feel her body reacting to the news of its own accord.

Trali nodded.

Raren leaned back from the parapet and wiped his mouth with the back of a trembling hand. He kept his eyes closed and his head tilted down. Renyra could see the grief pressing down on his body.

"I had her hand," he whispered. "As we ran. Then it was gone. I turned back, and—" He broke off, his face twisting in pain.

"There was nothing to be done." Trali laid a thick hand on Raren's shoulder. "It was quick."

A terrible silence followed these words. Renyra knew the same thought was flitting between them all, likely followed by the same guilt. Alura's death was a tragedy beyond comprehension, but this was not the time to mourn for her.

"I am ... I am sorry," Gellion said.

Raren did not respond, but took a deep shaking breath and stood straighter. Trali let his hand fall.

"We should never have tried to get at Kaelo through there. I thought —" Gellion raked his hands through his hair and shook his head. "It was reckless and risky. I thought the phoenix would land, or at least dip lower. And the animals—"

"None of us could have predicted that," Veldon said. "But now that we see what we are facing, what are we going to do?" He looked toward the phoenix. It was still high in the air, watching the sickening destruction of its own making.

Renyra balled her hands into fists. Was Kaelo satisfied by horror he had wrought? Was this revenge enough for him? Was this a worthy cost for his ambitions?

Gellion sighed and turned to Kyna. The woman was staring at Raren with pallid shock.

"I—" She blinked and looked back at the phoenix. "I don't know how we can make them land. There is no threat to them, no reason for them to join the battle when—" She trailed off, but the meaning of her words was evident.

When this army will crush the elves within the hour all on its own.

"Is that it then?" said Valder. Anger seemed to have replaced his shock. "We're just going to watch this slaughter?"

"What do you suggest?" Gellion snapped.

"Kyna says there is no threat to Kaelo and the phoenix. So we make a threat. We make them come to us."

"We have no threat." Gellion laughed bitterly. "The only threat we hold over that cursed bird at this point is knowledge, and we can hardly flaunt that over the top of a wall. Without Kaelo, we have nothing."

Renyra tried to tune out the argument, racking her brains for something—anything that could help them, that could draw a phoenix's attention. She thought of the magnetic blaster of the Remsgri, of Gellion's display of redstone in Morcanan. They were out of weapons and bereft of redstone. What of Kaelo, then? Could they get *his* attention, and by so doing draw the phoenix with him? She looked at Kyna out the side of her eyes.

"Maybe—"

Renyra's voice was drowned out by another sonorous blast from the horns of Telem Fier. She clapped her hands over her ears and looked around wildly, trying to see the reason for this second warning call. Had the phoenix's army reached the gates? Had they infiltrated the city?

She ran to the parapet and looked over the side. Cherufin and a handful of cats were indeed wreaking havoc among the Fieri soldiers now, but the main gate to the city was closed.

Still the horn sounded.

"What is it?" Renyra shouted, looking to Firas and then to Caerlyn.

The wall began to hum. Renyra took her hands from her ears and grasped the parapet, her heart leaping into her throat. Was this some new devilry of the phoenix? Would it collapse the walls of Telem Fier as Kaelo had collapsed Daro? Could it do that from such a distance? But then the city gate began to open, and Renyra realized it was only the mechanisms of the gate causing the vibrations.

She watched the gate with wide eyes. What was Cuvan thinking? Why would he open this last defense between the people of his city and the horrors on the battlefield outside?

Then the Lord of Telem Fier himself emerged from the gate. He was riding a burly horse, and on a horse next to him sat Auralia. They were each laden with what looked like bags. Each carried a short bow.

Auralia drew an arrow from a quiver on her saddle and reached into one of the pouches. Renyra could not make out what she pulled from the bag, but whatever it was, Auralia seemed to affix it to the end of her arrow. She nocked it and drew her arm back.

"Clear!" she yelled in a ringing voice.

The Fieri soldiers ahead of her melted to either side of her at once, leaving a space of cherufin and animals in the suddenness of their retreat. Auralia loosed the arrow into the middle of them.

The arrow hit no cherufin or cat, but struck the ground. There was no time for Renrya to wonder at the woman's aim, however. The moment the arrow struck the ground, the air around it seemed to explode in a ball of fire and soil.

Chunks of rock and limbs of animals soared into the air. Cats screamed and darted in mad circles, their coats aflame. Streaks of red and green spirits rose from crumbled heaps of stone.

Renyra's jaw dropped.

Auralia kicked her mount forward, Cuvan splitting off from her in another direction. Fieri cleared the way. The ground exploded. Again and again.

Cherufin started turning their attention to the two horses. After the fifth explosion, two of them charged Auralia, fists raised. Renyra gasped, but Auralia reached into another bag and threw what looked to be a glass ball at the cherufin. It hit one of the creatures and exploded. The impact of this explosion was more concentrated, but achieved Auralia's goal nonetheless. The cherufin split apart and crumbled.

Renyra let out a whoop. She turned to see Gellion grimacing at her.

"Looks like the craft competition came out with some good after all," he said.

Renyra's mouth formed an 'o.' She remembered the chemical compound Auralia had invented for the competition that now seemed centuries ago. A drop of the stuff had started a controlled fire. It appeared Auralia had expanded its use.

"Will this do for a threat?" Firas said to Valder.

Valder snorted but turned a worried glance toward the phoenix. It was facing the city gate, watching Auralia and Cuvan decimate any of its army that came too near to the city.

The horn sounded again.

The Fieri soldiers nearest the wall drew pouches out of their wraps, then ran forward into the battle that had finally reached them.

It was like fireworks. Pops of color, fire, and smoke filled the air. The wind blew the smoke toward the city, and Renyra smelled the acrid scent of burnt chemicals. Hope rose in her chest, but her smile faded as she watched the phoenix. What would it do? Elves were clearly still dying by the hundreds. Auralia's bombs may disrupt the phoenix's forces, but could they possibly do enough to change the outcome of the battle when the phoenix could just make more soldiers?

Explosions continued. The Fieri began to push away from the walls. Cherufin still marched toward the city at the same pace, but the corrupted animals were beginning to run from the balls of fire erupting around them. A small portion of the buval herd had made its way to the city now, but the beasts halted their attack when they saw the explosions. It seemed even corrupted spirits could not entirely override the instincts of the animals. Buval started to charge away from the city. In less than a minute, there was a veritable stampede. Renyra cringed as elves were trampled beneath the massive animal's hooves, but so too were cherufin and cats caught beneath their weight.

The phoenix screamed.

Renyra stepped back, reaching for Firas's arm as the horrifying sound filled her head.

The beast gave two massive beats of its wings and sent a cloud of crimson flame into the air, then tucked its wings to its sides and dove toward Telem Fier.

Renyra gasped. It took all her will to keep her legs from running the other direction. This is what they wanted. The phoenix was finally leaving its sky-bound perch. Kaelo was flying toward them, toward the ground. Yet much as she told herself these facts, Renyra could not seem to find it within herself to be glad of the demonic monster hurtling toward elves she cared about.

Come on Auralia. Do something. You must have known this would happen.

Renyra watched helplessly as the phoenix tore through the air toward the leaders of her kin. It would flatten them. Why weren't they aiming arrows at it? Did they not see the flaming, boat sized bird—hear its screeches of rage? Maybe if they hit it with one of their arrows—

The horn sounded yet again.

Renyra heard chanting shouts from the wall to their right. She turned to see a crossbow manned by half a dozen elves. A thick bolt sat ready in the machine. Its tip was glass.

"Auralia you wonderful woman," Renyra muttered to herself. She could have cried with relief.

The bolt swung to face the phoenix, which didn't seem to have noticed the commotion on the wall. It was close enough now that Renrya could see the molten depths of its eyes. It would hit the ground in a matter of seconds.

The chant of the Fieri archers ended, and the bolt flew.

BLOOD, FLAMES, AND TEARS

Kyna watched the arc of the bolt. Hope and horror twined and mingled within her, stifling her breath. The crossbow had fired true, yet somehow the progress of its arrow seemed to slow in the muted pressure now exerting itself against Kyna's ears and chest. Her eyes moved to the phoenix. Its focus was solely on Auralia. The beast's wings were flattened against its sides, and between the joints, Kyna saw the flash of her father's pale face. He did not face Auralia, but the bolt coming straight at him. He raised his sword as if to cut the bolt down, but there was nothing he could do.

The bolt hit the phoenix square in the chest.

The air exploded.

Kyna's hands flew up to shield her eyes. Where the phoenix had been, a new sun had come into being, drowning out the bird's flames with a light as powerful as lightning. The resounding crack that followed made Kyna's ears ring. The echo of the noise ricocheted off the walls of Telem Fier and echoed through the surrounding fields and hills. The ground shook.

Kyna squinted against the brilliant display, trying to discern the phoenix's shape. She thought she could hear shouts and screams—maybe the shrieking of a bird—but the sounds seemed far away and small. Rubbing her ears, Kyna blinked away the spots crowding her vision.

The explosion would not have killed the phoenix, but her father—

"Where are they?" Gellion said. "Can you see them?" He was leaning over the wall, squinting against the smoke.

"I can see flames," said Veldon. "There."

Kyna followed the line of his extended finger. She could just make out flares of crimson amid the haze.

There were definitely shouts now. Kyna could feel her hearing slowly returning. Some of the yelling came from the wall and the soldiers just below it. Shouts of victory. They were quickly overrun by the screams of terror further afield. Fireworks of light and fire started popping throughout the blanket of smoke.

The larger flames of the phoenix had grown brighter. A single piercing note rang out over the field. Kyna's blood ran cold. The Fieri had not killed the phoenix, they had enraged it.

The ground shook again, then the very atmosphere seemed to rend itself apart.

Kyna fell backward in a roaring rush of light and heat and sound. Covering her head, she huddled against the ground. The stones of the wall shuddered with the force of the explosion, but blessedly remained intact.

"Stay down!" Gellion's voice called somewhere to her right.

Kyna reached for him on instinct, desperate to feel the life of another elf in this world of smoke and screams. After several swipes through hot and grainy air, Kyna felt the reassuring structure of skin and bone meet her hand. Gellion jerked at the unexpected touch, but then his hand gripped her arm.

"Is everyone alright?" he said. Kyna could not tell if it was a whisper or a shout.

The smoke was beginning to thin, but Kyna could still barely make out Gellion's outline.

"What the hell was that?" said Valder.

No one answered.

Kyna felt a pressure beneath her arm. She tightened her grip around Gellion's elbow and stood on shaky legs as he helped her to her feet.

A fresh chorus of screams carried through the smoke. Gellion rushed to the parapet, pulling Kyna with him and grasping the ledge for support. The stone trembled beneath their hands.

A shiver rippled down Kyna's spine as she looked out over the veiled landscape.

Memories overshadowed the present. She remembered a rubble strewn street, the muted stillness imposed upon chaos by suspended particles in the air. Then she had found the effect mesmerizing. Now there was only horror, without and within.

A burst of flames shone through the smoke, and the shadow of the phoenix soared upward. It flew in a twisting ball of fire and reflected light, swirling and morphing the smoke around it into dizzying shapes. It stopped, beating its wings in powerful strokes. The smoke cleared in billowing sweeps.

Where the phoenix had been, the grass was charred and smoking. Bodies littered the space, though most could not be recognized as elf or animal. It was desolation.

In the blackest portion of the ruin, Kyna thought she could make out the remains of a horse.

"Auralia," Renyra choked.

Kyna could not make herself turn to Renyra's grief. It was clear what had happened, and it was sickening. By accident or will, the phoenix had come down upon Auralia with a force that had broken the woman's entire stock of explosives. The phoenix may have burned a few of the bodies now steaming in the ash, but it had been the Fieri's own weapons that created this devestation.

Slowly, the sounds of battle came once more from the further reaches of the field. Those elves nearest the walls of Telem Fier staggered and swayed in a momentary suspension of action.

The phoenix was climbing into the air again. The reality of their goal broke through Kyna's shock.

"Where is he?" she said. "Is he still on the phoenix?"

It didn't seem possible. The phoenix had gone down hard, and there had been so much fire, so much destruction.

"I don't see him." Gellion was shielding his eyes from the sunlight as he squinted toward the phoenix. "I can't imagine he could have stayed on its back through that."

Kyna was already scanning the ground around the blackened stain upon the field.

"He could have been thrown from the phoenix—fled before the second explosion." She looked for his armor, his hair, his sword, anything. All she saw were rainbows of wraps and dark skin.

The cherufin had begun to infiltrate the area again. Elves scrambled to find fallen weapons. Some had started to run.

"He still had his redstone," Kyna said. "Maybe—there!" Her heart lurched. She pointed at a fanned formation of stone rising from the flat ground. It was cracked and blackened. "Look! There's no way that's natural. It's my father—he shielded himself. He must have. Which means—"

"He's on the ground." Excitement lit Gellion's face. He turned to face the troupe, now gathered along the parapet. "We need to get back down there. Stay close to the walls if you can, but look for Kaelo. He's off the phoenix. It may come back for him any moment, but if we can find him before that happens—"

Everyone gaped at him. It was a plan no more formed than any they had pursued thus far, but it had a chance. It was their only chance.

Gellion looked at Kyna, and her breath hitched in her throat.

"Stay with me," he said.

It was the logical thing to do. Kaelo would be more likely to stay his hand, or at least hesitate upon seeing the two of them. They both knew how to use redstone if they could get their hands on it. Still, Kyna could not eradicate the hope and the longing that rose in her from Gellion's words.

Gellion was clearly waiting for her confirmation.

Kyna nodded once. Gellion turned toward the stairs, but hesitated a moment longer.

"Raren," he said. "If ... if you want to stay here, no one will—"

"I'm going," Raren said in a flat voice.

Gellion bowed his head in acknowledgment, then sprinted down the stairs.

Kyna's mind spun, grasping at images, sounds, and memories. There was no direction any more. Elves were on all sides. Cherufin were on all sides. Everywhere Kyna turned were corpses and blood and ashes. She held on to her cudgel like a child holding a butter knife among a pack of wolves. She was no warrior. In the battle at Arvain, she had lingered near the back of the army, planning to bide her time until the elves could retreat. The reality of that battle had unnerved her more than she would ever admit. This was worse. So much worse.

She tried to remember what Gellion had taught her of the A'vaeri, but the stances came to her in a jumbled mess of incoherent thoughts amid all that was happening around her. How in Riure was an elf supposed to remember balance and movements in the chaos of battle?

Beside her, Gellion moved with as much fluidity and precision as he had in Daro's arena. He hardly seemed to think as he maneuvered his halberd through the masses of bodies around them, somehow using the weapon as shield and blade simultaneously while distinguishing between animal, cherufin, and elf. Kyna stayed as close to him as she dared. She had lost sight of the others of their company several minutes before and now channeled all of her concentration into looking for her father, but the elven army had begun to mingle in the chaos. Turi elves dotted the Fieri, drawing Kyna's eyes with false hope and wasted time. She pictured her father's armor—black and crimson. She listened for rumbling ground and cracking stone.

The phoenix had not returned to the ground since its flight from the explosions. Her father could not have gotten far on foot in this mess. Surely he was fighting, and if so, he could be found.

Kyna glanced to the sky, and a bolt of panic coursed through her body. The phoenix was gone. She looked around frantically, but was forced to return her attention to the ground when a snapping dog came within inches of her arm. She screamed and beat at the beast's head with her cudgel. Its eyes shone crimson, and saliva streamed from its ebony teeth. Kyna smashed her weapon into its face again and again, dodging its mouth between each blow.

Please die. Please die.

She tried to chance a look back at the sky, even as she made sure Gellion was still within reaching distance. He had not noticed the mongrel still trying to rip out Kyna's throat. It took nearly a dozen hits before the vile thing fell beneath Kyna's onslaught, its head cracked nearly in two. Kyna recoiled and almost fell into Gellion. She could feel herself shaking.

What hell had she helped to create? These monsters had certainly never been part of the plan. Kyna had been as disturbed by their presence as the elves of Daro and still did not entirely understand what they were or where they came from.

Kyna forced her attention back to the sky. The phoenix was still gone. Had the bird swooped down somewhere without her seeing? Was Kaelo even now climbing back onto its back, ready to soar out of reach once more?

A brilliant flash of light came from the center of the battle. Kyna nearly shouted in relief as she saw the streaming flames of the phoenix. Her relief was short lived. The light that had drawn her eyes was not that of the phoenix's body, but of a colossal cloud of silver flames pouring from its beak. Tendrils of red and green shot through the mass of fire.

Kyna could not explain the dread that settled in her stomach. Never had she seen flames like this. This was something new. Yet some buried instinct told her it was also something terrible.

"Gellion!" she shouted.

Gellion jerked back toward her. Droplets of blood splattered his face, and his eyes were wild with the energy of battle. "What? Did you see him?"

"No," said Kyna. "No, but the phoenix—"

Gellion looked to the phoenix, now flying low over the battle and reigning its bizarre flames.

A cherufin swung at Gellion. Kyna gasped, but Gellion ducked the blow without even looking and brought the metal butt of his halberd down into the thing's knees. It buckled sideways, flailed its stubby arms for a few moments, then crumbled into a pile of rock when its legs broke apart. Kyna let out her breath.

"Whatever it's doing, we can't do anything about it." Gellion's eyes lingered on the phoenix a moment longer, then he shook his head. "We have to find your father. He's the only way to stop this now. Stay focused." His expression was softer than his words, but Kyna could see the desperation behind his eyes. He was afraid. The realization seemed an obvious one, yet it still struck a blow to Kyna's thinning hope.

They moved on, Gellion fighting their way through beasts of nightmare as Kyna feebly defended herself and scanned the face of every elf they passed. She tried to keep her attention away from the phoenix, but the flames were coming closer now, and their roaring was punctuated by what sounded like shrieks of terror.

Find your father. You can stop this if you find your father.

It seemed both hours and moments before she finally heard the crack of stone. Her head jerked toward the sound so hard it sent a snap of pain down her neck. The ground trembled. It was a subtle movement, nothing like the earthquakes in Daro, but Kyna was sure it was more than marching cherufin.

Calling to Gellion, Kyna started to run toward the sounds. Gellion was at her side in an instant. His brows were drawn over his eyes, but upon another ringing crack of rock, he gave a sharp intake of breath and increased his pace. The ground began to slope downward, lending a better view of the fighting further to the north. There were more cherufin here, but the fighting was more spread out.

The ground rumbled.

Kyna saw him.

Her father stood amid the melee, indistinguishable from the elves around him but for his armor and the crimson sword in his hands.

"Father!" The word escaped Kyna's lips before she could remember thinking it.

Her father's sword lowered, but he did not turn toward Kyna. Instead, he turned to face the east, and even from the distance between them, Kyna could see his body go rigid. She turned just in time to see the glare of silver flames before they engulfed her.

This fire was not like the current-driven red flames the phoenix used to unmake vierstone. It was like a light breeze, yet the brush of energy was evident upon Kyna's skin, and the roaring of the flames separated into tangled voices in her ears.

Then it was gone.

The phoenix continued its steady flight back toward the walls of the city.

Kyna looked down at herself, then at Gellion. She flexed her hands and blinked several times, but could not see or feel any change brought on by the flames. In a rush of panic, she grasped at Gellion's arm.

"The vierstone. Is it ok?"

Gellion blanched and plunged his hand into his pocket. He brought out a round of green in his palm. Kyna sighed with relief.

The silver flames had laid a lull of confusion over the battle, but the fighting was quickly returning to its former intensity. Still, the screams of terror from further afield were only growing louder. What had the flames done?

"Kyna." Gellion gave her a pointed look, then turned back to her father.

Two Fieri soldiers were coming at him with spears. Kyna nearly closed her eyes. She did not want to see this. In all this time, she had never seen her father kill directly by his own hand. It seemed a ridiculous detail to care about. Her father had caused the deaths of hundreds of elves by now, if not thousands. But he was backing away from the advancing elves. He held his sword aloft, but seemed to only be paying the Fieri mild attention. One of the Fieri threw their spear. Her father deflected the weapon with the flick of his sword and continued his retreat.

"Kyna!" Gellion had started running toward Kaelo, then turned back to see Kyna standing frozen to the spot. "What are you waiting for?" he said.

"I don't—" Kyna shook her head. Something was wrong. The flames. The screams. Why had nothing happened?

Then she saw it.

Behind Gellion, an elf had lain upon the ground in the blood soaked grass. Kyna had not even noticed the body among the gruesome landscape, but now her eyes followed it with horrified fascination. The elf was rising to her feet—a Fieri woman. Her wraps were torn and bloodied, and she held a spear.

"Gellion." Kyna's voice was a hoarse whisper. It felt like she was in a dream—one where she could not scream no matter how hard she tried. "Gellion." The whisper rose an octave.

The Fieri woman's throat was slashed through, as though by raking claws. The ravaged skin stretched as she raised her head. Kyna's heart stuttered. The woman's eyes were a luminescent red.

Gellion turned just as the woman lunged for him. Her spear grazed his shoulder as he turned away from her attack, and Gellion grunted in pain. He wheeled backward and brought his halberd around to crack over the woman's skull. She fell to her hands and knees, swayed, then started to get back up. Gellion was backing away. His eyes were wide and his face ashen.

"No. No, no," he muttered.

The screams had reached them in full. Kyna tore her eyes away from the horrible scene before her to see the stumbling, bloodied forms of elves pulling themselves from the ground all around. Their eyes were the same as the cherufin's. The same as the dog's.

"Riu above," Gellion breathed. His eyes were fixed on the dead woman groping for her spear. "Not again."

The Fieri's hand had not yet found her fallen weapon, but Gellion brought the blade of his halberd down on the woman's neck before her fingers brushed the metal. The red dimmed from her eyes as her head tumbled to the ground.

Kyna gagged. She remembered the stories she had extracted from a reluctant Gellion in Daro. He had talked of the demonic animals in the Great War, of the twisted elves who had sold their souls to be commanders in the phoenix's army. And he had talked of the elves who had not chosen to be in the army—those who had been possessed by spirits in death.

Wights.

It was happening again. All of it. The phoenix had recreated its reign of terror as before, only this time it had had help.

"What have we done," Kyna whispered. Tears blurred her vision as she looked to her father. He stood with his arms at his sides, looking around him as one lost in a crowd.

Gellion was still staring at the body of the woman he had beheaded.

His knuckles were white around the shaft of his halberd, and his knees looked close to buckling.

"Come on," Kyna said. "They're ... they're just bodies." Her voice shook. "We can still get to my father."

Gellion's eyes moved slowly from the prone body at his feet to Kyna. Was the disgust in their depths for what he had just done? For what the phoenix had done? Or was some of it reserved for the part he knew Kyna had played in bringing this to the elves? Tears spilled onto Kyna's cheeks. With a shuddering breath, she grasped her cudgel in both hands and ran past Gellion, sprinting down the slope that lead to her father.

Kaelo was further than he had appeared on top of the slope. Kyna struggled to keep sight of him as she dodged monstrosity after monstrosity. She could no longer tell which elves fought for their kin or the phoenix—not unless she could see their eyes, but that was entirely too close for her comfort. Tears still set a haze over her vision. She blinked them away in annoyance.

"Wait!" Gellion said.

Kyna's steps faltered. She looked over her shoulder to see Gellion making his way toward her. Tornac was beside him.

Gellion's brother looked far more ragged than Gellion. His hair was matted to the sides of his face, and his clothes were ripped and stained. He held the ornate sword Kyna had seen him carry on the journey to Maramor months before. It seemed out of place amid such ugliness, the blood on its blade an abomination.

"You have seen him?" Tornac said.

Kyna nodded and pointed behind her. She froze. She did not see her father. He wasn't in the same depression of land he had occupied since the wights began to rise. Curses flowed beneath Kyna's breath. She shouldn't have turned to Gellion's call.

"He was there," Kyna said. "In that bit of mud where the ground sinks. I—"

All worries of her father's whereabouts fled her mind. Half a dozen elves stood board straight, staring at her outstretched finger. She lowered her hand and took a step back. Their eyes shifted to her face. Crimson.

They charged.

Kyna ran backward, not bothering to look behind her. She didn't care if she ran into Gellion and Tornac. She hoped she did. They carried proper weapons. They knew how to use them.

"Stop!" Gellion yelled. "There are more behind us!"

Kyna's feet rooted to the trampled grass. She dragged her eyes away from the rushing wights in front of her to see two more already engaged with Gellion and Tornac. The wights carried spears and daggers. They did not seem to wield them with the same wit and skill that their living counterparts would have possessed, but the weapons were still dangerous. Kyna turned back to the charging wights. They were barely two strides away.

The cudgel swung in Kyna's hands. She deflected one spear and ducked beneath another. The metallic scent of blood washed over her as the bodies converged, and she fought not to retch.

A blade flashed to Kyna's left, taking down one of the wights. Tornac had stepped beside her. Another wight turned its attention to Tornac, but the other four were still intent upon running Kyna through. She tried to watch all of their weapons at once, reacting to each of their thrusts and swipes with barely enough speed to evade death. She yelled and swung her cudgel at the closest one's face. The resultant crunch both disgusted and elated her, but then a flash of pain at her side made her gasp and stumble back. One of the wight's blades had skated over her ribs, slicing through the skin beneath her shirt.

The pain was not excruciating, but it distracted her. One of the wights spun and twisted its spear and brought the butt of the weapon upward to catch her in the stomach. Kyna cried out as the blow stretched her injured skin and nearly lifted her off her feet. She stumbled and fell. The wights ran at her.

Kyna stared in horror. Time seemed to slow as death came for her in the glowing eyes of the elves she had inadvertently killed. She raised her hands only to realize her cudgel was not in either of them. She groped around her for the weapon, never taking her eyes off the wights, but she felt only soggy ground.

She looked for help. Gellion had turned to her shout. He watched her with wide eyes, and his mouth opened, but he was too far away, already engaged with a new wight who had appeared since the initial attack. Kyna could not hear what he said.

Then Tornac was standing in front of her. He looked from the desperate fear in Kyna's face to the anguish of his brother's, then nodded once to Gellion. He raised his sword to the rushing wights.

Kyna could only watch in numb horror as the creatures descended upon Tornac. He fought like a caged wildcat, twisting around the blows with lithe grace and slicing his blade through tendon and muscle, but the wights hardly seemed to notice. He could not get at their necks, not with so many, not with their spears.

Kyna thought her chest would burst from the force of her heart. She reached around her, still trying to find her cudgel. She had to help him. She had to stop this.

Tornac thrust his sword through the throat of one of the wights. Its head lolled to one side, and he kicked it in the middle. The body fell with a wet thud and did not rise again. Gellion was still shouting, trying to get to them, but two more wights now stood between him and his brother. He hacked at them, all the fluidity of his A'vaeri fled in his desperation.

Tornac staggered. One of the spears had sunken into his side. He raised his sword again and again, but it fell with decreasing speed and force.

Never in her life had Kyna felt so useless—so cowardly. She couldn't move. She had no weapon. She would have been no help to Tornac if she had. She simply watched as the man who had nearly driven her to madness with his resemblance to Gellion—who had fought demons with her on a boat running a fool's errand of her own design—whom she had betrayed in the forges of Tura—get cut to pieces by the dead bodies of his own kin.

Another head parted company with its body. There were only two wights now, and Gellion's red hair flashed behind them, but Kyna knew it was too late. Tornac was holding his side, nearly bent double. He held his sword aloft, but seemed unable to move it any further.

One of the wights drew back its spear, then thrust the tip upward through Tornac's body.

Gellion's halberd sliced through both of the wights' necks. All three bodies fell.

Kyna wanted to scream. She could feel a wail of grief rising in her throat, but it could not seem to escape her mouth. Her ears were ringing. Her skin had turned cold. She pushed herself forward until she was kneeling over Tornac.

Gellion had gotten to him first. He pulled his brother up by the shoulders, turning him onto his back. Kyna flinched and curled over the pain in her stomach. She remembered how pale Tornac had been after the leech attack. That was nothing compared to this. His skin was grey. The lack of color was even more stark against the blood on his lips.

Finally, Gellion's voice broke through the cushion that had enveloped Kyna since the wights' attack.

He was shouting his brother's name.

"Tornac!" He put his hand to the side of Tornac's head and tilted it toward him. "Tornac!" His voice lost volume with each utterance of the word, until he was whispering it. "Tornac—"

Tornac's eyes had found his brother's, but there was hardly any light to them. Gellion's voice broke off.

"*Please*," he mouthed. His whole face seemed to be trembling.

Tornac's lips parted, but he was clearly beyond words. His eyes rolled to Kyna. She looked back at him and choked on a sob. Then his gaze slid back to Gellion. Tornac's crimson lips moved, and the slightest breath escaped them, forming words just discernible by the shape of his mouth.

"I go to mine."

Then his eyes focused on a point beyond Gellion's tear-stained face, and his lips were still.

37

LIFESTONE

The sun dimmed. The sounds around Gellion mingled to a dull rush of wind. Even his own body seemed set apart from the pain ripping through his mind. Tornac's eyes were glazed and still, yet the crystalline jade of his irises was as rich and real as it had ever been in life.

Gellion had been close to death more times in his life than he could count. Never had he seen moments of his life flash before his eyes. It was the deaths of others that forced images, memories, and moments to the forefront of his consciousness. He could see Tornac in Tura—impossibly older than him, just as all the other elves had been impossibly older than Gellion. It had seemed odd that Gellion shared the same status of family and blood with that severe and accomplished man. He saw Tornac in his study in Maramor, saw him holding Valder as a baby, saw him setting a small and long legged Veldon on his shoulders. And he saw Tornac with Vyra. The woman had transformed him. Those altered pieces had never returned to Tornac after she died, leaving empty space and anger in their place. Now, lying in blood with the world ending around him, Tornac had not looked so peaceful for two hundred years. Gellion wished he could feel the same peace.

The vierstone in Gellion's pocket seemed to be burning through the fabric of his shirt, like it could sense the wellspring of emotion just beneath the fibers and longed to reach them, to stoke them, to drown Gellion in the strength of their embrace. He ignored it. He would not feed even this last remnant of Riure's vierstone with his pain.

"Gellion, we have to move." Kyna's voice was strained and scratchy. Gellion could hear the sobs behind her words.

He could not look at her. His hands still clasped Tornac's shoulder and face. Warmth still radiated from his brother's skin. Loath though Gellion was to feel that warmth leak away, he could not bear the thought of breaking his touch while any of it still existed.

"Gellion, please," Kyna said. "I'm sorry. I'm so sorry, but we can't stay here. We can't."

Forcing his eyes from Tornac's face, Gellion looked up. The battle had not ceased for Tornac's death. It seemed a disrespectful and cruel thing. Cherufin still trudged through fallen bodies, red eyed wild animals still prowled and ran across the sodden field. And the wights—

A terrible cold spread through Gellion's body, and his grip on Tornac tightened. What if the phoenix made a second pass with its silver flames?

Kyna's hand was wrapped around Gellion's arm now, pulling at him. Two more wights had spotted them and were making their way across the slope carrying a chipped sword and a bow. At least the archer seemed to have no arrows.

Gellion knew he had to get up, that he had to leave Tornac's body here, but the thought of his brother holding Vyra's sword with red eyes burned him beyond bearing. He looked to the north. They were near the edge of the battle. The valley in which they had seen Kaelo was the border of organized fighting. Beyond, the field swelled into more pronounced hills, and fighting bodies thinned to nothing. A few elves were fleeing across the golden slopes and into the rocky outcroppings.

"Help me get him off the field," Gellion said.

Kyna stared at him.

"I will not have his body desecrated," Gellion growled. "Either we cut his head off now or we get him away from the phoenix."

Kyna opened her mouth and began to shake her head. She glanced at the approaching wights with wide eyes before looking at Gellion. She nodded.

Laying Tornac gently on the ground, Gellion stood. His limbs still felt distant and sluggish, and his front was soaked in Tornac's blood. He picked up his dropped halberd and turned to face the two wights. These had been Morcani. Gellion drew on the boiling rage in his core and stepped forward into a defensive stance of the A'vaeri.

Control the fire.

Rage would do him no good if it threw off the precision of his movements, but channeled properly—

Gellion spun his halberd and shifted his weight from one foot to the other, building his energy with his movements and twisting to avoid the swipes from sword and bow. The archer was brandishing his weapon like a mallet. Gellion snapped the bowstring with the edge of his blade and brought the tip of his halberd up through the wight's throat, jerking his hands to the side so it severed the head. He stopped his momentum smoothly and spun to meet another blow from the swordsman. Parrying a swipe and a wildly placed stab, he brought the blunt end of his halberd around in a sweeping arc that cracked against the side of the wight's face, breaking its neck and sending it sprawling into the sticky mud.

For a moment, he just breathed, waiting for the crackling energy to leave his arms, then he turned back to Tornac and Kyna. Kyna had begun to lift Tornac, but was struggling under his weight. Gellion crouched behind his brother's shoulders.

"Take his sword," he said. "Grab his legs with your other arm."

It was a halting and desperate run down the slope. Tornac's body half dragged on the ground, and Gellion lost his grip more than once, fending off attacks. Kyna carried Tornac's legs and kept pace with Gellion without a word, managing even to behead a one-armed wight who came at them from behind. Her face was smeared with tears and ashes, but her expression was grim and determined. Whatever fear had possessed her after the wight attack had gone.

Gellion's chest gave an upward lurch quite apart from the rest of the emotions twisting within him. Covered in battle and carrying a bloodied sword, Kyna was as beautiful as on a summer's day in Daro. Then he remembered whose sword she carried. He set his jaw against a fresh wave of grief and ran on.

They were halfway across the valley when Kyna shouted, "Gellion he's there!"

Gellion almost said 'who?' Then he saw him. Kaelo. The man they had been tracking with such desperation before Gellion's world had changed.

Kaelo stood at the edge of the battle. His sword was drawn, its ruby blade glinting in the weakening sunlight, but he did not seem to be using it. The fighting was sparse around him. A dog rushed him, but was thrown back by a chunk of stone before it could get near. Kaelo took a step backward. His head moved slowly from side to side, taking in his surroundings.

Tornac's shoulders pulled in Gellion's arm and he turned to see Kyna moving toward her father, still clasping Tornac's legs. She paused at his resistance.

"Come on," she said.

Kaelo was stepping backward with greater speed now. Gellion gave his head a jerk, trying to refocus his mind. Kaelo. Redstone. Destroy the phoenix. These things were bigger than his personal anguish. These things were the cause of it.

He started to run again.

Kaelo had not yet seen them. As they drew nearer, Gellion got a clearer view of the man's face. As always, the familiarity of his old mentor struck him and twisted his stomach with anger and regret. But this time he knew the whole story. This time the anger was less, the regret more. The man could have done wonders for the elves. Would he have done wonders still if he had told the Turi the truth of Arela's death?

The man Gellion now saw backing away from a battle of his own creation was vastly different than the one who had confronted him in Tura. Kaelo's face was stained with as much blood and ash as any of the elves around him. His eyes darted back and forth and seemed to hold a horror as deep as Gellion's own at the scale of violence around him. As his eyes passed over Gellion and Kyna, they locked in place.

Kaelo's retreating steps jerked to a halt. He stood perfectly still, his legs parted in half a step, and his sword lifted in his hand. The black pools of his eyes bore into Gellion and Kyna.

"Father!" Kyna shouted.

Kaelo flinched. He started to back away again.

"No," Kyna said. "Wait. Just listen to us!"

Kaelo's gaze shifted back and forth between his pursuers and what Gellion assumed was the phoenix far behind them. Gellion did not dare turn around to find out. Demonic creatures still moved around them—some had turned their attention to Kyna's call—and Tornac's weight still dragged at him as he tried to close the gap between them and Kaelo. He pointed his halberd at a passing boar, but it streaked past him toward a group of Remsgri closer to the city.

"We aren't your enemy," Kyna said. "We can stop this!"

Kaelo pointed the tip of his sword at his daughter with unsteady hands. His head was moving back and forth as though trying to clear Gellion and Kyna from his vision—to erase Kyna's words from his mind.

Kyna did not slow. "Please," she said, softer this time.

Then Gellion was thrown into the air. He could not recall what had hit him, only that it had come with the force of a Rale car. He landed hard, bones vibrating with the impact and rattling through his frame. For several seconds, he lay stunned. His breath was stuck in his chest. Opening his mouth, he tried to free it, but his diaphragm refused to expand. Even in his panic, Gellion flailed his arms with reaching hands, trying to remember what he had been holding and why they had been important.

With a spluttering gasp, oxygen filled his lungs again. Blood rushed to Gellion's head, and his vision cleared. He saw horns. Pointed at him. Moving.

Gellion rolled out of the way before he could comprehend what was happening. Thundering hoofbeats shook the ground behind him. He leaped to his feet. A burning pain ripped through his shoulder and he remembered for the first time the wound the first wight had inflicted upon him. His fall must have widened the laceration. Shoving the pain to the back of his mind, Gellion scanned the ground for his halberd.

A gurgling bellow came from behind him. Gellion turned to face the biggest buval he had ever seen. His experience with the species was minimal to say the least, but he imagined this must surely be a bull. Its head was half as big as he was, and the horns curling down the side of its face extended forward in curved prongs as thick as Gellion's legs. Its eyes were red pinpricks in its massive face.

The buval charged.

Gellion looked around wildly for his weapon—any weapon. A glint of metal caught his eyes, and he saw Tornac's sword flash in Kyna's hand, but she was too far away. She was jabbing the sword at a pair of wights, limping away from their pursuit.

Is this how it would end? Had they come so close to Kaelo only to be trampled by a grassland beast and finished off by the bodies of elves? It was ridiculous. It was infuriating. He could not let it happen.

Gellion coiled his body to spring. If he could throw himself far enough to the side before the buval could follow his motion, he might be able to avoid the reach of its horns. Then at least he may have a chance of finding his halberd before the beast regained its bearings for a third pass. He stared straight at the buval's shaggy head for half a second longer, then jumped.

He waited for the pain, praying it would never come. Surely one of the beast's horns would catch his leg or his hip as he fell.

As Gellion felt the crunch of grass and the bite of rocky soil under his body, he heard a horrible crunching and snapping. He sucked in a breath of air and closed his eyes. Had that been his body? Had his spine split in two? His ribs splintered to kindling? But why was there no pain? Gellion blinked and twitched his hands and feet. They responded.

Another crack sounded, but this one held the distinctive rumbling of rock. Wet screams followed.

Gellion flipped onto his back and pushed himself up, swiveling to face the terrible sound.

His eyes met another's—dark and bright with crimson reflected against the irises. For the span of a heartbeat, Gellion was sure he was looking into the face of death—a demon commander from the Great War come again. Then he saw the outline of a sword in the reflection. Gellion dropped his gaze to the weapon. It was shining with a liquid indistinguishable from the rich color of its blade.

Kaelo was staring at his sword with what seemed to be the same shock that possessed Gellion. To his right, Kyna sat on her heels with

Tornac's sword held slack in her hand. She was staring at the ground by her father's feet. Two bodies lay headless.

Head reeling, Gellion tried to piece together what had happened. The stone—the *bones*. Stone jutted from the ground near Kyna, similar to the column Kaelo had once used to throw Gellion backward during their chase in Daro. He had attacked the wights from a distance then, and beheaded them thereafter. But the buval—

Gellion took a step back when he saw it. The rock Kaelo had brought from the ground was sheer and thick. A crack ran down the middle. On the other side of the rock was the buval. Its horns lay in shattered pieces around its head. Blood oozed from the edges of its face, which was smashed flat against the stone in a display almost comical in a grotesque and stomach lurching sort of way.

Kaelo had torn his eyes away from his sword; they moved over the sky behind Gellion.

"You were fools to come here," Kaelo said. "Go to the hills. There is no reason for you to die in this."

Kyna had risen to her feet. She winced as she stepped toward them.

"There is no reason for any *more* to die in this," she said.

Kaelo looked down at her.

For a moment, Gellion looked between the two and was struck by their identical looks of stubborn and angry defiance. So too mirrored was their pain.

"Do you not see what we have done?" Kyna's voice broke with the strain of volume and emotion. "Can you not see that this is bigger than us now—bigger than any of the elves or the Kindoms or even vierstone? We can't leave the world to ashes while we run to the mountains!"

Kaelo's nostrils flared.

"You lost sight of our goal," he said. "You chose *them*." A red light seemed to flash in his eyes. "Like all the others."

"Them?" Kyna shook her head with her mouth open. "Can't you see that the sides we once defined have changed? I'm not against you, father, I am against the monster that now controls you."

Kaelo snarled. "No creature controls me."

"This is you then?" Kyna swung an arm at the battle around them. "Is *this* truly what you want?"

Kaelo's composure fractured. "I can control her." Desperation laced his words. "It will just take more time. This battle—I—"

"You cannot control the phoenix," Gellion said. Motion caught his eye as another boar flailed across the grass toward them. Gellion looked again for his halberd and spotted it at last, ten feet away, next to Tornac. He drew up short. The sight of his brother stole the next words from his mouth. The crack of stone cut across his silence as Kaelo opened a chasm beneath the charging animal's feet. It fell with a squeal that cut off with a crunch as the chasm closed once more.

Gellion grasped for his previous argument, trying not to look at Tornac's face as he reached for his halberd. He turned back to Kaelo, gripping the weapon in white knuckled fists.

"You may have redstone, but the phoenix is made of the same stuff, Kaelo. You cannot bend its will, though over time I am sure it can bend yours."

Kaelo was shaking his head.

"We have lost control of this, father," said Kyna. Gellion could hear the soft control she was forcing into her words. "This has nothing to do with our plans any longer. What does vierstone and pain and hypocrisy matter when we're all ruled by a perpetual force of evil so powerful we no longer possess any say in our own lives? We all know how to destroy this phoenix."

Kaelo's eyes darted to Gellion and narrowed.

"And so, too, do we all know what will happen if we do," Kyna continued. "It will come back again, but we can pass on the knowledge this time, don't you see? The Great War lasted two centuries because the elves didn't know how to end it, but now we do. Destroying the phoenix may only buy us time, but if the elves know how to kill it each time it comes, it may never get the chance to spread its stain further."

A lingering sense of dissatisfaction rose in Gellion. Was it worth fighting for such a bleak future? It seemed like giving up somehow—like killing the phoenix was submitting to its will and its eventual victory. It wasn't enough.

"The phoenix grows," Kaelo said. "She learns. She will find a way."

"Then we will find new ways to fight the thing!" Kyna said. "But I will not stand back and watch the creature we brought back to this world destroy what little hope the elves have left to them."

It was growing difficult to focus on the conversation. They were running out of time. More wights had begun to pass to their side of the field, and Gellion could see several beginning to converge upon them. He chanced a glance at the walls of the city. Cherufin had reached their base and were pounding against them with their fists. The Fieri rained vials of explosives on the creatures, but for every crumbled cherufin, a new one took its place. The walls were cracking.

There had to be another answer. What had Renyra said?

Break the cycle.

Transform the phoenix. Change it. But it was risky. They had no way of knowing if redstone was even capable of changing the monster. If they could not control it, why should they be able to change it?

But we can destroy it.

Destroying the phoenix required a sole moment of power—of dominance. Maybe altering the phoenix was possible if he could do it in the same stolen moment. But how? How could he change it without destroying it?

Kaelo was staring at Kyna.

"After all I have done for you." His voice was a hoarse whisper. "After the life I made for you—a life of freedom beyond any an elf has lived in this world. Now you speak as one of the elves you once condemned. You speak as though you never pursued our goal with the same wisdom and desire as I."

There was pain in Kyna's eyes. She opened her mouth to respond, but Kaelo cut her off.

"Maybe you are right," he said, his eyes distant. His voice grew softer, lower. "Maybe we were fools, raising a monster we could not hope to understand, but maybe that ignorance brought about a fate more inevitable than the one we designed. This was always going to happen. It would have happened with or without us, in its own time. What does it matter if the world crumbles beneath the wings of the phoenix now or in a millennia? Maybe the world deserves to crumble. Maybe a fully broken world would be better than a fractured life of expectation and pointless hope."

"You don't mean that," Kyna said.

She took a step toward her father, reaching a hand to him like someone approaching a frightened horse. Kaelo stood still as stone. His eyes were heavy, and his shoulders sagged with the weight of life. A weight Gellion knew all too well.

A pair of wights had reached them. Gellion turned his halberd upon them. His body slipped into the A'vaeri without his noticing. He let the movements carry him through the fight and lashed some of the focus they brought to his thoughts.

Transform the phoenix.

But could redstone do it? Gellion had seen redstone destroy, break, attach, move—but he had never seen it *change*. Could he turn the phoenix from living stone to lifeless rock? Could he turn it to metal or to glass and preserve its body while stopping its current—somehow entrap the beast's life in the statue of a corpse? There was no way to know without trying, and if he failed he may lose his chance to destroy the beast.

"Please," Kyna pleaded. "Help us."

Gellion ripped his halberd free of the first wight's neck and slid away from a jab from the second's sword. He could not see Kaelo's reaction, but the silence was as loud as any answer. The man may no longer believe in what he was a part of, but nor was he possessed of the will to fight it. His hope had been replaced by obsession centuries ago, and now that obsession was meaningless.

Another way. There had to be another way. Change the phoenix. Alter the phoenix. Reshape the phoenix.

Kaelo's sword flashed in the corner of Gellion's eye, and he leaped backward, turning his own weapon on Kaelo without thinking. Kaelo ignored him. The redstone sword bit into the second wight's neck with an almost lazy swipe.

Gellion stared at the glassy surface of the crimson weapon.

Cold electricity shimmered over his skin and penetrated to his bones. The force of the revelation struck him with such force he felt stunned, yet the concept still danced at the tips of his fingers and the edge of his consciousness.

The answer.

"Vierstone," Gellion whispered.

Kaelo's eyes snapped to him, then narrowed.

"What?"

The excitement was building, but Gellion could not quite keep up with the significance of his thoughts yet. He spun to face Kyna and Kaelo.

"Vierstone!"

Yes.

It was starting to take shape.

"Your sword." Gellion pointed at the weapon. "It was vierstone. The elves in Tura said that you *changed* it to redstone." He turned to Kyna. "And you said that he made redstone *out of* vierstone." His eyes swiveled back to Kaelo. "How? How did you do it?"

Kaelo stared at him as though he had just been asked the secret to life.

"How, dammit?" Gellion did not have time to deal with suspicion or shock. There was no time left.

Kaelo's sword twitched, and Gellion realized he had inadvertently brandished his halberd in his excitement. He let its tip fall.

"Please," he said through gritted teeth. "I have an idea. How did you do it?"

Kaelo paused a moment longer, then spoke.

"I reversed the current of the vierstone—stopped it completely, then restarted it in the opposite direction."

Gellion felt a grin begin to stretch up his face. Kyna and Kaelo looked at him as though he were mad. Maybe he was. But this could work. He knew it. He just had to think through it.

"You changed it," he said.

Kaelo nodded slowly, eyes still wary.

"He *changed* it," Gellion said to Kyna with a significant look. She gaped at him. "Remember what Renyra said? We have to break the cycle. To kill the phoenix is to perpetuate its rebirth, but to change it—don't you see?"

"I—" Kyna was shaking her head, but then her eyes locked on a point beyond Gellion. He could see understanding beginning to color her expression.

"Redstone destroys the phoenix by forcing its current to stop," Gellion said. "But it's not the only substance capable of that feat, is it? We need to change the phoenix, but not to something other than itself. We need to change it into something *opposite* from itself."

Kyna's eyes widened. "Vierstone."

"We already know how to perform the reverse," Gellion said. "We know it works. Redstone's current can cancel and then replace vierstone's. Vierstone is the answer. We use it on redstone—on the phoenix. We stop its current, then restart it in the opposite direction. We use the vierstone to breathe transformed life back into the phoenix before it turns to ash—before it dies."

"There is no more vierstone." Kaelo said the words with slow deliberation, as though explaining a difficult concept to a student. "Even if this were possible—"

"There is," Gellion said.

"There is what?"

Without considering the prudence of the action, Gellion pulled out the piece of vierstone from his pocket.

He stiffened, realizing his two mistakes in one fell swoop. Heat spread through his fingers and into his bloodstream, bringing with it a sharpened edge to the grief he had momentarily set aside in his excitement. He flinched at the pain, nearly dropping the stone. Then he saw Kaelo's face.

The man had gone rigid; the blood drained from his face. He stared at the little green stone like it was the most disturbing and terrifying thing on the battlefield.

Gellion's hand closed over the vierstone, wishing he had mentioned its existence before presenting it so brazenly to the man who had set his life to destroying the substance—a man who had as yet made no clear indication of his loyalties. Even as he watched Kaelo's face and braced himself to react to any sudden changes in the man, Gellion ground his teeth against the waves of torment crashing against him. The vierstone was nearly burning his palm. He did not release his grip. This was too important. This was the answer. Tornac deserved his mourning, but now was not the time to give in to it. He took a long breath, and the waves of agony settled.

Kaelo stood immobilized. Slowly, his gaze shifted from Gellion's fist to his daughter. Kyna did not quell before her father's glare.

"I wanted to see what it was like before it was wiped from the world," Kyna said.

"And then you kept it?" Kaelo's voice held the merest quaver. The air around him seemed to cool and still until it seemed the lightest breath would shatter it.

Kyna's jaw worked. Gellion could see the effort it was costing her to hold her father's stare.

"Yes," she said.

Kaelo looked back at Gellion's hand, now dropped to his side behind the protection of his halberd.

"After all I have done for you," he said again. "You ask me to turn to the substance from which I saved you."

A weight fell in Gellion's stomach as he realized Kaelo's eyes were shining. The anger was bleeding out of his face, leaving only stark betrayal. When his gaze returned to his daughter, its accusation was sharp as glass.

"Its taint is clear upon you now. I should have known this day would come the moment you entered Daro." His eyes took Kyna in from head to toe. He looked at her like she was a stranger. "You are one of them now." He shook his head, a manic look in his eyes. "They do not deserve it," he whispered. "None of them."

"I know," Kyna said with half a sob.

"They who never *felt* as I did—they who could not touch my skill with metal and stone—they had it handed to them in greater strength than I could ever dream, and they *wasted* it."

A hoarse cry announced the charge of a burly wight flanked by two cherufin.

Kaelo's lip curled in a snarl, and he slammed the tip of his sword into the stony ground without turning to face the attackers. A fanned wall of stone shards exploded from the ground around them in an arc, catching the monsters from below. The cherufin broke apart. The wight screamed as its back cracked. Wisps of color rose from all three.

Kaelo moved his head to take in the horrors still surrounding them.

"Now there is nothing left for them to waste. They can no longer be the heartless hypocrites who judge and condemn and betray—who break the world with the force of their pain and their love. When this is over, we can live in this world as equals."

"At what price?" Tears were leaking down Kyna's face now. "What world will be left? The phoenix has deserted you, father. It doesn't care about your goals. We took vierstone from the elves, but replaced it with an evil far greater than grief and betrayal. But we can still make something good out of this. We can rid the world of a terror that would destroy it—truly destroy it. We can turn that terror into something good."

"Good?" Kaelo's mouth twisted into a grimace. The crimson light in his eyes had returned. "You would have me turn the phoenix into a creature of vierstone and you would call it *good*? Nothing about vierstone is good. I have tried to explain this to you your entire life, but I can see my efforts were in vain."

"Was your love for Arela not good?" Kyna said.

Kaelo's face broke. He took a staggering step backward as though struck.

"Was the work you created in Tura not good? The joy you felt and the knowledge you passed on?"

Kaelo shook his head as though trying to clear it of Kyna's words.

"All that is good turns to ash," he said, staring at the ground. "It is the way of this world. If all that is good inevitably turns to evil, was it ever truly good?"

"What happened to you was terrible, father," Kyna said. "But it was not the result of evil. It was the result of choices—yours, Bardan's, Arela's, Liera's. Broken choices, yes, but not evil ones. You can't blame vierstone for your suffering any more than you can blame good for the pain its absence causes." Kyna took a deep breath and balled her fists. "But you can blame the phoenix for destroying good. You can blame it for causing pain and suffering, and you can stop it. You can save this world from a fate worse than broken love."

Kaelo's arms hung limp at his sides. The light in his eyes had extinguished, leaving them nearly lifeless.

"I know why you did it," Gellion said.

Kaelo blinked and started, as though he had forgot Gellion's presence. He turned his dulled gaze to Gellion.

"I know," Gellion said. "It burns me, too." He held up his hand. "It has always burned me—not my skin perhaps, but my very soul." The chasm of memories loomed before Gellion, heat rising from its center and reaching to pull him in. The Great War. The death he had witnessed. The death he had caused. "It will tear you apart—to feel, to care." He let his eyes fall on Tornac's broken body. "To love. But it is a burden we must face, or it will pull us down until we cannot live for the effort and the pain of it.

"Kyna is right. Your anger is justified, but your blame is misplaced. You seek justice in a world in which justice is inherently broken. What vierstone enables in us is good, but its consequences are as broken as the world we inhabit. It is not the fault of love that our imperfect attempts at it so often impale us, nor is it the fault of empathy if we share in the pain of others more often than in their joy. We cannot blame vierstone, Kaelo. We cannot fix the world or ourselves through its destruction. We can only use it to eradicate that which corrupts its essence. We can use it to shape the world into something better."

Kaelo was shaking his head again. The sheen had returned to his eyes. He raised the quavering tip of his sword.

"I can't," he said. "It is over. It is too late."

"Please." Gellion laid his halberd on the ground. "Give the sword to me."

Kaelo did not move.

"Let me try." Gellion moved his hand closer to Kaelo's sword until his fingers brushed the glassy blade. With the vierstone burning in Gellion's other hand, he felt an odd buzzing against his skin.

Kaelo held Gellion's gaze for another agonizing moment, then let his eyes fall to the weapon.

Gellion pressed his fingers to either side of the sword and focused. He felt the familiar flow of vierstone's current pass through his body. It burned hot in his chest, and Gellion felt the pressure of his grief behind his eyes, but he pushed the current further, until it reached the tips of his fingers and met the blade.

The first time Gellion had tried to 'see' into redstone using vierstone, the clashing of the currents had been like an electric shock that had caused him to drop the stone. This time he did not hesitate. He did not reach with the current, but let it pour from him without direction. There was a moment of resistance—then the current extended through the blade with the eager energy of water released into a dry riverbed. The clashing frequencies sent vibrations through Gellion's hand and up his arm. He watched in fascination as the blade's color bled away, leaving black in its wake.

The moment the black spread through the hilt of the blade, the vibrations ceased in Gellion's hand. He did not, however, stop the flow of current. He pushed it harder, more frantically. For a moment nothing happened. Gellion could feel his precarious hope thinning, waiting to rip apart.

Then a brilliant rush of green spread down the blade.

Gellion gasped, and the sword slipped through his fingers as Kaelo jerked backward, but the green continued to flow until it reached Kaelo's hand.

The sword fell to the ground.

Kaelo's hand remained outstretched where it had held the weapon. Shaking breaths puffed from his nose as he stared down at the emerald blade.

A surge of warmth flowed through Gellion's body, temporarily obscuring his pain and his anguish. It had worked. Riu above, it had worked.

"Take it," Gellion said breathlessly. "You can take it. You can get to the phoenix like none of us can."

Kaelo raised his eyes to Gellion at last. The look within was twisted and shattered.

"You can end this," Gellion said. "You can end this forever."

Gellion's hope flared at Kaelo's hesitation, the meaning of what he had just done growing in its scope. They could bring it all back. Riure could be veined with vierstone once more—the cities, the earrings. The terror now surrounding them would fade to another distant nightmare.

Then Kaelo shook his head. His eyes fell to the sword lying in the dirt, and he stepped away from it as though it were a snake poised to strike.

"I will not bring it back," he said in a hoarse whisper. "I cannot bring it back."

"Vierstone is not the cause of your pain," Gellion said. "The elves—"

"They do not deserve it." Kaelo did not seem to be listening to Gellion. He spoke in a monotone litany, as though repeating mantras to himself. "I can never have it."

"Take it," Gellion snapped. Kaelo's face twitched, but his tortured stare did not waver. "Take it and bear it—accept it. Use it! Use it to pursue the justice you claim does not exist. Use it to accept your pain and move beyond it."

Gellion bent and grabbed the sword carefully by the blade. Kaelo took another jerking step back.

"Father." Kyna's eyes were set on her father's face. "Please."

Kaelo did not look at his daughter, but his face contorted in further pain.

Gellion held the sword's pommel level with Kaelo's hands.

Kaelo began to raise his hand toward it.

A deafening shriek split through Gellion's head.

The sword slipped through Gellion's hand as he threw his arms over his head, slicing his palm. A chunk of stone flew into his back and sent him crashing to the ground. Rubble and dust and heat swirled and flew around Gellion, all punctuated by a cry that sent slivers of ice through Gellion's blood.

He groped in the confusion, trying to find the vierstone sword. The small round of vierstone had fallen from his hand. Light flashed in front of him. He sat up and blinked the spots from his vision.

The spires of stone Kaelo had erected around them were a crumbled heap strewn in all directions. Kyna was on her knees near what had been the base of the wall, a hand to her head.

Red swirled around them. The phoenix had sunk its talons into the ground and was beating its wings in fury. Flames streamed from its feathers, and its throat glowed scarlet.

The sword. Find the sword.

Gellion twisted on his knees, his hands still reaching in all directions. He prayed and he cursed, until he finally caught sight of green amid the storm of red. The blade—and next to it another smudge of green. Heart racing, Gellion reached for the blade, but it moved away from his outstretched hand.

Kaelo knelt down, his body obscuring the weapon and his back arched as though in pain. Then he rose to his feet.

One of his hands was balled in a fist, the skin stretched over his knuckles. The other gripped the pommel of the vierstone sword. Every muscle in the man's body was taught and strung. His eyes were closed, and lines of agony spanned from their corners.

"Father!"

Kyna cowered before the phoenix. The creature's molten eyes were fixed upon her, and its beak opened wide, a glow of yellow visible inside its wicked curvature.

"Stop." Kaelo did not speak loudly, but the phoenix paused, then slowly wrenched its mouth shut.

Kaelo's arm was shaking. His mouth twisted in a grimace, and he took in a sharp breath of air.

The phoenix's head swiveled toward its former master. Kaelo opened his eyes with obvious effort. They shone brighter than they had before—lighter—yet so too did they show the anguish that sent tremors through Kaelo's body.

"You left me," he said through gritted teeth.

A ripple of light traveled over the bird's feathers.

"I knew you would not be harmed," it said scathingly. "Besides, I could not find you—until I saw your stonework." Its head cocked, fixing one glassy eye on the sword. "What is *that*."

Green reflected in Kaelo's eyes as he looked at the weapon. Then he looked at Gellion. His jaw was clenched, and his eyes watered with pain, yet for a moment Gellion saw the shadow of the man he had once known in Tura. The man he had respected and admired.

"An abomination," Kaelo said. He threw the sword to the phoenix's feet.

The phoenix eyed Kaelo, then rained a torrent of crimson flames onto the sword.

"No!" Kyna yelled.

Gellion closed his eyes.

When the flames dissipated, the sword lay black and lifeless.

"The child has fallen further," the phoenix said, ducking its head to regard Kyna. "Mourning the cleansing of this world." Its head swiveled back to Kaelo, and its throat glowed yellow.

"Leave her," Kaelo said. "She can do no further harm."

The phoenix hummed in annoyance.

Kaelo's gaze swept over the battle behind them. Gellion gasped at the change. The numbers on the field had thinned substantially. Elves ran toward the city. The walls of the city itself were broken in places, the rain of Fieri explosives now barely giving off a pop every few seconds.

Gellion looked back at Kaelo, a boiling rage rising in his chest. The man's face was a slate of stone, his eyes cold and distant. Yet his left fist was still clenched in an iron fist, and Gellion could sense the slightest tremor to his rigid expression.

"I grow tired of this," Kaelo said. "Let us finish this."

He turned his back on Gellion and strode toward the phoenix, picking up and sheathing the blackened sword before approaching the phoenix's side.

Gellion tried to summon words—words of accusation, of anger, of pleading—but his mouth had gone dry as sand.

The piece of vierstone.

Gellion started. There was still a chance, the slightest breath of a chance. The piece of vierstone had been next to the sword, he was sure. If he could get to it before the phoenix left the ground, if he could get a single finger on its glassy feathers before it turned to kill him—

His eyes roved the ground in a frantic search. He found the place. There was a smear in the dirt where Kaelo had dragged the blade toward himself.

The soil was bare. The vierstone was gone. Kaelo had not been so great a fool as to leave his enemy's last weapon lying on the ground.

It was over. They had failed.

"You told me you wanted to change the elves for the better." Kyna's voice reached Gellion through a haze. "You can still do that."

Kaelo had one hand on the phoenix's bowed shoulder. He was staring at the ground.

The phoenix hummed again, and when the light rippling along its feathers passed Kaelo's hand, he stiffened.

"Don't do this." Kyna had not moved from the phoenix's head. She stood straight, with defiance in her shoulders and pain in her face. "Please." Her voice broke.

"It is what I deserve." Kaelo raised his head to her. Though Gellion could not see his face, whatever Kyna saw in it brought tears to her eyes.

Kaelo pulled himself onto the phoenix's back.

The phoenix launched into the air, hovered for several wing beats, then twisted its sinuous neck and sent a waterfall of silver flames over them. Gellion threw his arms over his head, wincing at the brush of voices against his ears and the tingle of energy over his skin. He barely had time to comprehend the horror rising within him before the flames cleared.

The phoenix was flying toward the gates of Telem Fier.

Tornac was pulling his broken body from the ground.

Kyna sank to her knees.

3 8

———

FROM ASHES

"It is coming back this way." Firas shielded his eyes against the glare of the phoenix.

The sun was beginning to sink in the western sky, its light seeming to intensify as it cast its rays above the curve of the land rather than onto it. The gold light reflected off the phoenix's feathers and gave the effect of light shattering beneath the red flames streaming off its body.

"Did you see what happened?" Renyra stepped beside Firas and reluctantly let her gaze fall to the battle below.

Memories of their second foray into the nightmarish fighting assaulted her in a constant stream of images and sounds even as she watched its continued reality beyond the walls.

Wights.

Renyra had heard of the wights in the Great War, but seeing their bright and lifeless eyes in person held more horror than she could have imagined. The spirits she had always revered had turned upon her in the bodies of her own kin.

"No," said Firas. "The phoenix landed and caused a scene on the outskirts of the battle over there, but I could not see what it did, only that it let loose more of its silver flames."

Renyra shuddered. How could these terrors exist in the world—in a world formed by Riu's hand? She closed her eyes, wondering at the naiveté she had always denied. Well, no one could think her naive now. She had wanted to be a part of the elves' shared suffering. She had asked for a sip of wine and received a drowning flood of spirits.

Stepping back from the edge of the wall, Renyra looked out over Telem Fier sprawled behind her. Cherufin had broken through to parts of the city. She could hear breaking stone and screams of rage and fright. As a whole, however, the city looked almost normal. If she ignored the tumult of sounds and looked only over the tops of the buildings, she could imagine that it was merely the end of a day—a normal day. Swaths of colored fabric blew in the breeze.

"Should we move him?" Valder said. His voice was strained and choked.

"No," Firas said gently. "I don't think the city is any safer than the walls at this point."

Renyra turned back to face what remained of their company. Firas knelt next to Valder. Raren stood over the two, his broken eyes turned to the approaching phoenix.

At their feet, Veldon lay propped against the parapet. His eyes were closed, and his face was pale. A bloody rag dripped in Valder's shaking hand. Firas had done his best to bind the gaping wound in Veldon's middle, but Renyra could see the life draining away from the gentlest of Gellion's brothers. It was strange. She had thought Veldon dead for months after the battle at Arvain, yet his reappearance had somehow made him seem more alive than before. This second death struck deeper than the first, though she had never known the man as well as Gellion and Valder. She had liked him.

He is not dead yet.

There were healers somewhere in Telem Fier, but Renyra had no idea where to find them. Dragging Veldon over half the Great City would have killed him as surely as letting him lie here on the wall. At least this way he could lie in peace.

Renyra looked away. She could not bear the grief written upon her friends' faces. Raren had lost his sister. Valder had one brother seriously injured and two missing. None of them had seen Caerlyn or Trali since the battle had scattered all of them. Were they all still fighting for their lives while Renyra stood on the walls? Were they all laying dead? Or did their eyes now glow red with the light of spirits? She sank her face into her hands.

There had been no choice but to come back to the wall. They had lost sight of Gellion and Kyna completely and had no way of knowing where Kaelo had gone. Then Veldon had fallen.

Renyra cringed at the memory. Veldon had just finished off a wight. She had seen it. He had won the fight. He had been safe. Then the boar had come from nowhere. A boar. Of all the horrors on that battlefield, a stupid possessed pig had been the one to bring down another of their number. It had taken three of them to get the massive creature off Veldon and half a dozen stabs to incapacitate it. Renyra could still see the beast's dirty blood crusting on her wrists, could still see the mad gleam of its eyes.

Bringing Veldon out of the fighting had been more important than remaining in the battle. Their efforts had made no difference to the slaughter anyway.

The phoenix was close enough now that Renyra could see its eyes. Hatred welled within her. It was maddening, to be so close to the thing she wanted more than anything in the world to kill, and to know how to do it, but to have no way of carrying it out. Their hopes now rested on Gellion and Kyna. It had been so long since they disappeared. Could they have found Kaelo in the chaos of this battle? Even if they had, it seemed impossible they could save Telem Fier now.

"Kaelo," said Raren.

"What?" Renyra ran to his side followed his gaze. He was still staring at the phoenix.

"He is on its back."

Renyra squinted between the beast's wings. Light and shadows made it difficult to see, but as the bird drew nearer, the shape of an elf between its wings became increasingly clear.

They had failed. Gellion and Kyna. All of them.

"That's it then," Renyra said.

She knew she should be afraid, or angry or self pitying, but she felt nothing. It was as if she had become a hollow and cold shell. Even the pressure of Firas's hand on her shoulder did not break through her numbness.

The phoenix screamed and brought its wings out like sails just before the main gate of the city. A wall of hot wind hit Renyra, and Firas steadied her from behind.

They were closer to the main gates than they had been before. They had known the risk of being so near the city's greatest target, but this had been the fastest way up from their flight from the battlefield.

Red light glowed from the phoenix's gaping mouth. Kaelo had drawn his sword. They would destroy the city now. It was all that was left to be done now that the armies outside were so thoroughly decimated. Renyra would watch Telem Fier fall just as she had watched the rest of her world fall.

"His sword," Firas said.

"Yes," said Renrya, not bothering to look at the terrible weapon she had helped create. "The redstone we need, not fifty feet away. Shall you throw me over the wall to wrestle Kaelo for it?"

"It is black."

Renyra's brows drew together. Her eyes snapped to the sword. Firas was right. Against the brilliant shades of crimson swirling around the blade, it hovered as a dark smudge. Unmade? But why? How? Had Gellion and Kyna found Kaelo? Had Kaelo destroyed the sword himself to keep this last remaining weapon from their hands?

Red flames rushed from the phoenix's throat, obscuring the city gates from Renyra's view. She winced against the brightness, but tried to see past it to Kaelo. He was not watching the flames or the city but staring intently at his sword.

"Let's go closer." Renyra started to jog toward the fire.

"What?" Firas said. "Renyra!"

She could hear him running behind her.

"What are you doing?" he said. "Renyra, the gate!"

Her feet slid on the stone. The metal and stone of the city gate was *shimmering* within the flames. Renyra thought of the shattered glass of the Daro greenhouses before it had fallen. It was far more unnerving to see the effect on solid stone. The phoenix snapped its beak closed, and the flames disappeared. Then the gate disintegrated into fine rubble and ash, bringing down sections of the wall to either side with it.

Elves screamed as they fell through thin air where moments before had been solid wall.

"Sweet Riu," Renyra whispered. "It can turn the whole city to ash within the hour."

"We have to get off the wall." Firas grabbed her arm, but Renyra resisted.

"No, wait."

Renyra could see Kaelo clearly now, and she could see what he was doing, though her mind could not accept it. Color was bleeding up the blade from Kaelo's hands, but it was not red.

"Firas," she breathed.

He had gone still beside her.

The phoenix opened its beak once more. The flames came again. Renyra jumped back. It was attacking the wall now—their side of the wall. The stone twenty feet away from them began to shimmer. The phoenix twisted its head and aimed the flames further toward them.

"We cannot stay here." Firas pulled at Renyra's arm again. "Whatever is happening, we cannot wait for the phoenix to dissolve the stone beneath our feet!"

Renyra stumbled a step backward, but reached a hand to the parapet to counteract Firas's insistence. She could see Kaelo's face now. His eyes were squeezed closed—whether in concentration or in pain she could not tell. A brilliant green rippled to the tip of the sword.

"Vierstone," Renyra said. "Firas, it's vierstone!"

Kaelo's eyes flew open. He looked down at the sword in his hands as though shocked to see it there, then he looked up. His eyes met Renyra's. They were different eyes than Renyra remembered. These were not the cold black orbs of slate that had haunted her dreams and memories for months, but the clear and anguished eyes of an elf—of a man.

The phoenix screeched and let its flames dissipate once more, watching the wall crumble to dust with what Renyra could only interpret as satisfaction. Its eyes swiveled to the next section of the wall, then settled on Renyra. Its feathers ruffled with a flash of flames, and smoke curled from the holes in its beak.

"You."

The word sliced through Renyra's mind. She cringed back from it. There was no inflection to the word, only a simple acknowledgement that the phoenix knew who she was and would probably be more satisfied by her death than that of a nameless elf. The beast moved closer to them with a single beat of its wings, then opened its mouth.

Firas's grip on Renyra's arm finally wrenched her from the edge of the wall. She fell back against him, still staring into the mesmerizing depths of the phoenix's fiery throat. Flames billowed up its throat like smoke rushing through a pipe. They filled the phoenix's mouth.

Firas was dragging her along the wall now. She wished he would stop. Even if they sprinted along the wall, the phoenix would follow them. They could not escape this.

"No." Renyra ripped her arm from Firas's grasp and straightened. She would not fall running from the phoenix. Something had changed —in Kaelo and in the world. She did not know what had happened, nor did she care. She had seen vierstone return from a dead blade. She would face the phoenix with the knowledge that there was still hope in the world, even if she would not be there to see it.

The flames washed over her.

She felt the current in her skin. In her blood. It was like brushing the fur of a horse the wrong way. Gasping Firas's hand in hers, closing her eyes against the piercing light, she waited for the stone to melt beneath her feet.

The current stopped.

The light faded from the inside of Renyra's eyelids.

She opened her eyes, then immediately bowed her head and clapped her hands over her ears as the most terrible sound she had ever heard saturated the air.

The phoenix was screaming, but its voice had risen to a pitch near the end range of Renyra's hearing. It was a grating and torn sound, carrying with it the same wrongness of the current that had engulfed Renyra moments before.

Firas was at her side in an instant, pulling her away from the phoenix as it thrashed and exuded lashing whips of flame.

"What's happening?" Renyra shouted, though she was sure Firas could not hear her over the phoenix's screams.

Then she saw him. Kaelo was hunched over the phoenix's back, his sword sunk between its shoulder blades nearly to the hilt. He held onto the sword as the phoenix bucked beneath him and from the edges of the bird's wound, black began to spread. It started as a slow stain, then flowed outward with increasing speed. Where the red drained from the phoenix, its body stopped moving, frozen like a grotesque statue in the air. Its wings beat more furiously, and its head thrashed backward, as though trying to reach Kaelo at the base of its neck, but it was no good. Kaelo held to the beast's back with an iron grip, still hunched over the sword.

As the blackness spread up the phoenix's wings and neck, red flames began to swirl around its body in mesmerizing patterns, and the tips of its talons and tail started to dissolve into ash.

Renyra watched with a slack jaw and wide eyes. The phoenix was returning to ash. It was dying. The cycle would continue. But Kaelo had used vierstone. What did it mean?

The phoenix's cries choked off as its throat froze in a twisted rictus of agony. Another sound took its place. The sounds of effort, of pain, of anger and determination and frustration ripped from Kaelo's throat as he drove the blade still deeper into the phoenix. He looked like he was fighting to hold together the phoenix now disintegrating around him.

An odd stillness had settled over the battlefield. Renyra could still see the motion of fighting below her, but it seemed to have slowed— grown distant. The elves on the walls and streets of the city all stared in frozen fascination at the spectacle before them.

Kaelo let out a final yell that echoed over the city, then the blackness around his hands began to change. Light and color suffused the crumbling stone of the phoenix and flowed outward with shocking rapidity.

It was green. And emerald and jade and teal. Every shade of the color Renyra had ever seen swirled and mottled the phoenix's shining feathers and shone with a light less blinding yet more brilliant than the sun. The red flames around the phoenix began to evaporate, and where bits of the bird had fallen away as ash, new talons and feathers grew and glimmered.

Green flames engulfed the phoenix. The fire spun and licked and swirled, and a cry split the air that was entirely different from the hair raising shriek of the phoenix Renyra had known. It was clear and pure and filled Renyra with warmth.

The ball of fire exploded outward. For a moment, the phoenix seemed to turn entirely to ash. Its shape hovered in the air as millions of tiny particles, then a final burst of flames carried through the mirage, and it snapped into the solid and complete form of a bird, its wings flaring out to catch the wind.

Renyra held on to Firas, hardly daring to believe her eyes.

"They changed it, Firas. They did it." She let out a laugh that was nearly a sob. "*He* did it."

She could feel tears starting to rise, could feel hope—real hope—starting to heat her chest.

Then, through the last remnants of fire, she saw Kaelo fall.

39

ATONEMENT

Kyna stumbled every few steps. If it wasn't the corpse of some decrepit creature or elf in her way, it was the pain shooting up her stupid foot. Bruised certainly, sprained probably. A cursed rock had fell on it when the phoenix crashed into them. Her side stung, too, but the bleeding had slowed and nearly stopped.

The battle was still somehow going on. Did no one else understand that everything had changed? Did no one else care that her father was in the middle of the wild and fiery scene above what had been the gates of Telem Fier?

Of course they didn't. He was their enemy, wasn't he? He had caused all of this. But he had ended it. He had done it. He had not just saved Telem Fier from destruction, but saved the elves from a future of terror and suffering. The elves did not know this. They did not understand. Kyna did.

A herd of boars thundered in front of her. The beasts were massive. She cursed and tried to stop, but something wet and soft caught her feet, and she fell to her hands and knees.

She had to get to him. She had to get to the gates.

Pulling herself up, she kept running—stumbling, gasping, crying. She ran toward her father, and she ran from the terror behind her.

The wights made her skin prickle to the bone, but seeing those lifeless and glowing eyes in Tornac had nearly broken her. It had broken Gellion.

She risked a glance backward, but did not see Gellion. They had both run as soon as Tornac stood. She knew Gellion would not fight his brother, not even the dead shell of his body. The sorrow and agony in his face as he had seen Tornac move toward him with blank hatred in his eyes had twisted Kyna's gut. It was her fault. It was her fault he was dead, her fault he now walked again, her fault Gellion had endured so much pain.

A glare of emerald light flashed in the sky. It was working. It was actually working. She could see the outline of the phoenix now amid the swirling flames. It was like before—in the forges—only more beautiful and less terrible. Why, then, did she feel this frantic desperation, this fear?

The flames exploded—once, twice. Her father had been on the phoenix's back. Were these flames as harmless to the body as the crimson flames had been? Could her father survive the salvation he had enabled?

A new phoenix flung its wings to the sky with a cry that filled the battlefield. It was a warm sound, a haunting sound.

A shape fell through the air.

Kyna came to a jolting stop.

No.

It seemed such an insignificant thing, so far away. An object dropped from the top of the walls. Never before had Kyna considered how thin air was, how fast a body fell through it. One moment she saw him in the air, the next he was gone.

A hand fell on Kyna's shoulder. She did not jump or turn to the unexpected weight.

"Come on." Gellion's voice was low and calm, though a tremor shook through his hand.

Under the pressure from Gellion's hand, Kyna began to jog forward again on unfeeling legs. Gellion did not remove his hand from her shoulder and held his halberd to the side as they ran, though nothing attacked them.

Kyna saw her father on the ground—an indistinct heap surrounded by wary onlookers. Her steps slowed as she approached, then stumbled to a stop as Gellion's hand ripped from her shoulder. She looked back.

Tornac stood behind them holding a spear he must have picked up from the battlefield. The front of his shirt was soaked in dark blood, and his lips were smeared with red. Tornac was too recently dead for his appearance to cause shock, yet still Kyna knew he *was* dead. The face now contorted into an animalistic snarl was familiar yet alien, real yet wrong. He thrust the spear's tip at Gellion, who ducked backward.

"Gellion!" Kyna said.

He did not look at her. His eyes were transfixed on what had been his brother.

"You have to do it, Gellion. He won't stop." She glanced back at her father, longing more than anything to run to him, but she couldn't turn her back on this. She couldn't leave Gellion to face Tornac alone. "It will not desecrate his memory, Gellion. That isn't Tornac anymore."

Still Gellion retreated, shaking his head and deflecting blows.

"I can't," he croaked. "I can't."

Tornac aimed a well placed strike at Gellion's throat. Gellion twisted sideways and caught the spear's tip in the curve of his halberd, wrenching it out of Tornac's hands. Tornac did not try to retrieve his weapon, but lunged at Gellion with his bare hands. Gellion moved the shaft of his halberd between himself and Tornac, shoving at his brother's chest and leaning away from his clawing hands.

He did not move to strike Tornac. Tears were streaming down his face.

Kyna ran around the back of Tornac and grabbed him around the waist, trying to pull him off of Gellion. She managed to make him stumble, but his weight was too much. She twisted sideways, trying to tangle his legs. He stumbled again, then rounded on her.

Before Kyna had time to react, his hands were around her throat.

She could not scream. She could not breath. She could only stare into Tornac's terrible eyes and think how she deserved this. Even so, she pulled at his wrists and kicked at his shins. It did no good. He was so much bigger than her, and for all she knew, he was no longer capable of feeling pain.

Black spots floated in Kyna's vision. Her limbs began to feel distant.

The world seemed to be dimming ... dimming ... then it was lit with a brilliant green light. The pressure around Kyna's throat disappeared.

Was this dying, then? Pain fading away and light flooding out the darkness? This wasn't so bad.

The pain returned. Her knees hit the ground with a crack, and she drew in a rasping breath. The green light was gone. Kyna blinked clarity back to her vision and rubbed at her throat. Hands clasped her shoulders. She heard her name.

"Are you alright?" Gellion's face came into focus before her. Tears still stained his cheeks, and his face was cracked with anguish.

"I'm fine." Kyna winced as her voice scratched the inside of her throat.

"I'm sorry," Gellion said. "I'm sorry. I couldn't ... I—"

Kyna shook her head. What was he talking about? Gellion closed his eyes, then opened them and looked down. Kyna followed his gaze.

Tornac lay on his back, as whole as he had been as he attacked her, but the horrible glow had faded from his eyes, leaving them green and glassy as they stared at the sky. The form of the phoenix reflected in their pupils. Kyna looked up at the bird hovering above them. The light she had seen—had it been fire? Had the phoenix cleansed Tornac of the corruption its counterpart had inflicted upon him?

The phoenix.

The events leading to Tornac's attack came rushing back to her. Vierstone. The phoenix. Her father.

She scrambled to her feet, ignoring Gellion's attempts to help her. She ran the last steps to her father, her feet dragging to a stop before her knees buckled.

Kaelo lay on his side, unmoving.

Kyna reached a hand toward him, reluctant somehow to touch her father. The metal of his armor was cool and soft, giving way to Kyna's fingers like the finest chain mail. She turned him on his back as gently as she could.

A pained stream of air escaped Kaelo's lips.

"Father?" Kyna's heart raced. He was alive. Was he alive? She had heard a breath, but his face was white and still, and blood trickled from his mouth.

His eyes fluttered open, barely slits. They roamed the open air, settling straight above him.

The phoenix was still hovering. Its head was angled downward, as though watching the scene.

"You did it," Kyna said in a small voice. A presence at her side told her Gellion had knelt beside her.

The slits of Kaelo's eyes rolled toward her, the irises bright green specks between translucent lids. His breath came in shallow and short bursts. Suddenly desperate to feel the warmth of his skin, Kyna reached for his hand.

"You did it," she said. His face blurred through her tears. A drop fell onto her father's armor as wind buffeted them from above. Elves scattered. Some shouted in fright as the massive beast landed.

Kaelo looked toward the phoenix again, then his eyes closed, lines of pain webbing from their corners. He opened his mouth and moved his lips, but all that came out was another stuttering breath. The stream of blood running from his mouth thickened.

Kyna choked back a sob. "It's alright," she whispered. "It's over."

She thought she saw the slightest twitch of his head in a nod. She bent lower over him. The waves of emotions that coursed through her were beyond meaning. She could not distinguish anger or sadness or despair, she could only be still within the torrent of feeling so strong it seemed to drown her very identity.

Her father's hand tightened in her grip, then his breath hitched to a stop and his hand went still.

The rush of emotion broke in a final crash. Kyna wanted to throw up, to cry, to scream, but all she could do was hold her breath and endure.

She felt a hand on her back, a body close to her side. She sucked in a breath and leaned against Gellion. When she finally opened her eyes, she found them swollen and wet. She had not realized she had been crying. She had not even realized she had closed her eyes. Her father's hand slid through hers as she raised her palms to wipe the water and grime from her face.

A low hum made her look up.

The phoenix was perched on the ground on the other side of Kaelo.

It was watching them, the feathers of its throat undulating with movement and light.

Kyna had not properly looked at the beast since its transformation. Its form, in essence, was exactly the same as the redstone phoenix, yet somehow its features appeared different under the shades of green. The beak was still curved and sharp, but it appeared more graceful than wicked. Its eyes were still molten and mesmerizing, but Kyna found herself wanting to stare into them, rather than pulled against her will. She blinked and looked away.

Good or not, this phoenix had killed her father. She did not care just now that the transformation had been of her and Gellion's own design, that it had likely saved all of Riure. She cared that this phoenix had let her father fall after the sacrifice he had given.

The beast leaned forward, digging its talons into the ground for balance. It arched its neck and lowered its head until it was level with Kyna.

Kyna leaned harder against Gellion.

The phoenix's eye swiveled to regard Kaelo, then focused on Kyna.

"I am sorry."

Kyna flinched as the voice filled her mind. Like the phoenix's appearance, its voice was the same as before, yet different. Its pitch had not changed, but the inflection was altered—the *feel* was different.

"I could not hold my form through the transformation," the phoenix said. It bowed its head and touched its beak to her forehead.

Kyna gasped as a current flowed through her. For a moment, she thought the phoenix was trying to take away her pain. She reached for the current eagerly, craving the numbing release she had drawn so often from redstone. It did not come. She did not feel the release of her own emotions, but the addition of another's. The phoenix was showing her its pain. Kyna could feel its grief over the death of her father and its sadness over her own pain. Then the connection snapped off.

"Kyna?" Gellion was watching her warily.

Kyna nodded her head to indicate she was alright. She did not trust her voice. The breaking of the current had left her feeling drained, still burdened by her pain, but she found the cutting edges of her emotions had dulled somewhat.

"He had done his part," the phoenix said.

Gellion stiffened against Kyna, and she knew the phoenix spoke aloud now, so far as that was possible.

"Will you finish it?" the phoenix said.

Kyna looked to the east. What remained of the battle waged on, unperturbed by the scene of grief and change before the walls of Telem Fier. The cherufin were still there. Wights still raised arms against their kin. Animals still shrieked ethereal cries as they attacked. This was not finished. Not yet.

The phoenix crouched down and lifted one of its wings away from its body.

Kyna took a breath and started to rise, then looked down at her father. He was surrounded by once enemies and deranged demons. Suddenly, Gellion's reluctance to harm Tornac's body made more sense to her.

"I will stay with him," Gellion said. The understanding in his eyes nearly broke Kyna's composure anew. "Go."

Kyna stood and stepped around her father's body to the waiting phoenix. She placed her hands on the smooth stone of its wing and hoisted herself onto its back.

It was strange, lifting into the air again, without her father, without her fear. The ground fell away, taking with it the sounds of battle and the heavy sorrow in the air. Kyna breathed in the fresh wind and braced her hands against the glassy feathers of the phoenix's neck. The current beneath her hands was perceptible, but it did not pass into her skin. Under her touch, the mottled patterns of green shifted, molding to the shape of her fingers. She took her hands away and the patterns melded back to what they had been before.

Kyna lifted her eyes from the phenomenon and took in the sprawled battle below her.

Finish it.

She had not meant to begin it. Surely that counted for something? Even in her final days with the redstone phoenix she could never have imagined this battle awaited them. Would she have finished the phoenix then if she had? But then the creature now below her would never have come to be.

"Start with the battlefield," Kyna said. "Start here."

The phoenix bowed its head and snapped its wings flat to the sides. Green flames lit below it.

They flew in sweeping arcs over the fields, raining green sunlight upon the blood soaked grass and broken army. Kyna watched straight below her, where the flames cleared in misty wisps. Cherufin crumbled where they stood. Wights fell like puppets with cut strings. Howling and snarling beasts froze mid stride and looked around wildly at their surroundings.

Hundreds of ribbons of light spiraled upward as the army of demons disintegrated. Spirits cleansed. Spirits freed.

There was joy to the sight, and relief, but so too was it tainted by sorrow. Elves crouched over fallen friends, groaned in pain, died where they lay. Each one of them looked up as the phoenix flew overhead, and Kyna saw hope in their faces, even those of the wounded and grieving.

Kyna clung tighter to the phoenix and felt an answering vibration reach into her fingers. The current was not numbing, but it was comforting. She felt her pain validated, understood, and somehow found it easier to bear. An echo of the hope she had seen in the elves below her lit in her breast. She set aside her grief, looked into the emerald flames, and watched the world reshape.

When Kyna slid from the phoenix's back, it was to a field and a city stricken with silence.

The battlefield was still. The scene before the gates was unchanged. Gellion was still on his knees next to her father. Kaelo still lay pale and bloodstained. Dead. The sight of his unmoving face struck Kyna harder than she had expected. Gellion looked up as she approached.

"They are all gone?" he said. "The ... the spirits?"

Kyna nodded.

Gellion took a steadying breath, then nodded to her father.

"His earring," he said.

Kyna crouched next to Gellion and looked at the stone pierced through her father's ear. It was green.

"He took my vierstone when he picked up the sword, Kyna. He changed his own earring to vierstone and then restarted the current in the sword." He pointed.

Kyna had not noticed the sword lying a ways from her father's feet. It shone emerald against the dirt.

"It's all gone," Gellion said. "The redstone."

Kyna could only nod. This was an important revelation, she supposed, but just now she could not seem to summon any further emotion.

"It really is over," Gellion whispered. He looked dazed, as drained and overwhelmed as she felt.

They crouched together for several silent moments before a voice shattered the stillness.

"Gellion!"

Kyna felt her mouth twitch despite herself. Leave it to Renyra to survive a battle this terrible and come out of it smiling and shouting. When Kyna looked up to the little Fieri, however, there was no trace of a smile on her face. Firas trailed behind her, his expression just as grave.

Gellion stood, looking between his two friends and visibly relaxing when he saw they were both whole and well. Renyra's eyes slid to Kaelo as she approached, then to Kyna. It was amazing how the force of the woman's sympathy could still shock Kyna.

"You're alright?" Gellion said. "And the others?"

Firas's face sunk deeper into its lines of sorrow, and Kyna felt a stab of anxiety. Something was wrong.

"What is it?" Gellion's voice was sharp, strained.

As Firas opened his mouth to respond, his gaze drifted behind Gellion—to Tornac's body. All the breath seemed to rush out of Firas. He closed his eyes.

"Gellion—"

Gellion glanced at Tornac and winced.

"What is it Firas? Who is it?"

Firas opened his eyes and slowly lifted them to Gellion's face. The pain written within them was stark and frightening.

"Veldon," he said softly.

Gellion's shoulders went limp. Every ounce of energy remaining in his bearing seemed to drain away in a single breath. His lips moved to the shape of his youngest brother's name.

"You had better come with us." There was no hope to Firas's voice —no urgency. Only gentle condolence.

Gellion walked forward with a drifting gate, as though in a dream— a nightmare.

Unsure how much more of this she could take, Kyna swallowed, took a last look at her father, and followed.

***

When Kyna first saw Veldon, she was sure he was already dead. A greenish pallor hung over his face, and blood soaked strips of cloth wound about his middle. Only the slight and erratic flaring of his nostrils demonstrated any signs of life.

Gellion stared at his brother with the sort of slack expression that afflicts only those who have been beaten down so many times they can hardly feel the blows any longer.

"Oh Veldon," he whispered.

Valder was sitting next to Veldon, his back against the wall. Raren was pressed to his other side. It was several moments before the two noticed Gellion. A dim spark lit in Valder's eyes, and his lips twitched upward, but his relief at seeing Gellion was clearly not enough to overcome his worry.

"I don't know how you did it, Gellion," Valder said. "But at least we didn't lose him in vain."

Gellion flinched as though struck. "Is he—"

"Not yet."

The words were no comfort.

Valder's eyes wandered over those behind Gellion, pausing on Kyna. "Is Tornac with you?"

Gellion only shook his head. He lowered himself to his knees beside Veldon.

"Gellion?" Valder's eyes were wide with question and dread. When Gellion finally look at him, his answer was written clearly upon his face.

Valder sagged backward. The shock of loss was something they had all felt this day, yet Kyna still felt her chest constrict at Valder's renewed grief.

A rush of footsteps turned every eye from Veldon and his brothers.

"You're all here. Oh thank Riu." Caerlyn pushed into their circle of bodies. "We saw you from the field—going through the gate. Didn't know what happened to you after that second storm onto the field. We feared the worst."

Trali stepped up behind Caerlyn, holding one of his hands to his chest. A pang of queasiness hit Kyna's stomach. The hand was twisted and mangled.

Trali flashed a grin at Kyna's look of horror. "Do not punch a cherufin. Good lesson to know, though I think we will not need it now."

Kyna tried to force a smile, but it came out as a pained grimace.

"What happened?" Caerlyn said. "The phoenix—we saw—" She cut off, her eyes falling on Veldon and those around him. "Oh," she breathed. "Oh no."

Kyna felt herself spiraling into a depth of emotion so overwhelming she could hardly maintain the energy to stand. Was this victory? To lose friends and family and know you would have to live with their absence the rest of your life? At least her father's death had served a purpose. Even Tornac—she closed her eyes.

Don't think of that.

Taking a shuddering breath, Kyna lowered her face into her hands. Veldon's death was too much. It was intolerable. It was unfair.

Please. Kyna tightened her hands over her face and fought the sobs threatening to seize her. *Please!* She projected the thought around her, shouting it over and over in her mind. *Please. Please.*

A hand, small and warm, wrapped around Kyna's elbow. Kyna's hands fell away from her face, and she looked down to see Renyra standing beside her. Tears shone in the woman's eyes, but the hint of a smile glowed about her lips. She nodded toward the wall.

The phoenix was hovering in the air level with the parapet. Kyna drew in a sharp breath. In her anguish, she had not even felt the breeze from its wings. It reached its talons forward and carefully wrapped them around the parapet, settling its weight onto the wall.

Those nearest the bird took several steps back. The phoenix cocked its head and swiveled one eye to take in the scene. It looked at each elf in turn, its gaze lingering on Veldon. Finally, the liquid eye fell on Kyna. The phoenix opened its beak and let out a soft fluttering sound.

"Please," Kyna said in a hoarse whisper. "Help him."

The phoenix's head cocked further to the side until it was almost horizontal with the ground, then it righted its head and swiveled it toward Veldon, pushing Gellion gently out of the way. Gellion jumped back from the bird's touch, the indignation in his face fading as he watched the bird press its beak to Veldon's forehead.

The feathers on the phoenix's face ruffled and lit from beneath with shimmering light. The effect travelled down the bird's body in a smooth ripple.

No one moved. No one spoke. Every eye was staring at the phoenix, transfixed. There was no fire—no sudden burst of light or piercing call or flapping of wings—but Kyna felt the current. She felt it as an after-echo, a shimmering of the air's texture. Kyna watched Veldon with bated breath, looking for a change—some sign of movement, of life.

The first thing she noticed was a pinprick of green shining beneath his hair—his earring. He had never taken it off even after it had blackened. The realization brought tears of shame to Kyna's eyes.

Veldon's eyes opened.

The green of his irises seemed to glow and move in the reflection of the phoenix. He blinked and looked up at the bird. Wonder shone in his face.

Kyna found herself smiling.

Valder was laughing through his tears. He put a hand on his brother's shoulder and gave it a gentle shake. Veldon winced and gasped. The smile vanished from Valder's face and he whipped his hand back.

"He will need a healer." The phoenix's ringing voice filled Kyna's mind. "But he will live."

Veldon smiled through his grimace of pain. The horror drained from Valder's face, and a semblance of his grin returned. Gellion had taken one of Veldon's hands in both of his and was looking down at his little brother with a fondness that made Kyna look away for the privacy of the moment. Her eyes fell instead on Raren, who was watching the scene of joy and relief with a strained smile.

"Alura." Kyna turned to the phoenix. "Tornac—my father." She tried to control the hope blossoming in her chest. "Can you—can we go to them? Can you heal them?"

The phoenix straightened on its perch, then bowed its head with a low hum—a mournful hum. Kyna's excitement shattered. Casting a glance at Raren, she saw the same broken hope in him. She cursed herself for mentioning the possibility aloud.

"Why?" she said through gritted teeth.

"It is not my place to bring back those whose time has come to leave this world." The phoenix looked to Veldon. "This one was strongly tuned to the current already, and his fate was not yet sealed. Not all are so easy."

Grief washed anew through Kyna.

"Your father made his sacrifice." The phoenix's voice was smaller now—softer—only for her. "He made his peace. He met his fate with open eyes."

Kyna looked away. Renyra's hand found hers and squeezed it. After a few moments, she looked to the phoenix.

"The vierstone," Renyra said. "Will it come back? All of it? Like the sword?"

The phoenix did not answer, but turned its gaze to Kyna. Looking into the swirling depths of its eyes, Kyna found she knew the answer.

"It will," she said softly. "But not on its own. It will take time, but we will bring it back." Her hand tightened around Renyra's. "I will bring it back."

She had to do this, of that she was sure. She had helped her father break the world, and now she would undo it, but the prospect of weeks spent alone with her grief and her guilt—alone with this terribly familiar yet alien creature, was more daunting than she cared to dwell upon just now.

Renyra's hand slipped from Kyna's. A shadow fell over them and Kyna looked up to see Gellion standing in front of her. His face was serious.

"You are still determined to do everything on your own, after all this?" he said.

Heat rose in Kyna's cheeks. She did not know whether she was more incensed or shamed by Gellion's question. Either way, she hardly knew how to respond to him. They had weathered the horrors of the last hours together, but had their companionship only been the result of circumstance? Could he forgive all she had done in light of this new world she would help renew?

"*We* will bring it back," Gellion said. He paused, and his expression softened. "With the help of all the elves."

Gellion moved closer to her, and she felt her heartbeat rise as a new flush of heat spread from her face to her whole body. Gellion lowered his voice, and though reservation and pain still colored his countenance, sincerity radiated in his words.

"You are not alone in your pain," he said. "However strong or however new it may be. And you will not be alone in this world— however different or however broken it is."

Something spread over Kyna—a sensation both frightening and powerful. She cringed from the feeling, expecting a new onslaught of pain, but though the surge of *something* within her was consuming and piercing, it lifted her. It filled her not with the heat of anger or of loss, but with the suffusing warmth of comfort, of gratitude, of joy.

She hurt—body and soul, she hurt from this day, from the weeks and the months and the lifetime that had led to it, but for the first time, she could see something worth living for beyond it—something other than atonement for the suffering she had brought on the world. She smiled through her pain—a real smile—and let Gellion lead her to the phoenix's lowered wing.

The world was broken, but they could restore some part of it together. They would work to restore more of it the rest of their lives. They would start with Telem Fier.

4 0

CITY OF HEALING

Renyra tucked a lock of hair behind her ear, letting her fingers brush the vierstone backing of her earring. The stone was in constant contact with her skin, yet she could not seem to help herself touching it with her fingers once an hour or so and checking for its presence in every mirror she passed. Now she stood squared in a mirror, tilting her head from side to side as she checked the effect of her braids and the fall and pull of her wraps with each movement.

It was nice to put effort into her appearance again—nicer than she would ever admit to Firas. The Morcani would never properly appreciate the nuances and importance of appearance beyond clean lines and patterned hair. Firas could not know what it was to wear brand new wraps of silk in colors so rich she wanted to eat them. Simply to bathe on a regular schedule and put on fresh clothes every morning was a luxury Renyra had never fully appreciated before. Her hair was smooth and shining, her skin clean and fragrant. She was hungry, but pleasantly so, with the anticipation of ample food to come. She found herself smiling—a real smile. The first she had donned in a while.

The days following the battle in Telem Fier had been a solemn affair, with celebrations tempered by the gruesome reminder of the battlefield and the fresh grief of the city's inhabitants. Most prominent of all had been the absence of the Fieri's leaders. Both Auralia and Cuvan had been killed in their brave charge with the chemical explosives. Renyra had never particularly liked Cuvan, but his death still grieved her. He had cared for his people and been a good leader in the best way he knew. As for Auralia—

No. Not tonight.

Renyra blinked away the tears and narrowed her eyes at her reflection. Tonight she would start to move on. She would smile—laugh.

It was not a celebration exactly, this citywide commemoration spanning every dining hall, market, home, and quarter of Tura. Celebrating seemed a frivolous and callous thing in light of the thousands of elven lives lost at Telem Fier. It was an ode to their memory—a public display of normalcy and an acknowledgement of the last months of terror and uncertainty and grief. It was the beginning of healing—the beginning of a new start.

Renyra smoothed her hair once more, and the lamp above her reflected on the shining tattoos of her hands. Her hands slowly dropped back to her side. She sighed.

She had begun to realize that she would never get an explanation for the suffering she had witnessed and experienced these last months. She could not make sense of it by any prophetic words of wisdom or self reasoned justification. It had happened. It had hurt. And she had come through it. She had seen suffering, but she had also seen that suffering bring about more bravery and love and drive for justice and compassion than she had seen in all her life.

"Ready?"

Firas stood in the doorway in a Turi coat with long tails. His hair was freshly shorn on the sides with a smooth ponytail on top. He smiled as he took in Renyra's appearance.

"You look lovely," he said.

In answer, Renyra bounded toward him and kissed him on the lips. The sensation sent shivers down her spine, and warmth flowed from her ear. She held the kiss longer than she intended, relishing the feel of him —his emotions, his essence. When she pulled away, her heart was hammering against her ribs.

Firas's lips curved up, and his eyes sparkled.

"Perhaps *after* the dinner?"

Renyra rolled her eyes and pushed past him.

"Perhaps I will not be feeling so generous *after* the dinner."

Firas chuckled and followed her.

"Oh you will," he whispered in her ear as he closed the door behind them.

Heat rushed over Renyra's skin. She cleared her throat to repress an unbecoming giggle and strode into the cool night, hiding her ridiculous grin. He was right.

***

The hall on which Renyra had decided was an airy place near the Bathhouse of Tura. It was not large, but its high windows gave the impression of both size and grandeur, offering views of the stars beyond the soft strings of lamps within. In truth, it was the tables that had drawn Renyra to this hall. They were long and spaced in a way similar to the Dining Hall of Daro. The familiarity seemed appropriate, serving both comfort and remembrance.

The hum of conversation fell upon Renyra's ears as she made her way to her friends. Renyra and Firas were the last to arrive—probably due to Renyra's existential musings in front of her mirror. She smiled to see them. None had yet noticed her arrival.

Caerlyn leaned back on her bench, swirling a finger around the rim of her wineglass. Trali was talking with animation to Veldon. His hand was still bound in bandages, but his visage was as vital and buoyant as ever. Veldon's eyes danced as he listened to Trali's story, a soft smile on his face. Next to him sat Farra, and next to her—Renyra's grin widened when she saw Valder. He and Raren were removed from the others just enough to make their close proximity meaningful. Sides pressed together, the two shared an air of sorrow and of joy.

Renyra pulled Firas to the emptier side of the table, sliding in next to Kyna. The woman's face softened in relief when she turned to see Renyra. She had been sitting with her hands in her lap, following the conversation between Trali and Veldon with her eyes.

"Evening," Renyra said to her. "You look nice."

Kyna's sleek hair was swept into a pile on top of her head. Her dress was a simple cut of satiny fabric in a deep navy that matched the night sky. Her resemblance to Liera had never been more evident, but she bore the look with softer lines and more grace.

Kyna let a puff of air out her nose in response, but her lips twitched upward.

"You too," she muttered.

The woman had been reserved since she returned to Tura—more reserved than usual, that is. She and Gellion had been gone for weeks with the phoenix. Their return to the city had been as joyous and solemn an occasion as the festivities tonight. Renyra still felt an odd shiver through her core each time she thought of the vierstone phoenix. It had been beautiful, with a presence almost intoxicating in its intensity. A good as powerful as the evil from whence it had come. Now it was gone. The cycle was over.

Kyna had turned her eyes absently back to the conversation around her, though she did not seem to be listening. Renyra could hardly imagine what Kyna must be feeling. Her life up to now had served a pre-ordained and twisted purpose that was now obsolete, and the loss of her father could only be making matters worse, no matter what the man had been for most of her life.

Pain spiked through Renyra's middle. She had said she wouldn't think about these things tonight. Still, it was impossible not to think of Kaelo when one looked at Kyna. For months, the man's eyes had haunted Renyra's nightmares. They still did, only now the eyes were those she had seen from the back of a phoenix just before he sacrificed himself to save them all. She heard his cries of anguish and determination, saw the moment of his fall when the phoenix turned to suspended particles. Kyna had listened in silence to Renyra's account of her father's last moments. She had shed no tears, but nodded slowly and walked away with that empty and faraway look.

"So," Renyra said with as much cheer as she could muster. "When are you coming back to the training halls with us?"

Kyna's brow wrinkled. "What?"

"Come on, I saw how reluctantly you loved it last time. There's a Sira performer in you. We just have to bring her out."

Kyna raised an eyebrow, but the flush of pleasure in her face was evident.

"So you're staying in Tura?" she said.

"Well, I don't know really, but I think we might. After a trip to visit my family of course." She nudged Firas in the thigh and flashed him a smile.

"I look forward to it immensely." There was a tease in Firas's voice, but the look in his eyes was of genuine contentment—contentment with a light of mischief. Renyra felt herself blush when he winked at her. She grabbed a glass of wine and buried her face in it.

The food was delicious—poached eggs, fried fish, dishes of greens and rice and nuts and fruits. Roasted sea birds with crispy skin lined platters of onions, roots, and berries, and covered baskets gave off a heady aroma of yeast and flour. Renyra enjoyed the food and talked with her friends with the sense of being only half there. It seemed unreal after all they had been through, to talk and eat together without fear or dread. The laughter of the room was subdued, but it was still there. Its sound was more nourishing than the food.

After an hour or so, Renyra saw Valder raise his hand toward the front of the hall.

Gellion nodded in answer. He looked the proper Lord of Tura tonight. His coat was black and simple, but silver embroidery lent it a look of elegance and importance. Gellion did not proceed to the front of the room, nor did he come straight to their table. He stopped at the nearest group of elves he saw and began to talk with them. Renyra smiled. He would make appearances all over the city tonight. No presiding speeches, no pomp and circumstance. It was not what Dulon would have done. It was not what Liera would have done. It was absolutely and genuinely Gellion, and it was perfect.

"He's going to make a great Lord of Tura," Renyra said.

"Tell him that." Valder grinned. "Maybe if we all say it ten or twenty times a day he'll start to believe one of us."

By the time Gellion made his way to their table, Renyra had cleared away their plates and poured another round of wine. Gellion stopped across the table from Valder. Looking from his brother to Raren, he raised his eyebrows with a wry smile. Valder's face flushed crimson. Gellion let out a bark of a laugh.

"Do you see this Veldon?" he said, still grinning. "I've finally done it. I made Valder blush as violently as you, and without even saying a word."

The color in Valder's face deepened, and he scowled at Gellion, though a smile still hung about his lips. His eyes moved pointedly to Kyna.

"Should I counter the attack?"

Gellion cut off his laughter and abruptly changed the subject to the places throughout the city he had already been tonight. It sounded as though the entire city had banded together for this commemoration, every elf participating in some way or another. Gellion was obviously trying to hide his pride in the success of the evening, but he had every right to be pleased by the outcome of his efforts. When Renyra told him as much, he looked away and shrugged.

Soon Gellion dismissed himself to continue his rounds, but as he turned to walk away, he gave Kyna a lingering look. No one but Renyra seemed to have noticed.

She gave Kyna a sideways grin. Kyna flinched when she saw it.

"What?" she said quickly.

"Oh nothing," Renyra said. "I'm just happy." She winked. "For you."

Kyna's face made a supreme effort to match Valder's flush.

"Will you do anything besides Sira here?" she said in a voice of forced nonchalance.

Renyra nodded and allowed the shift of subject. Something told her she would have ample time to tease Kyna about Gellion.

"I've been walking around the gardens here. They have nice flowers, but they're useless for growing fruits and vegetables. There's not even a greenhouse in the city—not a proper big one anyway. I think I'll change that."

She smiled to herself as she thought of the beautiful greenhouses of

Daro. The city had been extravagant, but it had also been efficient and lovely and innovative. The agricultural system of Daro was not the only thing that could benefit the Great Cities of Faeran. She would have to talk to Gellion about it. But not tonight.

41

A WORLD RESHAPED

The metal was warm beneath Gellion's touch. He closed his eyes and spread his fingers over its smooth surface. The room was quiet. Still. Orange light flickered against Gellion's eyelids, and sweat beaded along the top of his brow.

He took a breath and focused on his fingers, then extended the focus outward. He could feel the push and pull of current through him, could feel its gentle vibrations through the metal. It was amazing to him that he had once been oblivious to the nuances of this current. He had still seen, he had still understood, but now he worked *with* vierstone, not through it. The structure of the metal fanned before him in an intricate and sightless image. He knew it. He knew he could work it in ways he would never have thought of before. It would meld to his coaxing and, in time, reshape to his vision. He took his hands off the metal.

Gellion had not come here to craft. Lord of Tura or not, he had every intention of returning to his metalwork, but tonight he only wanted to remember.

After the traveling and stress and action that had consumed Gellion's life since Kaelo's arrival in Daro, he would have thought weeks spent in a city safe from attack or emotional implosion would have been a relaxing luxury. Instead, he found himself more exhausted. He was no longer used to this life of constant socialization and decision making and movement. Following the evening commemoration two days before, he had run his first official Council meeting as Lord of Tura. Surprisingly, it had felt no different from the meetings prior to his ascent to leader.

He would have to expand the members of the Turi Council now that three of its previous members were gone. His mother had told him just before the meeting that it would be her last. She planned to step down from politics. Gellion was glad for her. Still, he would have a time of it trying to fill all the spots when he had been separated from Turi politics himself for so long. Fortunately, Reanan was proving an apt and knowledgeable second in command, though his disappointment in the loss of redstone as a building tool caused some discomfort to Gellion. He did not blame Reanan. Most of the elves now knew of the existence of redstone, but few truly understood what it had been, or the consequences of its use. Perhaps it was better that way.

Gellion wandered away from the furnaces and moved toward the work benches along the far wall. These forges were smaller than the open air forges by the river. They were meant for steady and regular work, for training. Gellion ran his hand along the waxed wood of a bench. A few tools lay strewn across its surface, but it bore the casual cleanliness of a well used space.

Once, Gellion had watched Kaelo work at this bench. He had looked up at the imposing and impressive man with wide eyes and a burning desire to one day handle those tools with the same surety and precision. Then, sunlight had streamed through the towering windows. Other metalworkers had scraped and pounded and poured at their own benches and anvils and furnaces. Were any of those elves still here? Had they died in the Great War centuries ago? Had they died on a field outside Telem Fier just weeks ago? Or if they were here now, somewhere in the city, did they remember working in this room with the man who had so strongly shaped the world of the elves? The man Gellion had buried on windswept cliffs far from the city.

Soft footfalls echoed through the workshop, and Gellion stepped away from the workbench. Kyna stood in an archway leading into the room. Her arms were wrapped around a bundle, pulled close to her middle.

"I've been trying to find you," she said softly. "Valder said you might be here."

Gellion just nodded. He could feel the sweat on his brow starting to bead again. His muscles tensed.

Gellion had hardly spent any time in the same vicinity as Kyna since he had released the phoenix. Their weeks together with the great bird had been a strange blur, suffused by grief, hope, and surprisingly little time to talk. In truth, Gellion had been grateful for the constant action, though the destruction and loss he had witnessed on their journey had affected him as deeply as the healing and hope the phoenix had breathed over the land.

The end of their journey had been bittersweet. It had been difficult for Gellion to let the phoenix depart from the world, but the creature had insisted upon its release once its purpose was complete. Gellion had not destroyed the phoenix. He had not unmade it as his father had. He still did not fully understand what he had done, only that it had been instinctual once he placed his hands on the bird's glassy feathers and felt its essence in his soul. It had showed him what to do.

The phoenix would not return, but the land would heal. The elves would heal. And so would he.

Gellion's muscles relaxed slightly as he looked at Kyna.

So will we.

"I wanted to give this back to you," Kyna said. She hugged her bundle closer to herself. "My father left it in Tura when we ... when the phoenix rose. It took me a while to find it, but—"

She lifted her hands. A tunic of woven metal shook out of its folds and hung with a gentle tinkling. It caught the glow from the room and cast light around itself as it moved, until Gellion could only detect a shimmering of the air in front of Kyna.

Gellion would have once been overjoyed to be reunited with the masterpiece over which he had toiled for weeks of the Kindom Council. Now he only felt a dull sadness. Once this tunic had seemed the most important thing in the world. It had meant pride, accomplishment, proof of his skill and ingenuity. It seemed a silly thing now.

"Did you take it?" Gellion said. "The night I finished it?"

Kyna did not lift her eyes from the still shimmering tunic.

"I'm sorry."

"You couldn't have waited another twenty-four hours?"

Kyna looked up at him, and her face softened at his sardonic smile.

"All the elves in Daro would have known about it," she said. "They may have recognized it when my father—" Her face fell again. "When he used it."

Gellion reached for the garment. It flowed through his fingers as he folded it.

"Thank you," he said.

They stood in silence. Gellion watched the flickering light of the furnace move across Kyna's skin. He burned to reach out and touch it.

"You're leaving for Maramor tomorrow?" she said.

Gellion dropped his hand, which had begun to lift toward her face of its own accord.

"Yes," he said.

Kyna nodded. She was studying the top of the workbench beside him, her eyes trained on its surface with too much concentration.

"Who's going?" Kyna said.

"My brothers. Mother. Farra."

Tornac.

The name hung in the silence.

Gellion's family had waited to bury Tornac until Gellion's return. His body now lay in Maramor, awaiting its final resting place.

Kyna nodded again.

"Could—I know it's your family, it's personal, but—could I come?"

Gellion blinked in surprise. "I had assumed you would."

Kyna's eyes snapped up from the bench. "You had?"

"Well, yes. I mean, you were there. You helped me with—and, you knew him." Suddenly Gellion found his own mastery of words as slippery as Kyna's seemed to be. "I want you to be there."

The truth of this statement surprised Gellion. He found that his resentment toward Kyna had gone brittle and thin over the last weeks. It simply didn't seem important anymore. His anger belonged to a different world—a different woman. With or without his will, more powerful and present feelings had begun to break away the last of his reservation. More shards of resentment shattered as he watched tears well in Kyna's eyes.

"I'm sorry, Gellion," she said. "I'm so sorry. It's my fault he's dead. It's my fault all of this—"

Gellion moved to her. She stiffened for a moment, then wrapped her arms around him. She did not sob, he did not even know if she cried, she just held him in a desperate embrace. He could feel the pain and guilt radiating off of her. It was still a disconcerting feeling, sensing Kyna's emotions. For months he had wished nothing more than to see a glimpse of what lay beneath her stoic face and opaque eyes. Now the force of her emotions was almost overwhelming.

"It was not your fault," Gellion said into her hair. "Tornac made his decision. He would not have done so wanting you to live with the guilt of his choice." Gellion fought the tears threatening to overwhelm his own composure. Tornac's death was not something he had allowed himself to dwell upon while he scrambled to put the world back together. He would have to face it, and soon, but now it was more important to let Kyna face it.

Gellion drew back from Kyna and lifted her chin.

"I know how useless it is to tell you not to blame yourself," he said. "I can only tell you that I have lived with that same blame most of my life, and it has done neither me nor anyone else any good."

He trailed his thumb over her cheek. It was smooth as velvet.

"You can do nothing to change the decisions and circumstances that brought you here," he said. "In fact, I would say you did a pretty damn good job with what you were given." He raised an eyebrow. "Circumstances have changed. You can mourn the past, or you can use your new life to move beyond it."

Kyna let out a long breath and leaned her face into his hand. After a few moments, she placed a hand over his fingers and moved his hand gently away so she could look around the workshop more fully.

"Is this where he worked?" She spoke like one in a tomb—a hushed reverence touched by discomfort.

Gellion nodded. "This is where he first taught me. He had his own workshop on a higher floor, but this is where all the apprentices began back then." He smiled. "I expect he did not want me messing up his tools and projects."

Kyna snorted. "I doubt you were ever that bad." Her eyes danced with the light of the furnace as she looked around the room. "I had wanted to see where he used to work. Where he used to live. I always wondered what he was like—before." The corners of her mouth turned down. "I was afraid to ask him. He hated talking about Tura. And when we were here—I didn't want him to catch me snooping around the places he had told me about in stories." She looked toward the furnace, her eyes wandering over the room, yet fixed on memories beyond it.

"I could show you—tell you," Gellion said. "If you want," he added when the sadness in her eyes only deepened.

A smile touched Kyna's lips, and she turned to face him. She placed a hand into his. Goosebumps trailed up his arm.

"I would like that," she said.

The trip to Maramor was a strange affair full of stories and silence. The river through Ard Gael was cold and frothy, laced with the beginnings of winter from the higher mountains. Already the trees along the gorge had begun to drop their leaves. The season seemed disjointed from the changes in the world. New life and hope had come to Riure—should the land not follow suit?

The spires of Marmor struck Gellion like spears to the gut. The effect was even more pronounced than Gellion's most recent reunion with the city. Maramor had formed so much of his life. Now two of those he loved would be buried beneath those spires. Gellion's newfound title meant he would never be able to reside in Maramor for long periods of time, but as he set foot on the floating platforms, he knew he could not have remained here even if he was not needed in Tura. Ghosts still walked this city for him. They would as long as he lived.

The funeral would be held at sunset—the time when Riu was closest to the world. An end. A flash of fire before darkness. It was hours away still.

Tenille and Farra split from the group to meet with other members of Maramor's Council. Valder trailed after them, and Gellion moved to follow, but Veldon stopped him.

"Can I show you something?" Pink touched Veldon's cheeks.

Gellion hesitated, glancing at Kyna. She shrugged.

"I know my way to the rooms I stayed in last time," she said. "And food. I could do with a rest anyway." She turned and walked toward the nearest lift without a backward glance, her hair swishing between her shoulder blades.

"She suits you," Veldon said.

Gellion narrowed his eyes. "You had something to show me?"

Veldon smiled and started to walk. Gellion had to check his pace to stay behind Veldon. Veldon's recovery had been swift given the severity of his wound, but he still tired easily, and two days in a rough boat had not been kind to him.

"The crafting halls?" Gellion said as they neared the intricate doors.

Veldon led the way into the shining halls without a word. He navigated hallways until he came to a slender door rimmed with gold leaf.

Gellion walked into a small room with arched ceilings and windows. Bookshelves lined the walls to either side of a hearth. A workbench stretched where one would expect to find a writing desk. Gellion drew his brows together and cocked his head.

"And this is?"

"It's ... it's my workshop," Veldon said to the floor. "Or study, or—I haven't decided what to call it yet I suppose. But it's mine."

"Oh." Gellion could see Veldon's touch on the room now. It was somehow both cozy and austere—practical yet comfortable.

"It's nice," he said.

"I set it up when we passed through on the way back from Telem Fier. When I knew we would be staying here—Farra and I."

Gellion's confusion must have shown on his face.

"Did mother not tell you?" Veldon cocked his head.

"Tell me what?"

Veldon's mouth quirked up. "Farra is to be Lady of Maramor."

Gellion's eyebrows rose to hover on his forehead while he took this in, then he laughed.

"What?" Veldon frowned, looking insulted.

"No." Gellion shook his head. "It's great. She is the obvious choice. I don't know why it never occurred to me." Gellion looked at the room again with new eyes. "So you're staying in Maramor then, and this will be your workshop." He nodded, trying to ignore the pang of disappointment in his middle. This was what he had wanted for Veldon after all—to return to Maramor with Farra after all this was over. Tura was a lot closer to Maramor than Daro. He would still find excuses to see his brother.

"It's a great space." He tried to think of a way to voice his confusion in a way that was not insulting. "So, what is it for?"

Until the craftsman competition in Daro, Gellion had never known Veldon to craft anything. He had never shown an interest in metalwork like his brothers, or stonework or glasswork or anything else traditionally pursued by the Turi.

Color rose in Veldon's face again. "It is for vierstone."

Gellion stood silent for a moment, baffled by his own thickness. Had he not been the one to encourage Veldon's study of vierstone in Tala? To craft vierstone—not to craft with vierstone but to work the substance itself—was a rare and difficult branch of crafting. It is what their father had done. It is what Aryn had done—the first elf to die in this terrible string of events. The world was indeed short of vierstone masters, and never had their importance been so apparent.

"That's perfect Veldon." He clapped his brother on the shoulder. "You'll be amazing. I'll bet you already know more than almost any vierstone master in Faeran after all this."

Veldon did not flush at Gellion's praise. He did not even smile. A seriousness had fallen over his features.

"There is so much to learn," he said. "So much we don't know or have always misunderstood. This is important, Gellion. I know it is. There is no more redstone in the world, and the phoenix will not rise again, but that does not mean evil is expelled from the world—it does not mean the world isn't as broken as it was before."

Gellion nodded slowly. Once he would have skirted a conversation like this—Veldon's favorite kind of conversation. The subjects of good and evil and morality and feelings still made Gellion uncomfortable, but he held his tongue and let Veldon continue.

"Think what more we could do with vierstone if we only understood it better." Veldon began to pace the room.

Gellion thought about the newfound awareness he had felt at the touch of metal days before. He nodded.

"The phoenix—" Veldon's steps slowed. "I am not saying we can use vierstone to heal—not like ... not like I was." His voice always dropped in pitch when he mentioned his healing atop the walls of Telem Fier. "But what if we used it more deliberately with other elves? If we used vierstone to extend beyond emotions? Maybe we cannot heal physical wounds with it, but could we better understand the elven body to heal them ourselves? Could we use it to heal emotional wounds?"

Veldon's excitement had begun to bleed into Gellion. He had never thought of these possibilities. It was an entirely new way of thinking about vierstone.

"The elves need to change their relationship with vierstone." Veldon's eyes seemed to shine as he spoke. The light beneath his irises had never fully faded after the phoenix's healing. "We have used it to make beautiful and incredible things—cities, art, technology—but vierstone is not meant to be used solely for extravagance and competition. It is meant to be used to improve the world and the elves. To improve ourselves. We let it become a commodity—something to be guarded and sought after and traded—but now we must treat it as it is meant. A gift. A means to a better world."

"To reshape the world," Gellion muttered.

Veldon smiled, and Gellion felt his own mouth curve in response.

"That phoenix knew what it was doing, healing you," Gellion said. "You'll change the world, little brother."

Veldon looked away. His eyes fell on the workbench.

"Oh!" He ran to the bench and opened a drawer. "This is why I really brought you here." He tucked something into his fist and turned back to Gellion. "I—well, we were here for over a week when you were off with the phoenix, and I was setting up the workshop and—here." He opened his palm to reveal a tiny vierstone earring. It was the most intricate earring Gellion had ever seen. Delicate leaves formed a fan that curved like the frond of a fern.

"Riu above Veldon, you made this?" He took the jewel between his fingers, afraid to break it, though he knew vierstone did not break—well, not usually.

"It's for Kyna," Veldon said. He was looking away again. Gellion thought the blood in his cheeks may have taken up permanent residence.

"She never had one, and that piece she's carrying around now—well, I thought this would be nicer."

Gellion curved his finger over the edges of the earring, thinking of the beautiful jewel against Kyna's skin. He shivered.

"It's perfect, Veldon," he said. "It's perfect."

The whole city came to Tornac's funeral. While Tornac had never held the formal title of Lord of Maramor, Gellion knew Tornac had been as much a part of the city's community and function as their mother. His death lay over the city like a shroud of mist. Few words were spoken. Those that were floated on the heavy air as song. The grief and underlying hope of the elves in attendance gave testament enough to Tornac's life and death, and as he was lowered into the ground next to Vyra, Gellion found himself smiling at the words his mother had once spoken to him in Daro.

Their family was not split, she had said, it was only living in different places. Gellion had found no comfort in the words at the time. He still didn't, really—not for himself—but the prospect of Tornac being with Vyra again, wherever they were, couldn't help but lift some of the pain in his chest.

The crowds began to thin as the last light of the sun faded from the sky, and the twinkling lights of Maramor began to shine in the darkness —a floating starscape. Gellion embraced the members of his family and accepted the condolences of elves he had not seen for centuries. He stood on the breezy mountainside with his back to the gorge until the shadows had faded around him and an arm slipped through his own.

Kyna did not speak. She merely stood with him. He stared at the fresh soil and finally let the tears fall in silent streaks down his face.

Death had tormented Gellion since the first moment he had seen its blank and sightless face. It had haunted his dreams and dragged at his waking mind in moments of grief and anxiety. Gellion had always shoved it away. He had run from it. He had done all in his power to pretend it did not exist—that it could not touch him. The same treatment he had given any emotion that frightened him with its power. Now he understood the power his avoidance gave his fears.

He had feared becoming Kaelo, but he had never known how very close he had already been to his master's fall. Only circumstance had kept Gellion from spiraling out of control. He would not run anymore. He had faced death. He would face his grief, and he would move on. For once, he would take his own advice. He would move beyond the past.

Gellion took a deep breath and turned his back on Tornac's grave. A cold breeze blew off the gorge. The tears turned icy on his cheeks. He wiped them away on his sleeve.

"I have something for you," he said to Kyna. Reaching into his pocket, he pulled out the earring Veldon had given him hours before. He took Kyna's hand and placed the earring in her palm. "Veldon made it."

Kyna tilted her hand so the lights of the city reflected off the vierstone. Her eyes widened.

"It's beautiful," she breathed.

Gellion looked at her. He followed the line of her jaw, the plane of her nose, the curve of her lips. Her hair blended with the night, and her eyes shone with wonder at the vierstone in her hand.

"It must be overwhelming," he said. She was close to him, though they were not touching. If she raised her head their faces would be barely a foot apart. "Being surrounded by vierstone after a lifetime without it. Touching it when you have never experienced it before."

Kyna closed her palm and let it fall to her side.

"It was—" She looked out over the gorge. The breeze blew her scent against Gellion, and he breathed deeply. "Difficult," Kyna finished. "But it did not all come at once. It began to affect me the moment I stepped foot in Daro. The moment we touched." She looked up at him at last and sucked in a breath at his proximity. She did not move away.

"When I shocked you?" Gellion chuckled.

"Yes," she said without smiling.

Gellion raised a hand and let his fingers brush her cheek. Warmth spread through his hand and shuddered through his body.

He kissed her.

Through the touch of her lips, he saw her. Her love rushed into him like a rush of sunlight, not wild or jolting or unrestrained, but steady—real. Enduring. As the surges of their emotions joined, grief and fear and sadness began to mingle with the joy, yet somehow it seemed to only strengthen the connection between them. Gellion wrapped one arm around Kyna's back and let his other hand run through her hair. He pulled her closer, relishing her warmth and the softness of her lips and her skin, then pulled back and looked into her eyes. He was afraid. He was drowning in his joy. He smiled, and she smiled back.

Up close, Kyna's eyes sparkled like jewels, even in the darkness. Green like the foam of the sea.

"I met your cousin," he said.

Kyna blinked. "Excuse me?"

"She said your hair was as shining as a seal's and your eyes were like jewels of the sea." He moved his fingers in her hair. "She was Kayda. She knew you as a young child. She loved you. I told her that if I saw you again I would ... well, I would tell you that."

Kyna stared at him, then laughed.

"And you decided to tell me this now? Right now?"

"I—your eyes made me think of it. I had forgotten until now."

Kyna's laughter continued, and Gellion felt his face growing warm. She shook her head and leaned against him, wrapping one arm around his back and resting her head against his chest.

"Thank you for telling me. And thank you for making me laugh."

Not sure if he should feel teased or mollified, Gellion lay a hand on her shoulder and looked back at the city. Lights were starting to wink out. Elves were going to their homes for the night, maybe even going to sleep. Gellion tilted his head until it lay against Kyna's. Her hair brushed against his face in the breeze.

"We could visit Suri Ranta come spring," he said.

It would be nice to give the Kayda proper thanks for their help—maybe send something on to Eurig. And Veldon would be overjoyed if Gellion returned with Kaelo's piles of vierstone books. It wouldn't hurt to ensure there was no more redstone hiding in that cave either.

"Maybe we will." Kyna pressed herself closer to Gellion as another gust of wind pushed past them.

Gellion hugged her to his chest and pressed his lips to her hair. There was so much he wanted to do before spring, but suddenly it did not seem so daunting. He pulled one arm from around Kyna and ran a hand through his blowing hair. His fingers brushed the vierstone in his ear, and a warm shiver passed over his skin and into his chest. He felt a flush of heat—of anticipation and grief and love—of hope.

"Let's go inside," he said.

Entwining his hand in hers, he led Kyna off the windswept slope.

ACKNOWLEDGMENTS

Writing a book is the most amazing and frustrating and wonderful thing. While most of the long hours are spent in solitude, it is astounding how many people it takes to turn an idea and some words into a novel.

There were those who helped shape the book itself—the words, the art, and the story. Equally important were those who supported me through the years of creating—the writing, the editing, the laughing and crying and fist shaking and celebrating. Thank you all. I couldn't have done it without you.

To Pamela, thank you for supporting this project and every project I have ever endeavored to pursue. To David, thank you for sharing your love of literature with me the last twenty-eight years and for being my first reader and reviser when my story was still a mess to behold.

Thank you Emma, for your words of encouragement each time I realized anew how hard writing a book was. You are an inspiration and a true friend.

Thank you Jake, for everything. For sharing me with my characters and my computer screen and supporting me in everything I do with undeserved confidence.

To my editor, Al, thank you for your hours of work and attention to detail, and your ability to see the art beyond grammar. To Emily, thank you for your beautiful illustrations that captured the characters and world in my head more perfectly than I could have imagined.

Last, but certainly dear to my heart, I want to thank the authors of every fantasy book I have ever read for showing me the beauty, magic, and power of stories. There are too many to name, but your influence shaped my world.

ABOUT THE AUTHOR

Haley Rylander is an author living in Denver, Colorado. It is her goal to write inspiring stories set in other worlds that reflect our own world in ways that can only be achieved through the magic and power of words. This is her first novel.

haleyrylander.com